♦ ♦ ♦ *The Pilgrim's Progress* ♦ ♦ ♦

The Pilgrim's

in the Allegory of a Dream

JOHN BUNYAN

Translated by Cheryl V. Ford

Tyndale House Publishers, Inc.
WHEATON, ILLINOIS

ACKNOWLEDGMENTS

I wish to thank my husband, Clay, for allowing
me to set apart the time necessary to complete
this project and also for the many hours he
himself devoted to helping me. I am grateful to
Dr. Wendell Hawley of Tyndale House Publishers
for granting me the opportunity to represent
such a fine publisher. I also want to express my
appreciation to the Tyndale staff who contributed
to this fine work, and especially to editors Robert
Brown and Dan Elliott, whose spirit of encouragement and dedication to excellence has made
invaluable contributions to this effort. Thank you
to those who have prayed for me in this undertaking, most of all my family and friends at First
Baptist Church in Arcata, California. Thanks
most of all to the Lord our God who is faithful
to His pilgrims and who never ceases to do all
things well.

Library of Congress Cataloging-in-Publication Data

Bunyan, John, 1628-1688.
    [Pilgrim's progress]
    The pilgrim's progress in the allegory of a
    dream / John Bunyan.
        p.   cm.
    Includes indexes.
    ISBN 0-8423-5145-0
    I. Title.
PR3330.A1 1991
828' .407—dc20   91-65400

Cover illustration from BFC PILGRIM'S
PROGRESS woodcut edition. Books for
Christians, P.O. Box 11943, Charlotte, NC 28220.

Calligraphy by Timothy R. Botts
Original hardcover edition 1991
© 1991 by Cheryl V. Ford
Printed in the United States of America

03   02   01   00   99
5   4   3   2   1

I sent

my prophets

to warn you

with many

a vision

and many

a parable

and

dream.

HOSEA 12:10

CONTENTS

◆◆◆◆◆◆◆◆◆◆◆◆◆◆

PREFACE TO
The Pilgrim's Progress
◆◆◆◆◆◆◆◆◆◆◆◆◆◆◆◆◆◆◆◆◆◆◆◆◆◆◆◆◆◆◆◆

Of the nineteen babies born in 1628 in a little English village called
Elstow, one, John Bunyan, was destined to become one of the leading preachers and writers of the century. His birth took place only a
mile from the Bedford prison which would, in its turn, be the birth-
ing place of one of England's greatest literary works. The son of a
simple tinker, a traveling mender of broken pots and tools, he had
a low social standing with only a limited education.

John Bunyan was sixteen years of age when his world turned
upside down. In the span of three short months, the death of
his mother was followed by his sister's death and his father's
remarriage. This same year he joined the army where he spent
his next three years. Following this period of change and
upheaval he became a wild profligate who, by his own admis-
sion, had no equal in lying and blaspheming.

Upon his return to civilian life, he too became a tinker. This
would have been the end of the story but for the fact that God
prefers to "shame the wise" by choosing "what is low and
despised in the world."

When Bunyan was about nineteen, he married a poor orphan
girl. He stated, "We came together as poor as poor might be, not
having so much household-stuff as a dish or spoon betwixt us
both." She did have a dowry, but it consisted only of two Christian devotional books. These contributed to his becoming a
deeply religious young man who went to church and read the
Bible. His attempts at reformation, however, put him on an emo-
tional roller coaster; visions of light and hope were followed by
seizures of depression, doubt, fear, and guilt. Later he would say,

"For this reason I lay so long at Sinai, to see the fire and the cloud and the darkness, that I might fear the Lord all the days of my life upon earth, and tell of his wondrous works to my children."

One day he was working at his trade when he overheard some women talking about the new birth and how God, through the love of Jesus, had changed their lives. He was acutely interested, so the women introduced him to their pastor, a Baptist minister, who provided him with instruction. He read Luther's "Commentary on Galatians," which had a profound affect upon him, and his mind stuck on one line of the Apostle Paul's, "He hath made peace by the blood of His cross." Christ had died for him! The new convert joined the little Baptist congregation and before long was a zealous member and deacon.

Eventually this fervent young man was ordained to preach. To him God was a God of wrath as well as of mercy. Sin, grace, and redemption were the consistent themes of his sermons. His own inner struggles and searchings of the Scriptures made him a compassionate and yet powerful guide. People risked arrest to hear him preach; crowds listened entranced. He is esteemed by historians as one of the great preachers of his time.

Shortly after he began his ministry, political change drastically altered the course of his life. Cromwell died, and Charles II came home to England. With the return of royal rule, the religious freedom of non-Anglicans was severely curtailed. "Dissenters" and "Irregulars" who refused to take part in state-sponsored religion were persecuted. Bunyan closed his chapel but went underground, continuing to preach. He was faced with a choice between obeying his conscience or the dictates of the Church of England.

One evening in November 1660 he was arrested after refusing to heed a warning to stop preaching. As he was led away, he said, "If I were out of prison today, I would preach the gospel again tomorrow by the help of God." His original sentence of three months in the Bedford jail extended to six years as he refused to repent of his "illegal" preaching. "I must venture all with God," he contended.

During this time in jail, concern for his family was a heavy burden. He saw himself as a man who was pulling down his house upon the heads of his wife and children, yet with no other choice. Upon his release, he was once again charged not to preach—but preach he must. There were well-meaning friends who would advise him to compromise, but, remaining true to his convictions, he was imprisoned once again for another six years. He wrote, "I have determined, the Almighty God being my help and shield, yet to suffer . . . even till the moss shall grow on mine eyebrows rather than thus to violate my Father and principles."

Why is it that God would allow such a dynamic young preacher to spend twelve of the best years of his life in a jail? How clear, over time, the sovereignty of God has become: what the magistrates meant for evil, God meant for good. There is a cost to wholehearted dedication, but God has used Bunyan's experience for a clear testimony to the reliability of His promises. Most assuredly, "We know that all things work together for good to them that love God, to them who are the called according to his purpose."

First of all, God did not forget Bunyan's impoverished family. His wife would go before the judges pleading for her husband's release so that he could support their four children. He was allowed to handcraft and market lace to help support them. At one point he was given permission to leave jail at will, but only until his preaching resumed. Especially dear to his heart was his firstborn, a little blind daughter who was allowed to visit him often. She would run her hands over his face, and if there were tears, she would kiss them away.

Next, like Paul, turning bitterness into blessing, he carried on a prison ministry from within his cell. He ministered to other prisoners and virtually became a prison chaplain to other preachers and Christians who had been jailed. There, in prison, Bunyan developed an insatiable appetite for reading, repeatedly poring over the Bible and a copy of Fox's Book of Martyrs. He wrote, "I never had in all my life so great an inlet into the Word of God as now. These Scriptures, that I saw nothing in before, are made in this place to shine upon me. Jesus Christ also was never more real and apparent than now; here I have seen and felt him indeed."

Like Luther a century before him, he began to write, turning out pamphlet after pamphlet which were in turn read by thousands.

During this period he published five books. His ministry was enriched beyond measure as he willingly suffered for the cause of Christ.

In 1672 Charles II relaxed religious oppression, and Bunyan was released. Public worship outside the establishment was once again permitted. He was called to be pastor of the Bedford church, and throngs gathered to hear him preach. He poured his energies into strenuous preaching tours, and churches as far away as London eagerly welcomed "Bishop Bunyan" as he was called. John Owen, a religious writer and scholar told king Charles II in a private conversation, "If I could possess that tinker's abilities for preaching, I would most gladly relinquish all my learning."

The political-religious climate of England briefly shifted again in 1675. Bunyan once more landed in prison for about six months, and again he turned to his pen. It was during this last confinement that he began to write a work of genius, simple yet profound, a breathtaking allegory that so riveted the interest, sparked the imagination, and energized the spirit that it became an instant best-seller. The book, originally entitled *The Pilgrim's Progress from This World to That Which Is to Come,* was so popular that within the first year, three editions were issued. In no time one hundred thousand copies were sold—a tremendous accomplishment for a book in seventeenth century England.

To Bunyan the Christian life was a pilgrimage. Of his own pilgrim's heart he wrote, "I have loved to hear my Lord spoken of, and wherever I have seen the print of his shoes in the earth, there I have coveted to set my foot, too." Thus the book is set in the context of a pilgrimage.

The major theme of the book is seen in the Christian's need for spiritual endurance along the path of life. From the moment of conception into the faith, we are homeward bound; every step we take along the road is a step toward life or toward death. As the reader journeys along with "Christian" and his other pilgrim friends, encountering a gallery of devils, heroes, saints, and pretenders, he will no doubt meet himself somewhere on the road. Through the pilgrims' struggles for truth, the tribulations they meet with, and the victories granted them, the reader will gain focus on his own life's pilgrimage.

Today's Christian is increasingly being drawn towards a clash of cultures. He finds himself in growing opposition to the surrounding culture not unlike the setting in which Bunyan found himself. Bunyan was imprisoned not only for his faith but for his faithfulness to it. This same kind of resolve to follow Christ regardless of consequences permeates the entire message of the book. His message sounds a timely alarm for radical discipleship, for loyalty and for faithfulness to defend to the death the honor and the cause of our great King.

Those who relish the path of ease will not appreciate the path of the pilgrim; nevertheless, those who are weak will find comfort therein. While the magnificent grace of God ever manifests itself, also evident is the narrowness of the path. We stand beholding the glorious cross of Christ; yet we are also forced to embrace the cross that the Christian, too, must carry.

More than sixty books were eventually published by John Bunyan. Included in this number was a second part to *The Pilgrim's Progress,* which depicts the story of Christian's wife, Christiana, and her companions. While the first story is primarily a drama of the individual soul, the second portrays the Christian life as a family experience, lived out together in true Christian fellowship. Today the two books are combined into one volume.

Evidently, some Christians of the time had counseled Bunyan against publishing the book because it was merely an allegory and not straightforward theology. The world has been grateful, however, that Bunyan chose to disregard his critics. *The Pilgrim's Progress* was destined to become one of England's greatest literary works. Proving its timeless appeal, it has been translated into more languages than any other book except the Bible—nearly two hundred—and it is second only to the Bible in all-time circulation. A copy was present in almost every home in England and in early America. The simple tinker-preacher who refused to be silenced had now gained a universal audience. Maintaining popularity as a classic for over three hundred years, *The Pilgrim's Progress* has touched the hearts and minds of millions and has placed John Bunyan among the literary immortals.

It is astounding that a man who lived in a class system with rigid expectations could rise above them. Despite a background of poverty, toil, and a poor education, John Bunyan fought hard and prevailed. According to C. S. Lewis, "One of the reasons why it needs no special education to be a Christian is that Christianity is an education in itself. That is why an uneducated believer like Bunyan was able to write a book that has astonished the whole world."

In 1874 Bunyan's hometown of Bedford honored their favorite son by erecting a ten-foot bronze statue weighing nearly three tons. Thousands of dignitaries from all over England gathered for the occasion. When the statue was unveiled, one could see a man, a minister of the gospel, standing straight and tall. He was holding open in his hands the book he loved best—the Bible. A broken chain lay at his feet, representing his long struggle to freely preach the gospel of Christ. The name engraved at its base is simply, John Bunyan. Perhaps ironically, the figure stands with his back to the elegant St. Peter's Church which rises in the background as a symbol of the established church that had dogged him most of his life. Upon the huge pedestal were inscribed these words from his famous book:

> *He had eyes uplifted to heaven;*
> *The best of books in his hand;*
> *The law of truth was written*
> *Upon his lips . . .*
> *He stood as if he pleaded*
> *With men.*

My first acquaintance with *The Pilgrim's Progress* was through a children's version which I read to my children when they were youngsters. I became more enthralled with the story than they and found myself making applications to my own life faster than I could read the lines. I never forgot the lessons that I learned from our nightly readings together from this simple adaptation. It was easy to see that this was, indeed, a story for all times and for all people.

Not long ago, sensing that God wanted to allow John Bunyan to plead his case once again, I introduced *The Pilgrim's Progress* to a high school Sunday school class. Ten years had passed since I had first read the story to my children, and now they were members of the class. I began to teach a series of lessons from the book. I soon became convinced that the truths Bunyan was attempting to communicate to his world had perhaps an even greater relevance today.

After doing a comparative study of several versions of the book, however, I concluded that there was a real need for a modern version that would be complete and faithful to the original, without taking great liberties to embellish the story on the one hand and without subtracting from it on the other. It would also need to communicate with our generation while still sounding like John Bunyan. So began the process that has led to this book.

Whenever we deal with truth, we are treading on holy ground. The publisher and I have taken our shoes off, so to speak, and trodden with reverence through the pages of this enduring classic of Christian literature. The end product is one that is easy to read yet true to the story—something with which I believe John Bunyan would be pleased.

THE AUTHOR'S DEFENSE OF HIS BOOK

When at the first I took my pen in hand
To write like this, I did not understand
At all that it would become a little book
In such a format; no, I had undertook
To make another; but when almost done,
Before I knew it, this I had begun.

And so it happened: I, writing of the way
And the race of saints, in this our gospel day,
Fell suddenly into an allegory
About their journey and the way to glory,
In more than twenty things which I set down:
This done, I had twenty more in my crown;
And they began again to multiply,
Like sparks from coals of a fire do fly.
"No," I thought, "if you breed so fast
I'll put you by yourselves, lest you at last
Should prove ad infinitum, and eat out
The book that I am already about."

So, that's what I did, but I didn't yet think
To show to all the world my pen and ink
In such a mode; I only thought to make
I didn't know what: nor did I undertake
To please my neighbor by it: no, not I;
I did it for my own self to gratify.

Only in vacant seasons did I spend
Time scribbling these thoughts, nor did I intend
But to divert myself in doing this
From worse thoughts which would lead me amiss.

So I set pen to paper with delight,
And quickly had my thoughts in black and white.
For my method I had down by the end,
But still thoughts came and so I penned
It down: until it came at last to be,
In length and breadth, the size you see.

Well, when I had thus put the ends together,
I showed them to others that I might see whether
They would either condemn or justify:
And some said, "Let them live"; others, "Let them die."
Some said, "John, print it"; others, "Don't do so."
Some said, "It might do good"; others, "No, no."

Now I was in a real fix, unable to see
Which was the best thing to be done by me:
At last I thought, "Since you are thus divided,
I will print it"; so the case was decided.

For I thought, some I see would have it done,
Though others in that channel do not run:
To prove, then, who advised for the best,
I thought it wise to put it to the test.

I further thought, if I now do deny
Those who want it, whom it would gratify,
I did not know if hinder them I might
Of that which would be to them a great delight.
I told those who were not for its coming forth,
"I want not to offend you with a thing of no worth;
Yet since your brothers pleased with it be,
Forbear to judge, till you do further see."

If you won't read it, then let it alone;
Some love the meat, some love picking the bone:
Yes, then that I might better them placate
With them I did thus expostulate:

May I not write in such a style as this?
In such a method too, and yet not miss
My end—your good? Why may it not be done?
Dark clouds bring waters, when the bright bring none.
Yet dark or bright, if they send silver drops
To fall on the earth, thereby yielding crops
Praise comes to both and no fault to either,
And treasures of fruit they do yield together.

You see the ways the fisherman takes
To catch a fish; what gear he makes!
Look how he engages all his wits
Also snares, lines, angles, hooks, and nets;
Yet there are fish which neither hook nor line,
Nor snare, nor net, nor any tool can make it thine:
They must be groped for, and enticed too,
Or they won't be caught, whatever you do.

"Well, yet I am not fully satisfied,
That this your book will stand, when soundly tried."

Why, what's the matter? "It's not clear." So what?
"But it's fiction." What of that? I'll rebut
Some by such tales, fictional as mine
Cause truth to glitter, and its rays to shine.
"But they lack solidness." Go on, speak your mind.
"This drowns the weak; metaphors make us blind."

Solidity, indeed, becomes the pen
Of one who writes divine things to men:
But do I lack solidness, just because
By metaphors I speak? Were not God's laws,
His gospel, in old times set forth
By types and shadows and metaphors?
Far be it that a sober man will find fault
With them, lest he be found waging assault
On the highest wisdom! Instead he stoops,
And seeks to find out how by pins and loops,
By calves and sheep, by heifers and by rams,
By birds and herbs, and by the blood of lambs,
God speaks to him; and how happy is he
That finds the light and grace that in them be.

Do not be too quick therefore to conclude
That I lack solidness—that I am rude:
All things that appear solid may not be
All things in parable despise not we,
Lest things most hurtful lightly we've received,

While our souls of the good are sadly bereaved.
My mysteries and shadows, indeed do hold
The truth, as cabinets enclose the gold.

The prophets used metaphors much to serve
To set forth truth: yes, any who observe
Christ, His apostles too, shall plainly see
That truths to this day in such cloaks will be.

And now, before I put away my pen,
I'll show the profit of my book; and then
Commit both you and it into the Hand
That pulls the strong down, and makes weak ones stand.

This book lays out before your very eyes
The man who seeks the everlasting prize:
Where he's from and where he's going are both shown
What he does and leaves undone are both made known:
It also shows you how he runs and runs
Until to the gate of glory he comes.

Also are the ones who in haste would life gain,
Seeming like the lasting crown they'd attain:
Here also you may see the reason why
They lose their labor, and like fools they die.

This book will make a traveler of you
If by its counsel you'll learn what to do;
It will direct you to the Holy Land,
If its directions you will understand:
It will cause the slothful to active be;
Also the blind will delightful things see.

Are you for something rare and profitable?
Would you like to see truth found in a fable?
Are you forgetful? Would you like to remember
From New Year's Day to the last of December?
Then read my thoughts, and they will stick like burrs,
And may be to the helpless, sure comforters.

This book is written in such dialect,
As may the minds of listless men affect:
It seems a novelty, and yet contains
Nothing but sound and honest gospel strains.
Would you divert yourself from melancholy?
Would you be peaceful, yet be far from folly?
Would you read riddles and their explanation?
Or else be drowned in your contemplation?
Do you love picking at meat? Or would you view
A man in the clouds, and hear him speak to you?
Would you be in a dream, and yet not sleep?
Or would you in a moment laugh and weep?

Would you lose yourself and meet nothing tragic,
And find yourself again without using magic?
Would you read yourself, and read you know not what,
And yet know whether you are blessed or not,
By reading the same lines? Oh then come, draw near,
Lay my book, your head, and heart together here.

J O H N   B U N Y A N

in the Allegory
of a Dream

•••

THE FIRST PART

CHAPTER 1

❖❖❖❖❖❖❖❖❖❖❖❖❖

As I walked through the wilderness of this world, I came to a place where there was a den. Inside, I lay down to sleep, and as I slept, I had a dream. In my dream I looked up and saw a man clothed in rags standing in a certain place with his face turned away from his home. He carried a Book in his hand and a great Burden on his back. As I watched, I saw him open the Book and begin to read. And as he read, he wept and trembled. Then, not being able to contain himself any longer, he cried out in anguish, asking, "What shall I do?"

The jail

Isa. 64:6
Luke 14:33
Ps. 38:4
Hab. 2:2

Acts 16:30

While still in this condition, he returned to his home. Not wanting his wife and children to perceive his distress, he restrained himself as long as he could. He couldn't hide it for long, however, because his anguish only increased. Finally, he bared his soul to his wife and children and began to talk to them.

"Oh, my dear wife, and my children, the fruit of my own body, I, your beloved friend, have lost all peace because of a great Burden weighing heavily upon me. What's more, I have been informed that our City is most certainly going to be burned with fire from Heaven. And unless some way of escape can be found by which we can be rescued, all of us—you, my wife and sweet children, as well as myself—will come to a dreadful end in this terrible destruction."

2 Thess. 1:5-10;
Heb. 10:26-27;
2 Pet. 3:7

At this his family was greatly perplexed—not that they believed there was any truth in what he was saying, but they feared he was losing his sanity. Since nightfall was approaching, they quickly helped him to bed, hoping that some sleep might settle his troubled mind. But the night was as disturbing to him as the day, and instead of sleeping, he groaned and cried all night. When morning came, his family asked him how he felt. "Worse and worse," he answered. Once again he began to tell them about his fears, but they were not receptive, and their hearts began to harden. They also thought that perhaps they could drive the mental illness away by treating him harshly and rudely. Sometimes they ridiculed him, sometimes they rebuked him, and sometimes they totally ignored him. Consequently, he began staying in his own room, pitying and praying for his family and also grieving over his own misery. At times, however, he walked alone in the fields, sometimes reading and sometimes praying. He spent several days this way.

Exod. 7–10;
1 Sam. 6:6;
Ps. 95:8;
Heb. 3:15; 4:7

Evangelist Appears

Now I saw that one day when he was walking in the fields, he was reading in his Book, as was his habit, and his mind was greatly distressed. As he read, he burst out as he had done before, crying, "What shall I do to be saved?"

Luke 4:16

Acts 16:30

I also saw him looking this way and then that, as if he would run, yet he stood motionless. I perceived that he must not have known which way to go. Then I looked and saw a man named Evangelist coming toward him. Upon reaching him, he asked, "Why are you crying?"

"Sir," he answered, "I can see by the Book in my hand that I am condemned to die, and after that I will be brought to judgment. I find that I

Heb. 9:27

am not willing to do the first, and not able to bear the latter."

Then Evangelist asked, "Why aren't you willing to die, since this life is so filled with evil?"

The man answered, "Because I fear that this Burden on my back will drive me lower than the grave and into Hell itself. And, sir, if I am not even able to face prison, then surely I cannot bear the judgment and its subsequent execution. Thinking about these things makes me cry."

Ezek. 22:14

Isa. 30:33

Evangelist then asked, "If this is your condition, why are you standing still?"

He answered, "Because I don't know where to go."

Then Evangelist gave him a Parchment Scroll inscribed with these words: "Flee from the wrath to come."

Matt. 3:7

The man read it and, looking at Evangelist very carefully, asked, "To where do I flee?"

Then, pointing his finger to a very wide field, Evangelist replied, "Can you see the Wicket-gate in the distance?"

Matt. 7:13

Christ and the way to Him can't be found without the preaching of the Word.

"No," the man answered.

Then the other asked, "Do you see that shining light?"

He said, "I think I do."

Evangelist continued, "Keep your eyes fixed upon that light, and go directly to it; then you will see the Gate. When you knock on it, you will be told what to do."

Ps. 119:105

2 Pet. 1:19

Pursued by Obstinate and Pliable

So I saw in my dream that the man began to run. He had not run far from his own house when his wife and children saw what was happening. They

Luke 14:26

Gen. 19:17
The world's
response to
those who
flee from the
wrath to come

Jer. 20:10

cried after him to return, but the man put
his fingers in his ears and ran on, crying, "Life!
Life! Eternal life!" He would not look behind him
but fled toward the middle of the plain.

The neighbors also came out to see him run,
and as he ran, some mocked and others threatened. Some, however, cried out for him to
return. Among these neighbors, there were two
who resolved to go after him and force him to

OBSTINATE

come back. The name
of one was Obstinate
and the other, Pliable.

By this time the man
had traveled a good distance from them, but
they still resolved to pursue him, and in a short
time they were able to overtake him.

"Neighbors," the man asked them, "why have
you come after me?"

"To persuade you to come back with us."

"No way!" he replied. "You live in the City of
Destruction where I also was born. If you stay
there, however, sooner or later you will sink
lower than the grave into a place that burns with

Rev. 19:20

fire and brimstone. Find peace, dear neighbors,
and come along with me."

"What!" Obstinate objected, "and leave our
friends and our comforts behind?"

"Yes," said Christian (for that was his name),
"because what you will leave is not worthy to be
compared with even a little of what I am seeking

2 Cor. 4:18

to enjoy. If you will come along with me and
not turn back, you will find blessing as I will,
for where I am going there is enough for all and

Luke 15:17

plenty to spare. Come away with me and see if
I'm telling you the truth."

"But what things are you seeking, for which
you would leave all the world to find them?"
Obstinate asked.

"I am seeking an inheritance that is not subject to decay and that cannot be tarnished and that will never fade away. It is kept safely in Heaven to be given at the appointed time to all who diligently seek it. If you will, you can read about it right here in my Book."

1 Pet. 1:4;
Heb. 11:16

"Ridiculous! Get your Book out of here!" responded Obstinate. "Are you going to come back with us or not?"

"No, I'm not," said Christian adamantly, "because I have already put my hand to the plow."

Luke 9:62

Then Obstinate turned and addressed Pliable. "Come on then, neighbor Pliable; let's turn back and go home without him. A lot of these crazy-headed fools get an idea in their head and think themselves wiser than seven reasonable men."

Prov. 26:16

"Don't insult him," Pliable answered. "If what Christian says is true, the things he is searching for are better than ours. I am inclined to go with him."

Heb. 11:15-16

"What?" demanded Obstinate. "Another fool! Listen to me and go back. Who knows where this sick-headed man will lead you? Go back! Go back if you have any sense at all!"

"Come with me, neighbor Pliable," Christian pleaded. "Besides the things I told you about, there are many other glorious things to be gained. If you don't take my word for it, read it here in this Book. And if you want to be sure of the truth expressed within it, look closely, for all is confirmed by the blood of Him who wrote it."

Christian and Obstinate compete for Pliable's soul.

Heb. 13:20-21

At that Pliable said, "Well, Obstinate, my friend, I am making a decision. I intend to go along with this sincere man and to cast my lot in with him." Then, turning to Christian, he asked, "But, Christian, my good companion, do you know the way to this desirable place?"

"I have been directed by a man named Evangelist to travel quickly to a little Gate up ahead where we will receive instructions about the way."

"Then come on, neighbor, let's go!" Pliable said excitedly. And they left together.

Obstinate called out after them, "And I will go back home. I refuse to be a companion to such crazed fanatics!"

Obstinate goes back scoffing.

Christian and Pliable Discuss Heavenly Things

Now I saw in my dream, that when Obstinate had left them, Christian and Pliable went walking on over the plain, talking as they went.

"So, Pliable, my neighbor," Christian said, "let me get to know you. I am glad you decided to come along with me. If Obstinate had been able to feel what I have felt of the powers and terrors of what is yet unseen, he wouldn't have so easily rejected us."

Pliable was brimming with questions. "Come on, Christian, since we're the only people here, tell me more! What things are we seeking? How will we enjoy them? Where are we going?"

"I can better imagine them with my mind than speak of them with my tongue," said Christian, "but since you want to know, I will answer from my Book."

God's things are beyond description.

"Do you believe the words in your Book are really true?"

"Absolutely. For it was written by Him who cannot lie."

Titus 1:2

"This sounds good. What are the things we're seeking?"

"There is an endless kingdom to be inhabited

and everlasting life to be given us so that we will
live in that Kingdom forever."

Isa. 45:17;
John 10:27-29

"Wonderful! What else?"

"There are crowns of glory to be given us and
garments that will make us shine like the sun
in the heavens above."

2 Tim. 4:8

"Excellent! What
else?"

"There will be no
more sorrow and
crying, for He who
owns the place will wipe all tears from our eyes."

Rev. 3:4;
Matt. 13:43

"And who will be there with us?"

Christian's face shined as he went on. "There we
will be with seraphim and cherubim—beings who
will dazzle our eyes when we see them. We will
also meet with the thousands and ten thousands
who have gone on before us to that place. None
of them will cause harm; all will be loving and
holy. Everyone there will walk before God and
stand approved in His grace and presence forever.
Furthermore, we will see the elders with their gold-
en crowns and the holy virgins with their golden
harps; and we will see men who by the world were
cut to pieces, burned in flames, eaten by beasts
and drowned in seas, all because of the love they
had for the Lord of the place. Everyone there will
be completely well, made whole, and clothed with
immortality as with a garment."

Isa. 25:8;
Rev. 7:16-17; 21:4

Isa. 6:2; Rev. 5:11

Rev. 7:9

Rev. 21:3

Rev. 4:4; 14:3-4

Heb. 11:37-39

2 Cor. 5:2-5

Pliable could hardly contain himself. "My
heart is seized with ecstasy at hearing all this. But
are these things really for us to enjoy? How can
we come to share in them?"

"The Lord, the Ruler of that Country, has given
the answer in this Book. It says that if we are truly
willing to receive it, He will freely give it to us."

Isa. 55:7;
John 7:37;
Eph. 1:6;
Rev. 21:6; 22:17

"Well, my good friend, I'm glad to hear all
these things. Come on, let's quicken our pace."

Christian sighed. "I can't go as fast as I would like to because of this Burden on my back."

The Slough of Despond

Now I saw in my dream that, just as they had ended their conversation, they approached a miry Slough (a muddy swamp) in the plain. Neither of them paid attention to it, and both suddenly fell into the bog. The Slough's name was Despond. Covered with mud, they wallowed in it for some time. And Christian, because of the Burden on his back, began to sink in the mire.

Ps. 69:2

"Oh, Christian, my neighbor!" Pliable cried out. "Where are you now?"

"To tell you the truth, I don't know," Christian answered.

Hearing this, Pliable became offended and angrily scolded his companion. "Is this the happiness you have told me about all this time? If we have such terrible misfortune here at the beginning, what are we to expect between here and the end of our journey? If I can possibly get out of here with my life, you can possess that wonderful Country for you and me both!"

It is not enough to be pliable.

With that, Pliable gave a desperate struggle or two and was able to get out of the mire on the side of the Slough that faced his home. So away he went, and Christian never saw him again.

Help Comes to the Rescue

Thus Christian was left to roll around in the
Slough of Despond by himself. Even then, however, he tried to struggle to the side of the Slough
that was farthest from his own home and closest
to the Wicket-gate. He continued to struggle but
couldn't get out because of the Burden that was
on his back. Then I saw in my dream that a man
named Help came to him, and he asked Christian what he was doing there.

"Sir," explained Christian, "I was instructed
to go this way by a man named Evangelist who
gave me directions to that Gate up ahead where
I might escape the coming wrath. As I was going
toward the Gate, I fell in here."

"But why didn't you look for the steps?" asked
Help.

The promises.

"Fear pursued me so hard that I fled this way
and fell in."

"Give me your hand."

So Christian reached out his hand, and Help
pulled him out. He set him on solid ground and
told him to continue on his way.

Ps. 40:2

Then I stepped up to the one who had pulled
Christian out and asked, "Sir, since this is the
way from the City of Destruction to the Gate,
why isn't this place fenced off so that poor travelers may go by more safely?"

And he answered me, "This miry Slough is
the type that cannot be fenced. It is the lower
ground where the scum and filth that accompany conviction of sin continually accumulate.
Therefore it was named the Slough of Despond
because, as the sinner is awakened to his lost
condition, many fears, doubts, and discouraging
anxieties arise in his soul. All of them come
together and settle here in this place, and that
is the reason this ground is no good.

"It is not the King's desire that this place should remain so bad. By the direction of His surveyors, His laborers have been working for almost two thousand years to fence off this patch of ground. Yes, and to my knowledge at least twenty thousand cartloads of profitable instructions—yes, millions of them—have been swallowed up here. In all seasons they have been brought from all places in the King's domain, and those who are knowledgeable say that these materials have the best potential for making the ground good. Nevertheless, it remains the Slough of Despond, and so will it be even when all has been tried and failed.

The promises of forgiveness and acceptance to life by faith in Christ.

"It's true that some good and substantial steps have been placed evenly throughout this Slough by the command of the Lawgiver. Even then, however, this place spews out so much filth that when the weather gets bad the steps can hardly be seen. And even if people do see them, because of confusion they step the wrong way and fall into the slime. In any case, the steps are there, and the ground is good once they go through the Gate.

1 Sam. 12:23

Now I saw in my dream that by this time Pliable had arrived back home, and his neighbors came to visit him. Some of them called him a wise man for coming back, and some called him a fool for endangering himself with Christian. Still others mocked his cowardice, saying, "Surely, if I had begun such a venture I would not have been so cowardly as to have given up because of a few troubles." So Pliable sat cowering among them until he finally gained enough confidence to raise an objection. At this, they immediately left him alone and began to insult poor Christian behind his back because of what had happened to Pliable.

CHAPTER 2

•••••••••••••

Christian Meets Mr. Worldly-wiseman

Now as Christian was walking on alone, he saw someone in the distance coming across the field toward him, and they met just as their ways crossed. The gentleman's name was Mr. Worldly-wiseman, and he lived in a very influential town called Carnal-policy. This town was near to the one from which

Christian had come. The man, upon meeting Christian, had some idea of who he might be, for the news of Christian's leaving the City of Destruction had become the talk of the town there and was even becoming much bandied about in some other areas as well. Thus, Worldly-wiseman, seeing Christian's intense effort to travel and listening to all his sighs and groans, guessed who it was. So he decided to start a conversation with Christian.

"How are you, sir? Where are you going in such a burdened state?"

"Yes, in as burdened a state as I can imagine a poor creature could be," answered Christian. "And since you asked where I am going, I will tell you. I am going to that Wicket-gate that lies ahead because I have been informed that I will find a way to get rid of my heavy Burden."

Matt. 11:28

"Do you have a wife and children?"

1 Cor. 7:29

"Yes, but I am so weighed down by this Burden that I cannot enjoy them as I once did. I feel as if I had none."

Worldly-wiseman looked deeply concerned.

Prov. 15:22; 20:18

"Will you listen to me if I give you some advice?"

"If it's good, I will," answered Christian, "because I definitely need some good advice."

"I would advise you to get rid of your Burden quickly. You'll never have peace of mind until you do, and you'll never enjoy the blessings God has given you until then either."

"That's what I am looking for, to get rid of this heavy Burden. But I can't get it off by myself, and nobody in our country can take it off my shoulders. So I'm going this way, as I told you, to get rid of my Burden."

"And who told you to go this way to get rid of your Burden?"

"A man who appeared to me to be a very admirable and trustworthy person. His name, as I recall, is Evangelist."

Now Worldly-wiseman became indignant. "I curse him for his counsel! There is not a more dangerous and troublesome way in all the world than the one that he has steered you toward. And that is what you will find if you allow yourself to be led by his counsel. I can tell that you've already had some trouble, for I can see the dirt of the Slough of Despond on you. That Slough is only the beginning of the sorrows that come to those who take this way. Listen to me, for I am older than you. If you take this way you will likely meet with fatigue, pain, hunger, dangers, nakedness, swords, lions, dragons, darkness, and, in a word, death. This is the truth, and it has been confirmed by many testimonies. Should a man be so careless as to throw his life away by giving heed to a stranger?"

Heb. 11:32-38

"Listen," Christian groaned, "this Burden on my back is more terrible than all these things you have mentioned. No, I don't care what I encounter on the way, as long as I can also find deliverance from my Burden."

Worldly-wiseman resumed his interrogation. "How did you first receive your Burden?"

"By reading this Book in my hand."

"I thought so. And it has happened to you just like to other weak people who, meddling with things beyond their understanding, fall into the same mental confusion and obsessive behavior as you have. This can only break a man down, and I can perceive this is the case with you. These people take off on desperate ventures seeking to receive something they know nothing about."

Worldly-wiseman does not like men to be serious in their Bible reading.

Christian, straining under the weight of his Burden, immediately replied, "I know what I am seeking—freedom from my heavy Burden!"

"But why do you seek for freedom in this way, seeing that it's so dangerous? If you

had the patience to listen, I could direct you to what you are looking for without the dangers that you'll encounter by going this way. Yes, the remedy is here. Besides, I might add, instead of those dangers, you'll find abundant safety, friendship, and contentment."

This sounded wonderful to Christian. "Sir, I beg you, please reveal this secret to me."

"Well, a short distance from here there is a Village named Morality. In this Village lives a man named Legality. This man has sound judgment and a very good reputation. He has skill in helping people like yourself get such burdens off their shoulders. Yes, to my knowledge, he has done a great deal of good this way. Why, he even has skill in curing those who are being driven to distraction because of their burdens. Like I say, you can go to him and be helped right away.

LEGALITY

"His house is less than a mile from here. If he is not at home himself, he has a son, an impressive young man named Civility. He can help you just as well as the old man. You will be able to find relief from your Burden there. If you don't want to go back to your former home, and I wouldn't blame you, you can send for your wife and children to come to this town. There are

Isa. 55:1   houses vacant at this time, and you can purchase one of them at a reasonable price. You can also buy good provisions there at low prices. All you need to make your life happy is there, and you will live by honest neighbors who are successful and of a good reputation."

Now Christian had come to a standstill, not sure what to do. Before long, however, he concluded that, if what the man was saying were true, his wisest course of action would be to take his advice. With that, he questioned the man further.

"Sir, how do I get to this honest man's house?"

"Do you see that high Hill over there?"   *Mount Sinai*

"Yes, very well."

"You have to go by that Hill, and then the first house you will come to is his."

So Christian turned out of his way to go to Mr. Legality's house for help. But when he drew near to the Hill, it seemed very high, and the path he was following passed under such an ominous-looking overhang that he was afraid to continue on for fear that it might fall on him. So he stood still, wondering what to do next. To make matters worse, his Burden now seemed even heavier than when he was on the way. Suddenly, flashes of fire came out of the Hill and made Christian   Exod. 19:16, 18; afraid that he would be burned. So he continued   24:17 to stand there, sweating and shaking with fear.   Heb. 12:21 Now he was sorry that he had ever taken Mr. Worldly-wiseman's advice.

Evangelist Delivers Christian from Error

All of a sudden, he saw Evangelist coming to meet him. The sight of him caused Christian to blush because he was ashamed. Evangelist came nearer and nearer, and Christian could see that he had a very stern and almost frightening look on his face.

"What are you doing here, Christian," asked Evangelist.

Christian didn't know how to answer, so he stood speechless in front of him.

CIVILITY

Evangelist continued, "Aren't you the man I found crying outside the walls of the City of Destruction?"

"Yes, dear sir, I am the man," Christian replied faintly.

"Didn't I instruct you to go to the little Wicket-gate?"

Gal. 1:6-7   "Yes, sir."

"Well, how can you be so quickly led astray? For now you are completely out of the way."

"I met a man soon after I had gotten past the Slough of Despond who convinced me that in the Village up ahead I could find a man who could remove my Burden."

"What was he like?"

"He looked like a gentleman and talked with me for quite some time, finally persuading me to come this way. When I got here, I saw this Hill and how it hangs over the way, so I stopped because I was afraid it might fall on me."

"And what did this man say to you?"

"Why, he asked me where I was going, and I told him."

"And then what did he say?"

"He asked me if I had a family. I told him I did, but that I was so weighed down by the Burden on my back that I could not even enjoy them anymore."

"And what did he say then?"

"He encouraged me to get rid of my Burden right away. I told him that relief was what I was looking for, therefore I was going to the Gate up ahead to receive further direction in how I might get to the place of deliverance. At that, he said he wished to show me a better way—shorter, and not so full of difficulties as the way that you offered me, sir. He told me his way would take me to the house of a gentleman who had skill in taking off these kinds of burdens. So I believed him and turned from that way into this so that I might soon be free of my Burden. But when I arrived here and saw how things are, I stopped, like I said, because of the danger I feared. And now I don't know what to do."

Evangelist said firmly, "Stand still and listen while I show you the words of God."

So Christian stood trembling, waiting for Evangelist to speak.

Then Evangelist said, "See to it that you do not refuse him who speaks. If they did not escape when they refused him who warned them on earth, how much less will we, if we turn away from Him who warns us from Heaven?" He also said, "But my righteous one will live by faith. And if he shrinks back, I will not be pleased with him."

Heb. 12:25

Heb. 10:38

Evangelist then explained and applied the words:

"You are the man who is running into this misery. You have begun to reject the counsel of the Most High and to shrink back from the way of peace, even risking utter destruction."

Then Christian fell down at his feet like a dying man, crying, "Woe is me, for I am ruined!"

Isa. 6:5

When Evangelist saw this, he took him by the right hand, saying, "Every sin and blasphemy will be forgiven men. Don't be faithless any longer. Believe!" Then Christian began to feel some relief, so he stood up, once again trembling before Evangelist.

Matt. 12:31

wicketgate

John 20:27

"You must take more seriously what I tell you," Evangelist continued. "I will now show you who it was that deceived you, and also to whom he was sending you. The man who met you is one called Worldly-wiseman.* His name is appropriate, partly because he respects only the values and wisdom of this world and therefore always goes to church in the town of Morality. Also, he

1 John 4:5

*When Christians to carnal men lend an ear,
They go out of their way and pay for it dear,
For Mr. Worldly-wiseman can only show
A saint the way to bondage and woe.

loves the wisdom of the world best because it

Gal. 6:12 spares him from facing the Cross. Also, because he is of a carnal disposition, he seeks to pervert my ways even though they are right.

"Now there are three things in this man's counsel that you must utterly abhor. First, his turning you out of the way. Second, his effort to make the Cross repulsive to you. And third, his setting your feet in the path that leads to death.

The Cross

"First, you must abhor his turning you out of the way—yes, and your own consenting to it, since it was rejecting the counsel of God for the sake of the counsel of a Worldly-wiseman. The Lord says, 'Work hard to

Luke 13:24 get in through the narrow Gate'—the Gate to which I sent you. 'The Gateway to Life is small, and the road is narrow, and only a few ever find

Matt. 7:14 it.' This wicked man turned you aside from this little Wicket-gate and from the way that leads to it and nearly brought you destruction. Therefore, you must hate how he turned you out of the way, and despise yourself for responding to him.

"Second, you must abhor his effort to make the Cross seem repulsive to you—for you are to desire the Cross more than the treasures of

Heb. 11:25-26 Egypt. Besides, the King of glory has told you that 'If you insist on saving your life, you will

Matt. 10:39; lose it.' And 'Anyone who wants to be my fol-
Mark 8:35; lower must love me far more than he does his
John 12:25 own father, mother, wife, children, brothers, or sisters—yes, more than his own life—otherwise

Luke 14:26 he cannot be my disciple.' I tell you, then, it is despicable for a man to try and persuade you that the truth shall lead to death, when, in fact,

John 14:6; 17:3 without it you cannot hope to find eternal life.

This teaching you must completely renounce.

"Third, you must hate the way in which he set your feet in the path that will surely deliver you to death. And because of this, you must consider the one to whom he sent you, and how unable that person was to deliver you from your Burden."

Prov. 14:12

Rom. 8:1-8

Legality and Civility Also Are Condemned

"The one named Legality, to whom you were sent for relief, is the son of a Slave-woman who is now in bondage along with her children. It is a mystery, but she is Mount Sinai, this high Hill which you feared would fall on your head. Now if she and her children are in bondage, how can you expect them to set you free? This man Legality, therefore, is unable to set you free from your Burden. No one has ever been set free from a Burden by him—no, and never will be. You cannot be justified by the works of the law, for by the deeds of the law no person alive will be able to find relief from his Burden. For these reasons, Mr. Worldly-wiseman is an alien and Mr. Legality is a cheat. As for his son Civility, in spite of his alluring appearance, he is no more than a hypocrite and cannot help you. Believe me, there is nothing in all this noise that you have heard from these stupid and foolish men but a design to deceive you away from your salvation by turning you from the way that I had set before you."

Gal. 4:21-27

Rom. 3:20;
Gal. 2:15-16

After this, Evangelist called aloud to the Heavens for confirmation of what he had said. With that, words and fire came out of the Mountain under which poor Christian stood, making the hair on his skin stand up. The words could be heard clearly: "All who rely on observing the law are under a curse, for it is written: 'Cursed is everyone who does not continue to do everything written in the Book of the Law.'"

1 Kings 18:36-38

Exod. 24:15-18
Job 4:15

Gal. 3:10

Christian Is Forgiven

Now Christian expected nothing but death, and he began to cry out miserably, even cursing the moment he had met Mr. Worldly-wiseman. He kept calling himself a thousand fools for listening to his advice. He was also very ashamed to think that this man's arguments, proceeding from the flesh alone, could have prevailed in his thinking so as actually to cause him to forsake the right way. Once again he turned to Evangelist.

"Sir, what do you think? Is there any hope? Can I return and resume my journey to the Wicket-gate? Will I now be abandoned and sent back in shame? I am sorry I gave heed to this man's advice, but can I be forgiven?"

Evangelist replied, "Your sin is very serious. By your action you committed two evils; first, you abandoned the good way, and then, you walked in forbidden paths. The man at the Gate, however, will receive you, because he wants the best for everyone. Do not turn aside again, or you might be 'destroyed in your way, for his wrath can flare up in a moment.'"

Gen. 19:2

Ps. 2:12

CHAPTER 3

♦♦♦♦♦♦♦♦♦♦♦♦♦♦

Christian determined to go back, and Evangelist embraced him, smiled, and wished him a blessed and successful journey. So he hurried along, refusing to speak to anyone on the way, even if someone asked him a question. The entire time he walked like one treading on forbidden ground. He wouldn't believe he was safe until he was back on the way which he had left to follow Mr. Worldly-wiseman's counsel. So eventually Christian arrived at the Gate. Now above the Gate was written: "Knock and the door will be opened to you." Therefore, he knocked* more than once or twice, saying,

Matt. 7:7

*"May I now enter here? Will he within
Open to poor me though I have been
An undeserving rebel? Then will I
Not fail to sing his lasting praise on high."*

Ps. 51:3-4
Ps. 30:12

Christian Meets Good-will and Enters at the Gate

At last a solemn-looking person came to the Gate whose name was Good-will. He asked Christian who he was, where he came from, and what he wanted.

**He who would enter must first stand without
Knocking at the gate, but with no need to doubt.
For he who is a knocker will surely enter in
For God will love him and forgive all his sin.*

Christian answered, "Here is a poor, burdened sinner. I come from the City of Destruction but am going to Mount Zion so that I might be delivered from the wrath to come. Sir, since I have been informed that through this Gate is the way there, I would like to know if you are willing to let me in."

1 Thess. 1:10

The Gate will be opened to brokenhearted sinners.

"I am willing with all my heart," Good-will quickly responded. With that he opened the Gate.

When Christian was stepping in, the man gave him a pull. "Why did you do that?" asked Christian.

The man replied, "Not far from this Gate stands a strong castle, of which Beelzebub is the captain. From there, both he and his allies shoot at those who approach this Gate, thus hoping to kill them before they can enter."

Eph. 6:16

Satan envies those that enter the straight Gate.

Then Christian said, "I rejoice and tremble." So when he was in, the man guarding the Gate asked him who directed him there.

"Evangelist encouraged me to come here and knock, and I did. He told me that you, sir, would tell me what I have to do."

Good-will said, "See, I have placed before you an open door that no one can shut."

Rev. 3:8

"Now I begin to reap the benefits of the risks I took."

"But why did you come by yourself?"

"Because none of my neighbors could see their danger as I had seen mine."

"Did any of them know that you were coming here?"

"Yes, my wife and children saw me first and called after me to turn back. Then some of my neighbors stood crying and calling after me to return. But I put my fingers in my ears so I could continue on my way."

"But did not any of them follow you and try to persuade you to turn back?"

"Yes, both Obstinate and Pliable; however, when they saw that they could not succeed, Obstinate went away scoffing, but Pliable came with me a little way."

"Why didn't he continue?"

"We did come together until we came to the Slough of Despond, into which we accidentally fell. Then my neighbor Pliable became discouraged and refused to venture farther. He got out of the Slough on the side facing his own home and told me I should go on alone and possess the blessed Country for him. So he went his way and I came mine, he following Obstinate, and I on to this Gate."

A man may have company when he sets out for Heaven and yet go there alone.

"Oh, the poor man!" exclaimed Good-will. "Is the celestial glory of so little value to him that he didn't count it worth the risk of hazarding a few difficulties in order to obtain it?"

"Honestly, I have told you the truth about Pliable, and if I should reveal all the truth about myself, it would appear that I am no better. It is true, he went back to his own house, but I also turned aside to go into the way of death, having been persuaded by the carnal argument of a Mr. Worldly-wiseman."

Prov. 16:25

Good-will looked somewhat surprised. "Oh! Did he happen to find you? How remarkable! He would have you searching for ease at the hands of Mr. Legality! Both of them are cheats. Did you take his advice?"

"Yes, as far as I dared. I went to find Mr. Legality until it seemed to me that the Mountain that stands by his house would fall on my head. So I was forced to stop there."

"That Mountain has been the death of many and will be the death of many more," said Good-will. "It is good that you escaped being dashed to pieces by it."

"Well," said Christian, "I surely do not know what would have become of me there if Evangelist had not come along again. I was standing there, depressed and confused, wondering what to do. But it was God's mercy that he came to me again, for if he hadn't come, I wouldn't have made it here. But here I am now, such as I am, indeed more worthy of death by that Mountain than to be standing here talking with you, sir. Oh! What a blessing this is for me, that I am still allowed to enter here."

Good-will smiled and said, "We do not reject anyone from entering here, in spite of all they may have done before entering. The King says, 'Whoever comes to me I will never drive away.' Therefore, good Christian, come with me awhile, and I will show you the way you must go. Look ahead of you—do you see this narrow way? It was constructed by the patriarchs and prophets, and by Christ and His apostles, and it is as straight as a ruler can make it. This is the way you must go."

John 6:37

"But are there no bends or turns so a stranger might lose his way?" Christian asked.

"Yes, there are many ways adjoining this, and they are crooked and wide. But you can distinguish the right from the wrong, since only the right way is straight and narrow."

Matt. 7:13-14

Then I saw in my dream that Christian asked Good-will if he could help him get the Burden off his back. For he still had not gotten rid of it and could not find any way to get it off without help.

Good-will told him, "As for your Burden, be content to bear it until you come to the place of deliverance. There it will fall from your back by itself."

Then Christian tightened his belt and began to prepare for his journey. So Good-will told him that, after walking some distance from the Gate, he would come to the House of the Interpreter,

There is no deliverance from the guilt and burden of sin but by the death and blood of Christ.

THE HOUSE OF THE INTERPRETER

at whose door he should knock. There he would be shown excellent things. Christian then said good-bye to his friend, and Good-will wished him success on his journey.

The Interpreter's House
Christian traveled on until he came to the House of the Interpreter, where he knocked repeatedly. At last someone came to the door and asked who was there.

"Sir," said Christian, "I am a traveler who was told by an acquaintance of the owner of this House that for my own benefit I should call here. Therefore, I would like to speak to the master of the House."

So he called for the master of the House, who, after a short time, came to Christian and asked him what he wanted.

"Sir, I am a man who has come from the City of Destruction, and I am on my way to Mount Zion. I was told by the man who stands at the Gate where this way begins that if I called here you would show me excellent things that would be of help to me on my journey."

The Man in the Picture
The man, who was called Interpreter, said, "Come in; I will show you what will be profitable to you." So he had his servant turn on some lights and beckoned Christian to follow him. He led him into a private room and told his servant to open a door. When he had done so, Christian could see hanging on the wall a Picture of a very intense-looking man whose eyes were looking toward Heaven. He had the best of books in his hand, the law of truth written on his lips, and the world behind his back. He stood there as if pleading with men, and a golden crown rested upon his head.

"What does this mean?" asked Christian.

Interpreter explained, "The Man in this Picture is one in a thousand. He can bring children into being, suffer birthpains with them, and nurse them himself after they are born. And since you see him with his eyes looking toward Heaven, the best of books in his hand, and the law of truth written on his lips, you may be assured that his work is to know and reveal hidden things to sinners. That is why

1 Cor. 4:15
Gal. 4:19

THE MAN IN THE PICTURE

1 Cor. 3:2;
1 Thess. 2:7

you see him standing there as if pleading with men. And you see that the world is cast behind him and that a crown rests upon his head. That

Gal. 4:12

The Room Filled with Dust

is to show you that by disregarding and despising the things of this present world because of the love he has for his Master's service, he will surely have glory for his reward in the world to come.

1 Cor. 9:25;
1 John 2:17

"Now," continued Interpreter, "I have shown you this Picture first because the Man in the Picture has authority to be your guide in all the difficult places you may come to on your way. He alone has been authorized by the Lord of the place where you are going. Therefore pay careful attention to what I have shown you, and always keep in mind what you have seen. For you may encounter someone on your journey who will pretend to lead you the right way; in reality, however, his path will lead to death."

Gal. 1:1

2 Tim. 1:1, 11

1 John 2:26; 3:7
Prov. 14:12

The Room Filled with Dust

Then Interpreter took him by the hand and led him into a very large Room that, because it was never swept, was full of dust. Upon inspecting it for awhile, Interpreter called his servant to sweep it. When he began to sweep, such a cloud of dust arose that Christian almost choked. Then Interpreter told a young woman who stood watching, "Bring some water in here and sprinkle the Room." After she had done so, the Room was easily swept and cleaned.

"What does this mean?" Christian asked.

"This Room is the heart of a man who was never sanctified by the sweet grace of the Gospel," answered Interpreter. "The dust is his original sin and inward corruptions that have defiled his entire person. The one who first began to sweep is the Law, but she who brought water and sprinkled it is the Gospel. Now remember you saw that no sooner had the first begun sweeping than the dust made such a cloud that the Room could not be cleaned by him—and you were almost choked by it. This is to show you that the Law, instead of cleansing the heart from sin by its works, revives and adds strength to sin. Even as that soul sees and tries to get rid of the sin, it has been granted no power to overthrow it.

Rom. 5:20; 7:5;
1 Cor. 15:56
Rom. 7:18, 25;
Gal. 3:10-14

"Again, you observed the young woman sprinkle the Room with water so that it could easily be cleaned. This is to show you that when the Gospel comes into the heart with all its sweet and precious influences—even as you saw the young woman still the dust by sprinkling the floor with water—sin is vanquished and subdued. The soul is cleansed through faith and is consequently fit for the King of Glory to inhabit."

Eph. 5:26
Acts 15:9
1 Cor. 3:16-17

Passion and Patience

I next saw in my dream that Interpreter took him by the hand and led him into a small room

PATIENCE

where two little children sat, each one in his own chair. The name of the older one was Passion, and the younger, Patience. Passion seemed to be quite discontent, but Patience was very quiet.

Then Christian asked, "Why is Passion so unhappy?"

Interpreter answered, "Their guardian wants them to wait for their best things until the beginning of next year, but Passion wants everything now. Patience, however, is willing to wait."

Then I saw someone come to Passion, offering him a bag of treasure and pouring it out at his feet. Passion quickly picked it up, rejoiced over it, and began to laugh scornfully at Patience. I noticed, however, that before long Passion had wasted all of his treasure and had only rags left for clothing.

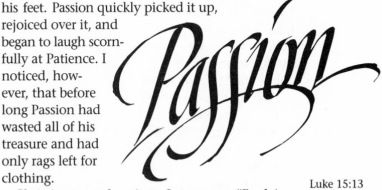

Luke 15:13

Christian turned again to Interpreter. "Explain this matter to me more fully."

"These two boys are symbols," answered Interpreter. "Passion represents the people of this world, and Patience represents those of the world to come. As you can see, Passion wants his treasures now, this year, that is to say, in this world. This is how the men of this world are; they must have everything they want right now. They can't wait until next year, that is, until the next world, for their good inheritance. That proverb, 'A bird in the hand is worth two in the bush,' carries more weight with them than all the divine promises of the blessings of the world to come. But as you observed, he quickly spent it all and was left with nothing but rags. And that is how it will be with all such people at the end of this world."

Luke 15:13-14

Christian said, "I can now see that for many reasons Patience has the best wisdom. First, because he waits for the best things, and second, because he will have glory, while the other has nothing but rags."

Titus 2:12-13

"Not only this," said Interpreter, "but you can add another. Know for certain that the glory of the next world will never wear out, but these present glories are suddenly gone. Therefore Passion did not have good reason to laugh at Patience simply because he had his treasures first. Patience will, in the end, laugh at Passion because he received his best things last. First must give way to last, because last is still yet to come, and last gives way to nothing, for there is nothing to follow. The one who receives his portion first, therefore, must of necessity spend it in its allotted time. But the one who has his portion last, will have it lastingly. It is said of a certain Rich Man, 'Son, remember that in your lifetime you received your good things, while Lazarus received bad things, but now he is comforted here and you are in agony.'"

Matt. 6:19-20

Matt. 20:16;
Mark 10:31;
Luke 13:30

Luke 16:25

"Then I can see," said Christian, "that it is best not to covet the things of this world but to wait for things that are to come."

Exod. 20:17;
Deut. 7:25;
Rom. 7:7;
1 John 2:16-17

Interpreter nodded. "You are speaking the truth. For the things that are seen are temporal, while the things that are not seen are eternal. But though this is true, since the present things and our own fleshly appetites are so compatible with each other, and since the things to come and our carnal senses are such strangers to each other, the first of these easily become friends while the latter are kept distant from one another."

2 Cor. 4:18

The Fire by the Wall

Then I saw in my dream that Interpreter took Christian by the hand and led him into a place where a Fire was burning against a wall. Someone was standing beside it trying to put the Fire out by constantly pouring great amounts of water upon it. Yet the Fire continued to burn, higher and hotter.

"What does this mean?" asked Christian.

Interpreter answered, "This Fire is the work of Grace that is formed in the heart. The one who throws water on it to extinguish it is the Devil. But as you can see, the Fire is burning higher and hotter in spite of this; and now you will see the reason why." So he took Christian around to the back side of the wall, where they saw a Man with a container of oil in His hand. Secretly this Man was continuously pouring oil into the Fire.

Then Christian asked, "What does this mean?"

Interpreter answered, "This is Christ, who with the Oil of his Grace, continually maintains the work already begun in the heart. Because of this, in spite of what the Devil can do, the souls of His people will continue to walk in His Grace. The fact that the Man was standing behind the wall to maintain the Fire is meant to teach you that it is difficult for those experiencing temptation to see how this work of Grace is being maintained in their souls." 2 Cor. 12:9; Phil. 1:6

The Beautiful Palace

I also saw that once again Interpreter took him by the hand and led him into a pleasant place where a stately Palace had been constructed. It was beautiful to behold, and when Christian saw it, he was greatly delighted. He observed some people walking up on the top of the Palace, and they were all clothed in gold.

Then Christian asked, "May we go in there?"

Interpreter took him and led him up toward the door of the Palace. At the door stood a great number of people, all desiring to enter but none

daring to try. There was a man sitting at a table
near the door with a Book and Pen, ready to take

Rev. 20:12-15 the name of anyone who would go in. Christian
saw also that many men in armor stood in the
doorway to guard it, having resolved to inflict
injury and mischief on those who would enter.
Christian was amazed!

At last, after every other man had drawn back
in fear, Christian saw a man with a resolute
expression come up to the one seated at the table.
He said, "Write down my name, sir," and it was
done. Then Christian saw the man draw his

Eph. 6:17 Sword and put a Helmet on his head. The man
rushed toward the door, and the armed men
came upon him with deadly force. Not at all dis-
heartened, he fought back, cutting and slashing
with fierce determination. After a bloody confron-

Acts 14:22 tation with those who sought to keep him out, he
fought his way through them all and pressed for-

1 Tim. 4:7 ward into the Palace. Then there could be heard
pleasant voices from within, even from the Three
that walked on top of the Palace. They said,

"Come in, come in,
Eternal glory you shall win."

Rev. 3:5 So the man went in and was clothed with
garments like their own.

Christian smiled and said, "I'm sure I understand the meaning of this. May I now go on
from here?"

"No, stay," said Interpreter, "until I have
shown you a little more. After that you can be
on your way."

The Man in the Iron Cage

Despair is like
an iron cage. So Interpreter took him by the hand and led him
into a very dark room where a man sat in an Iron
Cage.

32

By all appearances the man was very sad. He sat with his eyes staring at the ground and with his hands folded, sighing as if his heart would break.

Christian asked, "What does this mean?"

Interpreter told him to talk with the man.

Then Christian asked the man, "Who are you?"

The man answered, "I am what I once was not."

"What were you before?"

"At one time I was a man who professed Christ and whose faith was pure and growing, not only in my own eyes, but also in the eyes of others. I was, so I thought, fit for the Celestial City and even felt joy when I thought of my arrival there."   Luke 8:13

The Man IN THE Iron Cage

"Well, what are you now?"

"I am now a man of despair, and I am locked up in it as I am in this Iron Cage. I cannot get out. Oh, I cannot!"

"But how did you get into this condition?"

"I ceased to watch and be sober. I allowed myself to be driven by my lusts, and I sinned against the light of the Word and the goodness of God. I have grieved the Holy Spirit, and He is gone from me; I allowed an opening for the Devil, and he has come to me; I have provoked God to anger, and He has left me; I have so hardened my heart that I cannot repent."   Rom. 12:3
1 Tim. 6:9-10;
1 Pet. 2:11
Gal. 5:16-17;
Eph. 4:30
Eph. 4:27
1 Kings 16:2
Ps. 95:7-8;
Heb. 3:12-13

Then Christian asked Interpreter, "But is there no hope for a man like this?"

"Ask him," said Interpreter.

Turning again to the man, Christian asked, "Must you be kept in the Iron Cage of Despair? Is there no hope?"

"No, none at all."

"Why? The Son of the Blessed is very merciful."   Mark 14:61

Heb. 6:6
Luke 19:14

Heb. 10:29

Heb. 10:26-27

Luke 8:14

Eph. 6:18;
1 Thess. 5:6;
1 Pet. 5:8

"I have crucified Him to myself afresh; I have despised His very Person; I have despised His righteousness; I have counted His blood as an unholy thing; I have shown utter contempt for the Spirit of grace. Therefore, I have shut myself out from all the promises, and nothing remains for me but threatenings, dreadful threatenings, fearful threatenings of certain judgment and fiery wrath which shall consume me as an adversary."

Christian was greatly perplexed. "Why did you allow yourself to be brought into this condition?"

"For the lusts, pleasures, and profits of this world, in the enjoyment of which I promised myself great delight. But now every one of those things bites and gnaws at me like a fiery serpent."

"But can you not now repent and turn around?"

"God has denied me repentance. His word gives me no encouragement to believe. Yes, He has shut me up in this Cage, and not all the men in the world can set me free. Oh, eternity, eternity! How will I ever bear the misery that I must face in eternity!"

Then Interpreter looked at Christian and gave him this charge: "Remember this man's misery, and let it be a caution to you forever."

"Well, this is frightening!" Christian responded. "God help me to watch and be sober and to pray that I might shun what caused this man's misery. Sir, isn't it time for me to be on my way now?"

"Not yet," said Interpreter. "Stay until I show you one more thing, and then you may leave."

The Man with the Terrifying Dream

So he took Christian by the hand again and led him into a bedroom where someone was getting out of bed. As the man got dressed he shook and trembled.

Then Christian asked, "Why is this man trembling?"

Interpreter then told the man to explain to Christian why he was trembling.

THE MAN
WITH THE
Terrifying Dream

So he said, "Last night while I was sleeping, I dreamed, and suddenly the sky became completely black. The thunder roared and the lightning flashed in such a frightening way that I was filled with dread. Then I looked up and saw the clouds moving by at an unusual speed. Next, I heard a great trumpet blast and saw a Man sitting upon a cloud, accompanied by the hosts of Heaven. They were all arrayed in flames of fire, and the heavens were aflame as well. And I heard a voice, saying, 'Arise, you dead, and come to judgment.'

"With that the rocks split, the graves opened, and the dead within them came forth. Some of them were very glad and looked to the heavens; others tried to hide themselves under the mountains. Then I saw the Man seated upon the cloud open the Book, and He commanded the world to draw near. Yet, because of a fierce flame that issued forth from before Him, the dead were set at a distance from Him, like the span between a judge and the prisoners he will sentence.

"I heard it also proclaimed to those accompanying the Man on the cloud, 'Gather together the tares, the chaff, and stubble, and cast them into the burning lake.' And with that, a Bottomless Pit opened near where I stood. From the mouth of the pit spewed forth great amounts of smoke, coals of fire, and hideous noises. It was also commanded, 'Gather My wheat into the

Matt. 24:29

Rev. 20:11

1 Thess. 4:16;
Matt. 25:31;
Jude 14-15
2 Thess. 1:7-8
Matt. 24:30-31

Mark 13:14;
John 5:28-29

Rev. 20:12

Dan. 7:9-10;
Mal. 3:2-3

Rev. 9:1; 20:1-3

Matt. 3:12;
13:24-30;
Luke 3:17

barn.' Then I saw many caught up and carried away in the clouds, but I was left behind. I looked for a place to hide myself, but I was unable to do so because the Man who sat upon the cloud constantly kept His eye upon me. My sins also came to my mind, and my conscience accused me from every direction. After this, I awoke from my sleep."

Matt. 24:40;
1 Thess. 4:16-17

Rom. 2:14-15

"But what was it that made you so afraid of this sight?" Christian asked.

"Why, I thought that the day of judgment had come and that I was not ready for it. What frightened me most, however, was that the angels gathered some but left me behind. Also, the pit of Hell opened its mouth right at my feet, and my conscience continued to afflict me. It seemed that the Judge always had His eye on me, His face full of indignation."

Then Interpreter asked Christian. "Have you paid close attention to all these things?"

"Yes, and they fill me with both hope and fear."

"Well, keep all these things in your mind so that they may be a goad in your sides and prod you forward in the way you must go."

Eccles. 12:11

Then Christian tightened his belt and began to make preparations for his journey. So Interpreter blessed him, saying, "May the Comforter always be with you, dear Christian, to guide you in the way that leads to the City."

John 14:26

So Christian went on his way, saying,

"Here I have seen things rare and profitable
Things pleasant, yet awesome, to make me stable.
What I have begun to take in hand
Let me then think on and understand—
That I've been shown truth, so let me be
Thankful, O good Interpreter, to thee."

CHAPTER 4
◆◆◆◆◆◆◆◆◆◆◆◆◆◆

Christian Reaches the Cross

Now I could see in my dream that the High-way Christian was to travel on was protected on either side by a Wall, and the Wall was called Salvation. Burdened Christian began to run up the Highway, but not without great difficulty because of the load he was carrying on his back.

Isa. 26:1

He ran this way until he came to a place on somewhat higher ground where there stood a Cross. A little way down from there was an open Grave. And I saw in my dream that just as Christian approached the Cross, his Burden came loose from his shoulders,* fell from his back, and began to roll downward until it tumbled into the open Grave to be seen no more.

Rom. 6:5-7;
Col. 2:11-15

After this, Christian was glad and light. He exclaimed with a joyful heart, "Through His sorrows He has given me rest, and through His death He has given me life." Then he stood still for awhile to examine and ponder the Cross; for it was very surprising to him that the sight of the Cross alone had brought him complete deliverance from his Burden. So he continued to look and watch until springs of tears welled up in his eyes and came pouring down his cheeks.

When God releases us from our guilt and burden, we are as those that leap for joy.
Heb. 4:3; 5:8-9
1 Cor. 15:54-58;
Heb. 2:9

Zech. 12:10

Who's this? The Pilgrim! Oh, it's so true,
Old things are passed away, all is become new.
Strange! He's another man, you have my word,
They are fine feathers that make a fine bird.

Then, as he stood watching and weeping, three Shining Ones suddenly appeared and greeted him. "Be at peace!" The first announced. "Your sins are forgiven!" The second one stripped off his tattered clothing and dressed him in bright, new garments. After this, the third one set a mark upon his forehead and handed him a Scroll with a seal on it. He directed Christian to study the Scroll as he traveled and to present it upon his arrival at the Celestial Gate. They then left Christian, and he leaped for joy three times as he went on his way singing,

Mark 2:5

Zech. 3:4

Eph. 1:13;
Rev. 14:1

A Christian can sing, though alone, when God gives him the joy of his heart.

"I came this far burdened with my sin;
No, nothing could ease the grief I was in,
Until I came here; what a place is this!
Must here be the beginning of my bliss?
Must here the Burden fall off of my back?
Must here the cords that bound it to me crack?
Blessed Cross! Blessed grave! Blessed rather be
The Man who there was put to shame for me."

Even when alone a Christian can sing when God puts joy in his heart.

False Christians along the Way
After these things, I saw in my dream that Christian journeyed on in this happy state until he came

simple

to the bottom of a Hill where he saw, a little off the way, three men fast asleep with fetters on their feet. One was named Simple, the second was Sloth, and the third, Presumption.

When Christian saw them lying down like this, he approached them to see if he could possibly awaken them. He cried out, "You are like those who sleep on the top of a ship's mast. Can't you see that the deadly sea—a bottomless abyss—is beneath you? Wake up, then, and leave here! Have a willing heart, and I will help you out of your fetters."

Prov. 23:34

Continuing his exhortation, he said, "If he who goes about like a roaring lion comes by, you will certainly become prey to his teeth."

At that they looked up at him and began to reply. "I don't see any danger," said Simple. Sloth yawned as he said, "I just want to sleep a little bit more." Presumption arrogantly retorted, "Every barrel must stand on its own bottom." And so they lay down to sleep again, and Christian went on his way.

1 Pet. 5:8

There is nothing persuasion can do unless God opens the eyes.

Prov. 22:3; 27:12

Prov. 6:9-11; 24:30-34

Rom. 2:4

He was troubled to think, however, that men in such danger should have such little respect for one who so freely offered to help them. Not only had he awakened them and offered them wise counsel, but he had also been willing to help them remove their fetters.

While he was still troubling himself over these, he saw two other men come tumbling over the Wall on the left-hand side of the narrow way; they were able to quickly catch up with him. The name of one was Formality, and the other's name

PRESUMPTION

was Hypocrisy. So, like I said, they caught up with him, and the three began to converse.

"Gentlemen," asked Christian, "where have you come from and where are you going?"

They answered, "We were born in the Land of Vain-glory, and are on our way to Mount Zion to receive praise."

Prov. 27:2

"Why didn't you enter at the Gate that stands at the beginning of the way?" asked Christian. "Don't you realize it is written that 'anyone refusing to walk through the Gate, who sneaks over the Wall, must surely be a thief'?"

John 10:1

Formality and Hypocrisy answered that all the people from their country considered the Gate to be too far away. The usual way was to take a short-cut, just as they had done, by climbing over the Wall.

Christian was troubled by this and asked, "But since you are violating His revealed will, won't this be viewed as a trespass against the Lord of the City where we are going?"

They told Christian that he didn't need to worry about that because what they were doing was a custom dating back at least a thousand years, and, if need be, they could produce testimony that would bear witness to the correctness of their approach.

Those who come into the way but not by the door, think they can justify their actions.

"But will it stand up in a court of law?" Christian countered.

Formality and Hypocrisy replied that a long-standing custom over a thousand years old would by now undoubtedly be deemed legal by an impartial judge. "Besides," they argued, "what does it matter which way we take to get into the way, just so we are in it? If we are in, we are in. You, also, are in the way, though we perceive you came in at the Gate. But we are in the way, too, though we came tumbling over the Wall. Now, in what way is your condition any better than ours?"

Hypocrisy

At this, Christian challenged them. "I walk according to my Master's Rule; but you walk according to your own vain imaginations. The Lord of the way already counts you as thieves, so I doubt that you will be found to be true men at our journey's end. You have come in by yourselves without His direction, and you shall go out by yourselves without His mercy."

They didn't have much to say to this except to tell Christian to mind his own business. Then I saw that the three men walked on without much discussion with one another, except that the two men told Christian that as to laws and decrees, they would doubtlessly obey them as conscientiously as

Formality

he. "Therefore," they said, "except for the Coat on your back, which we trust was given to you by some of your neighbors to hide the shame of your nakedness, we don't see how you differ from us."

Again Christian made a swift retort. "Since you didn't come in by the door, you will not be saved by laws and decrees. And as for this Coat on my back, it was given me by the Lord of the place where I'm going. It was given, as you said, to cover my nakedness, and I received it as a token of kindness to me—I had nothing but rags before. Besides this, it encourages me as I journey on. I think to myself, 'Surely, when I arrive at the Gate of the City, the Lord of the place will know and accept me because I will be wearing His Coat.' It is a Coat that He freely gave me on the day that He stripped off my rags. Moreover, I bear a mark on my forehead that perhaps you haven't noticed. One of my Lord's most intimate associates fixed it there on the day that my Burden fell from my shoulders. In addition to this, I must tell you that they gave me a Scroll that bore a seal to authenticate it. It was given me to read for encouragement as I journey on the way. They

Gal. 2:16

Gal. 3:27

Rev. 14:1

told me, also, to present it at the Celestial Gate to prove that I am to be admitted without question. Though you need these things, I doubt you have them since you didn't come in at the Gate."

Formality and Hypocrisy had no answer to the things Christian had said; they just looked at each other and laughed. Then I saw that as they continued on their way, Christian went on ahead of the others. He had nothing more to say to them but spoke to himself, sometimes with sighs and sometimes with words of encouragement. He would often refresh himself by reading from the Scroll that one of the Shining Ones had given him.

Three Ways from Which to Choose

They all traveled on until they came to the foot of a Hill, at the bottom of which was a spring. In that place could be found two other ways besides the one that came straight from the Gate. There, at the bottom of the Hill, one way turned off to the left and the other way to the right. The narrow way, however, led straight up the side of the Hill, which was called Difficulty. Christian went to the spring and drank from it to refresh himself. Then, he began to move up the Hill, saying,

Deut. 5:32
Matt. 7:13-14

"The Hill, though high, I desire to ascend;
The difficulty will not me offend;
For I perceive the way to life lies here:
Come, be strong, heart, neither faint nor fear.
Better, though difficult, the right way to go,
Than wrong, though easy, where the end is woe."

The other two also came to the foot of the Hill. However, when they saw that the Hill was steep and high and that there were two other ways to go, they supposed that the three ways might once again converge on the other side of the Hill; therefore, they resolved to go the two

other ways. The name of one way was Danger, and the name of the other was Destruction. So one man took Danger and was led into a giant forest; the other went straight up the way to Destruction, and was led into a vast field full of dark mountains where he stumbled and fell to rise no more.

Shall they who begin wrongly rightly end?
Shall they have safety at all for their friend?
No, no, in headstrong manner they first set out,
And headlong they will fall in the end, no doubt.

Christian Loses the Scroll at the Pleasant Arbor

After this, I looked for Christian and saw him going up the Hill. I could see his pace slow from running to walking—and then from walking to crawling on his hands and knees—because the Hill was so steep. Now about halfway up the Hill was a Pleasant Arbor, a resting place made by the Lord of the Hill to refresh weary travelers. When Christian got there, he sat down to rest. Then he pulled out his Scroll from where he kept it hidden in his Coat next to his heart; he read from it for encouragement. He also looked over the bright new garments that were given to him when he stood at the Cross. After relaxing for awhile, he began to doze and was soon fast asleep. He was detained by his sleep until almost nightfall, and as he slept, the Scroll fell out of his hand.

A refuge of grace.

He that sleeps is a loser.

As he was sleeping, someone came and woke him up, saying, "Take a lesson from the ants, you

43

Prov. 6:6 lazy fellow. Learn from their ways and be wise!"
Upon hearing this, Christian suddenly leaped up
and hurried on his way, traveling swiftly until he
came to the top of the Hill.

Responding to Fear

Now when he had reached the top, two men
came running up hurriedly to meet him. The
name of one was Timorous and the other Mistrust. Christian asked, "Sirs, what is the matter?
You are running the wrong way." Timorous
answered that they had been going to the City
of Zion and had gotten past this difficult place.
"But," he said, "the farther we go, the more danger we meet. Therefore we have turned around
2 Tim. 1:7 and are going back again."

"Yes," said Mistrust, "for just ahead of us we saw
a couple of Lions lying in the way. We don't know
whether they are asleep or awake, but we couldn't
help but think that if we came within their reach,
they would immediately tear us to pieces."

"You are scaring me," said Christian, "but where
shall I run for safety? If I go back to my own country, which is awaiting fire and brimstone, I will
certainly perish there. If I can get to the Celestial
City, I am sure to find safety there. I must take the
risk. To go back is nothing but death; to go forward is fear of death, but beyond that lies everlasting life. I will continue to go forward."

So Mistrust and Timorous ran down the Hill,
and Christian went on his way. Reflecting on
what he heard from the men, however, he felt a
need to find comfort by reading from his Scroll.
He reached into his Coat to find the Scroll, but
it was gone. At this, Christian became deeply
distressed and didn't know what to do. He knew
that he needed the Scroll for encouragement,
and also to use as his pass into the Celestial City.

Recovering the Scroll

Finally, after much turmoil and confusion, he
remembered that he had fallen asleep in the
Pleasant Arbor on the side of the Hill. He fell
down on his knees and asked God to forgive him
for his foolishness. Then he started back to look
for his Scroll. But who could sufficiently express
the sorrow in Christian's heart as he journeyed
all the way back? Sometimes he sighed, sometimes he cried, and often he chided himself for
being so foolish as to fall asleep in the place that
was erected only for a little refreshment from his
weariness.

So he returned, searching carefully all along
the way, on this side and that, hoping to find
the Scroll that had been such a comfort to him
so many times on his journey. He traveled in
this way until once again he came within sight
of the Arbor where he had rested and fallen
asleep. But the sight of it compounded his sorrow by reminding him again of the evil of his
sleeping. He therefore expressed deep regret for
his sinful sleep, saying, "Oh, what a wretched
man I am, that I could sleep in the daytime!
And that I could sleep in the midst of diffi-   1 Thess. 5:6-8
culty! How could I so indulge myself so as to
use that rest to give ease to my flesh when the
Lord of the Hill erected it only for reviving the
spirits of pilgrims! How many steps I have
taken in vain! It happened like this to Israel;
because of their sin, they were sent back again
by way of the Red Sea. And I am now forced to   Num. 14:21-22, 25
tread these steps sorrowfully three times when
I could have happily walked them only once.
How far might I have been on my way by this
time! But now I am likely to be overtaken by   1 Thess. 5:4-5
nightfall, for the day is almost gone. Oh, that   Rom. 13:11-12
I had not slept!"

Now by this time he had come to the Arbor again where he sat down and wept for awhile. But finally, while looking under a bench, Christian's hopes were realized—he spotted his Scroll! When he saw it, he hastily grabbed it with trembling hands. How can one describe how joyful Christian was when he had found his Scroll again? For this Scroll gave him the assurance of eternal life and meant acceptance into the Celestial City. Therefore he held it close to his heart and gave thanks to God for directing his eye to the place where it lay. Then, with joy and tears he committed himself once again to his journey. And, oh, how swiftly he went up the rest of the Hill!

Titus 3:4-7;
1 John 2:25;
5:11-13

Heb. 13:14;
Rev. 21

Yet before he reached the top of the Hill, the sun went down on Christian. This made him again remember the stupidity of his slumbering, and once more he began to lament, "Oh, you sinful sleep! Because of you I will probably have to travel at night! I must walk without the sun and with only darkness covering the path for my feet, and I will have to listen to the sounds of the sad creatures of the night—all this because of my sinful sleep!"

Then he remembered the story that Mistrust and Timorous had told him, how they were frightened by the sight of the Lions. He thought, "These beasts roam about in the night for their prey, and if they should meet up with me in the dark, how would I be able to get them out of my way? How would I escape being torn to pieces by them?" He walked on in this way, but while he was still lamenting his foolish mistake, he looked up and saw a stately Palace ahead of him beside the High-way. Its name was Beautiful.

Facing Lions in the Way

So I saw in my dream that Christian moved quickly toward it, hoping to find lodging there. Before he had gone far, he entered a narrow pass, which was about two hundred yards from the Gatekeeper's Lodge. But then he saw two Lions in the way! "Now," he thought, "I can see the dangers that drove Mistrust and Timorous away." (The Lions were chained, but he was unable to see the chains.) He became very frightened and considered turning back to catch up with the others. For all he could see was death lurking in front of him. But the gatekeeper at the Lodge, whose name was Watchful, perceived that Christian had come to a halt as if he would turn back. Calling to him, Watchful said, "Are you so weak and timid? Don't be afraid of the Lions, for they are chained and have been placed there for a test of faith—to distinguish those who have it from those who do not. Keep to the middle of the path and you will not be hurt."

1 Pet. 1:3-9; 5:8-10
Deut. 5:32-33; Prov. 4:25-27

Difficult is behind, Fear is before
He is now up the Hill, but Lions do roar;
A Christian is never for long at ease,
When one fright's gone, another will him seize.

Then I saw that he moved on, trembling in fear of the Lions but heeding Watchful's advice. The Lions jumped up and roared, but they did him no harm. After this experience, Christian clapped his hands for joy and walked on.

CHAPTER 5

♦♦♦♦♦♦♦♦♦♦♦♦♦♦

Received at the Palace Beautiful

Christian arrived at the gate where Watchful stood waiting. Then Christian asked Watchful, "Sir, what is this place? May I sleep here tonight?"

He answered, "This House was built by the Lord of the Hill; He built it for the relief and security of pilgrims. Where have you come from and where are you going?"

"I have come from the City of Destruction and am going to Mount Zion, but because the sun is now set, I would like to stay here tonight if I may."

"What is your name?"

"My name is now Christian, but my name at first was Graceless. I am of the Race of Japheth, whom God will persuade to dwell in the tents of Shem."

Gen. 9:27

"But why have you come so late? The sun has already set."

"I would have been here sooner, but—I am such a wretched man!—I fell asleep in the Arbor that stands on the hillside! In spite of this, I would have been here much sooner, but while I was sleeping, I dropped the Scroll that had been given me at the Cross. I traveled all the way to the brow of the Hill without knowing it was gone. Then, when I felt for it and found it missing, with deep remorse I was forced to return to the place where I had fallen asleep. I found it there, and now I have finally arrived."

"Well," said Watchful, "I will call for one of the young women who lives here. If she accepts what you have to say, then, according to the House rule, she will bring you in to meet the rest of the family." So Watchful, the gatekeeper, rang the doorbell, and a serious but beautiful young woman named Discretion answered and asked why she had been called.

Watchful answered, "This man is on a journey from the City of Destruction to Mount Zion. He is weary, however, and it is dark outside. He asked me if he might sleep here tonight, so I told him I would call for you."

Discretion asked Christian where he had come from and where he was going, and he told her. Next, she asked him what he had seen and met with thus far on the way, and he answered her. Then she asked him his name.

"It is Christian," he replied, "and I have an even stronger desire to stay here tonight because I can tell that this place was built by the Lord of the Hill for the relief and security of pilgrims."

So she smiled, and tears began to form in her eyes. After a pause, she said, "I will call for two or three more members of my family." So she ran to the door and called for Prudence, Piety, and Charity, who, after a little more conversation with him, had him come join the family. And many of them met him at the entrance of the House, saying, "Come in, man blessed of the Lord. This House was built by the Lord of the Hill for the purpose of showing hospitality to pilgrims like yourself. Then he bowed his head in appreciation and followed them into the House. After Christian was seated, they gave him something to drink. Several members of the family— Piety, Prudence, and Charity—were appointed to discourse with Christian until dinner. And so they began to talk.

Matt. 25:34

Conversation with Piety

Piety first addressed him. "Come, good Christian, since we have welcomed you into our House tonight, let us hear more from you about all the things that have happened on your pilgrimage. Perhaps by listening to you we can be enriched. What first moved you to take on the life of a pilgrim?"

Rom. 1:11-13; Heb. 10:24-25

"I'm delighted that you're interested," answered Christian. "I was driven out of my native country by a dreadful sound in my ears. I learned that inevitable destruction awaited me if I continued to live there."

"But how did you happen to leave your country to come this way?"

"It was God's will; for when I became fearful of destruction, I didn't know where to go. But fortunately a man named Evangelist came to me as I was trembling and crying. He directed me to the Wicket-gate, which I never would have found on my own. He set me on the way that has led directly to this House."

"But didn't you pass by the House of the Interpreter?"

"Yes, and I saw things there that will stick in my memory for the rest of my life—three things in particular. I learned how Christ, in spite of Satan's efforts, maintains His work of grace in the heart. I learned about a man who had sinned beyond the point of hoping for God's mercy. And I saw a man who had a dream while he was sleeping and thought the day of judgment had come."

Phil. 1:6

Heb. 6:4-6

Rev. 20:11-15

"Why? Did he tell you his dream?"

"Yes, and I thought it was a dreadful one. My heart ached as he described it, but I'm glad I heard it."

"Was that all you saw at the Interpreter's House?"

"No, he showed me a stately Palace; all the

people inside were clothed in gold. A venturesome man came and cut his way through the armed guards that stood at the door to keep him out. Then he was invited to come in and win eternal glory. My heart got so carried away with these things that I would like to have stayed at the good man's House for a year! I knew, however, I had to continue on my journey."

Piety "And what else did you see as you traveled on the way?"

"After going just a little bit farther," said Christian, "I saw a vision of One hanging and bleeding on the Cross. The very sight of Him made my Burden fall from my back. Oh, I had groaned under a very heavy Burden, but then it just dropped off! This was a strange experience, for I had never before seen such a thing. Yes, and while I stood looking up—for I couldn't resist staring—three Shining Ones came to me. One of them declared that my sins were forgiven, another stripped off my ragged clothing and gave me this embroidered Coat that you see, and the third one affixed the mark that you see on my forehead and gave me this sealed Scroll."

Exod. 28:4, 39

Rev. 14:1

With that, he pulled the Scroll out of his Coat pocket.

"But you saw more than this, didn't you?" Piety asked.

"The things I've told you were the best. But, yes, I saw some other things. I saw three men—Simple, Sloth, and Presumption—just a little out of the way I was traveling on. They were lying sound asleep with fetters on their feet; but do you think I could rouse them? I also met Formality and Hypocrisy, who came tumbling over the Wall pretending to go to Zion, but they were quickly lost. I warned them, but they refused to believe me.

"Above all, however, I found that getting up this Hill was hard work; and passing by the Lions' mouths was just as difficult. I'm telling you the truth when I say that if that good man who stands by the gate had not been there, I'm not sure, after all I have been through, that I wouldn't have turned back again. But now, I thank God that I'm here, and I thank you for receiving me."

Conversation with Prudence

Then Prudence wanted to ask him a few questions.

"Sometimes don't you think about the country you came from?"

"Yes, but with much shame and abhorrence. It's true that if I had highly regarded the country that I came from, I might have returned at an opportune time. But now I desire a better Country, that is, a Heavenly one."

Heb. 11:15-16

"But don't you still waver sometimes when you think of the things you were accustomed to?"

"Yes, I struggle, but I don't want to. The inward and carnal thoughts—which all of my countrymen, as well as myself, delighted in—are especially troublesome. All those things are my grief now. If I could choose to have things my way, I would choose never to think of those former things again. But when I want to do what is best, that is when I find the worst is what motivates me."

Rom. 7:21-23

"Do you find that sometimes it seems as though those things have been subdued, but that other times they are your greatest entanglement?"

"Yes, but the former is seldom the case. The hours when I feel free are like gold to me."

"Can you remember how at times these agitating thoughts seem to be conquered?"

"Yes, when I remember what I saw at the Cross, that will do it; and when I gaze at this embroidered Coat, that will do it; and when I read the Scroll that I carry close to my heart, that will do it; and when I meditate about where I am going, that will do it."

"What makes you so eager to reach Mount Zion?"

"Why, there I hope to see the One who hung dead on the Cross alive again; and there I hope to be freed of all the things within me that are such a struggle to me. They say that there is no death there, and that I will live there with wonderful companions. To tell you the truth, I love Him because He delivered me from my Burden. And I am so tired of my inward sickness that I long to be where there is no more sin and death and where I will be in the fellowship of those who continually cry, 'Holy, holy, holy.'"

Rom. 7:21-25

Isa. 25:6;
Rev. 21:4

Isa. 6:3; Rev. 4:8

Conversation with Charity

Then Charity entered the conversation, asking Christian, "Do you have a family? Are you a married man?"

"I have a wife and four children."

"Why didn't you bring them along with you?"

Then Christian began to cry. "Oh, I wanted to! But all of them were utterly opposed to my going on this pilgrimage."

"But shouldn't you have talked to them and tried to show them the danger they were in by staying behind?"

"I did, and I also told them what God had shown me concerning the coming destruction of our City. However, they seemed to think I was joking and wouldn't believe me."

Gen. 19:14

"Did you pray that God would bless your counsel to them?"

"Yes, and with great love and emotion. I want you to know that my wife and poor children were very dear to me."

"But did you tell them of your own sorrow and of your fear of destruction? For I can imagine how clear the coming destruction was to you."

"Yes, over and over and over. I was so afraid of the judgment that was hanging over all of our heads that I know they could see the alarm on my face as well as in my tears. But none of this was enough to convince them to come with me."

Matt. 16:24-26;
Mark 8:34-38;
Luke 9:23-26;
1 John 2:15-17

"But why didn't they come? What did they have to say for themselves?"

"Well, my wife was afraid of losing this world, and my children were enjoying the foolish pleasures of youth. So for one reason or another they left me to wander in that anxious condition alone."

2 Tim. 2:22;
Heb. 11:25

"But did your own vain life weaken your ability to persuade them to go with you?"

"You're right; I cannot commend my life, for I am conscious of my many failings. I know that a man's own actions can quickly overpower whatever persuasive ability he may have to convince others for their own good. Yet I can honestly say that I tried to be very careful not to be a negative example in any way so that they would have no reason for not joining me on the pilgrimage. But for these very efforts they would tell me I was too exacting, that I denied things (for their sake) in which they saw no evil. No, I think I can safely say that if they were hindered by me, it was because of my great care not to sin against God or my neighbors."

Charity nodded. "Yes, Cain hated his brother

because his own deeds were evil while his brother's were righteous. And if your wife and children were offended with you for this, they were demonstrating their stubborn resistance to what is good, and so you are not responsible for their blood."

1 John 3:12

Ezek. 3:19

Conversation at Dinner

Now I saw in my dream that this conversation continued until supper was ready. When it was ready, they all sat down to eat at the table, which was spread with sumptuous foods and wine. Everyone talked about the Lord of the Hill—the things He had done and the reasons He had built the House. I learned that He had been a great warrior and had fought with and killed the one who had the power of death. His victory was not without great sacrifice to Himself, and hearing it made me love Him all the more.

Heb. 2:14-15

They related to Christian that His victory was accomplished only with the loss of much blood. And the thing that made His gracious sacrifice so beautiful was that all He did was motivated by pure love for His Country. Some of the members of the household told Christian that they had been with the Lord and had even spoken with Him since the time He died on the Cross. They had heard Him say with His own mouth that no one from East to West could be found who loves needy pilgrims more than He.

Heb. 9:22

John 13:1; 15:13

To demonstrate the truth of their story, they pointed out to Christian how He had stripped Himself of His glory to sacrifice His life for those who needed Him. They had heard Him say that He would not dwell in Mount Zion alone and that He had made into princes many pilgrims who by nature were born to live as beggars in garbage dumps.

Phil. 2:6-8

Rev. 14:1; 19:1, 6

1 Sam. 2:8;

Ps. 113:7;

1 Cor. 1:26-28

The Room Called Peace

They continued to talk until late that night, and
after committing their lives to their Lord's protection, they went to bed. Christian was taken to a
large upper Room with a window opened toward
the sunrise. The name of his Room was Peace.
Christian slept until daybreak, and when he
woke up, he sang:

Acts 20:7

Acts 20:32

Dan. 6:10;
Mark 14:15

"Where am I now? Is this the love and care
Of Jesus, for the ones who pilgrims are?
How He provides, that I should be forgiven!
And dwell already next door to Heaven!"

The Study and the Armory

In the morning they all got up, and after talking
some more, they told him that he shouldn't leave
until they had shown him some of the rare things
preserved there. First, they took him to the Study
where they showed him Records of the greatest
Antiquity. As I recall in my dream, the first thing
they showed him was the Genealogy of the Lord
of that Hill, revealing that He was the Son of the
Ancient of Days and descended from the eternal
lineage. His deeds were fully recorded, along with
the names of many hundreds who He had
received into His service. He had provided them
with permanent dwelling places that were not subject to decay by time or nature.

Matt. 1:1-17;
Luke 3:23-38

Dan. 7:13, 22

Heb. 5:5-6

John 14:2-3
1 Pet. 1:4

Then they read to him some of the praiseworthy
acts that some of the Lord's servants had done—
how they had subdued kingdoms, established righteousness, claimed promises, stopped the mouths
of lions, quenched the violence of fire, escaped the
edge of the sword, been courageous in battle, and
caused enemy armies to retreat.

Heb. 11:33-34

They read further in another part of the Records, where it was shown how willing their Lord

·THE·· ·DELECTABLE· ·MOUNTAINS·

would receive anyone with favor—yes, anyone—
even though previously he may have heaped

1 Tim. 1:15-16   insults against the Lord and His way. Christian
was able to survey the history of many other
notable things as well. He learned of things both
ancient and modern, along with prophecies and
predictions of things that are sure to be fulfilled,
both to the dread and amazement of enemies
and to the comfort and solace of pilgrims.

The next day they took him into the Armory
where they showed him all kinds of equipment
that the Lord had provided for pilgrims—Sword,
Shield, Helmet, Breastplate, All-prayer, and Shoes

Eph. 6:13-17   that would never wear out. There were enough
of these to equip many people for the Lord's

Gen. 15:5;   service—as many as the stars in the heavens.
Phil. 2:15

They also showed him some of the instruments
with which His servants had done wonderful

Exod. 4, 7–8,   things—Moses' Rod; the Hammer and Tent Peg
10:13; 14:16   used by Jael to slay Sisera; the Pitchers, Trumpets,

Judg. 4:1-22   and Lamps used by Gideon to put the armies of
Judg. 7   Midian to flight. They showed him the Ox Goad

Judg. 3:31   used by Shamgar to kill six hundred Philistines;
Judg. 15:15   the Jawbone used by Samson to do such mighty

feats; and the Sling and Stone used by David to
kill Goliath of Gath. They also showed him the
Sword with which their Lord will overpower the
man of lawlessness in the day of His coming confrontation. They showed him many other excellent things besides, which delighted Christian.
After this, they went to bed for the night.

1 Sam. 17

2 Thess. 2:7-9;
Rev. 19:15

A Look at the Delectable Mountains

Then I saw in my dream that when he got up
the next day to continue his journey, they again
asked him to stay until the next day. "If the
weather is clear," they told him, "we would like
to show you the Delectable Mountains." They
thought that seeing these Mountains would
encourage him since they were closer to his destination than where he was presently. So he consented and stayed. Early the next morning, they
took him to the housetop and told him to look
to the south. When he did, he saw far in the distance a very pleasant, mountainous Country,
made beautiful by forests, vineyards, fruit trees of
every kind, flowers, streams, and fountains—all
in all, a most delightful sight. Then he asked the
name of the Country. They answered, "That is
Emmanuel's Land, and like this Hill, it is to be
shared by all pilgrims. When you arrive there
from here, you will be able to see the Gate of the
Celestial City. The Shepherds who live there will
point it out to you."

Isa. 33:16-17

Isa. 8:8

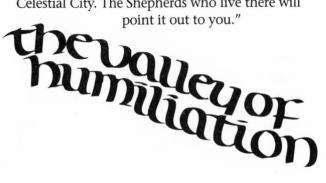

the valley of humiliation

Resuming the Journey in the Valley of Humiliation

Now it seemed to him that it was time to go, and they agreed. "But first," they said, "let us take you to the Armory again." When they got there, they equipped Christian from head to foot with all he would need in case he were attacked on the way. He then walked with his friends to the gate and there asked Watchful, the gatekeeper, if he had seen any pilgrims pass by.

"Yes," Watchful answered.

"Please tell me, was it someone you knew?" asked Christian.

"I asked his name," said Watchful, "and he told me it was Faithful."

"Oh, I know him!" said Christian. "He's from my hometown—a close neighbor. How far ahead do you think he is?"

"By this time he should be down the Hill."

"Well, kind sir, may the Lord be with you and bless you greatly for all the kindness you have shown me."

As he resumed his journey, Discretion, Piety, Charity, and Prudence decided to accompany him to the foot of the Hill. So they went out together, reviewing some of their previous conversations until they reached the place where the Hill began to descend.

Then Christian said, "It was difficult coming up the Hill, and as far as I can see, going down looks treacherous."

"Yes, it is," said Prudence. "It is a very difficult thing for a man to go down into the Valley of Humiliation and not slip on the way. That is why we want to accompany you down the Hill." So he began to make his way down very carefully, but even then, he lost his footing once or twice.*

Then I saw in my dream that when they reached
the bottom of the Hill, Christian's dear compan-
ions gave him a Loaf of Bread, a Bottle of Wine,
and a Cluster of Raisins. And he went on his way.   2 Sam. 16:1
While Christian was among his godly friends,
Their golden words sufficed to make amends
For all his griefs, and when they sent him to go
He was clad with steel from his head to his toe.

CHAPTER 6

❖❖❖❖❖❖❖❖❖❖❖❖❖

Christian's Encounter with Apollyon

Poor Christian was having a terrible time in the
Valley of Humiliation. He had ventured only a
little way before he noticed a foul Fiend—Apollyon   Rev. 9:11
—coming across the field to meet him. Christian
began to panic and debated whether he should
turn back or stand his ground. But then he
recalled that he had been given no armor for his   Eph. 6:11-17
back, and he realized that to turn back would
give his adversary an advantage. Apollyon would   Eph. 6:16
then easily pierce him with his arrows. So he
resolved to stand his ground and move forward   Eph. 6:14;
no matter what. For he thought to himself,   Phil. 3:12, 14
"Even if I had no more in mind than saving my
own life, this would still be the best choice." So
he went on, and Apollyon met him face to face.

The monster was hideous to look at, covered
with scales like a fish (and exceedingly proud of
them). He had wings like a dragon and feet like
a bear. Fire and smoke came belching up from
within his belly, and his mouth was like the   Rev. 13:1-2
mouth of a lion. When he drew close to Christian, he looked down upon him with utter disdain and demanded of him, "Where have you
come from and where are you going?"

Christian replied, "I have come from the City
of Destruction, which is the place of all evil, and
I am going to the City of Zion."

"I can tell by this that you are one of my subjects
since that whole country is under my authority—I   Luke 4:5-7

am the prince and god of it. How is it, then, that you have run away from your king? If I didn't believe you might still be of use to me, I would strike you to the ground right now with one blow."

Eph. 2:2

"It is true that I was born in your dominions," replied Christian, "but your service was hard and your wages were such that a man could not live

Rom. 6:23

on them, for the wages of sin is death. Therefore, when I came of age, I did like other people of discernment have done and looked for a way to straighten out my life."

"There is no prince who will take lightly the loss of one of his subjects," countered Apollyon. "Nor will I let you go. But since you complained about your service and wages, go on back, and whatever our country can afford, I hereby promise to give you."

"But I have given myself to another—to the King of Princes—and how can I in fairness go back with you?"

2 Tim. 3:15

"In doing this you have gone from bad to worse, as the proverb says. But it is typical for those who

1 Tim. 5:9-16;
2 Tim. 4:1-4;
Heb. 10:26-31;
2 Pet. 2:17-22

have professed themselves to be His servants to give Him the slip after awhile and return again to me. If you'll do this also, all will go well with you."

"I have given Him my faith and sworn my allegiance to Him," Christian responded. "How, then, can I go back from here and not be hanged as a traitor?"

"You did the same thing to me, and yet I am willing to forgive it all if you will now turn again and go back." Christian remained undaunted. "What I

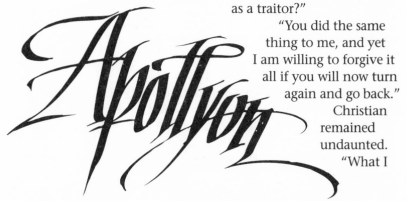

promised you was before I was of age. Besides,
I believe that the Prince, under whose banner
I now stand, is able to free me from my obligations to you and forgive me for what I did in
compliance with you. In addition to this, you
destroying Apollyon, to tell you the truth, I like
His service, His wages, His servants, His govern-
ment, His company, and His Country better than
yours. So forget about trying to persuade me further. I am *His* servant, and I will follow *Him*."

Rom. 8:2

Still, Apollyon persisted."Once you cool down
and reality sinks in, consider again what you will
likely meet with in the way you are going. You
know that, for the most part, His servants come
to a terrible end because they are violators of my
will and my ways. How many of them have been
put to a shameful death! You still believe His service is better than mine even though He has yet
to come from where He is to deliver any of His
servants from their assailants' hands. But as for
me, as all the world very well knows, I have
many times—either by power or by fraud—delivered those who faithfully serve me from Him
and His servants, though they were taken by
them. And I will also deliver you."

Christian answered firmly, "He presently
restrains Himself from delivering them in order
to test their love and see whether they will cling
to Him until the end. And as for the undesirable
end you say they come to, that is the most glorious credit to their account. They do not much
expect deliverance at present, but they remain
true for the glory coming to them—and they
shall have it when their Prince comes in His
glory and the glory of the angels."

James 1:2-3;
1 Pet. 1:6-7

Rom. 8:17-18;
2 Cor. 4:17;
Heb. 10:32-34

Matt. 24:30-31

"You have already been unfaithful in your
service to Him," Apollyon sneered. "How do you
think you can receive wages from Him?"

Rev. 12:10

"Oh, Apollyon, how have I been unfaithful to Him?"

"You weakened in your resolve when you first set out and were nearly choked in the Slough of Despond. You tried to go wrong ways to get rid of your Burden when you should have stayed on course until your Prince had taken it off. You sinfully slept and lost your treasured things. You were almost persuaded to go back at the sight of the Lions. And when you talk of your journey and of what you have heard and seen, you inwardly desire recognition for all you say or do."

"All this is true," answered Christian, "and much more that you have left out. But the Prince whom I serve and honor is merciful and ready to forgive. Besides, these shortcomings possessed me in your country, where I participated in them and groaned under their weight. I have been sorry for these things and have now received pardon by my Prince."

Ps. 86:15; 103:8;
Heb. 8:12

The Inevitable Conflict

Suddenly, Apollyon erupted into a fierce rage, shrieking, "I am an enemy of this Prince! I hate His Person, His laws, and His people! I have come out with this purpose—to stop you!"

"Apollyon, beware of what you do," warned Christian, "for I am in the King's High-way, the way of holiness. Therefore you had better watch yourself."

Num. 20:17,
21:22; Isa. 35:8

Then Apollyon spread himself out in such a way as to cover the entire width of the way, and challenged, "I am without fear in this matter. Prepare to die! For I swear by my infernal dwelling that you shall go no farther. I will destroy your soul right here."

And at that he hurled a flaming arrow at Christian's heart, but Christian had a Shield in his

The Prince

hand with
which he blocked the
arrow. Then Christian
drew his Sword and

Eph. 6:16

rouses himself for battle. Apollyon, with feverish
pace, began throwing arrows as thick as hail. It
was all Christian could do to avoid them, and,
even so, he was wounded in his head, his hand,
and his foot. This caused Christian to retreat

Matt. 27:29-30

somewhat. Seeing this, Apollyon fell upon him
with full and sudden fury. Christian regained his
courage, however, and resisted as gallantly as he
could.

This fierce combat went on for more than half
a day, until Christian's strength was almost completely spent. Because of his wounds, he grew
weaker and weaker. Apollyon saw his most opportune moment and drew up close to Christian. He
began to wrestle with Christian and threw him
forcefully to the ground. Christian's Sword flew
out of his hand.

Gloating, Apollyon said, "I am sure I have you
now." With that, he assaulted Christian nearly to

2 Cor. 1:8   the point of death so that he began to despair of life itself. But, as God would have it, while Apollyon was preparing to strike his final blow to completely annihilate his foe, Christian quickly stretched out his hand and grabbed his Sword, saying, "Do not gloat over me, my enemy!

Mic. 7:8   Though I have fallen, I will rise again!" With that, Christian gave Apollyon a deadly thrust that made him fall back as if mortally wounded. Seeing this, Christian attacked again, saying, "No, in all these things we are more than con-

Rom. 8:37   querors through Him who loved us." Apollyon then spread his dragon wings and sped away in

James 4:7   defeat, and Christian would see him no more.

A more unequal match could there be?
Christian must fight an angel, but you see
The valiant man by wielding Sword and Shield,
Does make him, though a dragon, quit the field.

No one could imagine, unless he had seen and heard the battle as I did, what yelling and hideous roaring Apollyon made the whole time;

Rom. 8:22-23   on the other hand, what sighs and groans burst forth from Christian's heart. In the struggle I never saw Christian even once give a confident look until he perceived he had wounded Apol-

Heb. 4:12   lyon with his two-edged sword—and then he actually smiled! It was the most dreadful fight that I have ever seen.

When the battle was over, Christian said, "I will give thanks here to the One who has delivered me out of the lion's mouth, to him who helped me against Apollyon." And he did, saying,

"So great Beelzebub, this Fiend's captain,
Had devised a plan that I'd never rise again.
He sent him out armed; he was enraged;
In hellish fight we fiercely engaged.

But blessed Michael helped me, and I,
By blow of Sword, quickly made him fly.
Therefore to Christ I'll give lasting praise,
And thank and bless His Name always."

Rev. 12:7-9

Then a hand reached out to him, holding leaves from the Tree of Life. Christian took the leaves, applied them to the wounds that he had received in the battle, and was healed instantly! After this, he sat down in that place to eat bread and drink from the bottle that had been given to him. Feeling refreshed, he prepared to go on with his journey. He kept his Sword drawn in his hand and said to himself, "There may well be some other enemy lurking nearby." But he had no more confrontations with Apollyon through the rest of the Valley.

Rev. 22:2

1 Cor. 11:26

The Valley of the Shadow of Death

At the end of the first Valley was another Valley called the Valley of the Shadow of Death. It was necessary for Christian to pass through it because it was the only way to the Celestial City. This Valley is a very solitary place. The prophet Jeremiah describes it as a Wilderness, a Land of Deserts and Pits, a

Ps. 23:4

Jer. 2:6

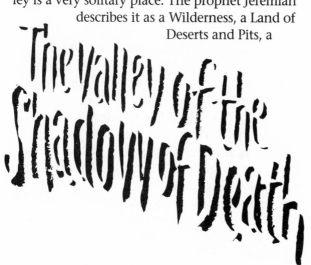

Land of Drought and of the Shadow of Death,
a Land that no one (except a Christian) is able
to pass through and where no one lives.

Heb. 13:5

Here, as you will see, Christian's testings were
even more severe than those he had encountered
with Apollyon. I saw in my dream that when Christian reached the borders of the Shadow of Death,
two men met him. They were Descendants of the
Spies who had brought back an evil report of the
Good Land, and they were in a hurry to go back.

Num. 13:31-32

"Where are you going?" Christian asked.

They answered, "Back, back, and we urge you
to follow us if you prize either life or peace."

"Why, what's the matter?"

"Matter? We were going along the same way
you are going and went as far as we dared,
almost past the point of no return. If we had
gone just a little farther, we would not have
made it back here to bring the news to you."

"But what have you met with?"

"Why, we were almost in the Valley of the
Shadow of Death, but just by chance we looked
ahead of us and could see the danger before we
came to it."

"But what did you see?"

"What did we see? Why, the Valley, itself,
which is pitch black. We could see Hobgoblins,
Satyrs, and Dragons of the Pit. We could also
hear in that Valley continual howling and
screaming—it sounded like people in indescribable misery who were bound in affliction and
chains. We also saw the depressing clouds of confusion hanging over the Valley; and death, with
wings spread, was hovering over it all. It is absolutely dreadful and in complete chaos."

Ps. 44:19; 107:10

2 Pet. 2:4-10

Job 3:5; 10:22

"From what you have said," replied Christian,
"I'm still not convinced that this isn't the way to
my destination."

"Have it your way," they said, "but we won't choose it for ourselves."

So they left, and Christian went on his way with his Sword still drawn for fear that he might be assaulted.

I then saw in my dream that there was a very deep Ditch along the right side of the Valley as far as it reached. It is into that Ditch that the blind have led the blind throughout the ages, and there both have miserably died. I could also see that on the left side was a very dangerous Quagmire; even a good person, should he fall in, will find no bottom for his foot to stand on. King David once fell in here and no doubt would have suffocated had not He who is able mercifully plucked him out.

Matt. 15:14;
Luke 6:39

Ps. 69:13-14

2 Sam. 11
Heb. 2:18; 5:7

The pathway was so narrow that Christian had to be very careful. When he tried in the darkness to avoid the Ditch on the one hand, he almost fell into the Quagmire on the other. However, when he tried to escape the Quagmire, unless he used great caution, he nearly fell into the Ditch. He went on this way, and I heard him sigh bitterly. For in addition to the dangers already mentioned, the pathway was so dark that often, when he picked up his foot to go forward, he had no idea where he should step next.

The Mouth of Hell was beside the way about midway through the Valley.

the Quagmire

Poor man, where are you now? Your day is now night.
Good man don't be downhearted, you are still right—
Your way to Heaven lies by the gates of Hell;
Cheer up, hold on, with you it shall go well.

So much fire and smoke continually came out, with swarms of sparks and hideous noises (things that gave no heed to Christian's Sword as did Apollyon) that he was forced to put his Sword away and use another weapon called "All-prayer." So I heard him cry out, "Oh, Lord, save me!" He continued praying like this for quite a while, but the flames kept reaching out toward him, and he heard sorrowful voices and rushing sounds around him. Sometimes he thought he would be torn to pieces or trampled down like dirt in the street.

Eph. 6:18
Ps. 116:4

Matt. 7:6

Christian experienced these terrors of sight and sound continuously for several miles. Then he came to a place where he thought he heard a band of Fiends coming forward to confront him. He stopped and began to think about his options. He had half a notion to go back, but then he thought that he might already be half-way through the Valley. He remembered also how he had already met and overcome many dangers, and it dawned on him that going back might be much worse than going forward. So he resolved to go on, but the Fiends seemed to come nearer and nearer. When they were almost face to face with him, he cried out very vehemently, "I will walk in the strength of the Lord God!" So they fell back and came no closer.

Ps. 73:23, 26

There is one other thing I must not omit. I noticed that poor Christian had become so confused that he no longer knew his own voice. This is how I noticed it: Just as he was passing the mouth of the burning pit, one of the wicked crea-

tures crept up behind him and whispered many
grievous, blasphemous suggestions in his ear.
This trial was worse than any of the others
because Christian thought these suggestions
had come from his own mind. How distressing   Rom. 2:15
it was for him to think that he had blasphemed
the One whom he had loved so much, but he
couldn't help himself. He didn't know enough
to close his ears, nor did he realize where the
blasphemies came from.

Christian Is Encouraged

After Christian had traveled in this disconsolate
condition for quite some time, he thought he
could hear a man's voice somewhere ahead of
him. The voice was saying, "Even though I walk
through the Valley of the Shadow of Death, I will
fear no evil, for You are with me." Then Chris-   Ps. 23:4
tian was glad for a number of reasons:

First, he gathered from this that he was not
alone but that others who feared God were in the
Valley as well. Second, he realized that God was
with them even though they were in a dark and
dismal state. He reasoned, "Even though I can't
feel His presence because of the hindrances in
this place, why wouldn't He be with me here   Job 9:11
too?" And third, he hoped that if he could soon
catch up with someone, he would then have
company. So he ventured on, calling out to whoever was up ahead. There was no answer, however; it was evident that the person thought he
also was alone.

Before long it was daybreak, and Christian
rejoiced. "He has turned the Shadow of Death   Ps. 143:8;
into the morning." Now that there was daylight,   Amos 5:8
he was able to look back, not that he wanted to
return, but to see what hazards he had gone
through in the dark. He could see more clearly

the Ditch that was on the one hand and the
Quagmire that was on the other. He also saw
how narrow the way was which led between
them. He could see the Hobgoblins, Satyrs, and
Dragons of the Pit, but they stayed far away after
daybreak and would not attempt to come near.
He could see these things, however, according
to what is written: "He reveals the deep things
of darkness and brings deep shadows into the
light." He had feared them so greatly, but he
could now view them clearly in the light of day.
Looking back, he was deeply moved by his deliverance from all the dangers he had encountered
on this desolate way.

Job 12:22

The sun's rising was also another mercy to
Christian, for though the first part of the Valley
of the Shadow of Death was dangerous, this second part which he now faced was worse. For
from where he now stood, the way to the end
of the Valley was beset on all sides with traps,
snares, instruments of torture, nets, pits and pit-
falls, deep holes, rocky cliffs, and ledges beneath
them. If he had possessed a thousand souls, he
would have lost them all if it was still as dark as
it had been when he traveled the first part. But,
as I said, the sun was rising. Christian said, "He
lighted the way before me and I walked safely
through the darkness." In this light he was able
to make it to the end of the Valley.

Job 29:3

Christian Passes the Place of Martyrs

I saw in my dream that at the end of the Valley
lay blood, bones, ashes, and mangled bodies of
pilgrims who had previously traveled this way.
While I was pondering the cause of this, I saw a
cave nearby where two Giants, Pope and Pagan,
had lived in ancient times. By their power and
tyranny, the men whose bones, blood, and ashes

THE PLACE OF MARTYRS

lay there were cruelly put to death. I wondered why Christian was able to pass by there with such little danger, but then I learned that Pagan had long since died, and that—although still alive—the other was very old. He had met with so many skirmishes in his younger days that he had grown rather crazy and was stiff in his joints. Now he could do little more than sit at the cave's mouth and grin at pilgrims as they went by and bite his nails because he couldn't go after them.

As Christian traveled on, he saw the old man sitting at the mouth of the cave. He didn't know what to think, especially when he heard him say, "You will never mend your ways until more of you burn." Christian held his peace, however, and went by unharmed. Then Christian sang:

"Oh, world of wonders (I can say no less),
That I should be preserved in the distress
That I have met with here! Oh blessed be
The hand that from it has delivered me!
Dangers in darkness, devils, Hell, and sin,
Did surround me, while this vale I was in;
Yes, snares and pits and traps and nets did lie
About my path, so that vain, foolish I
Might have been caught, entangled, and cast down:
But since I live, let Jesus wear the crown."

CHAPTER 7

◆◆◆◆◆◆◆◆◆◆◆◆◆◆

Christian and Faithful Meet in the Way

Now as Christian went on his way, he came to a little Hill placed purposely so that pilgrims could have a view of what lay ahead of them. So Christian went up the Hill, and from there he recognized Faithful journeying not far in front of him. Then Christian called, "Hello! Hold up, there! Wait, and I will be your companion!" At that, Faithful turned around and looked. Christian called again, "Wait, wait until I catch up with you."

But Faithful answered, "No, I am running for my life from one who is after me."

At this Christian became determined and put all his strength into catching up. He quickly reached Faithful and even ran beyond him so that the last was first. Then he smiled proudly because he had outrun his brother. While still gloating, however, Christian failed to watch his step, and suddenly he stumbled and fell. He was unable to get back to his feet again until Faithful came up to help him.

Matt. 19:30;
Mark 10:31;
Luke 13:30

Prov. 16:18

Then I saw in my dream that they went on together in brotherly love, sharing with each other about all that had happened to them on their pilgrimages. Christian began, saying, "Faithful, my brother whom I honor and love, I am glad that I have caught up with you and that God has so unified our spirits that we can walk as companions on this pleasant path."

Ps. 133:1

News from Home

"Dear friend," said Faithful, "I have desired your company ever since leaving our town, but since you left ahead of me, I was forced to come much of the way alone."

"How long did you stay in the City of Destruction before you set out after me on your pilgrimage?" asked Christian.

"Until I could stay no longer—for soon after you left, there was a great deal of talk that in a short time our City would be burned down to the ground by fire from Heaven."

"Really! Did your neighbors say this?"

"Yes, it was in everyone's mouth for awhile."

"What? Didn't anyone but you come away from there to escape the danger?"

"As I said, there was a great amount of talk, but I don't think they strongly believed it. For in the heat of the debate, I heard some of them speak derisively about you and your 'desperate journey'—that is what they called your pilgrimage. But I believed, and I still do, that fire and brimstone will fall from above to destroy our City; therefore I have made my escape."

Rev. 20:7-10

"Did you hear any talk of neighbor Pliable?"

"Yes, I did, Christian. I heard that he followed you until he came to the Slough of Despond, where some have said he fell in. He didn't want anyone to know this, but I'm sure that's the kind of dirt he was covered with."

"And what did the neighbors say to him?"

"He has been greatly ridiculed by all sorts of

people since his return. People mock and despise him, and he cannot even find employment. Now he's seven times worse off than if he had never gone out of the City."

"But why are they so much against him, since they also despise the way that he abandoned?"

"Oh, they say, 'Hang him; he is a turncoat; he wasn't true to what he professed!' I think God has stirred up enemies against him; they hiss at him and scorn him because he abandoned the way." Prov. 15:10

"Were you able to talk with him at all before you left?"

"I met him once in the streets, but he quickly looked away and crossed to the other side, obviously feeling ashamed of what he had done. So I didn't get a chance to speak to him."

"Well," said Christian, "when I first set out I had great hopes for that man, but now I fear he will perish along with the City when it is destroyed. For it has happened to him according to the true proverb, 'A dog returns to its vomit,'

and 'A sow that is washed goes back to her wallowing in the mud.'" Prov. 26:11; 2 Pet. 2:22

"Yes, I fear this too, but who can thwart the inevitable consequences of one's own foolish choices?"

Faithful's Confrontations with Temptation: Wanton

"Well, Faithful, my neighbor, let's talk about matters of more immediate concern to our own lives. Tell me about the things you've met with so far in the way. I know you've had some interesting experiences; if not, it would indeed be a marvel."

"I escaped the Slough that you fell into, and I reached the Gate without much danger. But I did encounter someone whose name was Wanton; she made every effort to allure and ensnare me."

"It is good you escaped her net; Joseph was severely tested by her. He escaped her like yourself, but it nearly cost him his life. What did she do to you?"

Gen. 39:11-13

"Unless you have already met her, you cannot imagine what a seductive tongue she has. She pressured me severely to turn aside with her, promising me all kinds of pleasure and contentment."

Prov. 5:3

Prov. 7:10-20

"She didn't promise you the pleasure and contentment of a clear conscience, did she?"

1 Tim. 1:3-5

"No, you know what I mean—only the pleasure and contentment that come from the gratification of carnal and fleshly desires."

"Thank God you escaped her snare; 'he who is under the Lord's wrath will fall into it.'"

Prov. 22:14

"Well, I don't know if I fully escaped or not."

"But why do you say this? I trust you didn't consent to her desires."

"No, I didn't defile myself. I remembered an old writing I had seen that reads, 'She leads you down to death and Hell.' So I shut my eyes because I didn't want to be enticed by her seductive looks. She cursed at me, and then I went on my way."

Prov. 5:5

Job 31:1

Faithful's Confrontations with Temptation: The Old Man

"Did you meet with any other assaults as you journeyed?" asked Christian.

"When I came to the foot of the Hill called Difficulty, I met a very aged Man who asked me who I was and where I was going. I told him that I was a pilgrim, on the way to the Celestial City. Then he said, 'You look like an honest fellow.

Will you be content to live with me for the wages that I will give you?' I asked him his name and where he lived. He said his name was Adam the First and that he lived in the town of Deceit. I then asked him what his business was and how much he would pay me to work for him. He said that his work was enjoyment and that his wages would be to inherit all that he had. I questioned further, asking what his House was like and how many others were employed in his service. He told me that his House was full of all the delicacies the world could offer and that his servants were his own children. Then I asked how many children he had. He said that he had only three daughters: the Lust of the Flesh, the Lust of the Eyes, and the Pride of Life, and he suggested that I should marry them if I so desired. I asked him how long he wanted me to live with him, and he said that it would be as long as he himself lived."

Rom. 5:14;
1 Cor. 15:22, 45

THE OLD MAN

1 John 2:16

"Well," said Christian, "what agreement did you and the Old Man finally come to?"

"Why, at first I found myself somewhat inclined to go with him, for I thought he spoke very sensibly. But then I looked at his forehead as I was speaking with him, and I saw written there, 'put off, concerning your former conduct, the Old Man.'"

"What happened then?"

Eph. 4:22

"Suddenly it came burning into my mind that no matter what he said and how he tried to entice me, I must resist him because his intention was to sell me as a slave. I told him to stop talking to me because I would not come near his House. Then he insulted me and told me that he

Gal. 4:3-7

would send someone after me to cause bitterness to my soul as I journeyed on my way. At that, I turned away from him, but just as I turned, he took hold of my flesh and gave me such a sharp jerk backwards that I thought he had pulled me apart and had part of me in his possession. This made me cry, 'What a wretched man I am!' Then I went on my way up the Hill."

Rom. 7:23-24

Faithful's Confrontations with Temptation: Moses

"When I had gotten about half way up the Hill, I looked behind me and saw someone coming after me, swift as the wind. He overtook me near where the Arbor stands."

"That is the place where I sat down to rest but was overcome with sleep," said Christian. "It was there that I lost my Scroll."

"But, my good brother," continued Faithful, "hear me out. As soon as the man overtook me, after saying only one word, to my surprise, he knocked me out cold with one blow. When I came to, I asked him why he had treated me this way. He said that it was because of my secret inclination toward Adam the First. Then he struck a powerful blow to my chest, and—continuing to punch me—he made me stumble backwards until I again lay at his feet like one dead. When I came to again, I cried to him for mercy, but he said, 'I don't know how to show mercy.' With that, he knocked me down again. He would doubtless have made an end of me had not that One come by and ordered him to stop."

Rom. 7:9, 11;
Rev. 1:17

Rom. 7:21-25

"Who was the One who made him stop?" asked Christian.

"I didn't know Him at first, but as He went by, I noticed holes in his hands and His side; then I concluded that He was our Lord. After that I went on up the Hill."

"That man who overpowered you was Moses. He doesn't spare anyone. He doesn't know how to show mercy to those who break his law."

"Yes, I know that very well," said Faithful, "and this wasn't the first time he has confronted me. Once he approached me while I was still living happily back home; there he threatened to burn my house down with me in it if I stayed there."

"I wonder, did you see the House that stood on top of the Hill facing the side that Moses met you on?"

"Yes, and the lions in front of it too, but I think they were asleep since it was about noon. Because I had so much daylight left, I passed by the gatekeeper and went on down the Hill."

"Yes," said Christian, "he told me that he had seen you go by. I wish you had come to the House; they would have shown you many rare and precious things that you would never forget till the day you die."

Faithful's Confrontations with Temptation: Discontent

"But please tell me, have you met anyone else in the Valley of Humility?"

"Yes," answered Faithful, "I met someone called Discontent. He tried to persuade me to go back again with him. His reason was that the Valley was altogether without honor. Besides this,

he told me that to go this way would offend the sensibilities of many friends, including Pride, Arrogance, Self-conceit, Worldly-glory, and others who he said he knew would be very much upset with me if I were to make such a fool of myself as to wade through this Valley."

"Well," said Christian, "how did you answer him?"

"I told him that even though all these that he had named might claim to be my friends and relatives—and it is true, because some of them are my relatives according to the flesh—since I became a pilgrim, they have already disowned me, and I also have rejected them. Therefore, they were now no more to me than if they had never been of my lineage. In addition, I told him that as to this Valley, he had really misrepresented it, because 'humility comes before honor' and 'a haughty spirit before a fall.' So I said to him, 'I would rather go through this Valley to receive what the wise count as honor than to choose what you consider most worthy of affection.'"

Prov. 15:33;
16:18

Faithful's Confrontations
with Temptation: Shame

"Well, did you have any other encounters in the Valley?"

"Yes, I met Shame; but of all those whom I have met on my pilgrimage, he, I believe, most bears the wrong name. After a little debate, others would have backed off some, but not so with this boldfaced Shame."

"Why, what did he say to you?"

"What didn't he say! He objected to our faith. He said it was a pitiful, low, cowardly thing for a man to give heed to religion. He said that a tender conscience was unmanly, and that for a man to be careful of his words and deeds would tie him down and rob him of the adventurous liberty to which the truly daring spirits of the times were accustomed. He said that such a person would be the laughingstock of our present-day society. He also objected that so few of the truly powerful, rich, or wise men and women were ever of my persuasion, and he contended that, of those of my persuasion, none had ever been powerful, wealthy, or wise prior to their conversion. He thought them to be fools who would voluntarily and eagerly decide to give up all they had for who knows what! He objected also to the lowly, inferior rank and condition of those who were pilgrims. He also said that the pilgrims were ignorant, especially in their understanding of the natural sciences. He confronted me about a great many more things in addition to those I have already related. He said that it was a shame to sit whining and mourning under conviction from the message of a sermon, and it seemed a shame to him to see pilgrims sighing and groaning as they returned to their homes. He thought it a shame for me to ask my neighbor for forgiveness for petty faults or to make restitution where I have taken advantage of someone. He said that religion separates a man from those who are great because of their few vices (which he called by finer names); and he said it makes him a member and friend to the lowbrows because of their common religious association. 'Is this not a shame?' he asked."

1 Cor. 1:26

Phil. 3:7-8

John 7:48

"Well, what did you say to him?"

"I hardly knew what to say at first. Indeed, he

was so convincing that I felt myself blushing. I felt like his point of view had beaten me. But then I began to consider how 'what is highly valued among men is detestable in God's sight.' And I thought again, 'This Shame tells me man's point of view, but he tells me nothing of what God or the Word of God says.' I thought, moreover, that at the day of judgment we shall not be doomed to death or presented with life according to the dictates of the lawless spirits of the world, but according to the wisdom and law of the Almighty. So I determined that what God says is best, even though all the world is against it. I realized then that God is the One who set forward this faith of ours. I saw that God esteems a tender conscience, that those who make themselves fools for the Kingdom of Heaven are wisest, and that the poor man who loves Christ is far richer than the greatest man in the world who hates Him.

"Then, I commanded, 'Go away, Shame! You are an enemy to my salvation. Should I give heed to you against my sovereign Lord? How would I then be able to look Him in the face when He comes? If I am now ashamed of His ways and His servants, how can I expect Him to bless me?' But this Shame was a bold and persistent villain, indeed. I could hardly shake him off. He kept haunting me and whispering in my ear about one or another weakness that goes along with religion. Finally, I told him that any further attempts to discredit the faith would be in vain, for it was in the very things he disdained that I was able to see the most glory. So, at last, I got past this stubborn menace, and having shaken him off, I began to sing:

"Oh, the hard trials that meet us all
Who do obey the heavenly call;

Margin references:

Luke 16:15

Ps. 51:17

1 Cor. 3:18

Mark 8:36;
Luke 9:25

1 Cor. 13:12;
1 John 3:2

Mark 8:38

They're many and suited to the flesh
Coming and coming again afresh,
That now or later we by them may
Be taken, overcome, and fall away;
So let the pilgrims, all pilgrims then,
Be vigilant, forsake self like men."

"I'm glad, my brother," said Christian, "that you so bravely withstood this villain. For, like you said, of all our enemies, he seems wrongly named. He is so bold as to follow us in the streets and attempt to make us ashamed before all people. He would have us be ashamed of all that is good. He is Shame, yet if he were not so audacious, he would never attempt to do as he does. But let us keep resisting him, for in spite of all his arrogant intimidation, he exalts none other than fools. Solomon said, 'The wise are promoted to honor, but fools are promoted to shame!'" Prov. 3:35

"Well," said Faithful, "I think we must cry for help against Shame to Him who would have us be valiant for truth upon the earth."

"You speak the truth," said Christian. "But did you meet anyone else in the Valley?"

"No, I didn't. I had sunshine all the rest of the way through it, and also through the Valley of the Shadow of Death." Ps. 23:4

Christian Recounts His Troubles

"Oh, you were well off. It was far different for me. I had an enduring season of trial. Almost as 1 Pet. 1:6 soon as I had entered into that Valley, I had a dreadful battle with that foul Fiend, Apollyon. Yes, I thought he was going to kill me, especially when he got me down and crushed me beneath him. It seemed he would crush me to pieces; then he threw me, and my Sword flew out of my hand. He told me his victory was certain, but

'this poor man cried out, and the Lord heard
Ps. 34:6   him, and saved him out of all his troubles.' After
this, I entered into the Valley of the Shadow of
Death and had no light for almost half the way
through it. I thought I would be killed there over
and over again. But at last the day broke, the sun
rose, and I went through the rest of the way with
far more peace and quiet."

CHAPTER 8

◆◆◆◆◆◆◆◆◆◆◆◆◆◆◆

Faithful and Talkative

Then I saw in my dream that as they went on,
Faithful looked to one side and saw a man whose
name was Talkative walking at a distance beside
them. For in this place there was room enough for
them all to walk. He was a tall man, and somewhat
more handsome from a distance than up close.

"Friend, where are you going?" called Faithful.
"Are you going to the Heavenly Country?"

"Yes, I'm going to that very place."

"Good; then I hope we can share your company."

"Yes, I will gladly be your companion."

"Come on then, let us go on together, and let
us spend our time discussing things that will be
beneficial to us."

Luke 24:13-27

"Ah," replied Talkative, "this is acceptable to
me. I will talk about good things with you or anyone else. I'm glad that I have found ones who like
such good conversation. For, to tell you the truth,
there are only a few who care enough to spend
their time this way while they're traveling. They
would much rather choose to speak about things
that are worthless, and this has troubled me."

"That is indeed lamentable," said Faithful. "For
what is more worthy of the use of the tongue
and mouth of men on this earth than the things
of the God of Heaven?"

"I am going to get along very well with you,
for your sayings are full of conviction. And, I
might add, what is more pleasant and what is

more profitable than to talk together of the things of God? What could be more pleasant to a man who delights in wonderful things? For example, if a man delights in talking about history, or the mystery of things, or if a man loves to talk about miracles, wonders, or signs, where will he find things recorded so delightfully and with such pleasing style as in the Holy Scripture?"

"That is true," answered Faithful, "but to profit spiritually from these things should be our main goal in discussing them."

"That is what I said. Talking of such things is most profitable, for by so doing a man may gain knowledge of many things, of both the futility of earthly things and the benefit of things above. So in general, but also in particular, by talking, a man may learn the necessity of the new birth, the insufficiency of our works, and the need of Christ's righteousness, among other things. Besides, by this a man may learn what it is to repent, to believe, to pray, to suffer, or the like. A man may also learn through conversing what are the great promises and consolations of the Gospel for his own comfort. Further, he may learn to refuse false opinions, to vindicate the truth, and also to instruct the ignorant."

"All of this is true, and I'm glad to hear these things from you," said Faithful.

"Alas! The lack of this is the reason that so few people understand the need for faith and the necessity for a work of grace in their heart in order to receive eternal life. They ignorantly live in the works of the law, by which no one can obtain the Kingdom of Heaven."

Gal. 2:16;
3:23-29

"But please permit me," Faithful responded. "Heavenly knowledge of these things is the gift of God; no one can attain them by human effort or merely by talking about them."

"I know that very well, for a man can receive nothing, except it be given him from Heaven. All is of grace, not of works. I could give you a hundred Scriptures to confirm this truth."

John 3:27;
James 1:17-18
Eph. 2:8-9

"Well, then," asked Faithful, "what topic shall we discuss at this time?"

"Ask what you will. I will talk of things in Heaven or things on earth; things moral or things spiritual; things sacred or things secular; things past or things to come; things foreign, or things at home; things more essential or things circumstantial—provided that it will be to our edification."

How impressive
you are,
O Talkative!

Phil. 4:8

Christian and Faithful Discuss Talkative's Walk

Now Faithful began to marvel at this man and stepped over to Christian, for Christian had been walking by himself during this time. He said to him softly, "What an admirable companion we've got! Surely this man will make a very excellent pilgrim!"

At this Christian modestly smiled and said, "This man with whom you are so impressed will, with that tongue of his, deceive almost anyone who doesn't know him."

"Do you know him then?"

"Know him! Yes, better than he knows himself."

"Then please tell me, who is he?"

"His name is Talkative. He lives in our town. I'm surprised you don't know him, but I guess our town is quite large."

"Whose son is he? And in what area of the City does he live?"

"He is the son of a Mr. Say-well. He lived in Prating-row, and he is known as Talkative by all his acquaintances in Prating-row. In spite of his fine tongue, he is a very sorry fellow."

"Well, he seems to be a very impressive man."

"Yes, to those who aren't fully acquainted with

him. For he puts on his best image away from home, but at home he is ugly enough. Your saying that he is an impressive man reminds me of what I have observed in the work of an artist whose work looks good at a distance but is displeasing up close."

"But I saw you smile, and I almost think you must be joking."

"I did smile, but God forbid that I should joke in this matter or that I should accuse anyone falsely. I will help you to understand him more fully. This man is ready for any companionship and for any conversation. As he talks with you now, so will he talk when he is at the tavern. And the more alcohol he has in his brain, the more of these things he has in his mouth. It is apparent that true faith has no place in his heart, in his house, or in his way of living. All he possesses lies in his tongue, and his religion is to make a great deal of noise with it."

"Well," said Faithful, "if what you say is true, then I am a man greatly deceived."

"Deceived, for sure! Remember the proverb, 'For they do not practice what they preach. For the kingdom of God is not a matter of talk but of power.' He talks about prayer, repentance, faith, and the new birth, but he knows only how to talk about them. I have visited his family and have observed him both at home and abroad, and I know what I say about him is the truth. His house is as devoid of true religion as the white of an egg is of flavor. He neither prays nor shows any sign of repentance from sin. Why, a poor beast, in his own way, serves God far better than he. He is the very stain, reproach, and shame of religion to all who know him. Because of him, scarcely can a good word be spoken of religion in all that end of town where he lives. Therefore,

Matt. 23:3;
1 Cor. 4:20

Num. 22:22-35

Rom. 2:17-24

the common people who know him say, 'A saint abroad and a devil at home.' His poor family finds it so; he is so unyielding, insolent, and unreasonable with his servants that they don't know what to do or how to speak.

talkative

"Those who have any dealings with him say that it is better dealing with a pagan than with him, that a pagan would deal more fairly than he. This man, Talkative, if given the chance, will manipulate, deceive, defraud, and take advantage of them. And besides all this, he is bringing up his sons to follow in his footsteps. And if he finds in any of them a 'foolish fear of danger' (for this is what he calls a tender conscience), he calls them fools or blockheads; further, he won't employ them much or recommend them to others. In my opinion, by his wicked example he has caused many to stumble and fall, and if God doesn't prevent it, he will be the ruin of many more."

"Well, my brother," responded Faithful, "I am obliged to believe you, not only because you say you know him, but also because when giving an account of the facts concerning people, you speak as a Christian should. I cannot believe that you speak these things out of ill will but because it must be as you say."

"Had I known him no longer than you," added

Christian, "I might, perhaps, have thought of him as you did at first. Yes, if I had received this report from the lips of the enemies of our faith, I would have thought it to be mere slander falling from an evil person's mouth upon a good person's name and faith. But from my own knowledge I can prove him guilty of all these things, yes, and a great many more as bad. Besides, good people are ashamed of him; they are unable to call him either brother or friend. Even his name called out among them causes embarrassment."

"Well, I see that words and deeds are two different things, and from now on I will make a better observation of this distinction."

"Indeed, they are two things and are as diverse as are the soul and the body. For as the body without the soul is but a dead carcass, so words, if they are alone, are nothing but a dead carcass as well. The soul of true religion is the part that puts it into practice. 'Religion that God our Father accepts as pure and faultless is this: to look after orphans and widows in their distress and to keep oneself from being polluted by the world.' Talkative is not aware of this; he thinks hearing and speaking, in and of themselves, will make him a good Christian; he thus deceives his own soul. Hearing is merely the sowing of the seed, and talking, alone, is not sufficient to prove that fruit is truly in the heart and life. Let us be assured that on the day of judgment, all people will be judged by their fruit. They will not be asked, 'Did you believe?' but, 'Were you doers, or merely talkers?' God will judge them all accordingly. The end of the world is compared to a harvest, and you know that those who do the harvesting care about nothing but the fruit. Of course, this does not mean that deeds, by themselves, which do not arise from faith are of any value either; I say this to you to show you how insignifi-

James 2:17, 26

James 1:27

James 1:26

Matt. 7:16;
25:31-46;
John 5:28

1 John 3:18-19

cant Talkative's words alone will be on that day."

Then Faithful replied, "This brings to my mind
Moses' description of animals that are clean—
those that part the hoof *and* chew the cud. Those   Lev. 11; Deut. 14
declared clean are not those that part the hoof
alone or chew the cud alone. The hare chews the
cud but is still unclean because it doesn't part the
hoof. This truly resembles Talkative. He chews the
cud, seeking knowledge, chewing on the Word,
but he does not divide the hoof. He professes true
faith with his mouth, but he does not live what he
professes. He refuses to part company with the way
of sinners, and thus he is unclean."

"I know you have discerned the true spirit
of the gospel," said Christian, "and I will add
another thing. Paul describes such people—those
known as great talkers—as resounding gongs and
clanging cymbals. Elsewhere he calls them life-   1 Cor. 13:1
less things, giving off only sound, strangers to   1 Cor. 14:7
true faith and the grace of the gospel, and consequently, even though their voices sound like the
voices of angels, they will never be received into
the Kingdom of Heaven among those who are
the true children of life."

"Well, Christian, I am sick of his company
now. What can we do to be rid of him?"   1 Tim. 6:20-21

"Take my advice. If you do as I say, you will
find that he will soon be sick of your company
too, unless God should somehow touch his heart
and change it."

"What do you want me to do?"

"Return to him and get involved in some serious discussion with him about the power of religion. Once he affirms the power of the gospel,
and he certainly will, ask him whether or not he
has experienced these things in his own heart,
or in his home, or in his way of life."

Faithful Confronts Talkative's Error

Faithful then walked back over to Talkative and asked, "How is it going now?"

"Well, thank you," answered Talkative. "But I thought that by now we would have enjoyed a great deal of conversation."

"Well, if you want, we can talk now. Since you left it with me to choose the subject, let it be this: How does the saving grace of God reveal itself when it is in one's heart?"

"I perceive, then, that our talk will be about the power of things. Well, it is a very good question, and I am willing to answer. Briefly stated, first, where the grace of God is in the heart, it causes a great outcry against sin. Second—"

"No, hold on, let us consider one point at a time. I think it might be better to say that it shows itself by inclining the soul to abhor its sin."

"Why, what difference is there between crying out against and abhoring sin?"

"Oh, a great deal. A man may make it his policy to cry out against sin, but he cannot really abhor it unless he has a godly aversion to it. I have heard many preachers cry out against sin from their pulpits while allowing it to abide safely within their own hearts, homes, and lifestyles. The wife of Joseph's master cried out against him with a loud voice as if she were quite righteous. In spite of this, however, she would have committed adultery with him. Some cry out against sin, like a mother crying out against the child in her lap, calling it ugly names like 'brat' and 'naughty girl.' And yet, later, the same mother is seen hugging and kissing the child."

Crying out against sin is no sign of grace.

Gen. 39:15

"It seems to me that you are trying to trap me," said Talkative.

"No, I'm not. I am only trying to set things straight. Now what is the second thing by which you would prove a work of grace in the heart?"

"Great knowledge of Gospel mysteries."

"I believe this sign should have been first, but first or last, I believe it is also false. For knowledge, even great knowledge, may be obtained concerning the mysteries of the Gospel, and yet there be no work of grace in the soul. Yes, even if a man has all knowledge, this is no guarantee that he is a child of God. When Christ taught His disciples, He made it clear that it was not enough simply to understand these things; He said, 'Now that you know these things, you will be blessed if you do them.' He makes it clear that they will be blessed, not because of their knowledge, but because of their doing. There is a knowledge that produces no doing. Indeed, there are those who know the Master's will but do not do it. A man may have knowledge like an angel of God and still not be a Christian. So I must say that your sign is not true. To know is something that pleases talkers and boasters, but to do is what pleases God.

1 Cor. 8:1-3; 13:2

John 13:17

Matt. 21:28-32
1 John 2:3

"Of course, a heart cannot be good without knowledge, for without it the heart is lost. Therefore, there is knowledge, and there is knowledge. One kind of knowledge rests in mere speculations about things; the other is accompanied by faith and love that moves a person to do the will of God from the heart. The first of these will

1 John 2:5; 5:3

97

serve the talker, but a true Christian cannot be content without the other. 'Give me understanding, and I will keep your law and obey it with all my heart.'"

Ps. 119:34

Feeling somewhat uncomfortable, Talkative answered, "You are once again trying to catch me in a trap. This conversation is not edifying or uplifting."

"Well then," answered Faithful, "why don't you propose another sign of how this work of grace shows itself in a life."

"No, I can see that we won't agree."

"Well, if you won't, will you allow me to give my proof?"

"You are free to do so."

"A work of grace in the soul shows itself either to him that possesses it or to those standing by. To the one who has it, it brings conviction of sin, especially of the defilement of the old nature, and of the sin of unbelief for which he will surely be damned if he does not find mercy from God's hand through faith in Jesus Christ. This experience of grace works in him a deep remorse and shame for sin. In addition, it is revealed to him that Jesus Christ is the Savior of the world, and he becomes aware of the absolute necessity of agreeing with and submitting to Him for eternal life. Consequently, he finds himself hungering and thirsting after Him who alone can satisfy those hungerings and thirstings as He has promised. Now, in proportion to the strength or weakness of his faith in the Savior, so will be his joy and peace, his love for holiness, his desire to know Him better and to serve Him more effectively in this world.

Mark 16:16;
John 16:8-9;
Acts 2:37

Ps. 38:18;
Jer. 31:19;
Rom. 7:24

Acts 4:12;
Gal. 2:16;
1 Tim. 4:10

Matt. 5:6;
Rev. 21:6

"Now even though I say that the work of grace shows itself within him, it is only seldom that he is able to perceive this work. The struggles with his own inner corruption, along with his distorted capacity to reason, cause his mind to misjudge the matter. So it is that very sound judgment is required before he can conclude with certainty that this is, indeed, a work of grace within him.

"Observers can first witness this work of grace in the believer's life through his confession of faith in Christ. Next, they must see a life that is consistent with that confession. This calls for a life of holiness: holiness in his own heart and life, holiness in his family life (if he has a family), and holiness in his conduct in the world. Thus he trains himself to abhor and deal with his own secret sins, to subdue sin in his family life, and to promote and exalt righteousness in the world. None of these can be attained by talk alone, as a hypocrite or a talkative person may try. On the contrary, there must be a practical submission of the heart, in true faith and love, to the power of the Word. And now, sir, as to this brief description of the work of grace, and also the means by which it can be perceived, if you have any objection, then object; if not, then please allow me to propose to you a second question."

Rom. 10:9-10

Phil. 1:27

Matt. 5:1-10;
Rom. 6:19;
1 Tim. 2:2;
Heb. 12:14;
1 Pet. 1:15-16

Ps. 19:12-13
Eph. 5:21; 6:4;
1 Tim. 3:4
John 17:21-23;
1 Pet. 2:12

John 17:17

Talkative replied, "No, my part is not to object now but to listen. Go ahead and ask your second question."

"It is this: First, have you truly experienced this first work of grace? And also, are your life and conduct consistent with that experience? Or does your religion stand on the power of word and tongue alone but not on the power of 1 John 3:18 actions and truth? Please, if you decide to answer me in this, say no more than what you know God above will say 'Amen' to and also nothing except what your conscience can justify. 'For it is not the one who commends himself who is approved, but the one whom the Lord com- 2 Cor. 9:18 mends.' Besides, to say, 'I am thus and so' when my conduct and all my neighbors tell me I am lying is great wickedness."

Talkative started to blush, but he recovered and replied, "You have now come around to the issues of experience, of conscience, and of God, and to our appealing to Him for justification of what we speak. I did not expect this kind of dis- cussion. I am not inclined to give an answer to such questions because I don't see that I am bound to do so, unless, of course, you take it upon yourself to be my teacher. But even if you should do so, I can still refuse to allow you to judge me. Will you please tell me, however, why you have asked me such questions?"

"Because I saw that you were eager to talk, and I didn't know whether or not you possessed any- thing more than mere notions. To tell you the entire truth, I have heard of you, that you are a man whose religion lies in talk, and that your conduct says that your mouth lies. It is said that you are a blemish among Christians and that the reputation of our faith has been hurt by your 2 Pet. 2:1-16 ungodly life-style. I have heard that some have already stumbled over your wicked ways and that, because of this, more are in danger of destruction. It is said that your kind of religion is compatible with the frequenting of bars, with covetousness and impurity and swearing and lying, with keeping bad company, and the like.

100

If this is true, the proverb that says a whore is a shame to all women is also true of yourself; you are a shame to all who profess Christ."

Talkative Chooses to Part Company

"Since you are so ready to listen to rumors and to judge so rashly," Talkative countered, "I cannot help but conclude that you are a faultfinding, unpleasant, and depressed person, not worthy of my conversation—so good-bye."

After Talkative had left, Christian approached his brother and said, "I told you how it would happen. Your words and his lusts could not agree. He would rather leave your company than reform his life. But he is gone, as I said, so let him go. The loss is no one's but his own. He has saved us the trouble of leaving him. For if he goes on as he is, and he most likely will, he would have been a blot to our fellowship. Besides, the apostle tells us concerning such men to 'keep away from them.'"

Jude 5-13

1 Tim. 6:5

"But I am glad we had this little discussion with him," said Faithful. "It may happen that he will think of it again. But if he doesn't, I have been honest and straightforward with him, and if he should perish, my conscience is clear."

Acts 28:25-27

"You did well to talk so openly with him. There is not enough of this kind of faithful dealing with people nowadays. It is no wonder that religion stinks in the nostrils of so many. There are so many fools who like to hear themselves talk, and whose religion is reduced to words alone, while their life-styles reflect only corruption and worthlessness. The fact that such people are welcomed into the fellowship of the godly is a confusing mystery to those in the world; it produces a dark blemish upon the name of Christianity and a deep grief in the hearts of sincere believers. I wish that all brothers and sisters would deal with such people as you have done. They would then either be forced to become more obedient to the faith, or else the fellowship of the saints would be too hot for their comfort."

Then Faithful said,

"How Talkative at first shows off his plumes!
What a show of words; oh, how he presumes
To persuade all who hear him! But just as soon
As I speak of heart-work, then like the moon
That's past it's full, will his light wane and go;
So it is with those who don't heart-work know."

CHAPTER 9

••••••••••••••

Evangelist Encourages the Pilgrims

So they went on, talking of what they had seen
on the way, and this made their travels more
enjoyable. No doubt the journey would other-
wise have been tedious because they were now
going through a Wilderness. When they had
passed nearly all the way through it, Faithful happened to glance back and saw someone coming
after them who looked very familiar. "Oh! Who
is approaching us?" he asked.

"Why, it's my good friend Evangelist," replied
Christian.

"Yes it is, and he is my good friend too; for he
is the one who sent me on the way to the Gate."

So Evangelist came and greeted them, saying,
"Peace, peace to you, and peace to your helpers!" 1 Chron. 12:18

"Welcome, welcome, Evangelist, my friend,"
said Christian. "Seeing your face reminds me of all
your kindness and patient
effort for my eternal good."

Then Faithful greeted
him. "And a thousand
welcomes, dear Evangelist!
How desirable your com-
pany is to us needy pil-
grims!"

"How has it been going with you, my friends,
since the time we last parted?" asked Evangelist.
"What have you encountered and how have you
conducted yourselves?"

Then Christian and Faithful told him about all the things that had happened to them in the way, and how and with what difficulty they had come to their present position.

"I am very happy," said Evangelist, "not that you have met with trials, but that you have been victors. In spite of having many weaknesses, you have continued in the way to this very day. Yes, I am happy for both my sake and yours. I have sowed, and you have reaped. 'What joys await the sower and the reaper, both together!' However, 'Let us not become weary in doing good, for at the proper time we will reap a harvest if we do not give up.' 'Run in such a way as to get the prize. Everyone who competes in the games goes into strict training. They do it to get a crown that will not last; but we do it to get a crown that will last forever.' There are some who set out to attain this crown, and after they have gone a good distance for it, they allow another to come in and take it from them. 'Hold on to what you have, so that no one will take your crown.' You are still within gunshot of the Devil. 'In your struggle against sin, you have not yet resisted to the point of shedding your blood.' Let the kingdom be always uppermost in your minds, and believe unflinchingly in the things that are unseen. Let nothing that is on this side get within and attach itself to your hearts. Above all, be very careful of your own hearts and the lusts that can hide there. 'The heart is the most deceitful thing there is, and desperately wicked.' So remember the words, 'Therefore have I set my face like flint, and I know I will not be put to shame.' Don't forget that you have all the power of Heaven and earth on your side."

Then Christian thanked Evangelist for his exhortation but added that they would like to

John 4:36

Gal. 6:9

1 Cor. 9:24-25

Rev. 3:11

Heb. 12:4
Matt. 6:33
2 Cor. 4:18;
Heb. 11:1

Jer. 17:9

Isa. 50:7

Matt. 28:18

have him speak to them further so that they could be strengthened on the rest of the way. They perceived that he was a prophet, and they asked him what dangers might lie ahead in the way and how to best resist and overcome them.

So Evangelist began to speak all that was on his mind. "My sons, you have heard the truth in the words of the Gospel, that 'we must go through many hardships to enter the Kingdom of God.' With Paul you can say 'prison and hardships are facing me.' You cannot expect to be able to go very far on your pilgrimage without facing hardships in one form or another. You have already experienced some of the truth of this testimony, but more will soon follow. See, you are almost out of this Wilderness, and you will shortly come to a town lying in front of you. There, you will be severely hemmed in by enemies. They will try hard to kill you, and to be sure, one or both of you must seal the testimony you hold with his blood. For our King says, 'Be faithful, even to the point of death, and I will give you the crown of life.'

"Whoever dies in that place, even though he will be murdered and will possibly suffer greatly, will be better off than his brother. For not only will he have arrived at the Celestial City soonest, but he will also have escaped the many miseries that the other will still face on the rest of his journey. After you have come to that town and the things I have related to you are fulfilled, then remember me, your friend, and remember my words. Persevere to the end like true men, and remember this word, 'So then, those who suffer according to God's will should commit themselves to their faithful Creator and continue to do good.'"

Acts 14:22

Acts 20:23

Rev. 2:10

1 Pet. 4:19

Vanity Fair

Then I saw in my dream that when the two had reached the end of the Wilderness, they could see a town stretching before them. The name of that town is Vanity, and in that town there is a perpetual fair called Vanity Fair. It bears this name first because the town where it sits is as superficial as vanity, and also because all that is bought and sold there is meaningless vanity. The saying of the wise is true, "Vanity of vanities, all is vanity."

Eccles. 1:2
Eccles. 1:9

This fair is no newly erected enterprise; it is a thing of ancient standing. Let me tell you of its

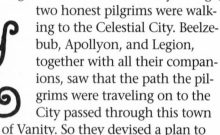

origin. About five thousand years ago, two honest pilgrims were walking to the Celestial City. Beelzebub, Apollyon, and Legion, together with all their companions, saw that the path the pilgrims were traveling on to the City passed through this town of Vanity. So they devised a plan to set up a fair within it, a fair in which all kinds of worthless vanity could be sold all year long.

See Vanity Fair! The pilgrims there
Are chained and stand beside;
Even so, our Lord passed here,
And on Mount Calvary died.

To this day all kinds of merchandise is still sold there—houses, lands, jobs, positions, honors, promotions, titles, countries, kingdoms, lusts, pleasures. And there are also enjoyments of all sorts to suit one's preference—whores, prostitutes, wives, husbands, children, masters, servants, lives, blood, bodies, souls, silver, gold, pearls, precious stones, and more. In addition, at this fair there can always be seen deceptive trickery, cheating, gambling, games, plays, amusements, fools, frauds, knaves, and rogues of every type—not to mention the numerous thieves, murderers, adulterers, and false witnesses of the basest sort.

Other fairs of less consequence have several rows and streets called by proper names that identify where certain items are sold. Likewise, here there are rows and streets named by countries and kingdoms where the desired merchandise can be found. There is the British Row, the French Row, the Italian Row, the Spanish Row, the German Row, and so forth. All sorts of vanities are sold in these places. But as in other fairs, one commodity is chief of all at the fair. So the Wares of Rome and her merchandise are greatly promoted at this fair. Only our English nation, with some others, have taken a dislike to it.

Now, as I have said, the way to the Celestial City passes right through this town where the lusty fair is held, and he who would like to bypass this town on the way to the Celestial City would have to leave the world altogether. The Prince of   1 Cor. 5:10
Princes Himself, when on earth, went through this town on His way to His own Country. I believe it was Beelzebub, the chief lord of the fair, who invited Him to buy from his vanities. Indeed, Beelzebub offered to make Him lord of the fair if only He would pay him homage as He went through the town. Because He was such a person of honor, Beelzebub took Him from street to street, in a short time showing Him all the kingdoms of the world. He tried to allure the Blessed   Matt. 4:8;
One into buying some of his vanities and thereby   Luke 4:5-6
cheapening Himself, but He had no interest in the merchandise.
He left the town without buying so much

as one penny's worth. So, you can see that this fair is ancient; nonetheless, its alluring power is still very great today.

Now Faithful and Christian would have to go through this fair, and so they set out. Even as they first entered the fair, however, all the people took notice. As a matter of fact, the entire town came together in a great commotion around them. There were several reasons for this.

First, pilgrims' clothes were so different from those that were traded at the fair that the people just stood and stared at them. Some said they were fools; others said they were lunatics; still others said they were very strange.

Second, just as the people marveled at their clothing, they also wondered at their speech, 1 Cor. 2:7-8 for only a few could understand what they said. This was because the pilgrims naturally spoke the language of Canaan, but those at the fair were people of the world. So from one end of the fair to the other, the pilgrims were thought to be uncivilized foreigners.

Third, the pilgrims showed little interest in the items displayed for sale, something not at all appreciated by the city's merchants. They did not care enough even to look at them, and when the merchants called upon them to buy, they would put their fingers in their ears and cry, "Turn my Ps. 119:37 eyes away from worthless things." They would then look upward, signifying that the only Phil. 3:19-20 things of interest to them were in Heaven.

The Pilgrims Cause a Commotion
One merchant, after observing them for a time, mockingly asked, "So, what will you buy?" But looking intently at him, they answered, "We will Prov. 23:23 buy the truth." This gave the people a reason to despise them even more. Some began mocking

the pilgrims, taunting them and discrediting
them, and they called on others to beat them up.
At last the situation became out of control, and
the commotion in the fair was so great that all
order was lost. Word then reached the manager
of the fair, who quickly came down and
appointed some of his most trusted friends to
take the men into custody for questioning since
they had disrupted the entire fair.   Acts 22

So the pilgrims were interrogated. They were
asked where they had come from, where they
were going, and why they were dressed in such
unusual garb. They answered the people that
they were pilgrims and strangers in the world,
and that they were on their way to their own
Country, which was the Heavenly Jerusalem.   Heb. 11:13-16
They explained that they had not given the
townsfolk or the merchants any reason to abuse
them and detain them from their journey. They
went on to explain that when asked by a merchant what they would buy, they answered only
that they would buy the truth. However, those
conducting the examination would not believe
that the pilgrims were anything better than troublemakers and madmen. How else could they have
brought the entire fair into such a state of confusion? Therefore, taking Faithful and Christian,
they beat them and smeared them with dirt. They
put them into a cage made for criminals and
made a spectacle of them to everyone at the fair.   1 Cor. 4:9

So Christian and Faithful sat in the cage for
quite sometime and were made to be the objects
of any passing person's amusement, bullying,
or revenge. The manager of the fair kept laughing at all that had befallen them. But the men
were patient and, holding their tongues, refused
to return evil for evil. On the contrary, they
returned blessing for insults, offering good words

Rom. 12:17, 21 in exchange for bad, and kindness for injuries
inflicted.

The Conflict of Opposing Sides

Some people at the fair who were more obser-
vant and less prejudiced than the rest began to
correct and confront the more depraved types
for their continual abuse of the two men. This
caused the ruffians to angrily attack them in
return, accusing them of being as bad as the men
in the cage and in league with them. They said
their behavior warranted their being tossed into
the cage along with the two pilgrims. The defenders answered that all they could see was that the
men were quiet and serious-minded, intending
nobody any trouble. They said that there were
many who traded in the fair who were far more
deserving of being put into the cage than these
poor, abused men. After much more angry argument, while the pilgrims continued to conduct
themselves wisely, the opposing sides finally
Acts 23:1-11 came to blows and began to harm one another.

After this, the two poor pilgrims were dragged
before their examiners once again, this time
charged with causing this latest ruckus. The
examiners beat them mercilessly, and, putting
them in iron chains, they led them by the chains
up and down the streets of the fair as an example
and deterrent to others who might try to speak
up on their behalf or, worse yet, join them.

But Christian and Faithful conducted themselves
even more wisely in the face of all the deep, personal disgrace and humiliation that was heaped
upon them. They responded with such meekness
and patience that it won to their side (though only
few in comparison) some of those in the fair. This
put the opposing side into such a great rage that
they concluded that these two men deserved the

death penalty. Thereupon they angrily presented their case that neither cage nor chains would do any good in reforming them, and that only death would do justice for all the damage and delusion that they had caused the fair. They were then ordered back to the cage until further action could be taken with them. Once inside the cage again, their feet were locked in chains.

Christian and Faithful Stand Trial

So the pilgrims called to mind what they had heard from their faithful friend Evangelist. Recalling his words encouraged them and confirmed to them that their way and their sufferings were not mistakes. They also comforted and reassured each other that if one of them were chosen to suffer and die, that one would have the higher blessing. So each man secretly desired that position. But, commiting their lives to the all-wise will of Him who rules over all things, they contentedly waited for the further unfolding of His will and purpose.

They were appointed to stand trial at a time convenient to the court. When the time had come, they were brought before their enemies and arraigned. The judge's name was Lord Hate-good. Though varying in form, the testimony was basically the same in substance. The content of the indictment handed down was this: That they were enemies and disturbers of their trade, that they had made a commotion and caused divisions in the town, and that they had won a group to their own most dangerous opinions in contempt of the law of their king.

Acts 18:13; 19:27

Then Faithful began to reply to the charges.

111

Now, Faithful, play the man, speak for your God;
Don't fear the wicked's malice nor their rod;
Speak boldly, man, the truth is on your side;
Die for it, and to life in triumph ride.

"I have set myself only against that which has set itself against Him who is higher than the highest. And as for disturbance, I have made none, being a man of peace. The persons who were won to our side were won by seeing our honesty and innocence, and they are only the better for it. And as to the king you speak of, since he is Beelzebub, the enemy of our Lord, I defy him and all of his angels."

False Witnesses Give Testimony

Then a proclamation was made that if anyone had anything to say for their lord the king against the prisoner at the bar, they should appear forthwith and give their evidence. So three witnesses came in—Envy, Superstition, and Talebearer. They were then asked if they knew the prisoner at the bar and what they had to say for their lord the king against the prisoner. Envy stepped forward and said, "My lord, I have known this man for a long time, and I will attest upon my word before this honorable bench, that he is—

"Hold up, there! Give him his oath," the judge interrupted.

So they swore him in, and the man continued, "My lord, this man, in spite of his credible name, is one of the most disgusting men in our country. He regards neither prince nor people, law nor custom; on the contrary, he does all he can to influence people everywhere with his disloyal notions, which, in general, he calls principles of faith and holiness. But specifically, I myself once heard him affirm that Christianity and the customs of our town of Vanity were diametrically opposed to one another and could never be reconciled. By such a statement, my lord, in one breath he not only condemns all of our praiseworthy ways but condemns us for following them."

Acts 24:1-8

"Do you have anything more to say?" asked the judge.

"Your honor, I could say much more, but it would only become tiresome to this court. Yet, if you need me, when the other gentlemen have given their evidence, if anything is lacking, I will return and enlarge my testimony lest this man be freed." So he was told to stand by.

Then they called Superstition and charged him to look at the prisoner. They asked him also what he could say for their lord the king against the defendant. They swore him in, and he began his testimony. "My lord, I am not very familiar with this man, nor do I desire to get to know him better. However, I do know from talking with him in town the other day that he is a very dangerous fellow. I heard him say that our religion is nothing and that no one could please God by it. In saying this, my lord, you very well know what must follow—that we still worship in vain, are yet in our sins, and shall eventually be damned. This is all I have to say."

1 Cor. 15:12-19

Superstition

Then Talebearer was sworn in and charged to say what he knew in behalf of their lord the king against the prisoner at the bar. "Your honor," began Talebearer, "and all you ladies and gentlemen, I have known this man for a long time and have heard him speak things that should not have been said. For he has insulted our noble Prince Beelzebub and has spoken contemptuously against all of his honorable friends whose names are, Lord Old Man, Lord Carnal-delight, Lord Luxurious, Lord Desire of Vain-glory, old Lord Lechery, Sir Having Greedy, along with all the rest of our nobility. Furthermore, he has said that if everyone was of his frame of mind, there would remain no living for any of these upstanding citizens in this town. Besides this, he has not been afraid to revile you, my lord, who are appointed to be his judge. Why, he has called you an ungodly villain, along with other slanderous names with which he has besmeared most of the aristocracy of our town."

These lords are all sins and great ones.

When Talebearer had finished his story, the judge directed his speech to the prisoner at the bar, saying, "You, renegade, heretic, traitor! Have you heard what these honest gentlemen have witnessed against you?"

Faithful answered, "May I speak a few words in my own defense?"

"Sir, you don't deserve to live a minute longer. You should be put to death on the spot! Yet, so that all men may see my fairness toward you, let us hear what you have to say for yourself."

"First, I say in answer to what Mr. Envy has spoken, I never said a thing except that any rules, laws, customs, or people who are not in harmony with the Word of God, are, in reality, diametrically opposed to true Christianity. If I have said something amiss in this, convince me of my error, and I will publicly recant.

"As to the second witness, Mr. Superstition, and his charge against me, I said only that to truly worship God, divine faith is required, but there can be no divine faith without a divine revelation of the will of God. Therefore, whatever is included in the worship of God that is not in agreement with divine revelation cannot be done except by a false, human faith, which is not beneficial for eternal life.

"As to Mr. Talebearer's charges, I have avoided terms that are insolent and abusive. But I did say that the prince of this town along with all the rabble that this gentleman named, are more fit for being in Hell than in this town and Country. And, so, may the Lord have mercy on me."

The Judge's Counsel
Then the judge called to the jury (who were listening and observing all the while). "Gentlemen of the jury, you see this man about whom so great an uproar has been made in this town. You have also heard what these worthy gentlemen have testified against him, and you have heard his reply and confession. It lies in your hands whether to hang him or save his life, but I think it is fitting for me to give you some instruction in our law.

"A decree was made in the days of Pharaoh the Great, servant of our prince, that, in order to prevent those of a contrary religion from multiplying and growing too strong for him, their males should be thrown into the river. A decree was also made in the days of Nebuchadnezzar the Great, Exod. 1:15-16

115

another of his servants, that whoever would not fall down and worship his golden image should be thrown into a fiery furnace. Further, a decree was made in the days of Darius, stating that whoever called upon any God but him should be thrown into the lions' den. Now this rebel has broken the substance of these laws, not only in thought, which cannot be allowed, but also in word and deed, which is absolutely intolerable.

Dan. 3:1-7

Dan. 6:6-9

"Now Pharaoh's law was based on supposition of what might happen, to prevent trouble, though no crime had yet been apparent. But, in this case, it is clear to all that a crime has been committed, and, as you have witnessed, he admittedly disputes and denies our religion. For the treason that he has confessed, he deserves to die."

The Jury Returns a Verdict

Then the jury went out to deliberate. Their names were Mr. Blind-man, Mr. No-good, Mr. Malice, Mr. Love-lust, Mr. Live-loose, Mr. Heady, Mr. High-mind, Mr. Enmity, Mr. Liar, Mr. Cruelty, Mr. Hate-light, and Mr. Implacable. All these expressed their opinions in the jury room and then agreed to return a unanimous verdict of guilty.

First, Mr. Blind-man, the head juror, spoke and said, "I see clearly that this man is a heretic."

Then Mr. No-good said, "Away with such a man from the earth."

"Yes," said Mr. Malice, "for I hate the very looks of him." Then Mr. Love-lust added, "I could never endure him."

"Nor I," said Mr. Live-loose, "for he would always be condemning my ways."

"Hang him, hang him," demanded Mr. Heady.

"He is a miserable bum," said Mr. High-mind.

"My heart swells with anger against him," said Mr. Enmity.

116

"He is a worthless person," said Mr. Liar.

"Hanging is too good for him," snarled Mr. Cruelty.

"Let's put him out of the way," suggested Mr. Hate-light.

Then Mr. Implacable said, "If all the world were offered me for reconciling with this man, I would be unable to. Therefore, let us immediately recommend the death penalty."

Faithful's Martyrdom and Departure

And so they did. Faithful was condemned to be put to death by the most cruel means that they could invent.

Faithful, so brave in what you've done and said,
Judge, witnesses, and jury have instead
Of overcoming you, only shown their rage,
When they're dead, you'll live from age to age.

So they brought him out to do with him according to their law. First, they whipped and beat him; then they cut him with knives and swords; after that they stoned him with stones; and, last of all, they burned him to ashes at the stake. Thus Faithful came to the end of his earthly life.

Then I saw that behind the crowd stood a chariot driven by horses waiting for Faithful, who, as soon as his enemies had finished with him, was ushered inside. With the sound of a trumpet, he was immediately carried up through the clouds—the nearest way to the Celestial Gate.

2 Kings 2:11

As for Christian, he was given a temporary delay and was ordered back to prison where he remained for a time. But He who overrules all things, having power over their rage in His hand, made it possible for Christian to escape. After Christian had escaped, he went on his way singing,

"Well, Faithful, you have faithfully professed
Your Lord, by whom you will surely be blessed;
When faithless ones with all their vain delights,
Are crying out under their hellish plights,
Sing, Faithful, sing, for your name will survive,
For though they killed you, you are yet alive!"

CHAPTER 10
◆◆◆◆◆◆◆◆◆◆◆◆◆◆◆

Hopeful Joins Christian

Now I saw in my dream that Christian did not have to go very far by himself. He was joined by one whose name was Hopeful, being made so by observing the examples of Christian and Faithful in what they said and did during their sufferings at the fair. The two of them entered into a covenant with one another, vowing to be companions. So following the death of one who died bearing testimony to the truth, another was raised up out of his ashes to be a companion with Christian in his pilgrimage. And Hopeful related to Christian that before long many more people from the fair would set out to follow them.

The Pilgrims Meet Mr. By-ends

Not long after they had left the fair, I saw that they overtook one who had been traveling ahead of them. They asked him, "Where are you from, sir? And how far are you traveling this way?" He answered that he had come from the town of Fair-speech and that he was on his way to the Celestial City.

Prov. 26:25

"From Fair-speech?" asked Christian. "Are there good folks living there?"

"Yes, I certainly think so," he answered.

"Tell me, sir, what may I call you?" asked Christian.

"Oh, I am a stranger to you, as you are to me. If you are going to be traveling this way, I will be glad to have your company, but if not, I will have to be content."

"This town of Fair-speech," Christian said, "I have heard of it; as I recall,

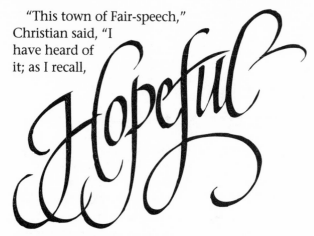

people say it's a wealthy place."

"Yes, I assure you that it is, and I have many rich relatives there."

"Who are your relatives there, if you don't mind my asking?"

"Well, almost the whole town. Let's see, some of the more notable ones are Lord Turn-about, Lord Time-server, and Lord Fair-speech (from whose ancestors the town first took its name); also, there are Mr. Smooth-man, Mr. Facing-bothways, and Mr. Any-thing. Our pastor, Rev. Two-tongues, is my mother's own brother. To tell you the truth, I have now become a gentle-man of high standing, even though my great-grandfather was only a boatman—looking one way and rowing another. Actually, I received most of my estate from those of the same occu-pation."

"Are you a married man?" asked Christian.

By-ends smiled proudly. "Yes, and my wife is a very fine and virtuous woman who is also the daughter of such a woman. She is Lady Feign-ing's daughter and so comes from a very honor-able and prestigious family. She has acquired such a high degree of poise and sophistication that she knows precisely how to conduct herself with both prince and peasant alike."

Mr. By-ends's Religion

"It is true, our faith differs in some respects from those of the stricter sort, but only in a couple of minor points. First, we go with the flow; we never strive against the wind or current. Second, James 1:6 we are always more zealous for religion when it is refined and elegant—wearing silver slippers, so to speak. We love to walk boldly in the streets with religion when the sun is shining upon it and people are applauding it." Matt. 6:2, 5

After hearing this, Christian stepped aside to talk to his friend Hopeful. "It dawns on me that this man may be Mr. By-ends from Fair-speech. If it is, we have in our company as tricky and deceitful a person as lives in all these parts."

"Well, ask him," said Hopeful.

"I don't think he will be ashamed of his name."

So Christian returned to him again and said, "Sir, in listening to you talk about yourself and your views, if I am not mistaken, I have a pretty good idea who you are. Are you Mr. By-ends of Fair-speech?"

"That is not my name, but, yes, it is a nickname that was given to me by some who cannot stand me. I must be content to bear it as a reproach as other good people have had to before me."

"But did you ever give anyone good reason to call you by this name?"

"Never, never! The most I ever did to give reason for calling me this name was that I have always had the good luck to be able to adjust my views to the present trends of the times. Whenever I have had a chance to gain, I have employed this ability, and if I have prospered in this way, let me count it a blessing. But don't let those who are malicious burden me with their scorn."

"I thought you were the man I had heard of," Christian responded. "Let me tell you what I think; I fear this name is more appropriate for you than you are willing for us to believe."

They Must Part Company

"Well," said By-ends, "I cannot help what you think. You will still find me a good traveling companion if you allow me to continue walking with you."

"If you will travel with us," said Christian, "you will have to go against the wind and current, and I believe this is contrary to your belief. You must also embrace this faith, not only when it wears silver slippers, but also when it is dressed in rags. You must stand by it when it is cast into prison as well as when it parades triumphantly through the streets and receives applause."

Phil. 4:11-12

Matt. 5:11, 16;
1 Pet. 2:12;
4:12-16

"But you shouldn't impose your views on me, nor lord it over my faith," responded By-ends. "Allow me to walk in my liberty and at the same time continue on with you."

"No," said Christian. "Unless you intend to do what I have presented to you, as we intend to do, we won't be traveling another step together."

Then By-ends said, "I will never desert my old principles; not only are they harmless, but they are also very profitable for me. If I cannot go

with you, I must continue on as before and go
by myself until someone comes along who will
enjoy my company."

Mr. By-ends's Three Friends

Now I saw in my dream that Christian and
Hopeful left him and went on ahead, keeping
their distance from him. After awhile, one of
them happened to look back and saw three men
following Mr. By-ends. As they caught up with
him, they greeted each other warmly. Their
names were Mr. Hold-the-world, Mr. Money-
love, and Mr. Save-all. Mr. By-ends had known
all of them previously. In their younger years
they had been schoolmates and had been
taught by Mr. Grasp-man. He was a teacher
from the town of Love-gain, a center of commer-
cialism in the northern County of Coveting.
This teacher had trained them well in the art of
getting ahead by whatever means, whether by
violence, cheating, flattery, lying, or by putting
on an external appearance of religion. These
four had excelled to such a degree in their teacher's art that each of them could have run such a
school by himself.

They Evaluate Christian and Hopeful

After they had greeted one another, Mr. Money-
love asked Mr. By-ends, "Who are they on the
road ahead of us?" For Christian and Hopeful
were still within view.

Mr. By-ends replied, "They are men from a distant country who are, in their own way, going
on a pilgrimage."

"Too bad! Why didn't

MR. MONEY-LOVE

they wait so that we could enjoy their company?" asked Mr. Money-love. "After all, aren't we all going on a pilgrimage?"

"Yes, we are indeed. But those men up ahead are very rigid and dogmatic. They love their own opinions to such an extent that they have precious little regard for anyone else's. A person could be very godly, but if he doesn't agree with them on every point, they will thrust him completely out of their fellowship."

"Well, that's bad," said Mr. Save-all. "However, we have read about some who are overly righteous. The extreme legalism of this type of person drives them to judge and condemn everyone else but themselves. But, please tell me, on what and on how many points did you differ?"

"True to their headstrong manner," replied Mr. By-ends. "They have concluded that it is their duty to rush forward on their journey no matter what the weather; I, on the other hand, am for waiting for favorable wind and current. They are for risking all for God at the snap of a finger; I am for taking advantage of every opportunity to secure my life and estate. They are for holding to their ideas even though all the world would be against them; I, however, am for religion insofar as the times, conditions, and my safety allow it. They are for religion when walking in rags and abuse; I am for it when it walks in silver slippers, in sunshine, and with applause."

At this, Mr. Hold-the-world spoke up. "Ah, yes, Mr. By-ends, hold to your position. In my opinion, whoever has the freedom to keep what he possesses but is unwise enough to lose it is a fool!

Let us be wise as serpents. Make hay when the sun shines. And can't you see how the bee lies still all winter but rouses herself again only when she can enjoy her gain? Sometimes God sends rain and sometimes sunshine; if they are such fools as to go through the rain, let us be content to take the good weather along with us. As for me, I like that religion best that will favor the security of God's good blessings to us. Can anyone who listens to the dictates of common sense imagine that God, who has bestowed on us the good things of this life, does not want us to keep them for His sake? Abraham and Solomon grew rich through their religion, and even Job says that a good man shall 'lay up gold as dust.' But these great men differ from those two ahead of us if they are as you have described them."

Matt. 10:16

Matt. 5:45

Job 22:24

"I think we all agree concerning this matter, so there is no need to discuss it any further," concluded Mr. Save-all.

Mr. Money-love agreed. "No, we need not waste any more words over this matter. For he who believes neither Scripture nor reason—and we have both on our side—neither knows his own liberty nor seeks his own safety."

A Question from Mr. By-ends

"My brothers," said Mr. By-ends, "as you know, we are all going on a pilgrimage, and for a positive diversion from unpleasant things, allow me to propose this question: Suppose a person—a minister, a businessman, or other—should have an opportunity to get the good blessings of this life. However, the only way he can attain them, it seems, is to become extraordinarily zealous in certain religious matters that he previously had shown no interest in. Can he still be an honest man while taking advantage of this means to achieve his end?"

At this, Mr. Money-love quickly replied, "I can see your purpose in asking this question, and if you gentlemen will permit me, I will propose a suitable answer. First of all, I would like to speak to your question as it concerns a minister. Suppose a minister, a worthy person, has received very little compensation but has set his sights on a much higher standard of living. Suddenly he has the opportunity of getting it—but by being more studious, by preaching more frequently and zealously, and by altering some of his principles in order to accommodate the disposition of his listeners. As far as I am concerned, I see no reason why a man may not do this, and even a great deal more, provided he has a calling from God. He is still a man of integrity, and here are my reasons why:

"First, no one can argue the legality of his desire for greater compensation, and God Himself has set before him the opportunity to improve his lot. So, then, he may get it if he can do so without any question of conscience.

"Second, his desire for more money makes him more studious, and thus a better teacher and a more zealous preacher. He has therefore greatly improved himself and is a better man for it—and this is obviously in accordance with the will and purpose of God.

"Third, his accommodation to the dissenting opinions of his people by yielding some of his principles in order to serve them will exemplify a self-denying spirit and a gentle yet winning demeanor. Thus he will demonstrate that he is all the more fit to fulfill the obligations of ministry.

"Fourth, I will conclude by saying that a minister who exchanges a little for much should not be judged as covetous for doing so. Rather, since he has improved his lot in life and, in so doing, has

also improved his level of competence in his work,
then let him be viewed as one who diligently
pursues his calling and makes the most of every
opportunity that has been given him to do good.   Eph. 5:15-16

"And now to the second part of the question,
concerning the businessman you mentioned.
Let's suppose his business has been meager in
this world, but by becoming religious, his market
may improve dramatically. He may be able to
get a rich wife or more numerous and perhaps
wealthier customers. I am of the opinion that
there is no reason why this could not be legiti-
mately done, and this is why: First, to become
religious is commendable, regardless of the
means by which a person does so. Second, there
is nothing wrong with getting a rich wife or
more and better customers. Another way of looking at it is that the one who receives these blessings by becoming religious gets good things from
good people by becoming good himself. So, here
we have a good wife, good customers, and a
good livelihood—all by becoming religious—and
that is good! My conclusion, then, is that it is a
very good and profitable objective to become a
devout person for the purpose of receiving all
these benefits."

Christian Answers the Question

Mr. Money-love's answer to Mr. By-ends's question
was well received and highly applauded by all of
his companions. They heartily endorsed all of his
conclusions and thought them to be extremely
insightful and profitable. The thought occurred
to them that no one would be able to refute these
arguments. And because Christian and Hopeful
were still within earshot, and in light of their earlier opposition to Mr. By-ends, they all decided to
quickly catch up with Christian and Hopeful in

order to present the same question to them. So they called after the two until they stopped and waited for them.

Meanwhile, as they were walking to meet them, it was decided that old Mr. Hold-the-world would pose the question to them instead of Mr. By-ends. They didn't want Christian and Hopeful's answer to be influenced by the heat of controversy kindled between them and Mr. By-ends at their earlier parting.

The group caught up with the two, and after a friendly greeting Mr. Hold-the-world posed the question to Christian and his friend, inviting them to answer it if they could.

This was Christian's reply: "Even a baby in the faith can answer ten thousand such questions. For if it is wrong to follow Christ for loaves and fish—as it is—how much more an abomination it is to use Him and religion as a means to get and enjoy the world! Only pagans, hypocrites, devils, witches, and sorcerers are of such an opinion. Let me explain: First, let me tell you about pagans. Hamor and Shechem wanted Jacob's daughter and his cattle as well, but they saw that there was no way to obtain them except by being circumcised. They told their friends, 'If every male among us is circumcised as they are, won't all their cattle, money, and everything of theirs become ours?' In seeking to obtain daughters and cattle, they used religion as a pretense to get what they wanted. You can read the whole story.

"Then there are the hypocritical Pharisees. They were of this same faith. Long, impressive prayers were their pretense, but their intent was to cheat widows out of their houses. God will judge them with greater damnation.

"Third, there are the devils of which Judas was one; he was also of this religion. He was religious

John 6:26-27

Gen. 34:20-23

Luke 20:46-47

so that he could carry the common purse, hoping that he might possess what was inside. But he was lost, cast off, the very son of perdition.

John 13:27-29; 17:12

"Then, fourth, are the witches and sorcerers. Simon was of this religion, for he desired to receive the Holy Spirit only for the money he hoped to gain with His power. Peter sentenced him accordingly.

Acts 8:19-22

"Fifth, I cannot help but believe that the person who takes up religion in order to gain the world will also throw it away

Mr. Hold the world

just as quickly in order to gain the world. Judas, for example, hoped to gain the world by embracing the faith, but he subsequently sold his faith—as well as his Master—for the same purpose. Therefore, to answer this question affirmatively, as I perceive you have done, and to say that such a motive can be viewed as acceptable and authentic faith, seems to me to be pagan, hypocritical, and devilish. If you adhere to this position, your reward will be according to your works."

At this, they just stood staring at each other! No one knew how to answer Christian, so there was a prolonged silence between them. Hopeful was pleased with the soundness of Christian's reply, but Mr. By-ends and his friends lagged behind in order to keep a good distance between Christian and Hopeful and themselves. Christian said to his brother, "If these men cannot stand before mere mortals, how will they stand before God? And if they are silenced by mere earthen vessels, what will they do when they are rebuked by the One whose tongue is a consuming fire?"

Isa. 30:27

CHAPTER 11

◆◆◆◆◆◆◆◆◆◆◆◆◆◆

In the Plain Called Ease

Christian and Hopeful continued on their way until they came to a lovely plain called Ease. They were very happy to travel there, but the plain was small and they passed through it quickly. At the far side of the plain there was a little Hill called Lucre, and in that Hill was a Silver-mine. Some of those who had gone that

The ease that pilgrims have is but little in this life.

PLAIN CALLED
ease

way previously had been attracted by the mine's uniqueness and had turned aside for a better view. Having gone too near the edge of the pit, however, the ground underneath them was deceptively untrustworthy, and it had given way. Some had fallen to their deaths, while others had been maimed for life.

The Appeal of Demas

Then I saw in my dream that a little way off the road, close by the Silver-mine, a distinguished-looking man named Demas stood ready to call travelers to come and take a look. He called to Christian and Hopeful, "Hello, there! Turn aside over here. I have something to show you."

"What is so important that it warrants our going off of the way to see it?" Christian replied.

"This is a Silver-mine, and some are digging in

it for treasure. If you come, with a little effort you can provide richly for yourselves."

"Let's go see," said Hopeful.

"Not I," said Christian. "I have heard of this place before and of the many who have died there. Besides, that treasure is a snare to those who seek it, for it hinders them in their pilgrimage."

Matt. 6:19-21, 24

Then Christian called to Demas, "Isn't this place dangerous? Hasn't it hindered many in their pilgrimage?"

Hos. 4:18

"Not really," Demas replied. "It's only dangerous to those who are careless." But he blushed as he spoke.

Then Christian said to Hopeful, "Let's keep on our way and not take even one step toward him."

"I agree with you, brother, but I'll just bet you that when By-ends comes here and receives the same invitation, he will go there to look."

"No doubt," said Christian, "for his principles lead him that way. A hundred to one that he dies there."

Then Demas called to them again, saying, "But won't you come over and take a look?"

So Christian bluntly answered, "Demas, you are an enemy of the righteousness of the Lord of this way, and one of His Majesty's judges has already condemned you for your own turning

2 Tim. 4:10

aside. Why are you seeking to bring us under a similar condemnation? Besides, if we turn aside at all, our Lord the King will certainly hear about

Luke 9:62

it. We would then stand before Him ashamed, whereas we could have stood before Him with

1 John 2:28

full confidence."

Demas cried again, pleading with them to understand that he was also one of their brotherhood, and that if they would but stay a little while, he would walk with them.

"What is your name?" asked Christian. "Isn't it the same as I called you?"

132

"Yes, my name is Demas; I am a son of Abraham."

"Well, I know you; Gehazi, Elisha's servant, was your great-grandfather, and Judas was your father. You are walking in their footsteps. Your father hung as a traitor, and you deserve no better. Be assured that when we come to the King, we will inform him of your behavior." After this, they went on their way.

2 Kings 5:20

Matt. 26:14-15; 27:1-6

By this time By-ends and his companions were again in sight. At Demas's first call, they went over. Now I'm not certain whether they fell over the edge of the pit or whether they went down inside to dig, or whether they were asphyxiated by the gases that commonly arise from the bottom. One thing I observed, though, was that they were never again seen in the way.

Then Christian sang a song:

"By-ends and silver-hearted Demas both agree;
One calls and the other runs, that he may also be
A sharer in his lucre, so he will also
Leave the Way for the world, and no farther go."

The Pillar of Lot's Wife

Now I saw that on the other side of this plain, just beyond the Silver-mine, the pilgrims came to a place where an old Monument stood along the roadside. Upon seeing it, they were both intrigued by its appearance. For it seemed as though it had been a woman who was now transformed into the shape of a Pillar. They stood there gazing at it, not knowing what to make of it. Eventually Hopeful noticed some unusual writing above its head, but he couldn't make it out. After careful scrutiny, Christian was able

Luke 17:32

Gen. 19:26 to decipher these words: "Remember Lot's wife." They both concluded that this must have been the Pillar of Salt that Lot's wife had been turned into when, fleeing for safety, she had looked back upon Sodom with a covetous heart. It was an incredible sight.

"Oh, my brother!" said Christian, "this is certainly a timely sight. Its appearance so suits the invitation Demas gave us to come over to view Lucre Hill. If we had gone over as he wanted us to—and as you, my brother, were inclined—we may well have turned out like this woman—a spectacle to all who come after."

"I'm sorry I was so foolish," said Hopeful, "and it's a miracle that I'm not like Lot's wife now. For what is the difference between her sin and mine? She only looked back, but I had a desire to go and look. Let grace be cherished, and let me be ashamed that such a thing was ever in my heart."

"This lesson may be of future usefulness, Hopeful. Let's take note and not forget what we see here. This woman escaped one judgment—the judgment that fell on Sodom—yet she was destroyed by another. May we always remember this Pillar of Salt."

"Yes," Hopeful answered. "She should be both a caution and an example to us. A caution because we should shun her sin, and an example of the judgment that will overtake those who disregard the caution. Likewise, Korah, Dathan, and Abiram, along with two hundred and fifty others, perished in their sin and became an example Num. 16;
26:9-10 telling all to beware. But one thing I marvel at, above all others, is how Demas and his friends can so confidently look for that treasure when this woman, only looking behind her—we don't read that she stepped one foot out of the way— was turned into a Pillar of Salt. The judgment

that overtook her is an example within plain sight of them all, and they can't help but see her if they look up."

The River of God

Christian added, "It is a mystery, and it goes to show that their hearts are in a desperate condition. I don't know whom best to compare them with: one who pick-pockets in the judge's presence, or one who greedily grasps for more gain while on his way to being executed. It is said that those in Sodom were terrible sinners because they were sinners 'before the face of the Lord,' that is, within His eyesight—and this in spite of all the kindness He had shown them, for the land around Sodom at that time was like the Garden of Eden. This provoked the Lord even more to jealousy and caused their plague of fire from Heaven to be as hot as the Lord could make it. It must be concluded that those who sin in the sight of God, despite many examples to warn them to the contrary, will come under the severest judgments."

Gen. 13:13

Gen. 13:10

"You have doubtless spoken the truth," said Hopeful. "But what mercy God has shown us, that neither you nor especially I have made such an example of ourselves. Let us thank God right now, and fear Him, and let us always remember Lot's wife."

The River of God
Then I saw that they went on their way to a pleasant River, which King David called "the River of God" and which the apostle John called "the River of the Water of Life." Since their way

Ps. 65:9
Rev. 22:1

135

went alongside its bank, Christian and Hopeful

Ezek. 47:7-12   walked there with great delight. They drank from the pleasant water in the River, and their weary spirits were revitalized. In addition to this, there were green trees with all kinds of fruit lining the banks of the River. The leaves were edible and were beneficial like medicine for the healing of various maladies. On both sides of the River were Meadows that were perpetually green and covered with lovely lilies. They lay down here and slept awhile because here

Rev. 22:1-2   they had found safety. When they awoke, they
Ps. 23:2;   gathered some fruit to eat, and they drank again
Isa. 14:30   from the water of the River. Needing more rest, they once again lay down to sleep. They continued this routine for several days and nights, and they sang:

"See here how this crystal River does glide,
To comfort pilgrims by the High-way side.
The Meadows are green with a fragrant smell,
Yielding refreshment, and they will all tell
What pleasant fruit and leaves these trees do yield;
They will soon sell all to purchase this field."

When they were ready to go on (for they were not yet at their journey's end), they ate, drank, and set out once again.

Temptation to Leave the Rough Way

Now I saw in my dream that they had not gone very far when the River and the way parted for a time. This made them very sorry, yet they dared not go out of the way. Now the way from the River was rough, and because their feet were already sore

from their travels, they became very discouraged.
They continued to press on but began to wish for
a better way. Before long they saw, lying in front of
them on the left side of the road, a Meadow; it was
called By-path Meadow. Then Christian said to his
brother, "If this Meadow lies alongside our way,
let's go into it." He climbed up some steps that led
over a fence so that he could take a good look, and
there he saw a path that lay parallel to the way but
was on the other side of the fence. "This is the way
I want to go," he said, "because it will make our
traveling much easier. Come on, Hopeful, let's go
on over."

Num. 21:4

*One temptation
makes way for
another.*

"But what if the trail over there leads us out
of the way?" asked Hopeful.

"That's not likely. Look, doesn't it go alongside
of the way?"

In By-path Meadow

So Hopeful was persuaded by his friend and followed him over. Once they were inside, they
found it was very easy on their feet. Soon they
were able to see a man ahead of them walking the
same path. His name was Vain-confidence. They
called out to him and
asked him where
this way led.
He replied,
"To the
Celestial
Gate."
Christian
turned to
Hopeful and said, "See, didn't I tell you? Now you
can be sure that we made the right decision." So
they followed, and he kept ahead of them. But
soon night began to overtake them, and it grew
so dark that they lost sight of the man.

*Strong Christians
may lead weak
ones out of the
way.*

*Watch what
happens when
you too suddenly
join strangers.*

A pit to catch the proud in.

Isa. 9:16

Vain-confidence, not being able to see the way clearly, fell into a deep pit. It was put there on purpose by the owner of the grounds to catch presumptuous fools, and there Vain-confidence would die. Now Christian and Hopeful both heard the man fall. They immediately called out to find out what had happened, but there was no answer, only a faint groaning. "Where are we now?" cried Hopeful. Christian remained silent, fearing that he had led them both out of the way. Then a dreadful storm came, with rain, thunder, and lightning, and the water began rising quickly.

Hopeful groaned to himself, saying, "Oh, that I had kept on my way!"

"But who could have thought that this path would have led us out of the way?" Christian asked.

"From the very first I was afraid of it," replied Hopeful, "and that's why I gave a gentle caution. I would have spoken more forcefully, but you are older than I."

"My dear brother, please don't be offended with me," pleaded Christian. "I'm sorry I have brought you out of the way and led you into such imminent danger. Please, brother, forgive me, for I didn't do it with an evil intent."

Rom. 8:28

"Take comfort, Christian, my brother, for I forgive you, and I believe that this will work out for our good."

"I'm glad I have such a merciful brother with me, but we must not stand here like this; let's try to go back again."

"But let me go first," said Hopeful.

"No, please let me go first so that if there is any danger I might come to it first since this is all my fault."

"No," replied Hopeful, "I cannot let you go first because your mind is troubled, and it might lead you astray again."

Then they heard a voice, and they were encouraged as they heard the voice saying, "Let your hearts be toward the High-way; the same way that you came, turn back to." But by this time the waters had risen greatly, which made going back very dangerous. (Then, in my dream, I thought to myself that it is easier going out of the way when we are in it than it is going in when we are out of it!)

Jer. 31:21

Now the pilgrims seek to gratify the flesh,
But by seeking its ease, Oh! how they afresh
Find many new griefs they've plunged head on into.
Seek pleasing the flesh, and your life you'll undo.

So they ventured back, but it was so dark and the flood so high that they nearly drowned nine or ten times. Not only that, but no matter how they tried they couldn't get back that night to the steps that led over the wall. Finally they found a little shelter and decided to sit there until daybreak. Being very tired, however, they fell asleep.

Seized by Giant Despair

Not far from the spot where they were sleeping was a castle called Doubting Castle. The owner of it was Giant Despair, and it was on his property that they were sleeping. The Giant got up early the next morning, and walking up and down his grounds, he spotted Christian and Hopeful sleeping there.

Then with a fierce, threatening voice, he woke them up and demanded where they had come from and what they were doing on his property. Christian and Hopeful answered shakily that they were pilgrims and that they had lost their way. Then said the Giant, "You have committed an offense against me by trampling in and lying on my property last night. Therefore, you must come with me." So they had no choice but to go with him because he was much stronger than they. They also had little to say in their own defense since they knew they were guilty.

The Giant forced them to walk in front of him until they reached the castle. There he threw them into a very dark dungeon, which the two men found disgustingly foul and smelly. They lay there from Wednesday morning until Saturday night without even a crumb of bread or drop of water; there was no light at all, and they had no one to ask what would become of them. They were, therefore, in a very evil situation, far from all friends and acquaintances. Christian felt doubly sorrowful because it was his ill-advised haste that had brought them into this distress.

Ps. 88:18

Distrust's Persuasions

Now Giant Despair had a wife, and her name was Distrust. When the Giant went to bed, he told his wife that he had taken a couple of prisoners and cast them into the dungeon for trespassing on his grounds. Then he asked her what else he should do to them. She asked who they were, where they were from, and where they were going, and he told her. Then she advised him that first thing in the morning he should beat them unmercifully. So when he got up he took a wooden club and went down to the dungeon. Even though they never said a word to provoke

him, he started ridiculing and insulting them as
if they were dogs. Then he beat them fiercely and
mercilessly, and he so devastated them that they
could do nothing to help themselves. They were
unable to even roll over on the floor. When the
Giant had finished his attack, he left them there
to mourn and grieve in their misery and distress.
That entire day was spent in nothing but sighing
and bitter lamentations.

*Giant Despair
beats his
prisoners on
Thursday*

The next night, talking with her husband
about them further, and finding out that they
were still alive, the Giant's wife further advised
him to counsel them to kill themselves. So when
morning came, he went to them in a fierce manner as before. Seeing that they were in pain from
the beatings that he had given them, he advised
them that, since they were likely never to come
out of that place, their only option would be to
do away with themselves immediately. "I am
leaving you a knife, a rope, and some poison;
you choose which means of death you prefer.
Why should you choose life, seeing that it
involves so much bitterness and pain?"

*On Friday, Giant
Despair counsels
Christian and
Hopeful to kill
themselves.*

They begged and pleaded with him to let them
go, but he only glared at them with frightening
eyes; then he rushed at them again. He would doubtless have killed them himself, but he suddenly fell
into one of his seizures, which he sometimes fell
into in sunny weather. This caused him to lose the
use of his hands for a time, so he once again left
them to themselves. Then the two prisoners con-
sulted between themselves as to what they should
do. Should they take the Giant's advice or not?

Hopeful Refuses to Abandon All Hope

"Oh, my brother," said Christian mournfully,
"what shall we do? The life we are now living is
miserable. As for me, I don't know whether it is

best to live like this or to die on the spot. My soul would rather choose to die than to live, and the grave will be easier for me than this dungeon. Shall we live our lives in bondage to this Giant?"

Job 7:15-16;
Phil. 1:21-26

"Indeed, our present condition is dreadful," replied Hopeful, "and death would be far more welcome to me than to live like this for the rest of my life, but let us reconsider a moment. The Lord of the Country to which we are traveling has commanded that we shall not murder anyone. How much more, then, are we forbidden to take this counsel and to kill ourselves. Besides, he that kills another can only kill his body, but he who kills himself, kills his body and soul together. Furthermore, my brother, you speak of ease in the grave, but have you forgotten the Hell where all murderers will certainly go? 'You know that no murderer has eternal life in him.'

Exod. 20:13

1 John 3:15

"Let us also remember that all authority does not lie in the hands of Giant Despair. As far as we know, others may have been taken by him and yet escaped out of his hand. Who knows but that the God who made the world may cause the Giant to die, or that at some point the Giant may forget to lock us in, or that he may shortly have another seizure and lose the use of all his limbs? And if this ever happens again, I am resolved to take courage like a man and try my utmost to get out from under his hand. I was a fool that I didn't try to do it before. So, my brother, let's be patient and endure for awhile. The time may come that will give us a blessed freedom, but let's not be our own murderers." With these words Hopeful stabilized Christian's mind. So they continued sitting together in the darkness in their sad and despondent condition.

Matt. 28:18

Rom. 12:12;
James 5:7

Toward evening the Giant went down into the dungeon again to see if his prisoners had taken

his advice. But when he came there, he found
that they were still alive—but barely. Because
they had been given no food or water, and
because of the wounds they had received when
he beat them, they could do little more than
breathe. Even so, upon seeing them alive, the
Giant fell into a terrible rage, screaming that
since they had disobeyed his counsel it would be
worse for them than if they had never been born.   Job 3:3

They trembled greatly at this, and I think
Christian even fainted; however, when he came
to again, he and Hopeful renewed their discussion about the Giant's counsel, wondering
whether it would be best to take it or not. Now
Christian again seemed in favor of doing it, but
Hopeful made his second appeal, saying, "My
brother, don't you remember how brave you
have been before? Apollyon could not crush you,
nor could anything that you heard, saw, or felt in
the Valley of the Shadow of Death. What hard-
ship, terror, and consternation you have already
gone through! And now are you just a bag of
fears? You see that I'm in the dungeon with you,
and I'm a far weaker man by nature than you
are. This Giant has wounded me as well as you,
and I have no bread or water either. I mourn
without the light along with you, but let's exer-
cise a little more patience. Remember how you
stood tall at Vanity Fair; you weren't afraid of
chains, the cage, or even of a bloody death. If
only to avoid shame—which is not proper for a
Christian to be found in—let's bear up under it
patiently as well as we can."   1 Pet. 4:12-19

It was nighttime again, and the Giant and his
wife were in bed. She asked him if the prisoners
had taken his counsel. He replied, "They are
sturdy rascals; they choose to bear all the hard-
ship rather than to do away with themselves."

Then she said, "Take them to the castleyard tomorrow and show them the bones and skulls of those we've already killed. Make them believe that, before a week comes to an end, you will tear them to pieces as you have done to those before them."

So when morning came, the Giant returned to them. As his wife had told him, he took them to the castleyard, showed them the bones, and said,

DISTRUST

"These once were pilgrims like yourselves, and they trespassed in my grounds as you have done. When I thought it a fitting time, I tore them to pieces. Within ten days I will do the same to you, so get back down to your quarters and wait." With that he kicked and beat them all the way down to the dungeon. They lay there all day Saturday in a terrible state.

Remembering the Key of Promise

Now when night had come, and when Giant Despair and his wife, Distrust, had gone to bed, they began to renew their discussion of the prisoners. The old Giant wondered why he couldn't bring the pilgrims to an end either by his blows or his counsel. His wife said, "I fear that they live in hopes that someone will come to set them free. Or maybe they hope to find a way to pick the lock and escape."

"Since you mention it, my dear, I will go down and search them in the morning," the Giant replied.

But it so happened that on Saturday at about midnight the pilgrims began to pray and continued in prayer until almost daybreak. Then Christian, a short time before daylight, became astounded and passionately exclaimed, "What a fool I am! Here I lie in a stinking dungeon when

I could be walking in complete liberty! I have a Key in my pocket called Promise that I am sure will open any lock in Doubting Castle."

Gal. 3:22;
2 Tim. 1:1;
Heb. 6:15;
1 John 2:24-25

"That's great news, my brother!" cried Hopeful. "Get it out right now and try it!"

Escape from Doubting Castle

So Christian pulled it out and went to the prison door. He put the Key in the lock and turned it, and the door flew open easily. Christian and Hopeful both stumbled out. Next, they went to the outer door that leads into the castleyard, and Christian used his Key to open that door also. Finally, they went to the iron gate and put the Key in that lock, and although it was extremely stubborn, it too opened. As they thrust open the gate, it made such a loud noise that it awakened Giant Despair, who hastily arose to pursue his prisoners. He was struck by one of his seizures, however, and his limbs failed so that there was no way he could go after them. Then they went on until they got to the King's High-way, and so, being out of the Giant's jurisdiction, they were safe once again.

This Key will open any lock in Doubting Castle.

Now after they had gone back over the steps they had originally come in on, they began to plan what they should do to prevent those who would come after them from falling into the hands of Giant Despair. So they agreed to build a Monument and engrave this sentence upon it: "Take these steps over the wall, and you will be on your way to Doubting Castle, which is kept by Giant Despair, who despises the King of the Celestial Country and seeks to destroy holy pilgrims." Many, therefore, following after, read

what had been written and escaped the danger.
This done, they sang the following:

"Out of the way we went, and then we found
What it was to tread upon forbidden ground;
So let them that come after please take care,
Lest heedlessness makes them, as we, to fare;
Lest they, for trespassing, his prisoner's are,
Whose Castle's Doubting, and whose name's
Despair."

CHAPTER 12

❖❖❖❖❖❖❖❖❖❖❖❖❖❖❖

The Delectable Mountains

Christian and Hopeful went on their way until
they came to the Delectable Mountains, which
belong to the Lord of the Hill. So they went up
to the Mountains to look at the gardens and
orchards, the vineyards, and the fountains of
water. They drank of the water and washed themselves in it, and they freely ate from the vineyards.
Upon the mountaintops, close to the Highway,
there were Shepherds feeding their flocks.

The Mountains Delectable they now ascend,
Where Shepherds are, which to them do commend
Allurements and cautions; learn to keep clear;
Pilgrims are kept steady by faith and by fear.

The pilgrims approached the Shepherds and
asked, "Whose Delectable Mountains are these,
and whose sheep are you feeding?"

They replied, "These Mountains are Emmanuel's
Land, and they are within sight of His
City; the sheep are also His, and
He laid down His life for them."

John 10:11

"Is this the way to the Celestial City?" asked Christian.

"Yes, you are right on the
way."

"How far is it from here?"

"Indeed, too far for
any but those who will
get there."

"Is the way safe, or is it dangerous?"

Hos. 14:9

"It is safe for those for whom it is to be safe, 'but sinners trying it will fail.'"

"Is there anywhere for weak and weary pilgrims to find rest and renewal?"

Heb. 13:1-2

"The Lord of these Mountains has given us a charge that we 'not forget to entertain strangers.' Therefore, every good thing of this place is set before you."

I also saw in my dream that when the Shepherds realized that the men were travelers, they questioned the pilgrims about where they were from, how they had gotten into the way, and how they had been able to persevere thus far. For only a few who begin on the way are ever seen in these Mountains. When the Shepherds heard their answers, they were very pleased, and they looked upon the pilgrims with love and favor, saying, "Welcome to the Delectable Mountains."

The Shepherds, whose names were Knowledge, Experience, Watchful, and Sincere, took them by the hand, led them to their tents, and served them a meal. Then they said, "We would like you to stay here for awhile that we might get better acquainted and also to allow you to gain more solace here on these Delectable Mountains." So the pilgrims agreed to stay, and they then went to bed because by this time it was quite late.

A Mountain Called Error

Then I saw in my dream that in the morning the Shepherds beckoned Christian and Hopeful to walk with them upon the Mountains. So they went off together, enjoying the lovely views that were on every side. Then the Shepherds said to one another, "Shall we show these pilgrims some wonders?" They decided to do so and carefully escorted them to the top of a Mountain called Error. It was very steep on its farthest side. They told them to look down to the very bottom. So Christian and Hopeful looked down and saw at the bottom several dead bodies that had been dashed to pieces; these had fallen all the way from the top.

"What does this mean?" asked Christian.

One of the Shepherds replied, "Haven't you heard of those who listened and were deceived by Hymenaeus and Philetus, who promoted a false doctrine concerning the resurrection of the body?" 2 Tim. 2:17-18

The pilgrims answered that they had. Then the Shepherds said, "Those whom you see dashed to pieces at the bottom of this Mountain are they. To this day they remain unburied, as you can see, as an example for others to heed. Climbing this Mountain can be treacherous, especially when one goes too high or ventures too near the edge."

A Mountain Called Caution

Then I saw the Shepherds take them to the top of another Mountain, the name of which was Caution. They told them to look far off in the distance. When they did, they thought they could see several people walking up and down among tombs that were there. Because of the way they sometimes stumbled over the tombs and couldn't seem to find their way out from among them, the pilgrims deduced that they were blind. Then Christian asked, "What does this mean?"

One of the Shepherds answered, "Did you notice a short distance below these Mountains on the left side of the way some steps that led over a fence into a Meadow?"

They answered, "Yes."

"From the steps there is a path that leads directly to Doubting Castle, which is owned by Giant Despair." Then one Shepherd pointed at the men among the tombs and said, "All these people were once on a pilgrimage to the City, as you are now, until they came to those steps. Because the right way was rough in that place, they chose to go out of it into that Meadow, and they were taken by Giant Despair and cast into Doubting Castle. After they had been kept awhile in the dungeon, he at last put out their eyes and led them among the tombs, where to this very day he has left them to wander so that the saying of the wise man might be fulfilled: "A man who strays from the path of understanding comes to rest in the company of the dead." Then Christian and Hopeful looked at one another and burst into tears, but they said nothing to the Shepherds.

Prov. 21:16

A By-way to Hell

Then I saw in my dream that the Shepherds took them to the bottom of the Mountain. There was a door in the side of a Hill. The Shepherds opened the door and told the pilgrims to look inside. When they did so, they saw that it was very dark and smoky inside. They also thought they heard a sound like a roaring fire and the eerie cries of people suffering in torment. In addition, there was a strong odor of sulfur.

"What does this mean?" asked Christian.

A Shepherd answered, "This is a By-way to Hell, a way through which hypocrites enter—namely, those who sell their birthrights along with Esau; those who sell their Master along with Judas; those who blaspheme the Gospel along with Alexander; and those who lie and hide under false appearances along with Ananias and Sapphira."

Gen. 25:29-34
Matt. 26:14-16;
Mark 14:10-11;
Luke 22:3-6
1 Tim. 1:20
Acts 5:1-11

Then Hopeful said to the Shepherds, "I perceive that each of these appeared to be on a pilgrimage, even as we are now. Is this true?"

"Yes," said one of the Shepherds, "and they held that appearance for quite some time, too."

"Well, how far did they succeed on their pilgrimage before they came to such a miserable end?"

"Some got farther than these Mountains and others not so far."

Then the pilgrims said to each other, "We have a great need to cry to the Strong One for strength."

"Yes," added another of the Shepherds, "and you will need all that you can get."

A View of the City

By this time Christian and Hopeful had a desire to go forward in their pilgrimage, and the Shepherds also desired this for them. So they walked together toward the end of the Mountains. Then the Shepherds said to one another, "Let's show the pilgrims the Gates of the Celestial City from here—that is, if they have the skill to look through our perspective glass."

So they led them to the top of a high Hill called Clear and offered the glass to them. The pilgrims   1 Cor. 13:12
gladly accepted it and both attempted to see through it. Because of the memory of the last thing that had been shown them, however, their hands were shaking. Though they were unable to have a clear and steady gaze through the glass, they did think they saw something like the Gate and perhaps even some of the glory of the City. After this, they began to descend the Hill, and the pilgrims sang this song:

"Thus by the Shepherds secrets are revealed,
Which from other men are kept quite concealed;
Come to the Shepherds, then, if you would see
Things deep, things hid, and that mysterious be."

When they were about to resume the pilgrimage, one of the Shepherds gave them written instructions to guide them on their way. Another told them to beware of the flatterer. A third told them to be careful not to sleep on the Enchanted Ground. Then the fourth wished them God's blessing on the journey. So then I awoke from my dream.

CHAPTER 13

◆ ◆ ◆ ◆ ◆ ◆ ◆ ◆ ◆ ◆ ◆ ◆ ◆ ◆

Walking with Ignorance

I again fell asleep and had a dream. I saw the same two pilgrims going down the Mountains along the High-way toward the City. Now a little beyond these Mountains on the left hand lay the Country of Conceit. A little crooked lane came from that country and joined the way in which the pilgrims were walking. At that junction they met a very lively young man from that country whose name was Ignorance, and Christian asked him where he came from and where he was going.

He replied, "Sir, I was born in the country that lies over there, a little to the left, and I am going to the Celestial City."

"But how do you think you will get in at the Gate?" asked Christian. "You may find some difficulty there."

"I will get in as other good people do."

"But what do you have to show at the Gate so that it may be opened for you?"

"I know my Lord's will and have lived a good life. I pay back every debt, I pray and fast, pay tithes and give to charities, and I have left my country behind in order to reach my destination." Luke 18:9-14

"But you didn't come in at the Wicket-gate that is at the beginning of this way. You came in here through this crooked lane. I fear that, in spite of how you may see yourself, when the day of reckoning comes, you will be counted as a thief and robber and will not gain entrance into the City."

John 10:1

"Gentlemen, you are absolute strangers to me; I don't know you. Please be content to follow the doctrine of your country, and I will be content to follow the doctrine of mine. I wish you well. But as for the Wicket-gate you mention, all the world knows that it is a long way from our country. I don't think a single person in our whole region even knows the way to it. Nor do they need to worry about whether they do or not, since we have, as you can see, a fine, pleasant, green lane that comes down from our country into the way."

When Christian saw that the man relied on the wisdom of his own conceit, he whispered to Hopeful, "Do you see a man wise in his own eyes? There is more hope for a fool than for him. 'Even as he walks along the road, the fool lacks sense and shows everyone how stupid he is.'" Then he asked, "What do you think? Shall we talk further with him or go ahead of him for awhile and leave him to think about what he has already heard? We could stop and wait for him later and see if, by correcting him a little at a time, we can do him any good."

Prov. 26:12

Eccles. 10:3

Then Hopeful said,

"Let Ignorance for a little while muse
On what's been said, and let him not refuse
To embrace good counsel lest he remain
Still ignorant of what's the greatest gain.
God says of them who discernment have waived,
He's their Maker, but they will not be saved."

Hopeful added, "I don't think it will be good for us to say too much to him all at once. If it is all right with you, let us pass him for now and

talk with him another time if he is open to it."
So they both went on ahead of Ignorance.

A Man Being Carried Away

They had not gone far when they entered a very
dark lane, where they saw a man whom seven
demons had bound with seven strong cords. The
demons were carrying him back to the door on
the side of the Hill that the pilgrims had been
shown earlier. Trembling, Christian attempted to
see if he knew him, and it looked like it might be
Turn-away, who lived in the town of Apostasy.
He couldn't see his face clearly, however, because
he was hanging his head like a captured thief.
But after they had gone by, Hopeful saw a sign
on his back with these words, "Self-indulgent
professor, and damnable apostate."

Matt. 12:43-45;
Prov. 5:22

The Story of Little-faith

Then Christian said to his companion, "Now I
remember what someone told me about a thing
that happened to a good man in these parts. The
name of the man was Little-faith, but he was a
good man and lived in the town of Sincere. As
I recall, the story goes like this: At the
entrance of this passage, there comes *little-faith*
down from Broad-way Gate a lane
called Dead-man's Lane. It is called this
because of the murders that commonly take
place there. This man Little-faith was going on
a pilgrimage as we are, and he happened to sit
down there and sleep.

"Now at that time, three big bruisers were
coming down the lane from Broad-way Gate.
Their names were Faint-heart, Mistrust, and
Guilt—three brothers. They saw Little-faith,
who had just awakened and was getting ready
to resume his journey, and they came racing

up to him. Approaching him with threatening language, they told him to stand up. At this, Little-faith turned as white as a sheet, and he had no strength either to run or fight. Then Faint-heart said to him, 'Give us your wallet.' But, being reluctant to turn over his money, he moved too slowly. Mistrust therefore ran up to him and, thrusting his hand into Little-faith's pocket, pulled out his wallet and grabbed his money.

"Little-faith cried out, 'Thieves! Thieves!' With that, Guilt struck Little-faith on the head with a large club that he held in his hand. Little-faith fell flat on the ground, where he lay bleeding profusely and looking as though he might bleed to death. All this time the thieves just stood there, but then they heard someone coming up the road. They feared that it might be Great-grace from the City of Good-confidence, so they took off running and left Little-faith there to fend for himself. Somehow he got up and managed to go on his way. This was the story I heard."

"But did they take from him everything he owned?" asked Hopeful.

"No, he had his Jewels hidden, so he was able to keep them. But I was told that he was very upset over his loss because the thieves had gotten most of his spending money. He had a little bit of money left, but not enough to bring him to his journey's end. No, if I am not misinformed, just to keep himself alive he was forced to beg as he journeyed along. For he refused to sell his Jewels, and, in spite of begging and doing what he could to scrape by, he went hungry most of the rest of the way."

"But isn't it a marvel that they didn't get his certificate for admittance at the Celestial Gate?" asked Hopeful.

"Yes, it is a marvel; they didn't miss it because of any cunning on his part. He was so unnerved at their coming that he had neither power nor skill to hide anything. It was the providence of God more than his own endeavor that saved the certificate."

2 Tim. 1:13

"It must be of great comfort to him that they didn't get this Jewel from him," said Hopeful.

"It might have been of great comfort to him if he had used it as he should have, but those who told me the story said that he made little use of it all the rest of the way because of the dismay he felt over the loss of his money. He even forgot about it for the better part of the rest of the journey. Besides this, whenever he thought of it and he began to be comforted, fresh thoughts of his loss would come to his mind, and he would once again be overwhelmed."

2 Pet. 1:19

"Oh, the poor man! This must have caused him great grief."

"Grief? Yes, grief indeed! This would have been the case for any of us had we been so cruelly robbed and wounded in a strange place. Poor soul, it is a wonder that he didn't die with grief. I was told that he spent most of his remaining time on the way mourning and complaining bitterly, telling all those he met where the robbery happened, how it occurred, who had done it, what was lost, how he was wounded, and how he had barely escaped with his life."

Hopeful Misjudges Little-faith

"It's a wonder," said Hopeful, "that he didn't, out of necessity, end up selling or pawning some of his Jewels to help relieve his misery."

"You're talking like one who isn't seeing clearly," Christian responded. "For what price should he have pawned them? Or to whom should he have sold them? His Jewels were not highly valued anywhere in the country where he was robbed. Also, he didn't want the relief that such a transaction would bring. Had his Jewels been missing at the Gate of the Celestial City, he knew that he would have been excluded from an inheritance there. That would have been worse for him than the confrontation of ten thousand thieves."

"Why do you speak so sharply, brother?" asked Hopeful. "Esau sold his birthright for a serving of stew, and that birthright was his greatest Jewel. If he did it, why not Little-faith also?"

Gen. 25:34;
Heb. 12:16

"Esau did indeed sell his birthright as do many others," said Christian, "but, like that wicked man, they exclude themselves from the chief blessing. However, you must recognize the difference between Esau and Little-faith and their situations. Esau's birthright was earthly, whereas Little-faith's Jewels were not; Esau's belly was his god, but Little-faith's belly was not so; Esau's desire lay in his fleshly cravings, Little-faith's did not. Besides, Esau could see no further than fulfilling his lusts. He said, 'When a man is dying of starvation, what good is his birthright?' But Little-faith, though he had only a small amount of faith, by that small amount was not only kept from such indulgences but was able to see and prize his Jewels more than selling them like Esau did his birthright.

Gen. 25:32

"You cannot read anywhere that Esau had so much as a little bit of faith. So where the flesh alone holds sway—as it will in the person who has no faith to resist with—it is no wonder if he sells his birthright and his very soul to the Devil of Hell. He is like a jackass that, because of its nature, cannot be turned away. When his mind is set upon lust, he will go for it, whatever the cost. But Little-faith was different from that. His mind was on the things of God, and his means of support came from what was spiritual and above. Therefore, there would have been no reason for him to sell his Jewels simply to fill his mind with worthless things.

Jer. 2:24

Col. 3:1-4

"Will a man pay a dollar to fill his stomach with hay? Or can you persuade the Turtledove to live on dead flesh like the Crow? For carnal lusts, faithless ones might be driven to pawn, mortgage, or sell what they have—along with their very lives to boot. But those who have faith, saving faith, though only a little of it, cannot do so. So here, my brother, is your mistake."

"I admit it," said Hopeful, "but your strong reaction almost made me angry."

"Why would you get angry? I only said you were acting like a man who wasn't seeing clearly. But please forgive me, and let's forget about this and return to the subject we have been discussing."

Hopeful's Idealism

"But, Christian, I am persuaded in my heart that those three thieves were nothing but cowards. Why else would they run at the sound of someone coming up the road? Why didn't Little-faith muster up greater courage? I think he should have at least tried to fight them, and if he couldn't win, then yield."

Hopeful swaggers.

"Many have said that these three are cowards," answered Christian, "but few have found it to be the case in their own time of trial. As for a great heart, Little-faith had none. And, my brother, I think that if you had been the man, you perhaps would have had a short skirmish but then yielded. In addition, it is one thing to think we

There is no great heart for God where there is only little faith.

159

have courage when things are easy but quite another to have it when we are suddenly afflicted. You might have second thoughts if you were suddenly in that man's shoes.

"And consider also that these are hired thieves. They serve under the King of the Bottomless Pit, who, if need be, will himself come to their aid 1 Pet. 5:8 with a voice like that of a roaring lion. I myself have been confronted as Little-faith was, and I have found it to be a terrible thing. These three villains set upon me once, and when I began to resist like a Christian, they called their master, and he immediately came. As the saying goes, I would have given my life for a penny, but, thank God, in accordance with His will, I was clothed with the armor of assurance. Yet even though I was so equipped, I still found it difficult to stand firm. No one knows what it's like to go through such combat except the one who is in the battle himself."

"But they ran, you see," explained Hopeful. "They fled as soon as they thought the one called Great-grace was coming."

"That is true; both they and their master have often fled when Great-grace has appeared, and no wonder, since he is the King's Champion. But I trust you will allow for some difference between Little-faith and the King's Champion. Not all the King's subjects are champions, nor are they able, when tried, to do such feats of war as Great-grace. Is it fitting to think that a toddler should 1 Sam. 17 handle Goliath as David did? Or that a wren should have the strength of an ox? Some are strong, some are weak; some have great faith, some have little. This man was one of the weak and so he went to pieces."

"I wish Great-grace had appeared to them," said Hopeful.

GREAT Grace

"If he had, he might have had his hands full," said Christian. "For I have to tell you that even though Great-grace is very highly skilled at using his weapons and has been able to do well against them as long as he can keep them at the tip of his Sword, his victory is never assured. For if Faint-heart, Mistrust, or Guilt can get by his Sword, they can throw him down. And once a man is down, what can he do? If you look closely at Great-grace's face, you can see numerous scars that prove what I say. Yes, once I heard that he said in combat, 'We despaired even of life.'

2 Cor. 1:8

"And how these same criminals and their friends made David groan and mourn! Yes, and Heman and Hezekiah, who were champions of the faith in their day, were forced to rally when they were assaulted by them as well. In spite of their stand, they were not without bruises. Once Peter thought he would see what he could do, but even though some say he is the prince of the apostles, when they were through with him he was afraid of his own shadow.

Ps. 88

2 Kings 20:1-7

Matt. 26:69-75

"Besides, their helper comes at their whistle. He is never out of hearing range, and whenever they are hard-pressed, he comes to help them immediately, if possible. Of him it is said, 'When he rises up, the mighty are terrified; they retreat before his thrashing. The sword that reaches him has no effect, nor does the spear or the arrow or the javelin. Iron he treats like straw and bronze like rotten wood. Arrows do not make him flee; slingstones are like chaff to him. A club seems to him but a piece of straw; he laughs at the rattling of the lance.' What can one do in a case like this? It is true, if a man could have Job's horse, along with the skill and courage to ride him, he could do notable things. For 'he paws fiercely, rejoicing in his strength, and charges into the fray. He laughs at fear, afraid of nothing; he does not shy away from the sword. The quiver rattles against his side, along with the flashing spear and lance. In frenzied excitement he eats up the ground; he cannot stand still when the trumpet sounds. At the blast of the trumpet he snorts, "Aha!" He catches the scent of battle from afar, the shout of commanders and the battle cry.'

"But for those of us who walk on the ground, let us never desire to meet with an enemy, nor boast as if we could do better than another when we hear of their failings. Let us not flatter ourselves with thoughts of our own boldness, prowess, or power, for those who do this are often the ones who fall hardest under trial. Take Peter, for example, whom I mentioned before. His foolish mind convinced him that he would do better and stand more faithfully for his Master than all the others. In spite of his worthless boasting, he was soundly defeated by these villains.

"When we hear of such robberies taking place on the King's High-way, I believe there are two things we should do. First, we must go out fully equipped, and this includes taking a shield with us. Without a shield, how can we hope to stand

Job 41:25-29

Job 39:21-25

Gal. 6:1-5

Matt. 26:33

against one such as Leviathan? If we have no shield, he thinks nothing of us. Therefore, as one highly skilled in warfare has said, 'In addition to all this, take up the shield of faith, with which you can extinguish all the flaming arrows of the evil one.'

Eph. 6:16

"Second, I believe that it is good also to desire a convoy of the King's forces to accompany us for our protection. Indeed, we should petition the King Himself to go with us. This caused David to rejoice in the Valley of the Shadow of Death, and Moses would rather have died than to have gone one step without his God. Oh, my brother, if He will go with me, 'I will not fear the tens of thousands drawn up against me on every side.' But without Him, even the proudest warriors fall into the ranks of the slain.

Ps. 23

Exod. 33:15

Ps. 3:6; 27:1-3

Isa. 10:4

"As for me, I already have some experience in this warfare, and through the abundant grace of Him who is greatest, I am still very much alive, as you see. But I cannot boast of any strength on my part. As a matter of fact, I would be very greatly relieved if I never had to experience any such attacks again. I fear, however, that we have not yet gone beyond all danger. But, as the lion and the bear have not yet devoured me, I trust that God will also deliver us from the next 'uncircumcised Philistines,' those enemies of God that seek our destruction." Then Christian sang,

1 Sam. 17:26

"Poor Little-faith! Have you been among thieves?
Were you robbed? Remember, if you believe,
You'll get more faith; then a victor you'll be
Over ten thousand, and not a mere three."

CHAPTER 14

◆◆◆◆◆◆◆◆◆◆◆◆◆◆◆

The Pilgrims Are Deceived

So they traveled on, with Ignorance following
along behind them, until they came to a place
where another way joined the way that they
were on, and both ways seemed to lie as straight
as the way they were supposed to go. They were
confused, unsure which of the two to take, so
they stopped there, wondering what to do.

As they were thinking, a man wearing a white
robe approached them and asked why they were
standing there. They told him that they were
going to the Celestial City but were confused as
to which of the ways to take. "Follow me," said
the man. "I am going there." Impressed by his
appearance, they followed him in the way that
joined the way they had come on. That way gradually turned, and by degrees it turned them away
from the City. In a short time their faces were
turned in the opposite direction, but they continued to follow him. Before they realized what was
happening, the man led them into a net. They
got so tangled up in it that they didn't know
what to do. At that, the white robe fell off the
man's back, and they saw the error of their way.
They lay there crying for some time because they
didn't know how to free themselves.

Eventually Christian said to Hopeful, "Now I
can see that I am in error. Didn't the Shepherds
warn us to beware of the flatterers, those deceivers
who give false hope and deceitful encouragement?

They are able to persuasively entice the careless
into following their ways. As the saying of the
wise man goes, we have found that 'whoever flat-
ters his neighbor is spreading a net for his feet.'"

Prov. 29:5

Then Hopeful said, "The Shepherds
also gave us instructions so
that we wouldn't have
trouble keeping to the
way. But we were care-
less and forgot to read
them and therefore
haven't kept our-
selves from the
destroyer's path. David
was wiser than we are, for
he said, 'By the word of Your

Ps. 17:4-5 lips, I have kept away from the paths of the
destroyer.'"

Encounter with a Shining One

So they lay there helpless in the net, crying over
their captivity. At last they noticed a Shining
One coming toward them with a whip in his
hand. When he came to where they were, he
asked them where they had come from and how
they got there. They answered that they were
poor pilgrims on their way to Zion, but they had
been led out of their way by a man clothed in
white who told them to follow him because he
was going there also.

Then the Shining One with the whip said, "He
is Flatterer, a false apostle who has transformed
himself into an angel of light." He then tore the
net and let them out, saying to them, "Follow
me so that I may lead you back to the way." So
he led them back to the way, which they had
left to follow the Flatterer. Then he asked them,
"Where did you sleep last night?"

2 Cor. 11:13-14;
2 John 7

"With the Shepherds on the Delectable Mountains," they answered.

He then asked them if the Shepherds hadn't given them a sheet of directions to direct them on the way.

"Yes," they answered.

"But didn't you pull it out and read it when you were confused about which way to go?"

"No."

"Why not?"

"We forgot."

"Didn't the Shepherds warn you to beware of the flatterers?"

"Yes, but we didn't imagine that this fine-speaking man was one."   Rom. 16:18

Then I saw in my dream that he commanded them to lie down, which they did, and he gave them a whipping to teach them the right way to walk. He said, "Those whom I love I rebuke and   Heb. 12:5-6
discipline. So be earnest, and repent." This done,   Rev. 3:19
he sent them on their way advising them to pay careful attention to the other directions given by the Shepherds. So they thanked him for all his kindness and went carefully along the right way, singing:

"Now come here, you who walk along the way,
See how the pilgrims fare who go astray:
Taking lightly good counsel, they forget
And are soon caught in an entangling net;
It's true they were rescued, but still you see,
They're whipped to boot: let this your caution be."

Meeting Atheist

Now after awhile they could see someone far in the distance coming toward them. Christian said, "There is a man with his back toward Zion, and he is coming to meet us."

"I see him," said Hopeful. "Let's be careful now; he may prove to be a flatterer also." So he drew nearer and nearer until at last he came to them. His name was Atheist, and he asked them where they were going.

"We are going to the Mount Zion."

At that, Atheist began to laugh uncontrollably.

"Why are you laughing?" asked Christian.

 "Ha! Ignorant people like you make me laugh. You take upon yourselves such a tedious journey only to end up, in all likelihood, with nothing but your travels for all your pains."

"Why, sir," asked Christian, "don't you think we'll be received?"

"Received! There is not such a place as you dream of in all this world!"

"But there is in the world to come."

"When I was at home in my own country, I heard about your belief, and afterward I decided to pursue it. I have been seeking this City for twenty years but can find no more of it than I did the first day I set out."

Eccles. 10:15

"We have both heard, and believe, that there is such a place to be found," responded Christian.

The atheist finds his satisfaction in this world.

"If I hadn't believed when I was at home, I wouldn't have come this far to seek for it. But finding nothing—and I would have if it were there—I'm going back again and will seek to refresh myself with the things I had formerly cast away for those vain hopes."

Then Christian said to Hopeful, "Do you think what this man is saying is true?"

"Be careful," replied Hopeful, "for he is one of the flatterers. Remember what it has cost us already for listening to this type of fellow. What!

168

No Mount Zion? Didn't we see the Gate of the City from the Delectable Mountains? Aren't we now to walk by faith? Let's go on, lest the man with the whip overtake us again! You should have been the one to teach me this lesson, but I will whisper it in your ears: 'Stop listening to teaching that contradicts what you know is right.' My brother, I say, stop listening to him, and let us believe and thus secure the salvation our souls."

2 Cor. 5:7

Remembering past discipline helps with present temptations.

Prov. 19:27

Heb. 10:39

"My brother," said Christian, "I didn't ask the question because I doubted the truth of our belief, but to test you, and to draw out the fruit of integrity from your heart. As for this man, I know that he is blinded by the god of this world. Let us both go on, secure in the fact that we believe the truth, knowing that 'no lie comes from the truth.'"

2 Cor. 4:4

1 John 2:21

Then Hopeful said, "Now I rejoice in my hope of seeing the glory of God." So they turned away from the man, and he went his way, laughing at them.

On the Enchanted Ground

I saw then in my dream that they went on till they came into a certain country where the air naturally tended to cause drowsiness in those unaccustomed to it. Hopeful's mind began to grow dull, and he became very sleepy. He then said to Christian, "I'm getting so drowsy that I can hardly keep my eyes open. Let's lie down here and take a short nap."

"No way!" said Christian. "If we sleep here, we may never wake up."

"Why not, my brother? Sleep is sweet to one who is exhausted. We may be refreshed if we take a nap."

"Don't you remember that one of the Shepherds warned us to beware of the Enchanted Ground? He meant that we should beware of sleeping there, 'So then, let us not be like others, who are asleep, but let us be alert and self-controlled.'"

1 Thess. 5:6

"I admit my fault," said Hopeful. "If I had been here alone, I would have run the risk of death by falling asleep. I see that what the wise man said is true, 'Two are better than one.' Up to this time your company has been a gift of mercy to me; 'you shall surely have a good reward for your effort.'"

Eccles. 4:9

Matt. 10:40-42

"You have blessed me too," said Christian, "but to keep the drowsiness of this place from overcoming us, let's keep talking about those things that edify our spirits."

"Indeed, I agree with all my heart," Hopeful replied.

"Where shall we begin?" asked Christian.

"Where God began with us. But you start the discussion, if you will."

Then Christian said, "First, I will sing you this song:

"When the saints grow sleepy, let them come here
And listen how two pilgrims' words remain clear.
Yes, let them learn from these and become wise,
So to keep open their dull, slumbering eyes.
The fellowship of saints, if managed well,
Keeps them awake, in spite of all Hell."

CHAPTER 15

◆◆◆◆◆◆◆◆◆◆◆◆◆◆◆

Hopeful Tells His Story

"I will ask you a question," Christian said. "How did you first decide to begin this pilgrimage?"

"Do you mean, how did I first come to care about my soul's welfare?" asked Hopeful.

"Yes, that's what I mean."

"For a long time I continued to delight in those things that are seen, which were sold at our fair—things that I now believe would have drawn me into Hell and destruction if I had continued with them."

"And what were those things?" asked Christian.

"All the treasures and riches of the world. Oh, I also found great pleasure in riotous behavior, wild parties, drinking, swearing, lying, immorality, Sabbath-breaking, and other things that contribute to the soul's destruction. But I heard from you and also from beloved Faithful, who died in Vanity Fair for his faith and righteous living, that

the consequence of the things I was doing is
death. I heard that, on account of these things,
the wrath of God is coming on those who are
disobedient. Then I considered these and other
things pertaining to God."

Rom. 6:21, 23

Eph. 5:6

"And did you at once fall under the power of
this conviction?"

"No, I wasn't immediately willing to admit the
evil of sin or to acknowledge the damnation
resulting from it. At first, when my mind began
to be shaken by the Word, I tried to shut my eyes
to its light."

"But what was the cause of your continuing to
hold on to the sin when God's blessed Spirit was
first beginning to work on you?" asked Christian.

"The causes were as follows: First, I was ignorant of the fact that God was acting upon me.
Second, sin was still very desirable to my flesh,
and I didn't want to part with it. Third, I didn't
know how to break off relationships with my old
friends; their companionship and the things we
enjoyed together were very important to me.
And fourth, the times I was under heavy conviction were so disturbing and frightening to me
that I couldn't bear the thought of them, even
for a moment."

"But then," said Christian, "it seems that at
times you were freed from the turmoil."

"Yes, this is true, but it would again return to
my mind, and then I would be as bad—no, even
worse—than I had been before."

Ps. 51:3

"Why, Hopeful, what was it that brought your
sins to mind again?"

"Many things, such as if I met a believer in the
street, or if I heard anything read from the Bible,
or if my head began to ache, or if I was told that
a neighbor was sick, or if I heard the bell toll for
someone dead, or if I thought of dying myself, or

if I heard of the sudden death of someone else—
but especially when I thought of myself soon
facing the judgment."

"Were there any times when you could easily
dispel the feelings of guilt that came over you in
these ways?"

"No, none at all. For they got an ever-tighter
grip on my conscience, and if I even thought of
continuing in sin, it would mean double torment
for me."

Attempted Reforms and Renewed Conviction
"Well, what did you do then?" asked Christian.

"I thought I must make every effort to change
my ways or else I would surely be damned."

"And did you try to change?"

"Yes, and I fled not only from my sins but
from my sinful friends as well. I began to per-
form religious duties such as praying, reading,
weeping for sin, and telling my neighbors the
truth. I did these things and many others that
are too numerous to relate."

"Did you feel good about yourself then?"

"Yes, for awhile, but finally my burden came
tumbling down upon me again,
despite all my efforts
to reform."

"What renewed
the conviction, see-
ing that you now
thought yourself
to be reformed?"
asked Christian.

"Oh, there were
several things that brought it upon me, especially
such sayings as these: 'All of us have become like
one who is unclean, and all our righteous acts are
like filthy rags; we all shrivel up like a leaf, and

Isa. 64:6 like the wind our sins sweep us away.' 'Know that
Gal. 2:16 a man is not justified by observing the law, but by
faith in Jesus Christ.' 'So you also, when you have
done everything you were told to do, should say,
Luke 17:10 "We are unworthy servants; we have only done
our duty."' I heard many other sayings like this
also. From these I began to reason with myself
along this line: 'If all my righteous acts are like
filthy rags, and if no one can be justified by obeying the law, and if, when we have done everything we can, we are still unworthy, then it is
foolishness to think that I can ever see Heaven
by trying to be good.'

The Debt and Power of Sin

"Then I thought, 'If someone once charged thousands of dollars worth of merchandise at a clothing store, and since that time has paid all his
other bills, still, if this old debt remains on the
ledger, the store may sue him and he may even
go to prison until the debt is paid.'"

"Well," asked Christian, "and how did this
apply to your condition?"

"Why, I thought to myself, 'Because of my
sins, I have accumulated a lot of debt on God's
ledger, and even if I now reform, it will not pay
off the balance. Therefore, I will still go under
despite all the good changes I have brought
about in my life.' So I asked myself, 'How then
shall I find freedom from the prospect of damnation that my former sins have caused me?'"

"That was good thinking, but please go on,"
said Christian.

"Another thing that troubled me was that, if
I looked carefully at even the best of what I was
accomplishing during my efforts at reform, I
could still see sin—new sin—mixing in and taint-
ing the good within me. I was, therefore, forced

to conclude that despite my former self-conceit and pride in my accomplishments, I could now recognize that I was presently committing enough sin in one day to send me to Hell, even if I had been previously faultless."

Phil. 3:1-11

A Savior Is Needed

"And what did you do then?" asked Christian.

"Do! I didn't know what to do. I poured out my heart to Faithful because we were well acquainted. He told me that if I could not obtain the righteousness of a man who had never sinned, then neither my own righteousness nor all the righteousness this world possesses could save me."

"And did you think he was telling you the truth?" asked Christian.

"If he had told me this when I was pleased with myself and my reforms, I would have called him a fool for worrying about such a thing. But since I could now see my own malady and the sin that would latch on to my best efforts, I was forced to accept his opinion."

"But when he first told you this, did you think that a person existed of whom it could justly be said that he had never committed sin?"

"I must confess that at first these words sounded strange, indeed, but upon further discussion with him, I became convinced of their truth."

"Did you ask him who such a Man could be and how you could hope to be justified by Him?"

"Yes, and he told me it was the Lord Jesus, who sits at the right hand of the Most High. 'So,' he said, 'you must be justified by Him, and this through trusting in what He did in the days of His flesh by hanging and suffering on the tree.' Then I asked him how that one Man's righteousness

Ps. 2; Phil. 2:9-11

Heb. 10:19-22;
1 Pet. 1:3-5

could be so effective as to justify another person before God. He told me that this one Man was the Mighty God, and that He lived the life He lived and died the death He died not for Himself, but for me. Then he added that the inestimable value of what He had done would be credited to me if I put my trust in Him."

Col. 1:15-20

Rom. 6:8-10

Rom. 4:23-25

An Invitation Extended

"What did you do then?"

"I had objections that were a hindrance to my believing; I thought He was not willing to save me."

"And what did Faithful say to you?"

"He told me to go to Him and see. I answered that this would be presumptuous of me, but he said that wasn't true since I had been invited to come. Then he gave me a Book that Jesus had authored to encourage me to come more readily. He told me that every word in the Book, down to the minutest details, stood firmer than Heaven and earth. So I asked him what I would have to do when I went to Him. He said that I must fall on my knees and ask the Father, with all my heart and soul, to reveal Him to me.

Matt. 11:28

Matt. 24:35

Ps. 95:6;
Dan. 6:10;
Jer. 29:12-13

"Then I asked him further how I should entreat Him. He said, 'Go, and you will find Him sitting on a mercy seat; He sits there all year long to give pardon and forgiveness to those who come to Him.' I told him that I didn't know what to say when I approached Him, and he told me to say something to this effect: 'God, have mercy on me, a sinner and help me to know and believe in Jesus Christ. For I see that if Christ had not been righteous, and if I don't have faith in that righteousness, then I am utterly without hope and have been cast away. Lord, I have heard that You are a merciful God and have ordained that Your Son, Jesus Christ, should be

Exod. 25:22;
Lev. 16:9;
Num. 7:8-9;
Heb. 4:16

Luke 18:13

the Savior of the world. Moreover, I have heard
that You are willing to bestow Him upon such
a miserable sinner as I am. Yes, I am a sinner
indeed. Lord, take this opportunity and glorify
your grace by saving my soul through Your Son,
Jesus Christ. Amen.'"

Hopeful's Struggle

"And did you do as you were told?"

"Yes, over and over and over
again."

"And did the Father
reveal His Son to you?"

"No, not the first
time, nor the second,
third, fourth, fifth, or
sixth time either."

"Well, what did you do then?"

"What did I do? Why, I didn't know what to do."

"Did you have any thoughts of giving up praying?"

"Yes, at least a hundred times over."

"Why didn't you?"

"I believed that what had been told me was
the truth: that, without Christ's righteousness, all
the world could not save me. So I reasoned with
myself, 'If I give up, I will die, and I dare not die
except at the throne of grace.' Then the words
came to me, 'Though it linger, wait for it; it will   Hab. 2:3
certainly come and will not delay.'"

He Receives a Revelation

"So," Hopeful added, "I continued to pray until
the Father showed me His Son."

"How was He revealed to you?"

"I didn't see Him with my human eyes, but the
eyes of my understanding. This is how it hap-   Eph. 1:18-19
pened: One day I was very sad; sadder, I think,

than at any other time in my life. This sadness was the result of a new awareness of the enormity and ugliness of my sins. I then expected nothing but Hell and the eternal damnation of my soul, but suddenly I thought I saw the Lord Jesus, looking down from Heaven at me and saying, 'Believe in the Lord Jesus, and you will be saved.'

Acts 16:31

"I replied, 'But, Lord, I am a great—a very great—sinner.' He answered, 'My grace is sufficient for you.' Then I asked, 'But, Lord, what does it mean to believe?' He replied, 'He who comes to Me will never go hungry, and he who believes in Me will never be thirsty.' Then I concluded that believing in Christ and coming to Him were one and the same, and that the one who comes to Him, whose heart and affections pursue Christ and His salvation, is indeed one who believes in Christ.

2 Cor. 12:9

John 6:35

"At this realization tears filled my eyes, and I further asked, 'But, Lord, may such a great sinner as I truly be accepted and saved by You?' And I heard Him say, 'Whoever comes to Me I will never drive away.' Then I asked, 'But, Lord, in my coming to You, how must I regard You so that my faith will rest properly on You?' Then He said, 'Christ Jesus came into the world to save sinners.' 'Christ is the end of the law so that there may be righteousness for everyone who believes.' 'He was delivered over to death for our sins and was raised to life for our justification.' He 'loves us and has freed us from our sins by His blood.' He is the 'one mediator between God and men.' And 'He always lives to intercede for them.'

John 6:37

1 Tim. 1:15

Rom. 10:4

Rom. 4:25

Rev. 1:5

1 Tim. 2:5

Heb. 7:25

"From all these words I gathered that I must look for righteousness in His person alone and for satisfaction of the penalty for my sins through His blood alone. I saw that what He had done in obedience to His Father's law, by submit-

Eph. 1:3-14;
Heb. 10:12-14

178

ting to the penalty therein, was not for Himself but for all who will gratefully accept it for salvation. By this time my heart was full of joy, my eyes were filled with tears, and my emotions were overflowing with love for the Name, the people, and the ways of Jesus Christ."

"This was indeed a revelation to your soul. But tell me, what effect did this have on your spirit?"

"It became clear to me that the world and all its standards of righteousness stand condemned. I saw that God the Father, although He is just, can legally absolve and justify any sinner who humbly comes to Him. I was greatly ashamed of the vileness of my former life, and I felt a strong sense of shame for all my ignorance. I had been so blind that I had never before considered the glorious beauty of Jesus Christ. I suddenly had a compelling love for the holy life and longed to do something for the praise and honor and glory of the Lord Jesus. Yes, I now felt that if I had a thousand gallons of blood in my body, I could have spilled it all for the sake of Jesus, my Lord."

CHAPTER 16
◆◆◆◆◆◆◆◆◆◆◆◆◆◆◆

The Pilgrims Discuss
Justification with Ignorance

Then I saw in my dream that Hopeful glanced back and saw Ignorance still following, but at a good distance behind. "Look," he said to Christian, "Ignorance is dragging his feet and lagging far behind."

"Yes, I see him. He doesn't care for our company."

"But I don't think it would have hurt him to have kept pace with us."

"I don't think so either, but I'm sure he thinks otherwise."

"I can agree with that, but let's wait for him."

So they waited, and when Ignorance was within earshot, Christian called to him, "Come on, man! Why do you linger so far behind?"

And Ignorance called out, "I take more pleasure in walking alone than with others—unless I enjoy their company."

Then Christian said to Hopeful in a low voice, "Didn't I tell you that he doesn't care for our company? But let's wait for him anyway."

When Ignorance approached them, Christian said, "Join us, and let's talk away the time in this lonely place. How are you doing now? How is your relationship with God?"

Ignorance replied, "Well, I hope; for I am always engaging in positive mental activities to encourage myself as I walk."

"What kind of mental activities?" asked Christian.

"Oh, I think about God and Heaven."

"That is good, but are you aware that the demons and those who will suffer damnation do this also?"

James 2:19

"But I think about them and desire them."

"I am sure you are aware that many desire them who will never be accepted there. For 'the sluggard craves and gets nothing.'"

Prov. 13:4

"But not only do I think of them; I have left everything for them."

"Can you really say that?" asked Christian. "For leaving everything behind is a very difficult matter—yes, a harder matter than most of us are even aware. But why do you believe you have left all for God and His Kingdom?"

Prov. 28:26

"I know it in my own heart."

"Did you know that the wise man says, 'He who trusts in his own heart is a fool'?"

"That is spoken of an evil heart; but mine is a good one."

"But how can you prove that it is good?"

"It comforts me with hopes of Heaven."

"But that may be through it's deceitfulness; for a person's heart may minister comfort to him in hopes of something for which he doesn't yet have grounds for hope."

THE WORD OF GOD

"But my heart and life both agree; thus, there are good grounds for me to hope."

"Who told you that your heart and life are in agreement?"

"My heart tells me so."

"Ask your heart if I am a thief. Does your heart tell you so? Unless the Word of God bears witness in the matter, no other testimony will be of any value."

"But isn't it a good heart that will have good thoughts? And isn't it a good life that is lived according to God's commandments?"

"Yes, a good heart has good thoughts and a good life is lived according to God's commandments. But it is, indeed, one thing to possess these things and quite another to merely think so."

"Please tell me what you determine to be good thoughts and a life lived according to God's commandments," said Ignorance.

"There are many kinds of good thoughts—some concerning ourselves, some of God, some of Christ, and some of many other things."

"What are good thoughts concerning ourselves?"

"Those that agree with the Word of God," said Christian.

"When do our own thoughts of ourselves agree with the Word of God?" asked Ignorance.

"When we pass the same judgment upon ourselves that the Word of God passes. Let me explain myself. The Word of God says of a person in his natural condition, 'There is no one righteous, not even one,' 'that every inclination of the thoughts of his heart was only evil all the time,' and that his 'bent is always toward evil from his earliest youth.' Now then, when we agree with these conclusions concerning ourselves, our thoughts are good because they are in agreement with the Word of God." | Rom. 3:10

Gen. 6:5

Gen. 8:21

"I will never believe that my heart is that bad," said Ignorance.

"Then," replied Christian, "you don't really have one truly good thought concerning yourself. But let me go on. As the Word passes judgment on our hearts, it also passes judgment on our ways. When the thoughts of our hearts and the way we live both agree with the Word of God's assessment of them, then both are good, because they are in agreement with it."

"Spell out what you mean."

Prov. 2:12-15;
Rom. 3:9-18

"Why, the Word of God says man's ways are crooked—not good, but perverse. It says they have not known the good way and therefore are naturally out of it. Now when a man views his ways from this perspective with wisdom and humility, then he has good thoughts concerning his ways because his thoughts now agree with the perspective of the Word of God."

"What are good thoughts concerning God?" asked Ignorance.

"As I have said concerning thoughts about ourselves, so it is with our thoughts about God. We must agree with what the Word says about Him. We must think of His being and His attributes only in the light of the Word. I cannot discuss this in depth at this time, but I will speak about Him as it regards us. We have a right view of God when we believe that He knows us better than we know ourselves and that He can see sinfulness in us when we see none in ourselves. We also have a right view of Him when we believe that He knows our inmost thoughts, and that our heart, with all its hidden depths, can hide

1 Chron. 28:9;
Ps. 7:9

nothing from His eyes. Also, we have a right view of Him when we believe that all our own righteousness stinks in His nostrils, and that, because of this, He cannot tolerate seeing us stand before Him with any self-assurance, even

Isa. 65:5

if we present ourselves in our finest form."

"Do you think that I am such a fool as to think that God can see no farther than I can, or that I could come to God through trusting in my own best effort?" asked Ignorance.

"Why? How do you view this matter?"

"Well, in short, I think I must believe in Christ for justification."

The Righteousness of CHRIST

"For what reason? How can you think you must believe in Christ when you are unable to see your need of Him? You don't see either your original sin or your existing malady. Your opinion of yourself and of your efforts plainly exposes you as one who has not as yet seen his need of Christ's personal righteousness to justify him before God. How can you then say, 'I believe in Christ'?"

"I believe," replied Ignorance, "that Christ died for sinners and that I shall be justified before God from the curse through His gracious acceptance of my obedience to His law. Or, if that is not enough, Christ will make my religious duties acceptable to His Father by virtue of His merits, and so I shall be justified."

1 Tim. 1:15

"Please let me give a response to this confession of your faith," said Christian. "First, you believe with an imaginary faith; for this faith is nowhere described in the Word. Second, you believe with a false faith; it takes away justification from the personal righteousness of Christ and applies it to your own. Third, this kind of faith doesn't allow Christ to be the justifier of your person, but rather the justifier of your actions; it renders your person justified by your actions. This is false. Last, therefore, this faith is deceitful. It will lead you to wrath on the judgment day of the Almighty God. For true justifying faith puts the soul, which because of the law has become perceptive of its

185

lost condition, fleeing to Christ's righteousness
for refuge. And His righteousness is not an act of
grace which makes your obedience acceptable to
God. No, it is His personal obedience to God's

Rom. 8:3-4   law, in doing and suffering for us what the law
required of us. True faith accepts this righteousness, and under its skirt the soul is hidden and is

Eph. 5:25-27   presented as spotless before God. The soul, therefore, is accepted and thereby acquitted of all guilt
and condemnation."

"Come on!" exclaimed Ignorance. "Would you
have us trust only in what Christ in His own person has done without us? This ill-founded
notion would loosen the reins of our lust and
allow us to live however we wanted. For it
wouldn't matter how we live, so long as we may

Rom. 6:1, 15   be justified by Christ's personal righteousness
when we believe it."

"Ignorance is your name, and it fits you perfectly," said Christian. "Even your answer demonstrates what I say. You are ignorant of what
justifying righteousness is; you are just as ignorant of how, through faith, to secure your soul
from the terrible wrath of God. Yes, you are also
ignorant of the true effects of saving faith in this
righteousness of Christ, those effects being a bowing and surrender of the heart to God in Christ, a
love for his Name, His Word, His ways, and His
people—and not as you ignorantly imagine."

Then Hopeful said to Christian, "Ask him if he
has ever had Christ revealed to him from Heaven."

"What!" exclaimed Ignorance. "You believe in
revelations? I believe that what both of you, and all
the others like you, have to say about this matter is
nothing but the fruit of insanity in your brains!"

"Why, man!" declared Hopeful. "Christ is so
hidden in God from the perceptions of the natural man that He cannot be known, and salvation

in Him cannot be attained by any unless God the
Father gives a revelation of Him to them."

Matt. 11:25-27;
1 Cor. 2:6-10

"That is your faith, not mine," countered Ignorance. "Just because I don't have as many whimsical doctrines turning my head as you doesn't
mean that my faith isn't as good as yours."

"Allow me to say one more thing," said Christian. "You shouldn't show such disregard for this
matter. For I will boldly affirm, just as my good
friend has done, that no one can know Jesus Christ
except through a revelation of Him by the Father.

Matt. 11:27;
1 Cor. 12:3

And another requirement for knowing Christ is
faith that is fashioned by 'the exceeding greatness
of His power.' By such faith the person whose

Eph. 1:19

heart is right is able to lay hold of Christ. And I per-

Phil. 3:12-14

ceive, poor Ignorance, that you are still ignorant of
the working of such faith. Be awakened then; see
your own wretchedness, and flee to the Lord Jesus.
By His righteousness, which is the righteousness of
God—for He, Himself is God—you shall be deliv-

Rom. 3:21-26;
8:1; Phil. 3:7-14

ered from all guilt and condemnation."

"You go so fast that I can't keep up with you,"
Ignorance responded. "You go on ahead, for I
must stay behind for awhile."

Then Christian and Hopeful said,

"Well, Ignorance, will you foolish remain,
Slighting good counsel, given once and again?
If you still refuse it, you'll surely know
Before long the evil of your doing so.
Remember in time, man—bow, do not fear;
Good counsel well taken, saves, therefore hear.
But if you still slight it, you'll surely be
The loser, Ignorance, most assuredly."

After this, Christian said to Hopeful, "Well,
come on, brother, it looks as if we will once
again be walking by ourselves."

So I saw in my dream that they went on a

ways ahead, and Ignorance came walking lamely behind them. Then Christian said to his companion, "I am deeply grieved for this poor man; it will certainly not go well for him when he reaches the end."

"It's tragic," replied Hopeful. "In our town there are an abundance of people in this condition. There are whole families, yes, whole streets, including pilgrims too. And if there are so many like this in our region, how many do you think there are in the area where he was born?"

Christian added, "Indeed, the Word says, 'He has blinded their eyes and deadened their hearts, so they can neither see with their eyes, nor understand with their hearts.'"

John 12:40

They Discuss Godly Fear

"Now that we are by ourselves, Hopeful, what do you think of such people? Do you think that at any time they feel the conviction of sin and fear that they are in a dangerous condition?"

"No, you answer your question since you are the older one."

"Then I will say that I think sometimes they may. But they, being naturally ignorant, don't understand that such convictions are for their good. Therefore they desperately try to stifle and hide them and presumptuously continue to soothe their egos in the best way they know how."

"I believe as you do," said Hopeful. "I also believe that fear can be very beneficial in prompting them to begin their pilgrimage on the right foot."

Job 28:28;
Ps. 111:10;
Prov. 1:7

"Without a doubt, if it is godly fear, for the Word says, 'The fear of the Lord is the beginning of wisdom.'"

"Will you elaborate on what you believe is the right kind of fear, Christian?"

"Well, I believe godly fear is recognized by

three things: First, by what causes it—the type
of conviction of sin that leads to salvation. Next,
you can see that it drives the soul to grasp and
cling tightly to Christ
for salvation. And
finally,

Godly Fear

it brings to birth
and maintains
within the soul a deep reverence for God, His
Word, and His ways, keeping the heart tender
and making it afraid to turn from these things.
That person will turn neither to the right nor
to the left. He won't want to do anything that
might bring dishonor to God, interrupt his peace
with God, grieve the Spirit of God, or give an
enemy reason to speak scornfully of God or His
kingdom."

Deut. 5:32

Eph. 4:30

"Well said," Hopeful responded. "I believe that
you have spoken the truth. Do you think that we
are almost out of the Enchanted Ground?"

"Why? Are you getting tired of this discussion?" asked Christian.

"No, definitely not, but I would like to know
where we are."

"I don't believe we have more than two miles
farther to travel on this ground, but let's return
to our subject. . . . Those who are ignorant don't
realize that such convictions, which are intended
to instill fear in them, are for their own good.
Therefore, they seek to stifle those feelings."

"How do you think they seek to stifle them?"
asked Hopeful.

"One way is by thinking that such fears were
brought about by the Devil, but the truth is
that they are from God. In thinking this they

consequently begin resisting the fear as if it were a threat to their very existence.

"A second way is to think that these fears will spoil their faith, when, in fact, these unfortunate people possess no true faith anyway. So they harden their hearts against the fear.

"A third way is to presume that they should project an image of courage; so they harden their hearts, repress the fear, and choose to become presumptuously confident.

"A fourth way is that when they notice that such fears tend to erode confidence in their sense of personal righteousness, they determine to resist them with all their might."

"I know something of this, myself," said Hopeful. "Before I understood these things, I was just like that."

They Discuss Backsliding

"Why don't we leave our neighbor Ignorance by himself for now," suggested Christian. "Let's discuss another beneficial question."

"Yes, that's a great idea, but you go ahead and choose the topic of discussion again."

"Well," Christian began, "about ten years ago, there was a man named Mr. Temporary living in your region. He was a very impulsive sort of man. Did you know him?"

"Yes, I certainly did," answered Hopeful. "He lived in the town of Graceless, about two miles from Honesty. I believe he lived next door to a Mr. Turn-back."

"That's him! Actually he lived under the same roof with Mr. Turn-back. I believe that he once experienced an awakening in his life where he suddenly had some insight into his sins and the wages that they would bring him."

Rom. 6:23

190

"Yes, I believe that's true," said Hopeful. "My house wasn't over three miles from his, and he would often come to me in tears. I really felt for the man and even had some hope for him. But, as we all may see, 'not everyone who cries, "Lord, Lord," will enter the Kingdom of Heaven.'"

Matt. 7:21

"He once told me that he had resolved to go on a pilgrimage," said Christian. "But then he suddenly got acquainted with one called Save-self; after that he treated me like a stranger."

"Since we are talking about him, why don't we try to figure out why he and others suddenly backslide," offered Hopeful.

MR. TEMPORARY

"It may be of some profit, but you go ahead and begin."

"Well," said Hopeful, "in my judgment there are four reasons for it. First of all, though the conscience of such a person is awakened, their minds remain unchanged. Therefore, when the strength of the guilty feelings wears off, that which drove them to be religious ceases. So, quite naturally they return to their former ways again. This is like a dog that is sick from what he has eaten. As long as the sickness persists, he will keep vomiting it up. He doesn't do this on purpose but because his stomach is upset. But as soon as the sickness is over and his stomach is soothed, because his desires are not at all alienated from his vomit, he turns around and licks it right back up. So, what is written is true, 'A dog returns to its vomit.'

2 Pet. 2:22

Therefore, I think that they are eager for Heaven only out of a sudden sense of and fear of the torments of Hell. But as soon as this sense of Hell and fear of damnation is gone, their desire for Heaven and eternal happiness dies also. At that point they simply return to their former course.

"Another reason is this: They have an oppressive fear that is overpowering to them—I am speaking of the fear that they have of men, for the 'fear of man will prove to be a snare.' So, although they seem to be on fire for the Kingdom of Heaven as long as the flames of Hell are lapping around their ears, when the terror subsides, they begin to have second thoughts. Namely, they think that it is good to be wise and not run the risk of losing so much for who knows what. If not fearing they will lose all, then they at least fear they will bring themselves into unavoidable and unnecessary conflict. So they once again fall back into step with the world.

Prov. 29:25

"A third reason is that the scorn that so often accompanies a sincere religious experience is a stumbling block to them. They remain proud and haughty while true religion remains low and contemptible in their eyes. So when they have lost their sense of Hell and the wrath to come, they again return to their former course.

"Fourth, I believe that facing their guilt and contemplating the terrors to come are unbearable to them. They don't want to face their misery before the time comes. If they would heed the warning that has been given them, they would flee to where the righteous flee and find safety. But because they shun these thoughts of guilt and terror, once their realization has been effectively suppressed, they gladly harden their hearts and choose ways that will harden them more and more."

Then Christian said, "I think you are close to the mark, for the bottom line is that they need a change in their minds and in their wills. They are like the felon who stands before a judge. He will shake and tremble, repenting heartily. Underneath, however, there is the fear of punishment, not loathing for his offense. This soon becomes evident because, if you give the man his freedom, he will go right back to his criminal activities. If his mind had been truly changed, his actions would be quite different."

"And now," said Hopeful, "since we have discussed reasons for their backsliding, you tell me how it happens."

"I will try," said Christian. "I believe it happens by degrees. First, they try, as much as they can, to pull their thoughts away from remembering God, death, and the coming judgment. Then, they gradually cast off their personal obligations such as closet-prayer, curbing their lusts, being watchful, being sorry for sin, etc. Next, they begin to shun the company of active and zealous Christians. Then they grow indifferent to their public obligations, such as attending church and other gatherings of believers. After this, they start nit-picking and look for the faults in other Christians. They find a flaw in them and thereby get an excuse to cast their faith behind their backs. Next, they often begin to run with a carnal, hedonistic crowd. After this, they give way to secret and profane discussions. And, incidentally, they are glad if they can find those with good reputations doing the same things. This enables them to use that person's example as an excuse to sin. Then they can easily begin to play with little sins openly. Finally, being hardened, they show themselves as they are. Once again they have been launched into the gulf of misery, and unless a miracle of grace prevents it, they will everlastingly perish in their own deceit."

CHAPTER 17

•••••••••••••••

Enjoying the Country of Beulah

Now I saw in my dream that by this time the pilgrims had gotten past the Enchanted Ground. They were now entering into the Country of Beulah, where the air is sweet and refreshing. Since their way lay directly through it, they enjoyed some peace and comfort there for a time. They enjoyed every day they spent in that place, seeing lovely flowers and hearing the continual singing of birds. In this Country the sun shines night and day; thus it is beyond the Valley of the Shadow of Death. It is also out of the reach of Giant Despair; they could not so much as catch a glimpse of Doubting Castle.

Isa. 62:4

Song of Sol. 2:10-12

Rev. 21:22-25

Quite the contrary, here they were able to see the City of their destination. Because it was on the border of Heaven, the Shining Ones commonly walked in this Land. Also, in this Land the covenant between the Bride and the Bridegroom was renewed. Yes, here, as a bridegroom rejoices over his bride, so their God rejoices over them. Here they had no lack of food or wine, for the place is filled with an abundance of all they had been seeking in their pilgrimage. They were able to hear voices from the City—loud voices

Rev. 21:1-2

Isa. 62:5

Isa. 62:8

proclaiming, "Say to the daughter of Zion, 'Surely, your salvation is coming! Behold, His reward is with Him!'" All the inhabitants of the Country called them "the Holy People, the Redeemed of the Lord."

Isa. 62:11

Isa. 62:12

Now as they walked over this Land, they did more rejoicing than they had in all the other places in their journey put together. As they drew near to the City, they had an even more wonderful view of it. It was constructed of pearls and other precious stones, and they could see a street paved with gold. The beauty of the City and the radiance of the sunbeams coming from it were such a glorious sight that Christian became sick with intense longing. Hopeful also was stricken with the same affliction, and because of their pangs they lay there for some time crying out, "If you find my beloved one, tell him that I am sick with love."

Rev. 21:9-21

Song of Sol. 5:8

After a time, however, their strength was renewed and they were more able to bear their sickness, and so they continued on their way. As they came nearer and nearer to the City, they saw beautiful orchards, vineyards, and gardens with gates opening into the High-way. As they approached one such gate, a gardener was standing there, and they asked, "Whose lovely vineyards and gardens are these?"

He replied, "They are the King's, and they are planted here for His delight and also for the comfort of pilgrims." So the gardener invited them into the vineyards and told them to refresh themselves with the delicious produce. He also showed them the King's walks and arbors where He delighted to visit. They lingered here and fell asleep.

Now I saw in my dream that they talked more in their sleep at this time than they ever had in all their journey. Because I was in deep thought over this, the gardener spoke to me and said,

"Why do you contemplate this matter? It is the nature of the fruit of the grapes of these vineyards to go down 'smooth and sweet, causing the lips of those who are asleep to speak.'"

Song of Sol. 7:9

Two Shining Ones
When they woke up, I saw that they determined to go up to the City. Being of pure gold, the City was so extremely bright and glorious that they could not look directly at it except through a special instrument that veiled its brilliance. I saw that as they went on, two Shining Ones met them. They were dressed in clothing that shone like gold; their faces also shone like the light.

Rev. 21:18

2 Cor. 3:18

These two asked the pilgrims where they came from, and they answered. They also asked them where they had lodged, what difficulties and dangers they had experienced, and what comforts and pleasures they had met in the way. The pilgrims answered all their questions. Then they said, "You have only two more difficulties to meet with, and then you will be in the City."

Christian and Hopeful asked the Shining Ones to go along with them, and they told them they would. "But," they said, "you must obtain it by your own faith." So I saw in my dream that they went on together until they came to within sight of the Gate.

The Unavoidable River
Then I saw a River that flowed between them and the Gate. There was no bridge for crossing over, and the River was very deep. The pilgrims

*Death is
not naturally
welcome, but
by it we pass
out of this
world and
into glory.*
Gen. 5:24;
2 Kings 2:11
1 Cor. 15:51-52

were astonished by the sight of the River, but the Shining Ones said, "You must go through it or you cannot approach the Gate." The pilgrims then began to inquire as to whether there was any other way to the Gate. They answered, "Yes, but there have been only two, Enoch and Elijah, who have been permitted to walk that path since the foundation of the world; it will not happen again until the last trumpet shall sound."

Then the pilgrims, and especially Christian, began to lose hope and become despondent. They looked this way and that but could find no way to escape the River. They asked the Shining Ones if the River was of the same depth in every place. The men answered, "No, but we cannot help you in this case either because the waters are of greater or lesser depth, depending on your faith in the King of the place."

Passing through the River

Christian and Hopeful finally resolved to go into the water. Upon entering, however, Christian began to sink. Crying out to his good friend, Hopeful, he said, "The engulfing waters threaten me, the deep surrounds me. The waves of death swirl about me; the torrents of destruction overwhelm me."

Jon. 2:5
2 Sam. 22:5

Then Hopeful said to him, "Cheer up, my brother, I can feel the bottom, and it is firm."

Christian responded, "Oh! my friend, the sorrows of death have surrounded me; I shall not see the Land that flows with milk and honey." At that, a great darkness and horror fell upon Christian. It was so intense that he could not see a thing ahead of him. Also, to a great degree he lost his senses, and he was able neither to remember nor to talk rationally about any of the blessings and encouragements that he had met with

in the way of his pilgrimage. Every word he
spoke engendered a terror of mind and heart that
he would surely be lost in that River and never
obtain entrance at the Gate. Here also, as those
who stood watching perceived, he was troubled
greatly by thoughts of the sins he had committed, both before and since he had become a pilgrim. It was also observed that he was being
afflicted with visions of Hobgoblins and Evil
Spirits; he talked endlessly about them.

Hopeful, therefore, had quite a task keeping
his brother's head above water. Sometimes he
would be completely under the water, and then,
for awhile, he would rise up again, half dead.
Hopeful also would try to encourage him, saying,
"Brother, I see the Gate and men standing by it
to receive us." But Christian would answer, "It is
you, it is you they are waiting for; you have been
Hopeful ever since I met you."   Isa. 57:2

"And so have you, Christian," Hopeful would
answer.

"Ah, brother," Christian responded, "surely if
I was righteous, He would now arise to help me;
but because of my sins He has brought me into
a snare and left me."

"But, my brother," said Hopeful, "you have
completely forgotten the Text where it is said
of the wicked, 'For there are no pangs in their
death, but their strength is firm. They are not in
trouble as other men, nor are they plagued like   Ps. 73:4-5
other men.' These troubles and distresses that
you are going through in these waters are no
sign that God has forsaken you. They are sent
only to test you to see whether you will remember what you have received of His goodness up
to this time and whether you will lean on Him
in your time of distress."

Then I saw in my dream that Christian was

thoughtful for awhile. And Hopeful, adding another word of exhortation, said, "Be of good cheer, for Jesus Christ is making you whole." Immediately Christian yelled with a loud voice, "Oh, I see Him again, and He tells me, 'When you pass through the waters, I will be with you; and when you pass through the Rivers, they will
Isa. 43:2 not sweep over you.'" Then they both took courage, and after that the enemy was as still as stone until they had crossed over. Therefore, Christian was able to find ground to stand on, and so it followed that the rest of the River was shallow. Thus they got over.

On the Other Side
Now upon the riverbank on the other side they saw the two Shining Ones again, waiting for them. When they came up out of the water, the two greeted them, saying, "We are 'ministering
Heb. 1:14 spirits sent to serve those who will inherit salvation.'" So they went along together toward the Gate.

Now I would have you take note of the fact that the City stood upon a mighty Hill. The pilgrims, however, went up the Hill with ease because they had these two Shining Ones leading them up by the arms. They also had left their
2 Cor. 5:1-4 mortal garments behind them in the River. For though those garments entered the River with them, the pilgrims came out without them. Therefore they moved forward with great agility and speed in spite of the fact that the foundation upon which the City was built was higher than the clouds. So they went up through the regions of space, happily talking as they went, being much comforted that they had safely gotten over the River and had such glorious companions to help them.

What the Pilgrims Can Expect Ahead

The Shining Ones described to them the glorious splendor of the place. They told them that the beauty and glory of it was inexpressible. They said, "You are coming to Mount Zion, to the Heavenly Jerusalem, the City of the living God and to thousands and thousands of angels in joyful assembly and to the spirits of righteous men made perfect. You are now going to the paradise of God where you will see the Tree of Life and eat of its never-fading fruit. White robes will be given to you upon your arrival, and every day you will walk and talk with the King— even throughout

Heb. 12:22-23

all the days of eternity. There you will never again see such things as sorrow, sickness, affliction, and death, 'for the old order of things has passed away.' You are now going to join Abraham, Isaac, Jacob, and the prophets—ones who were taken away by God from the evil to come and who are now cradled in eternal rest and walking in eternal righteousness."

Rev. 2:7

Rev. 3:4

Rev. 21:4

Hopeful and Christian then asked, "What will be required of us in this holy place?"

"You must receive consolation for all your toil and receive joy for all your sorrow. You must reap what you have sown—the fruit of all your prayers and tears and suffering for the King on the way. In that place you must receive your treasures and wear crowns of gold. You will receive perpetual joy from beholding the Holy One; for there you shall see Him as He is. You will also

Gal. 6:7

Rev. 4:4, 10

1 John 3:2

serve Him there continually with praise, shouting, and thanksgiving. You so desired to serve Him in the world, but it was very difficult because of your human frailties.

"Your eyes will be delighted by seeing and your ears with hearing the Mighty One. You will once again enjoy your friends and loved ones who have gone there before you. And not only that, you will have the joy of receiving every one who follows after you into that holy place. You will be clothed with glory and majesty, and you will be suitably equipped to ride out with the King of Glory. When the trumpet sounds and He comes in the clouds upon the wings of the wind, you will come with Him. And when He sits upon His throne of judgment, you will sit beside Him. Yes, and when He passes sentence upon all the evil-doers, whether angels or men, you will also have a voice in that judgment because they were your enemies as well as His. And when, at the sound of the trumpet, He again returns to the City, you will return also, and you will be with Him forevermore."

So now see how the holy pilgrims ride!
Clouds are their chariots, angels their guide;
Who for this joy wouldn't all hazards run?
What provision there is when this world is done!

A Glad Procession to the Gate
Now as they drew ever-closer to the Gate, a throng of the heavenly host came out to meet them. The two Shining Ones addressed them and said, "These are the men who have loved our Lord when they were in the world and who have left all for His holy name. He has sent us forth to receive them, and we have brought them this far on their desired journey so that they may go in and look with joy into the face of their Redeemer."

1 Thess. 4:13-16

Jude 14

Dan. 7:9-10

1 Cor. 6:2-3

Rev. 22:5

Then the heavenly host gave a great shout, saying, "Blessed are those who are invited to the wedding supper of the Lamb!" At this same time, several of the King's Trumpeters came out to meet them. They were clothed in brilliant white raiment, and blowing their trumpets, they welcomed Christian and Hopeful from the world with ten thousand shouts and trumpet blasts; the Heavens resounded with their loud and melodious sounds.

Rev. 19:9

After this the pilgrims were surrounded by a joyful procession. Some were in front of them, some behind, and some on either side, as if guarding them while they traversed the upper regions. As they walked along, the Trumpeters continually sounded their trumpets, filling the Heavens with their jubilant sounds. It would have seemed to any observer that all of Heaven had come down to meet them. So they all proceeded together, and Christian and Hopeful could see how exceedingly great was the joy of the crowds as they came to meet them and how welcome the two of them were in their fellowship. It seemed to the men as if they had already reached Heaven before they had come to it! They were overwhelmed with joy and lost in wonder at seeing the angels and listening to their heavenly music. They could see the City, and it seemed to them that they could also hear all the bells within it ringing to welcome them. But what gave them the greatest joy of all was the thought that they themselves could be so fully accepted as to be invited to make their own dwelling here with such companions—not just for a short time, but for ever and ever. Oh, how could tongue or pen ever express such rapturous joy!

They Gain Entrance to the City

Rev. 22:14 So they approached at the Gate, and when they arrived at it, they saw written above it in gold letters,

"BLESSED ARE THOSE WHO DO HIS COMMAND-MENTS, THAT THEY MAY HAVE THE RIGHT TO THE TREE OF LIFE, AND MAY ENTER THROUGH THE GATES INTO THE CITY."

Then I saw in my dream that the Shining Ones told them to knock at the Gate. When they did, some who lived inside looked over from a vantage point above the Gate—Enoch, Moses, Elijah, and others. The Shining Ones said, "These pilgrims have come from the City of Destruction because of the love that they possess for the King of this place."

Then the pilgrims presented the certificates that had been given them at the beginning. The certificates were brought to the King, and upon reviewing them, He asked, "Where are the men?"

The messengers answered, "They are standing outside the Gate."

The King then gave a command to open the Gate, saying, "Open the Gates that the righteous nation may enter, the nation that keeps faith."   Isa. 26:2

Now I saw in my dream that these two men went in at the Gate, and as they entered they were suddenly and gloriously transfigured! The clothes they now wore shone like gold! They were met by some who presented them with harps and crowns. The harps were given them for praising the King, and the crowns were bestowed upon them for their own honor. Then I heard in my dream that all the bells in the City rang out again for joy, and I heard it said, "Enter   Matt. 25:23 into the joy of the Lord." I could also hear Christian and Hopeful, along with the multitudes, singing with loud voices, "To Him who sits on the throne and to the Lamb be praise and honor and glory and power, for ever and ever!"   Rev. 5:13

Now, just as the Gates had opened to let the men in, I looked in after them, and I could see that the City shone like the sun. The streets were paved with gold, and on them walked many saints with crowns on their heads and palm   Rev. 7:9; 21:21 branches in their hands. They were playing golden harps as they sang praises to God. I could also see there were those with wings, and they addressed one another continually, saying, "Holy, holy, holy is the Lord Almighty." I wished   Isa. 6:3; Rev. 4:8 that I myself was among those whom I had seen, but after this, the Gates were once again closed.

Final Outcome of Ignorance

Now while I was still pondering all these things, I turned my head to look back, and I saw Ignorance approaching the far bank of the River. Soon he was able to cross over with less than half the difficulty that the other two men had experienced, for it just so happened that there was a ferryman waiting there named Vain-hope, and he ferried Ignorance across. So Ignorance, like the others, ascended the Hill to reach the Gate. He came alone, however; no one met him with the least bit of encouragement. When he approached the Gate, he looked up at the writing above and then began to knock, supposing that he would quickly be admitted.

The men on top of the roof looked down and asked, "Where have you come from and what do you want?" He replied, "I ate and drank in the presence of the King, and He taught in my streets."

Then they asked him for his certificate so that they might take it in and show it to the King. So he fumbled in his clothing for one but found none.

Then they asked, "Don't you have one?"

Ignorance remained silent.

So they told the King, but He would not come down to see him. Instead, he commanded the two Shining Ones who had escorted Christian and Hopeful to the City to go out and take Ignorance and bind him hand and foot and have him carried away. So they seized him and carried him through the air to the door that I had seen in the side of the Hill, and there they cast him. Then I saw that there was a way to Hell, not only from the City of Destruction, but even from the Gate of Heaven itself.

Matt. 22:1-14

At this I awoke . . . and I realized it had all been a dream.

The Conclusion
Now reader, I have told my dream to thee;
See if you can interpret it to me
Or to yourself or your neighbor, but take heed
Of misrepresenting, for that, indeed,
Will bring you no good but, instead, abuse;
By misinterpreting, evil ensues.

Take heed also, that you don't be extreme
In playing with the limits of my dream.
Don't let this allegory now conclude
By sending you laughing or causing a feud;
The childish or fools in this way can be,
You, though, the substance of my work must see.

Draw back the curtains, look within my veil;
Ponder my metaphors, and please do not fail;
There, if you seek them, are things you will find
That will be helpful to an honest mind.

So what if my dross you find there, be bold;
Throw it away, yet preserve all the gold.
What if my gold is wrapped up in ore?
Who tosses the apple because of the core?
But if you cast all away as just vain,
I do not know when I might dream again.

THE AUTHOR'S WAY OF SENDING FORTH
HIS SECOND PART OF THE PILGRIM

Go now, my little Book, to every place
Where my first Pilgrim has shown his face;
Call at their door: if any say, "Who's there?"
Then answer them, "Christiana is here."
If they invite you in, then enter now,
With all her boys; and then, as you know how,
Tell who they are and from where they came:
Perhaps they'll know them by their looks or name.
But if they should not, ask them yet again,
If formerly they did not entertain
Christian, a Pilgrim, and if they say
They did, and were delighted in his way;
Then let them know, these are related to him:
Yes, his wife and children, his own kin.

Tell them that they have left their house and home,
Are turned Pilgrims; seeking a world to come;
That they have met with hardships in the way;
That they meet troubles both night and day;
That they have trodden on serpents, fought devils
Have also overcome so many evils;
Yes, tell them also of those who behave
For love of pilgrimage, as stout and brave
Defenders of that way; and how they still
Refuse this world, to do their Father's will.

Go tell them also of the pleasant things
That to the Pilgrim a pilgrimage brings.
Make them acquainted, too, with how they fare
As beloved of their King, under His care;
What lovely mansions for them He provides;
Though they meet with rough winds and swelling
    tides,
How fine a calm they will enjoy at last,
Who to their Lord, and by His ways hold fast.

Perhaps with heart and hand they will embrace
You as they did my firstling, and will grace
You and your fellows with such cheer and care
That love for Pilgrims they'll prove they share.

My Pilgrim's book has traveled land and sea,
Yet it has never been perceived by me
That it was slighted, or turned out the door,
By any kingdom, whether rich or just poor.
In France and Flanders, where men kill each other,
My Pilgrim is esteemed a friend, a brother.
In Holland, too, it's said, as I am told,
My Pilgrim is to some worth more than gold.
Highlanders and wild Irish can agree
My Pilgrim should familiar with them be.
In New England it's made such an advance,
Receiving there such loving countenance,
As to be trimmed, newly clothed, decked with gems,
That it might show its features and its limbs.
Now so popular is my Pilgrim's walk,
That of him thousands daily sing and talk.

Yet some still say, "He laughs too loud."
And some say, "His head is in a cloud."
Others say, "A cloud is in his head,"
But it shows that Wisdom's covered instead
With its own cloaks, just to stir the mind
To a search for what it desires to find.
Things that seem to be hid in words obscure
Do but the godly mind the more allure
To study what those sayings might contain,
That speak to us in such a cloudy strain.

Besides, what my first pilgrim left concealed,
You, my fine second pilgrim, have revealed!
What Christian left locked up and then went his way,
Sweet Christiana opens with her key today.

Go then, my little book, and show to all
Who open and give you a welcome call,
That what you keep shut up from the rest,
You want to show them so they may be blessed.
For their own good, may they choose to be
Better pilgrims by far than you or me.

When you have told the world all of these things,
Then turn about, my book, and touch those strings;
Which, if but touched, will such music make,
That the lame will dance, a giant will quake.

Those riddles that lie couched within your breast,
Freely propound, expound; and for the rest
Of your mysterious lines, let them remain
For those whose nimble fancies shall them gain.

Now may this little book a blessing be
To those that love this little book and me;
And may its buyer have no cause to say,
His money has been lost or thrown away.
Yes, may this second Pilgrim yield such fruit
As may with each good Pilgrim's fancy suit;
And may it persuade some who go astray
To turn their foot and heart to the right way.

Is the hearty prayer of The Author,
J O H N   B U N Y A N

*in the Allegory
of a Dream*

• • •

THE SECOND PART

CHAPTER 18

◆◆◆◆◆◆◆◆◆◆◆◆◆◆◆◆

Courteous Companions,
Some time ago I shared with you the content of
the dream I had about Christian the pilgrim and
his perilous journey toward the Celestial Country.
It was a pleasant experience for me, and I trust
that it was profitable for you. In that dream I also
related to you what I saw concerning his wife and
children—how they were unwilling to go with
him on the pilgrimage and how, on account of
that, he was forced to go ahead without them.
For he dared not stay with them and run the risk
of experiencing the terrible destruction that he
feared would come upon the City of Destruction.

Unfortunately, because of so much pressing
business, I have been greatly hindered and have
been unable to travel as I would have liked into
those parts where Christian went. Although I
wanted to tell you what has happened to those
he left behind, I haven't had an opportunity to
make further inquiry about them until recently.
However, because I have experienced a renewal
of concern about them in recent days, I went
down that way again. Having become weary
from the journey, I found shelter in the woods
about a mile from the place, and there I fell
asleep. Once again I began to dream.

A Meeting with Mr. Sagacity
In my dream, I suddenly saw an aged gentleman come by where I was lying. Because he was

planning to go part of the way that I was traveling, I dreamed that I got up and went with him. As we walked, we began to converse, and our talk happened to be about Christian and his travels. I had begun the conversation this way:

"Sir," I asked, "what is the name of the town that lies below here on the left-hand side of our way?"

Then Mr. Sagacity (for that was his name) answered, "It is the City of Destruction, a large City full of people who, though in a terrible predicament, are yet surprisingly complacent."

"Yes, I thought it was that City," I said. "I once went through that town, myself, and I know that your perception is true."

"Only too true! I wish I could speak better of those who live there and still be truthful."

What People Say about Christian

"Well, sir," I said, "I perceive that you are a good-hearted person, one who enjoys listening to and telling about things that are good. Please tell me then, did you ever hear what happened in that town to a man named Christian who, some time ago, went on pilgrimage up toward the higher regions?"

"Hear of him!" exclaimed Mr. Sagacity. "Yes, and I also heard about all the abuse, troubles, battles, captivities, cries, moans, terrors, and fears that he encountered on his journey. And further, I must tell you that the sound of his name resounds throughout my Country. Most households have heard of him and of his efforts, and they have actually sought after and found information about his pilgrimage. I can say that his hazardous journey won many admirers. Although everyone labeled him a fool when he was still here, now that he is gone, he is highly praised by all, for it is said that he lives royally where he now is. Indeed, there are many who have resolved never to hazard such risks and yet their mouths water as they think of the treasures he now possesses."

Then I said, "They certainly think correctly if they think he is living well where he is. For he now lives at, and actually within, the Fountain of Life. He enjoys what he now has without labor and without sorrow, for there is no hint of grief there. But please tell me further, what do they say about him?"

Rev. 22:1-2

Mr. Sagacity answered, "Well, the people say truly amazing things about him. Some say that he now walks in white, that he has a chain of gold around his neck, and that he wears a pearl-studded gold crown upon his head. Others say that the Shining Ones, who sometimes appeared to him on his journey, are now his companions and that he is as familiar with them in that place as we neighbors are one with another here. Besides this, it is confidently affirmed concerning him that the King of the place where he now lives has already bestowed on him a rich and pleasant residence in his court. And that, also, he eats and drinks and walks and talks with Him every day, and he receives smiles and favors from Him who is the Judge of all who are there.

Rev. 3:4

Zech. 3:7;
John 14:2-3
Luke 14:15

"It is expected by some in these parts that Christian's Prince, the Lord of that Country, will soon come here and inquire as to the reason, if they can give any, why his neighbors stood by him so little and scorned him so much when they discovered his intent to become a pilgrim.

Jude 15

"For they say that now Christian is so loved by his Prince, and that his Sovereign is so seriously concerned over the indignities that were heaped upon him when he became a pilgrim that He will regard all the abuse as if it had been done to His own Person. And no wonder, because it was for the love that Christian had for his Prince that he ventured forth as he did."

Luke 10:16

"I am glad to hear this," I said. "He now has rest from his labors, and he reaps with joy the benefits of the tears he shed. He is now beyond the range of fire from all his enemies, and beyond the grasp of any who hate him—how happy this makes me! I am also happy that a rumor is circulating all over the area concerning him. Who knows but that it may work for some good on behalf of those who were left behind? But please, sir, while it is fresh in my mind, do you hear anything about his wife and children? Poor people! I wonder what they are doing."

Rev. 14:13
Ps. 126:5-6

Good News about Christian's Family

"Who? Christiana and her sons? Why, they are likely to do as well as did Christian himself. For though they all played the fool to begin with and refused to be persuaded in the least bit by any of Christian's tears or entreaties, second thoughts have done a wonderful work in them. They have now packed up and gone after him."

"This is getting better all the time!" I said. "But what? Wife, children, and all?"

"It's true. I can tell you all about it because I was there when it happened and have stayed abreast of the entire situation."

Then I said, "It seems that one could merely report that this was true."

"Don't be afraid to affirm the truth of my words; they have truly left on pilgrimage—the woman and her four boys. And since it appears that we will be going a considerable distance

CHRISTiana

together, I will tell you the whole story." Thus, Mr. Sagacity gave me the following account:

Christiana's Misery

Her name is Christiana, called that from the day she and her sons committed themselves to the pilgrim's life. After her husband had passed through the River, and she was unable to hear of him any more, thoughts concerning him began to stir in her mind. First, she thought about how she had lost her husband; the loving bond between them had been completely broken. For, as you know, our human nature makes those who are alive become deeply preoccupied with thoughts of loved ones who have recently departed. So these thoughts of her husband cost her many tears.

Mark this, you who show contempt for your godly relations.

But this was not all; Christiana began to wonder whether her inappropriate behavior toward her husband was a reason that he was gone and had been taken away from her. She became obsessed with memories of her unkind, unnatural, and ungodly behavior toward her dearest friend. Her conscience became clogged with conviction; she was overwhelmed with guilt. She was also broken by the remembrance of her husband's restless groanings, salty tears, and self-regret, and by the memory of how she had hardened her heart against all his pleas and loving persuasions that she and her sons go with him. Yes, there was not one thing that Christian had said or done in her presence during the time his burden hung on his back that did not return to her memory like a flash of lightning. Her heart was especially torn over his bitter lament, "What shall I do to be saved?" His words kept ringing sadly in her ears.

Acts 16:30

Then she said to her children, "Sons, our lives are falling apart because I have sinned your father away from us. He is gone, but he wanted us to go with him. I was stubborn and would not go myself, but I also hindered you from finding life." At that, the boys burst into tears and cried out that they wanted to go after their father. "Oh!" said Christiana, "if only we had gone with him! Then things would surely be better than they are now. I foolishly imagined that your father's troubles had come from a silly whim or a melancholy mood, but now I cannot get it out of my mind that, in very truth, they sprang from another source—from the Light of Life that had been revealed to him. And because of this, I believe he has escaped the snares of death." Then they all wept again and cried out, "Oh! Woe is the day we let him go without us!"

Matt. 23:13

John 1:4
1 Cor. 15:56-57

Her Distressing Nightmare and Blessed Dream

The next night Christiana had a dream. Lo and behold, she saw a large Scroll open before her. In it were recorded all the deeds of her life. She thought her crimes looked very dark and ugly indeed. Then she cried out in her sleep, "God, have mercy on me, a sinner!" and her children heard her.

Luke 18:13

After this, she thought she could see two ill-favored ones standing by her bed and saying, "What should we do with this woman? For she cries out for mercy when awake and asleep. If she continues on like this, we will lose her as we

The quintessence of hell

have lost her husband. Therefore, in one way or another, we must seek to get her mind off the thoughts of things to come. If we fail, there will be nothing in the world to keep her from becoming a pilgrim."

She awoke with a start, sweating and trembling, but after awhile she fell asleep again. Then she dreamed that she saw Christian, her husband, in a place of bliss and surrounded by many immortals. He was standing before a throne with a harp in his hand, and he was playing the harp for the One seated there who had a rainbow about His head. She also saw Christian bow his head with his face to the pavement that Rev. 4:3 lay under his Prince's feet. He was saying, "My Lord and King, I thank you with all my heart for bringing me here safely and for receiving me into this place." Then a large number of those standing around Him shouted and played their harps. No one alive could tell what they were shouting except Christian and his companions. Rev. 14:2-3

The Visit by Secret

Next morning, Christiana got up, and after she had prayed to God and talked with her boys for awhile, someone pounded loudly on the door. She called out, "If you come in God's name, come in."

"Amen, I do!" he replied and opened the door. He greeted her, saying, "Peace to this house. Christiana, do you know the reason I have come?"

She began to blush and tremble, and her heart grew strangely warm as she wondered where he had come from and what his business was with her.

He continued, "My name is Secret, and I dwell with those who are on high. There is talk among those I live with that you have a desire to go there. It is also reported that you are aware of the evil you formerly did to your husband in hardening your heart against his way and in keeping your young ones in their ignorance. Christiana, the Merciful One has sent me to tell you that He is a God ready to forgive and that He takes great delight in pardoning all of your offenses. He also wants you to know that He invites you to come into His presence, to His table, so that He can feed you and you may 'feast on the inheritance of your father Jacob.'

Exod. 34:6-7;
Ps. 86:5

John 6:35;
Rev. 3:20
Isa. 58:14

"Your husband, Christian, is there with multitudes of companions, ever beholding that face that ministers life to all who gaze upon it. They will all rejoice greatly when they hear the sound of your feet stepping over your father's threshold."

At this Christiana lost all confidence in herself. Feeling greatly ashamed, she humbled her face to the ground.

The visitor proceeded and said to her, "Christiana, here also is a letter I have brought you from your husband's King."

The Invitation to Christiana

Taking the letter, she opened it, and she could smell the fragrance of what seemed the finest of perfumes. The letter was written in gold letters, and its message was an exhortation from the King, who wanted her to do as Christian had done; for the way he had gone was the way to the King's City. He wanted her also to come and dwell in His presence with joy forevermore. At this she was overcome with emotion and cried out to her visitor, "Sir, will you take me and my children with you, so that we too may go and worship this King?"

Song of Sol. 1:3

Then the visitor said, "Christiana, you must

taste the bitter before the sweet. You must enter
the Celestial City through troubles, as did Christian who went before you. Therefore, I advise you
to do as he did: Go to the Wicket-gate out over
the plain, for it stands at the beginning of the
way that you must travel. And I wish you great
success! Also, I advise that you keep this letter
safe and close to your heart, and that you read it
to yourself and to your children until it takes root
deep within you. It is one of the songs that you
must sing while you are still in your body, the
earthly tent of your pilgrimage. You will also need
this letter at the Gate of the Celestial City."

Ps. 71:20

Ps. 119:11, 54

2 Cor. 5:1-5

Now I saw in my dream that this old gentleman, Mr. Sagacity, was deeply moved as he proceeded to tell me the story.

The Family Makes a Decision
Christiana called her sons together and said to
them, "My sons, as you are probably aware, my
soul has been in great turmoil recently over the
death of your father. I do not doubt his happiness, and I am sure now that he is well. But I
have been deeply affected with thoughts about
our own condition and have concluded that it is
truly desperate. My behavior toward your father
in his time of distress has become a great burden
on my conscience, for I hardened both my own
heart and yours against him and refused to go
with him on his pilgrimage.

"Remembering these things would kill me outright if it weren't for a dream I had last night and
the encouragement this stranger has given me
this morning. Come, my sons, let's pack up and
set out for the Gate that leads to the Celestial
Country. Then we will see your father and be
with him and his companions in peace according
to the laws of that Land."

Then the boys burst into tears of joy because of their mother's decision to go. So their visitor said good-bye, and they began to prepare for their journey.

The Neighbors Oppose Christiana's Decision

When they were about ready to leave, two women who were Christiana's neighbors came and knocked at her door.

She said as before, "If you come in God's name, come in."

The neighbors were stunned, for they weren't used to hearing Christiana use this kind of language. They came in, however, and found her preparing to leave her home. They said, "Neighbor, please tell us, what is the meaning of this?"

Christiana directed her answer to the eldest, whose name was Mrs. Timorous. "I am preparing for a journey."

Mrs. Timorous was the daughter of the man who, on the Hill Difficulty, had advised Christian to go back for fear of the Lions. She asked Christiana, "What journey are you preparing for, may I ask?"

Christiana answered, "I am going after my good husband," and then she began to weep.

"I should hope not!" exclaimed Mrs. Timorous. "My good neighbor, your children need you. Don't throw yourself away."

"This isn't the case, for my children are going with me. Not one of them is willing to stay behind."

"I wonder in my heart who—or what—could have driven you to this state of mind!" exclaimed Mrs. Timorous.

"Oh, my neighbor! If you knew as much as I do, I have no doubt that you would go with me."

"Please tell me," asked Mrs. Timorous, "what

new knowledge have you received that is driving you away from your friends and causing you to go to who knows where?"

Christiana replied, "I have been terribly afflicted since my husband left me, but most especially since he passed over the River. What troubles me most is the memory of my rude behavior toward him when he was in his distress. Besides this, I am presently in the same state he was in then, and nothing will satisfy me except going on this pilgrimage. Last night I dreamed that I saw him. Oh, if only my soul could be with him! I saw him living in the presence of the King of that Country. He sits and eats with Him at His table. He has become a companion of immortals. He has been given a house to dwell in, to which the grandest palace on earth, if compared, would look like a garbage dump. The Prince of the Place has also sent for me with a promise to receive me if I will come to Him. His messenger was just here and brought a letter inviting me to come." At that, she pulled out the letter, read it to them, and asked, "Now, what do you have to say about this?"

Rev. 19:7-8

2 Cor. 5:1-4

"Oh, the insanity that has possessed both your husband and now you, to drive you into such difficulties!" exclaimed Mrs. Timorous. "I am sure you have heard all that your husband met with, even from the first step he took on his way. Our neighbor Obstinate can attest to this, for he went along with him, and so did Pliable. But they, like true wise men, were afraid to go any farther. We also heard about how Christian met the Lions, Apollyon, the Shadow of Death, and many other things. And don't forget the danger he met at Vanity Fair. For if he, though a man, was so hard-pressed, what can you do, being just a frail woman? You need to consider also that these four sweet children are your flesh and blood; therefore, even though you would be so rash as to throw your own life away, for the sake of your children you should stay home."

But Christiana answered her, "Don't tempt me, my neighbor. I have been shown what there is to gain, and I would be the greatest fool if I did not take heart and seize this opportunity. Your telling me of all the troubles that I am likely to encounter in the way cannot dissuade me—they will only convince me that I am in the right. The bitter must come before the sweet, and that will serve only to make the sweet sweeter. Therefore, since you did not come to my house in God's name, as I said, please leave me alone and don't trouble me any further."

A pertinent reply to the appeal of fleshly reasonings

Mercy's Decision

Then Mrs. Timorous began to insult her and said to her friend, "Come, neighbor Mercy, let's leave her to herself since she scorns our counsel and company."

But Mercy stood still. She couldn't so readily comply with her neighbor for two reasons. First, her heart was filled with compassion for Christiana, and she thought to herself that she ought to go with her a little way to help her. Second, her heart yearned for her own soul, for Christiana's words had made an impression on her. So she told herself, "I need to talk further with Christiana; if I find truth and life in her words, I will go with her with all my heart."

So Mercy said to Mrs. Timorous, "Neighbor, it's true that I came with you to see Christiana this morning. But, as we both can see, she is saying her last farewell to her Country, and I want to walk with her a little way on this bright, sunshiny morning. Perhaps I can help her along on her way."

She did not tell her
the second reason,
however, but kept it to herself.

"Well, I see you have a mind to carry on like a
fool too," said Mrs. Timorous. "But listen to wisdom
and take heed before it's too late. While we're out of
danger, we're out, but when we're in, we're in."

Mrs. Timorous and Her Neighbors

So Mrs. Timorous returned to her house, and
Christiana resolved to begin her journey as soon
as possible. When Mrs. Timorous got home, however, she sent for some of her neighbors, namely
Mrs. Bats-eyes, Mrs. Inconsiderate, Mrs. Light-
mind, and Mrs. Know-nothing. When they got
to her house, she began to tell them all about
Christiana and the journey she was planning.

"Neighbors," she said, "I had very little to do
this morning, so I went to visit Christiana. When
I got to her house, I knocked on her door as is
customary. She answered, 'If you come in God's
name, come in.' So I went right in, thinking all
was well, but I found her preparing to leave town
with her children. I asked her what was the
meaning of this, and she told me, in short, that
she had now decided to go on a pilgrimage just
as her husband had done. She also told me about
a dream she had and how the King of the Country where her husband was had sent her an invitation to come there."

Then Mrs. Know-nothing said, "What? Do you
think she'll really go?"

"Yes," replied Mrs. Timorous. "I believe that she'll go, come what may. I earnestly tried to persuade her to stay home by telling her about the troubles she will likely face on the way, but she acted as if these were reasons to go. She said that the bitter must come before the sweet and that this makes the sweet seem even sweeter."

"Oh, this blind and foolish woman!" said Mrs. Bats-eyes. "Won't she be warned by her husband's afflictions? In my opinion, if he were here and had it to do over again, he would rest content and never run into so many hazards again. It just makes no sense."

Mrs. Inconsiderate also gave her opinion: "Away with these starry-eyed fools from our town! I say good riddance to her! If she were to stay here and hold such thoughts in her mind, who could live peacefully around her? She would either be moping around, depressed and unneighborly, or rambling on about these matters in a way that no wise person could tolerate. So, in my opinion, I will never regret her departure; let her go and let someone better move in. The world has never been a good place since these whimsical fools began to dwell in it."

Mrs. Light-mind added, "Come on, let's forget about this discussion. I was at Madam Wanton's house yesterday where we were as happy as larks. For who do you think was there? Besides me there were Mrs. Love-the-flesh, Mr. Lechery, Mrs. Filth, and three or four others. We enjoyed music and dancing and everything else that was available for having a good time. Madam Wanton is an admirable and well-bred lady, and Mr. Lechery is quite a handsome man!"

CHAPTER 19

•••••••••••••••

Their Pilgrimage Begins

By this time Christiana and her children had
started on their journey. Mercy went along with
them, and Christiana and Mercy began to talk.
"Mercy," said Christiana, "what an unexpected
blessing this is for you to come outside to accompany me for a little while on my way."

"You know," said young Mercy (for she was but
young), "if I thought there was good reason to go
with you, I would never go near the town again."

"Well, Mercy," said Christiana, "come join me,
and we will venture together. I know very well
what awaits us at the end of our pilgrimage; all
the gold mines in Spain could not lure my husband away from where he is. The King who has
sent for me and my sons will not reject you, even
though you go by way of my invitation 'because
He delights in mercy.' And besides, if you agree
to it, I will hire you, and you can go along with
me as my helper. Even so, we will share all things
in common if you will only go with me."

"But how can I be certain that I also will be
accepted?" asked Mercy. "If someone could guarantee this hope, I wouldn't make an issue of it. I would
go, no matter how tiresome the way, and I know
that I would be helped by Him who is able to help."

"Well, kind Mercy," Christiana responded,
"I'll tell you what you should do. Go with me
to the Wicket-gate, and I will further inquire for
you there. If you aren't encouraged there, I will

Mic. 7:18

*The Gate is
Christ.*

certainly understand if you decide to return home, and I will gladly pay you for all the kindness you show me and my sons for as long as you accompany us in our way."

"Then I will go with you and accept what follows. May the Lord grant that my inheritance will be awaiting me, and that the heart of the King of Heaven will go out to me."

wicketgate

This made Christiana very happy—not only that she had a companion, but also that she had convinced this poor, young lady to be deeply concerned for her own salvation.

Mercy's Concern for Others

As they went on together, Mercy began to weep.

"My sister, why are you crying like this?" asked Christiana.

"Alas! How can I help but grieve when I honestly consider the state and condition of my poor relatives who still remain in our sinful town? And what makes my grief all the more unbearable is that they have no one to teach them or to tell them what is to come."

"Compassion is befitting for pilgrims, Mercy. You are doing for your friends as my dear Christian did for me—He mourned because I would not listen to or heed him, but his Lord and ours gathered up all of his tears and put them into His bottle. And now both you and I, along with my sons, are reaping the fruit and benefit of them. Mercy, I believe that these tears of yours will not be lost, for the Word of Truth has said, 'Those who sow in tears shall reap in joy. He who continually goes forth weeping, bearing seed for sowing, shall doubtless come again with rejoicing, bringing his sheaves with him.'"

Ps. 126:5-6

Then Mercy said,

"Let the Most Blessed be my Guide,
If it be His blessed will,
On to His Gate, into His Fold,
Up to His holy Hill.
And let Him never allow me
To swerve, or turn aside
From His free grace and holy ways,
Whate'er shall me betide.
And let Him gather those of mine,
That I have left behind;
Lord, make them pray they may be Thine,
With all their heart and mind."

They Cross the Slough of Despond

Now my old friend, Mr. Sagacity, proceeded to tell me his account. He said that when Christiana came up to the Slough of Despond, she wondered what to do. For she said to herself, "This is the place where my dear husband was almost smothered by mud." She perceived also that despite the King's command to make this place good for pilgrims, it was now even worse than before.

I asked the old gentleman if this was the case. "Yes, too true," he said, "for there are many who pretend to be the King's laborers and who say they are all for mending the King's High-way, but who, instead of bringing stones,

Carnal conclusions instead of the word of life

bring more filth and manure into it. They mar instead of mend, and they do more harm than good."

So Christiana, along with her boys, came to a standstill. But Mercy said, "Come on, but let's be careful." So very cautiously and carefully, taking one step at a time, they managed to get across the Slough. Even so, Christiana almost fell in a number of times. They had no sooner gotten across when they thought they heard words that said to them, "Blessed is she who has believed that what the Lord has said to her will be accomplished!"

Luke 1:45

As they resumed their pace, Mercy said to Christiana, "If I had as much ground for hope of a loving reception at the Wicket-gate as you do, I don't believe any Slough of Despond would discourage me."

"Well," Christiana answered, "you know your weakness, and I know mine. And, my good friend, we will each have enough evil to contend with before we come to our journey's end. Is it conceivable that those who set out to gain such excellent glories as we do, and whose ultimate joy will be so envied, can expect to escape every fear, snare, trouble, and affliction with which those who hate us will try to assault us?"

Arriving at the Wicket-gate

At this point in my dream, Mr. Sagacity left me to dream out my dream by myself. Then I thought I saw Christiana, Mercy, and the boys approaching the Gate. On their arrival, they began to debate how they were supposed to call at the Gate and what should be said to the One who would open it. They concluded that, since Christiana was the oldest, she should knock on the Gate to gain entrance, and that she should also be the spokesman for them to the One who opened it.

Prayer should be made with consideration and fear, as well as with faith and hope.

So Christiana began to knock, and, like her husband, she knocked and knocked again, but no one answered. Then they all thought they heard a Dog barking as if it were coming after them. It sounded like a very large Dog, and the women and children were frightened. For a while they didn't dare knock anymore for fear the guard Dog would charge at them. They were greatly tumbled up and down in their minds for a while, not knowing what to do. They dared not knock for fear of the Dog, and yet they dared not go back for fear that the Keeper of the Gate might see them going back and be offended with them.

The Dog is the Devil, an enemy to prayer.

At last they decided to knock again, and this time they knocked harder than before. Then the Keeper of the Gate called out, "Who's there?" At that, the Dog stopped barking, and He opened the Gate to them.

They are perplexed about prayer.

Christiana and Her Sons Gain Entrance

Then Christiana fell on her knees and humbled herself before him. "Please, our Lord, don't be offended with your servants for knocking at Your princely Gate."

"Where do you come from?" asked the Keeper. "And what do you want?"

Christiana answered, "We have come from Christian's hometown, and we seek the same destination as he. That is to say, if it pleases you, we would like for you to graciously admit us by this Gate into the way that leads to the Celestial City. My Lord, I am Christiana, the wife of Christian who is now above."

With that the Keeper of the Gate marveled, saying, "What! Has she now become a pilgrim, who only a short time ago abhorred that life?"

She bowed her head and said, "Yes, and so have these, my dear sons."

Then He took her by the hand, led her in, and
said, "Let the little children come to me." And
with that He shut the Gate. This done, He called
to a trumpeter who was stationed above the Gate
to entertain Christiana with shouts of joy and
trumpet sounds. So he obeyed, and the sounds
filled the air with joyful melodies.

Luke 18:16

Luke 15:7

Mercy's Fear of Rejection

Now all this time poor Mercy stood outside,
trembling and crying for fear that she had been
rejected. But after Christiana had gained admittance for herself and her sons, she began to intercede for Mercy. "Sir," she said, "I have a companion
who is still standing outside, and she has come here
for the same reason as I have. She is quite dejected
because she believes she has not been invited,
whereas I was sent for by my husband's King."

Mercy became very impatient, and each minute that passed seemed to her as long as an hour.
She interrupted Christiana's intercession for her
by knocking at the Gate herself. She knocked so
loudly that Christiana was startled. Then the
Keeper of the Gate asked, "Who is there?" And
Christiana said, "It's my friend."

*The delays make
the hungering
soul more fervent.*

So He opened the Gate and looked out, but Mercy
had fainted out there because of her fear that the
Gate would not be opened to her. Then He took her
by the hand and said, "My child, arise."

Luke 8:54

"Oh, Sir," she said, "I feel so faint; there is
scarcely life left in me."

But He answered her, "Someone once said,
'When my life was ebbing away, I remembered
you, Lord, and my prayer rose to you, to your
holy temple.' Don't be afraid, but stand to your
feet and tell Me the reason you have come."

Jon. 2:7

"I have come for that which my friend Christiana was invited. Her invitation was from the

King, but mine was only from her. Therefore I fear that I have been presumptuous."

"Did she want you to come with her to this Place?" asked the Keeper.

"Yes, and as you can see, I have come. So if there is any grace and forgiveness of sins to spare, please allow Your poor servant girl to share in them."

Mercy Is Admitted

Then He took her again by the hand and gently led her inside, saying, "I pray for all those who believe on Me, by whatever means they come to Me." Then He said to some standing by, "Go get something for Mercy to smell, to keep her from fainting again." So they went out, and when they returned they gave her a bundle of myrrh, and in a short time she was revived.

John 17:20

So Christiana, her boys, and Mercy were all received by the Lord at the beginning of the way, and He spoke kindly to them. They told Him, "We are sorry for our sins, and we beg our Lord's forgiveness. Please grant us further instruction about what we must do."

He replied, "I grant you pardon because of My word and because of My deed—by My word, because it promises forgiveness, and by My deed, because of what I did to obtain it. Take the first from my lips with a kiss, and the latter as it will be revealed to you."

John 15:3
John 17:1-5
Song of Sol. 1:2;
John 20:20

Christiana and Mercy Discuss Their Experiences

Now I saw in my dream that He said many wonderful things to them, and their hearts were lifted with great joy. He also took them up above

Christ crucified seen afar off

the Gate where He showed them by what deed they were saved. He told them that they would see that sight again as they went along on the way, and this was of comfort to them. After this He left them for awhile in a room below.

"How glad I am that we have gotten in here!" exclaimed Christiana.

"You very well may be," replied Mercy, "but I, of all people, have reason to leap for joy!"

"At one point as we were standing at the Gate," said Christiana, "when I knocked and no one answered, I feared that all our labor had been for nothing—especially when that ugly beast barked so ferociously at us."

"But, Christiana, my worst fear came when I saw that you were received into His favor and I was left behind. I thought that what is written is

Matt. 24:41

fulfilled, 'Two women will be going about their household tasks; one will be taken, the other left.' It was all I could do to restrain myself from crying out, 'Ruined! I am ruined!' I was afraid to knock any more, but then when I looked up and saw the words written over the Gate, my courage was renewed. I thought that I must either knock again or die; so I knocked, but I don't know how—for my spirit was struggling between life and death."

"Tell me how you knocked," said Christiana, "for your knocks sounded so earnest that the sound startled me; I thought I had never heard such knocking in all my life. I thought you would

Matt. 11:12

come in violently and take the kingdom by storm!"

"Good grief!" exclaimed Mercy. "Could any-one in my situation help doing the same? You saw the door shut in my face and that cruel Dog nearby. Could there be anyone as fearful and

Christ is pleased with loud and restless prayer.

fainthearted as I who would not have knocked with all his might? But, please, what did my Lord say? Was He angry about my rudeness?"

"Well," replied Christiana, "when He heard your urgent pounding on the Gate, He smiled gently. I truly believe that what you did pleased Him and maybe even aroused His admiration toward you, for He showed no sign to the contrary."

They Question the Gatekeeper about the Dog

"But I wonder why He keeps such a Dog," Christiana continued. "If I had known about it before, I'm not sure I would have had the courage to venture this far. But now we are here, we are inside, and I am glad with all my heart."

"If you like," said Mercy, "next time He comes down to see us I will ask Him why He keeps such a filthy beast in His yard. I hope He won't take the question wrongly."

Christiana's sons had been listening intently, and one of them spoke up. "Yes, please do ask Him, and try to persuade him to kill that beast. We're afraid he'll maul us when we leave here."

At last He came down to see them again, Mercy fell with her face to the ground before Him and worshiped, saying, "Let my Lord accept my 'sacrifice of praise—the fruit of lips that confess His name.'"   Heb. 13:15

He answered her, "Be at peace; stand up."

But she continued on her face, saying, "You are always righteous, O Lord, when I bring a case before You. Yet I would speak with You about Your justice." Why do You keep such a cruel Dog   Jer. 12:1
in Your yard, at the sight of which women and children like ourselves are ready to flee in fear from the Gate?"

He answered her, saying, "Although that Dog is kept near here, he has another owner, and he actu-   *The Devil*
ally lives on that person's property. My pilgrims

hear his barking, but he belongs to the castle that you can see there in the distance. By coming up to the walls of this place, he has frightened many an honest pilgrim, but this has served only to strengthen their resolve at the Gate. Thus they are actually brought from a weaker to a stronger condition by his ferocious barking. The one who owns him does not keep him because of any good will toward Me or Mine; his real intention is to keep the pilgrims from coming to Me by making them afraid to knock at this Gate for entrance. The Dog sometimes has broken out and frightened some that I love, but at present I am patient with this.

"I always give my pilgrims help in sufficient time so that they are not overcome by what this beast tries to do to them. But, my purchased one, if you had known this beforehand, I don't think you would have been afraid of a Dog. Beggars who go from door to door will willingly face the hazard of a growling, barking, and biting Dog rather than lose the alms they hope to receive. And shall a Dog in another man's yard, a Dog whose barking I turn to the pilgrim's advantage, keep anyone from coming to Me? I deliver them from the Lions; I will certainly deliver them from the power of the Dog."

A check to carnal fears of pilgrims

Then Mercy said, "I confess my ignorance. I spoke about something I didn't understand. I acknowledge that you do all things well."

Dan. 6

Wise christians acquiesce to the wisdom of the Lord.

Job 42:3

The Pilgrims Venture Onward

After this, Christiana began to talk about their journey and inquire about the way. He fed them and washed their feet, and then He set them in the way of His steps, just as He had done with her husband before. Then I saw in my dream that they walked on along their way, enjoying

the beautiful weather that had been provided
them. Then Christiana began to sing a song:

"Blessed be the day that I began
Wishing a pilgrim to be;
And blessed also be that man
Whose example moved me.

True, it was long before I began
To seek to live forever;
But now I run as fast as I can.
It's better late than never.

To joy from tears; to faith from fears,
We've turned, as we can see;
So from our beginning it now appears
Just what our end will be."

CHAPTER 20

❖❖❖❖❖❖❖❖❖❖❖❖❖

The Unauthorized Fruit

On the other side of the wall that bordered the way on which Christiana and her companions were going was a Garden belonging to the one who owned the barking Dog. Branches from some of the fruit trees that grew in the Garden reached over the wall, and many who traveled on the way, upon seeing the fruit, would stop and gather the fruit, eating it to their own detriment. One of Christiana's sons was attracted by the appearance of the trees and their fruit, and, as a boy would be inclined to do, he picked some fruit and began to eat it. His mother scolded him for this, but he refused to take her seriously.

The Devil's Garden

Gen. 3

"Well," she said, "you have crossed the boundary and have taken someone else's property—that fruit is not ours." She was unaware, however, that the fruit belonged to the enemy, a fact that, had she known of it, would have caused her great fear. Fortunately, however, they passed by without incident.

The Attack by Two Ill-favored Ones

They were only a short distance onto the way when they saw two ill-favored ones coming swiftly down toward them. Christiana and Mercy covered their faces, and they all huddled together as they pressed forward on their journey. The men approached them and walked right up to the women as if they would embrace them. "Stand back, or go peaceably on by as you should," said Christiana. The two men seemed to be deaf, however, and they ignored Christiana's words. Instead, they began to grab at Christiana and Mercy. Christiana became very angry at this and began to kick at them fiercely. Mercy and the boys did what they could also. Christiana again demanded, "Stand back and go away; we are pilgrims, and therefore, we have no money but live on the charity of our friends."

Then one of the men said, "We are not after your money; if you will grant us but one small favor we ask of you, we will make real women of you forever."

Now Christiana, wondering what this could mean, answered them again, saying, "We will not listen to you or regard what you say or yield to anything you ask of us. We are in a hurry and cannot stay. Our undertaking is a matter of life and death." So again they tried to go on past the men, but they stood in their way.

"We don't intend to hurt you," said the ill-favored ones. "We want something else."

"Yes," said Christiana. "I can tell that you want to take us, body and soul, for that is why you have come. But we are willing to die on the spot rather than allow ourselves to be brought into your snares; we will not risk our eternal well-being." Christiana and Mercy then both began crying out, "Murder! Murder!" Thus they put themselves under the laws provided for the pro-tection of women. But the men continued to press their attack, seeking to overpower them. So they continued to cry out.

Deut. 22:13-28; 24:1-4

A Reliever Comes to Their Aid

Since the pilgrims had not yet gotten very far on their journey, their voices could be heard from the Gate. Some of those inside the house came out to see what was happening. Recognizing Christiana's voice, they ran quickly to her aid. By the time they were in sight of them, the pilgrims were involved in an all-out brawl.

It is good to cry out when assaulted

Then one of those who came to their aid called out to the ruffians, "What do you think you are doing? Would you cause the Lord's People to sin?" He attempted to capture the men, but they escaped over the wall into the Garden, and the Dog became their protector.

The Reliever came to Christiana and Mercy and asked them how they were. They answered, "We give thanks to your Prince; we are all right, but we have been somewhat frightened. We thank you also for coming to our defense; other-wise we would have been overcome."

Their Need of a Guide

The Reliever said to them, "When you were enter-tained at the gate, I knew you recognized your frailty, and I wondered why you didn't ask the Lord for a guide to protect you. Had you done so, you might have avoided these troubles and dan-gers, for He certainly would have granted you one."

"Goodness!" exclaimed Christiana. "We were so thrilled with the blessings we were experiencing that we completely forgot about the dangers and snares ahead. Besides, who would have ever thought that such awful men would lurk so close to the King's Palace? We very definitely should have asked our Lord for a guide; but, tell me, since our Lord knew it would be to our advantage to have one, why didn't He offer to send one along with us?"

The Reliever

"It is not always wise to grant things that are not requested," said the Reliever. "By doing so these things are often taken for granted and not appreciated. But when we feel the need for something, our estimation of it is more in line with its true worth, and thus when we ask for it and receive it, we appreciate it and use it with gratitude. If my Lord had granted you a guide before you felt a need for one, you would not have realized or regretted your oversight in not asking for one. So all things work for good and contribute to your being more cautious."

Rom. 8:28

Then Christiana asked, "Should we then go back again to the Lord and confess our foolishness and ask Him for a guide?"

"I will present the confession of your foolishness to Him. You do not need to start over. All along the way you will have no lack of provision, for preparations have been made in each of my Lord's lodgings for the reception of His pilgrims. All that is needed to arm pilgrims against every attack has been provided for. Like I said, how-

ever, He desires that you ask Him for these
things. If something is not worth asking for, it is
deemed cheap and inferior." When he had finished saying these things, he returned to his
place, and the pilgrims went on their way.

"What a jolt this has been!" exclaimed Mercy.
"I thought we were past all danger and that we
would never again have to face sorrow."

"My sister, your innocence may excuse you,"
replied Christiana, "but I knew better, and for
that reason I am more at fault. I saw the danger
before I ever walked out my door, and yet I
didn't think to get help from where it was readily
available. I am very much to blame."

"I'm confused," said Mercy. "How did you see
this before you left your home?" said Mercy.

"Well," answered Christiana, "one night before
I left, I was lying in my bed, and I had a dream.
I thought I saw these same two men; they were
standing at the foot of my bed plotting how they
might prevent my salvation. I was in great turmoil, but I can still remember their words. They
said, 'What shall we do with this woman? In her
waking and in her sleeping she cries out for forgiveness. If she is allowed to continue on as she
has begun, we will lose her as we lost her husband.' That dream should have made me careful
to ask for help when it was available."

"Well," said Mercy, "this experience has given
us an opportunity to discover our own imperfec-
tions, and our Lord has used it to reveal to us the
riches of His grace. It is clear to see that in accordance with His will and pleasure, and in spite of
our carelessness, He has showered His kindness
upon us. I had heard said that He will 'redeem
them from the hand of those stronger than they,'
and so He has done with us."

*Mercy makes use
of the neglect of
their duty.*

Eph. 1:7

Eph. 1:5-6

Jer. 31:11

CHAPTER 21

◆◆◆◆◆◆◆◆◆◆◆◆◆◆◆

Arrival at the Interpreter's House

After they had talked awhile longer, they drew near to a House standing in the way that had been built for the refreshment of pilgrims. This was the House of the Interpreter who was described in the first part of this story. When they came to the door, they heard some people talking inside. Listening carefully, they thought they heard Christiana mentioned by name, though the people inside had no idea she was standing at their door. News concerning Christiana and her boys and their pilgrimage had preceded them, and those inside were very pleased because they had heard such a good report about Christian's wife—the very woman who some time ago had been so set against going on such a pilgrimage.

After standing there for awhile longer and listening to the good things being said about her, Christiana finally knocked on the door as she had done at the Gate before. A young woman named Innocent opened the door and saw them standing there.

"With whom would you like to speak?" asked Innocent.

"We have been told that this is a place of privilege that has been prepared for those who have become pilgrims," answered Christiana. "We who now stand at your door are pilgrims, and we ask that you please allow us to share in your hospitality. As you can see, the day is past, and we don't want to go any farther tonight."

"May I please tell the Master of the House who is calling?"

"My name is Christiana. I was the wife of the pilgrim who traveled this way several years ago. These are our four sons, and this young woman is accompanying us on our pilgrimage as well."

INTERPRETER

Then Innocent ran in and said to those inside, "Guess who is at the door! It is Christiana with her children and a friend. They are asking for lodging here tonight!"

They all jumped for joy and went and told their master. So he came to the door, and upon seeing her he asked, "Are you the Christiana whom Christian, the good pilgrim, left behind when he accepted the pilgrim's life?"

"Yes, I am that woman who was so hardhearted as to make light of my husband's anxieties and who let him go on his journey alone, and these are our four sons. But now I have come on the pilgrimage, too, because I am convinced that this is the only right way."

Then Interpreter, the master of the House, said, "Then the word has been fulfilled that was written of the man who said to his son, 'Son, go and work today in the vineyard.' 'I will not,' he answered, but later he changed his mind and went."

Matt. 21:29

"So be it. Amen!" said Christiana. "May God grant that this saying be true of me and grant that I may be found at peace with Him in the end, 'without stain or wrinkle or any other blemish, but holy and blameless.'"

Eph. 5:27

They Are Invited Inside

"But why do you stand at the door like this?"
asked Interpreter. "Come in, daughter of Abraham. We were just talking about these things, for
we had heard the news that you had become a
pilgrim. Come, boys, come in; come, young lady,
come in." So he received them all into his House.

*Old saints are
glad to see young
ones walk in
God's ways.*

Once inside, they were told to sit down and
rest awhile, and those in the House came back
into the room to see them. One smiled, and then
another, until they were all smiling for joy that
Christiana had become a pilgrim. They warmly
received the boys as well, and they treated Mercy
also with tender love.

Their Tour of the House

After awhile, the Interpreter took them into his
Significant Rooms and showed them what Christian had seen some time before. They saw the
Man in the Cage, the Man and his Dream, the
Man that cut his way through his enemies, and
the Picture of the greatest of them all, together
with the rest of those things that had been so
profitable to Christian.

The Man with the Rake

Following the tour, the Interpreter gave them
some time to digest what they had seen. Then he
took them into a room where they
saw a man who could look only in
a downward direction. In his
hand he held a Rake, and Someone was standing over his head
with a celestial crown in His hand,
offering to trade it for the Rake. The man,
however, never looked up, nor did he acknowledge the offer, but he kept raking the straws,
small sticks, and dust that were on the floor.

"I believe I understand what this means," said Christiana. "Isn't this a figure of a man of this world, good sir?"

"You have answered correctly," said Interpreter. "His Rake illustrates his carnal mind. As you can see, he would rather rake up straws and sticks and the dust on the floor than obey Him who is calling from above with the celestial crown. The point of this is to show that for some Heaven is no more than a fairy tale; they think that only those things that are here on earth are real. In view of the fact that he can only look down, you can recognize the truth that earthly things, when they are allowed to control people's minds, have the power to carry their hearts completely away from God."

Col. 3:2

"Oh, deliver me from this Rake!" cried Christiana.

"That prayer," said Interpreter, "has been so little used that it is almost rusty. Scarcely one in ten thousand will pray, 'Keep me from the snare of earthly riches.' The straws, the sticks, and the dust of this world are greatly prized, and most people seek after them."

1 Tim. 6:17

Mercy and Christiana both wept and cried out, "Oh! It is only too true!"

The Spider on the Wall

After the Interpreter had finished showing them this, he took them into the very best room in the House—a very fine room, indeed. He told them to look around and see if they could find any-thing profitable there. They looked all around the room but could find nothing that they thought useful. There was a very large Spider on one of the walls, but they overlooked it.

"Sir, I see nothing at all," said Mercy. But Christiana said nothing.

"Look again," said Interpreter.

So Mercy looked around one more time and said, "I see nothing but an ugly Spider clinging to the wall."

Then he said, "Is there only one Spider in all this spacious room?" Then Christiana's eyes began to mist, for she was a woman with sharp understanding. She said, "Yes, Sir, there are more here than one—ones whose venom is far more destructive than that one's."

Then Interpeter looked very pleased at her and said, "You have spoken the truth." This made Mercy blush and the boys also, because now they were all beginning to understand the mystery.

Then Interpreter said, "As you see, the Spider's arms fasten themselves even to the walls of kings' palaces. And why do we take note of this except to show you that it doesn't matter how full of the venom of sin you might be, yet by the arm of faith, you may lay hold of and dwell in the best room that belongs to the King's House above."

Prov. 30:28

"I thought it meant something like this," said Christiana, "but I couldn't imagine it all. I thought that we were like Spiders, and that we looked like ugly creatures no matter how fine the room we were in. But it didn't enter my mind that by this Spider—this venomous and ugly creature—we were to learn a lesson about faith. It has taken hold with its hands, as I can see, and lives in the best room in the House. God has made nothing in vain."

They seemed happy after that; nevertheless, tears were in their eyes. They looked at one another and also bowed before the Interpreter.

The Hen and Her Chicks

He then ushered them to another room where there was a Hen and her Chicks. He instructed them to observe them for awhile. They saw one of the Chicks go to the trough to drink, and every time it drank, it lifted up its head and eyes toward Heaven.

"See what this little Chick does and learn from it," said Interpreter. "Acknowledge where the mercies you enjoy come from by looking up as you receive them. Take another look and listen closely." When they did, they noted that the Hen had four different methods of calling her Chicks. First, she had a call that she used normally all day long; second, she had a special call that she used only occasionally; third, she made a brooding sound; and, fourth, she had a cry of alarm.

Deut. 4:39-40

The Hen and her Chicks

"Now," said Interpreter, "compare this Hen to your King and these Chicks to His obedient ones. For, like her, He has His own methods that He uses to call His People. He has a normal call that simply lets you know His presence is there; with His special call He always has some new gift or insight to bestow; He also has a brooding voice to comfort those who are under His wing; and last, He has a cry of alarm to warn His children when He sees an enemy approaching."

Matt. 23:37;
Luke 13:34

The Compliant Sheep

"Please, sir, let us see some more," said Christiana.

So he took them into a Slaughter-house where a Butcher was killing a Sheep. But the Sheep was quiet and accepted her death patiently. Then Interpreter said, "It is important for you to learn from this Sheep how to suffer and to put up with injustice to yourselves without grumbling and complaining. See how quietly she receives her death; she doesn't even offer an objection. Your King has called you His Sheep."

Isa. 53:7

James 5:10;
1 Pet. 2:22-23;
3:9; 4:19

Ps. 100:3;
John 10:1-16

The Flowers in the Garden

After this, he led them into his Garden where there was a great variety of Flowers. "Do you see all these?" he asked.

"Yes," said Christiana.

Then he said, "Look at how different they are in size and shape, in beauty and quality, and in color and fragrance. Though some may be more desirable than others, nevertheless they each stand happily where the Gardener has planted them, neither competing with nor striving against one another."

The Grain in the Field

He next took them to his Field where he had sown Corn and Wheat. But they could see that all the tops had been cut off, and only stalks and straw remained. He said, "This ground was properly fertilized, plowed, and sowed, but what shall we do now with this crop?"

"Burn some of it, and plow under the rest," offered Christiana. Then Interpreter said, "Fruit, you see, is what we look for; because there is none, you either condemn it to the 'unquenchable fire' or 'to be thrown out and trampled by men.' Take heed that in this you do not condemn yourselves."

Matt. 3:8;
Rom. 7:4
Matt. 3:12
Matt. 5:13;
Luke 3:9;
John 15:2

The Robin with the Spider

As they were coming in from the Field, they noticed a little Robin with a huge Spider in its beak. Interpreter said, "Look at this." Mercy was baffled and said nothing, but Christiana remarked, "What a disgusting sight! How this pretty little Robin red breast, which is esteemed above many other kinds of birds and likes to get along peaceably with men, has disgraced and demeaned himself in our eyes. I thought they lived upon crumbs of bread or other harmless matter. I like him much less than I did before."

Interpreter replied, "This Robin is a symbol; it very appropriately exemplifies some of those who profess the faith. Like this Robin, they look good on the surface: they are pretty in color, well-behaved, and pleasant to listen to. They also seem to have great love for those who are sincere in the faith. Above all, they desire to associate with them and be their friends, as if they could live upon the good man's crumbs. They make a pretense, and therefore they are frequently found in the House of the Godly, and are seen doing the Lord's business. But when they are by them-selves, like the Robin, they can catch and gobble up Spiders; they can change their diet, drink in-iquity, and swallow sin like water."

The Interpreter's Proverbs

Pray, and you will get at that which lies unrevealed.

When they had arrived back at the House, din-ner was not yet ready, so Christiana asked Inter-preter to continue teaching them things that might be helpful to them.

Interpreter began to talk, saying, "The fatter the sow is, the more she desires the mud; the fat-ter the ox is, the more playfully he goes to the slaughter; the more healthy the lustful man is, the more prone he is to do evil.

1 Tim. 2:9-10; 1 Pet. 3:3-5

"Women have a desire to go out looking neat and lovely, and it is especially attractive for them to be adorned with what is of great value in God's sight.

Matt. 10:22

"It is easier to be a good night watchman for a night or two than to stay responsible for an entire year; likewise, it is easier to do a good job of professing the faith in the beginning than to carry it through to the end as it should be done.

"Every ship's captain, when in a storm, will willingly throw overboard everything of the smallest value; who, however, will throw the best out first? Only the one who doesn't fear God.

"One leak can sink a ship, and one sin can destroy the one who is sinning.

"He who disregards his friend is ungrateful to him; but he who disregards his Savior is unmerciful to himself.

"He who lives in sin and looks for happiness hereafter is like the man who sows weeds and hopes to fill his barn with wheat or barley.

Gal. 6:7-8

"If a person would seek to live well, let him always keep in mind his last day and clutch it to himself as a companion.

"Gossiping and double-mindedness prove that sin is in the world.

Rom. 1:29;
Ps. 119:113

"If this present world that God set into existence is counted of value to men, think of what Heaven is like, which God so highly regards!

"If we are so reluctant to let go of this life which is accompanied by so many troubles, think of what the life above will mean to us!

"Everyone extols the goodness of man, but how many are, as they should be, preoccupied with the goodness of God?

"Seldom do we sit down to eat without leaving leftovers; likewise, in Jesus Christ there is more justification and righteousness than the entire world will ever need."

The Rotten Tree
When the Interpreter was finished, he took them out into his Garden again and showed them a Tree. The Tree's insides were rotted away, yet it had leaves and was still growing. Then Mercy asked, "What does this mean?"

"This Tree," said Interpreter, "which is lovely outside but rotten inside is like many who are in the Garden of God. They speak on God's behalf

with their mouths, but they don't really do anything for Him. Their leaves are pleasing, but their hearts are good for nothing but to be tinder for the Devil's tinderbox."

Christiana Shares How She Became a Pilgrim
Now supper was ready, and everything was set on the table. After giving thanks, they sat down to eat. It was Interpreter's custom to entertain those he hosted with music at meals, so the musicians played throughout their dinner. There was also a singer with a fine voice, and this was his song:

"The Lord alone is my support,
And He never fails to feed;
How can I then want anything?
What is there that I need?"

When the song and music were ended, Interpreter asked Christiana what had moved her to take up the pilgrim's life.

Christiana answered, "First, the loss of my husband came to mind and gave me great grief, but that was only natural affection. After that, all his troubles leading up to his pilgrimage and then the pilgrimage itself weighed heavily on my mind. Also, I remembered how unyielding I had been. Guilt took hold of my mind and would have drawn me down to the pits, but just in time I had a dream that he was all right. After this, an invitation was sent to me by the King of that

Country where my husband dwells. The dream
and the invitation together so prevailed upon
my mind that I was forced to go this way."

"But didn't you run into any opposition before
you left?" asked Interpreter.

"Yes, a neighbor, Mrs. Timorous. She was
related to a man who tried to persuade my husband to go back because he was afraid of the
Lions. She belittled me and called my pilgrimage
a desperate adventure. She also tried to discourage me by pointing out the
hardships and trials my *Mrs. Timorous*
husband had endured. I
got over this soon enough, but then I
had a dream of two wicked men who were plotting how to ruin my journey. This greatly troubled me at the time, and I still can't get it out of
my mind. It makes me afraid of everyone that I
meet for fear that they will try to do me harm
and turn me out of the way. I don't want everyone to know this, but I will tell you, that between
here and the Gate by which we came into the
way we were so terribly assaulted that we both
screamed, 'Murder!' The two who assaulted us
were like the two I had seen in my dream."

"You have made a good beginning," said Interpreter, "and by the end of your journey you will
have greatly increased in strength and confidence."

Mercy Shares How She Became a Pilgrim

Interpreter then turned to Mercy and said, "And
what moved you to come here, my dear?"

Mercy blushed and trembled and remained
silent for awhile.

Interpreter soothed Mercy's mind by saying,
"Don't be afraid; only believe, and say what is on
your mind."

She answered, "The truth is that my inexperience makes me want to keep quiet. That same reason fills me with fears of falling short in the end. I cannot testify of visions and dreams like my friend Christiana can; nor do I know what it is to mourn over my refusal of the advice of those who were insightful relatives."

"What was it then, dear one, that convinced you to make the choice you have made?"

"Well, when our friend Christiana was packing up to leave our town, another woman and I, without knowing what was going on, went to visit her. We knocked at the door and went in, but when we saw her packing, we asked for an explanation. She said she had been sent an invitation to join her husband. She then went on to tell us how she had seen him in a dream; he was living among immortals in a strange place, wearing a crown, playing on a harp, eating and drinking at his Prince's table, and singing praises to Him for bringing him there. While she was describing these things, my heart burned within me, and I told myself, 'If this is true, I will leave my father and mother and the land of my birth, and, if I may, I will go along with Christiana.' So I inquired further of her about the truth of these things, and I asked whether or not she would let me go with her. I had come suddenly to the realization that I could no longer live in our town without risking utter ruin. Nevertheless, I left with a heavy heart—not that I regretted leaving, but out of concern for all my loved ones who were left behind. Yet I have come with all my heart, and, if allowed, I will go with Christiana to her husband and his King."

"Your initial dedication is commendable, for you have given heed to the truth. You are a Ruth, who, out of love for Naomi and for the Lord her God, left the land of her birth to join herself to a

Luke 24:32

Mark 10:28-31

258

people she had never known. 'May the Lord God of Israel, under whose wings you have come to trust, bless your work and honor you with a full reward.'"

Ruth 2:11-12

By this time they had finished eating dinner, and preparations were made for sleeping. Christiana and Mercy were given one room, and the boys slept in another room. Although Mercy had gotten in bed, she could not sleep because of the joy she felt. Her doubts about her being accepted

were put to rest, and she was able to relax more than at any other time. So she lay there blessing God and praising Him who had shown her such favor.

The Bath in the Garden
In the morning the pilgrims arose with the sun and prepared for their departure. But Interpreter wanted them to linger a little while. He said, "You should be well-groomed before you leave." He then asked the young woman who had first opened the door to them to take them to the Bath in the Garden and have them washed, cleansing them from all the dirt they had gathered in their traveling. So she did as he had said. She explained that this was what he required of those who called at his House who were going on a pilgrimage. After they had washed, they came forth not only smelling sweet and clean, but their bodies felt invigorated and strengthened.

Sanctification

1 Cor. 6:11

They returned to the House looking much love-
lier than they had looked before. When Inter-

Song of Sol. 6:10 — preter saw Christiana and Mercy, he said, "Fair as
the moon." Then he called for the seal that was

2 Cor. 1:22; — used to seal those who had been washed in the

Eph. 1:13 — Bath. The seal was brought to him, and he set his

Rev. 7:3 — mark upon them, a mark that would be recognized in all the places through which they were
yet to travel. Now the seal had the significance
and power of the Passover that the children of
Israel ate when they were brought to freedom

Exod. 13:8-10 — from the land of Egypt. The mark was affixed
between their eyes and greatly added to the
attractiveness of their faces. It also enhanced
their dignity and made their countenance
resemble that of angels.

They Are Given New Clothing

Then Interpreter told the young woman who
had waited upon them, "Go into the closets and
get appropriate garments for these people. So she

Rom. 13:14; — went and came back with clean white clothing

Gal. 3:27 — made of fine linen, and she laid them before
him. He then commanded them to go put on the
clean clothing. When they did so, they became
awestruck and even fearful of one another, for
although they could see no change in them-

2 Cor. 3:18 — selves, they could see the glory of God in each
other. For this reason, they began to esteem each

Phil. 2:3 — other better than themselves. "You are more full
of grace," said one. "You are more pure," said
another.

They Are Given a Guide

Interpreter then called for one of his male servants whose name was Great-heart. He told him

Eph. 6:13-17 — to take a Sword, a Helmet, and a Shield, and said,
"Take these children of mine and escort them to

GREAT HEART

the House called Beautiful, which is where they will next stop to rest. So the servant took his weapons and prepared to leave. Interpreter said, "God bless you on your way." Then all those who belonged to the family sent them off with many good wishes, and they went on their way, singing:

"This has been our trip's second stage;
Here we could hear and glean,
Those good things that from age to age
Were hid, but we have seen.

The Raker, Spider, and the Hen,
The Chicks, also, I see
Have taught a lesson: let me then
Conformed to it now be.

The Butcher, Garden, and the Field,
The Robin and his prey,
Also the Rotten Tree did yield
Teachings that heavily weigh;

To move me so I'll watch and pray
To strive to be sincere:
To take up my cross day by day,
And serve the Lord with fear."

CHAPTER 22

❖❖❖❖❖❖❖❖❖❖❖❖❖❖

A Question about Forgiveness

Now I saw in my dream that they traveled on, and
Great-heart went ahead of them. They came to the
place where Christian's Burden had fallen off his
back and tumbled into a Grave, and they paused
here for awhile to bless and thank God. "Something we were told at the Gate now comes to mind,"
said Christiana; "namely, that we receive forgiveness by both word and deed; by word, because it
promises forgiveness, and by deed, because of what
was done to obtain it. I understand something of
the promise, but what does it mean to have forgiveness by deed, or in the way that it was obtained?
Mr. Great-heart, I suppose you know, so, will you
please tell us what you know about this?"

Great-heart's Explanation

Great-heart answered, "Forgiveness, or pardon,
by a deed done is forgiveness obtained by one
person for another who needs it. It is not
obtained directly by the person who needs it, but
Justification
by the act or deed of another. So then, to speak
to your question more particularly, the forgiveness that you and Mercy and these children have
received was obtained by another—namely, by
Him who let you in at the Gate. And He has
obtained it in a twofold way: first, He has cov-
Rom. 3:22; 8:3-4
ered your need of righteousness with His own,
Rom. 3:25;
and second, He has shed His own blood that you
Titus 3:5;
may be washed in it."
Heb. 9:12-14

"But if He imparts His righteousness to us, what will He have left for Himself?" asked Christiana.

"He has more righteousness than you have need of, or than He needs for Himself," answered Great-heart.

"Please explain what you mean," said Christiana.

"I will try as best I can," said Great-heart. "But let me begin by saying that the One of whom we are about to speak is unique. He has two natures in one Person, easy to distinguish but impossible to divide. There is a righteousness that belongs to both of these natures, and each righteousness is essential to that nature, so that one might as easily kill that nature as to separate its righteousness from it. Therefore, we are not made partakers of these righteousnesses, nor are they imparted to us; so these aspects of His righteousness are not those that cause our justification or give us life.

John 14:10;
Phil. 2:6-8;
Heb. 4:15

"There is also another righteousness besides these that this Person has. It is a righteousness derived from the joining of His two natures into one. It is not His divine righteousness as distinguished from that of His manhood, nor His human righteousness as distinguished from the divine righteousness, but rather, it is a righteousness that stands in the union of both natures. This is the righteousness that is essential to His being called by God to fill the demands of the office of Mediator between God and man. Without His first righteousness, He parts with His divinity; without His second righteousness, He parts with the purity of His manhood; and without the third, He parts with the perfection that qualifies Him for the office of Mediator.

1 Tim. 2:5

"Finally, He has a fourth righteousness, one which centers in and is derived from His obedi-

MEDIATOR

ence to the revealed will of His Father. It is this righteousness that He bestows upon sinners and by which He covers their sins. Therefore, it is said, 'For just as through the disobedience of the one man the many were made sinners, so also through the obedience of the one man the many will be made righteous.'"

Rom. 5:19

"But are His other forms of righteousness of no use to us?" asked Christiana.

"That is right. Because they are essential to His natures and calling, they cannot be shared with others. Yet, it is on account of them that the righteousness that justifies is effective for us. The righteousness of His divine nature gives virtue to His obedience; the righteousness of His human nature gives His obedience the capacity to justify us; and the righteousness that comes from the union of these two natures and which uniquely qualifies Him to be our Mediator, gives authority to that righteousness to do the work that it is meant to accomplish.

"So, then, we have a righteousness that Christ, as God, has no need of, for He is God without it. We also have a righteousness that Christ, as man, does not need, for He is a perfect man without it. Then, we have a righteousness of which Christ, as the God-man, has no need, for He is perfectly righteous without it. So here we have forms of righteousness that Christ as God, as man, and as God-man does not need in and of Himself. Thus,

He can spare the righteousness that justifies us: He gives it away because He has no need for it, and for this reason, it is called the 'gift of righteousness.'

Rom. 5:17

"Since Christ Jesus the Lord was placed under the Law, this righteousness must be given away. For the Law not only demands that those bound to it live righteously, but that they do so in love. So, according to the law, if someone has two coats, he should give one of them to someone who has none. Now our Lord surely has two coats—one for Himself, and one to spare—and so He freely gives one to those who have none. Therefore, Christiana and Mercy, and the rest of you who are here, your pardon comes by deed, or by the work of another Man. Your Lord Jesus Christ is He who has worked and is willing to give what He has gained to the next poor beggar He meets.

Gal. 4:4-5
Lev. 19:18;
Deut. 6:5;
Matt. 22:37-40;
Rom. 13:8-10

Luke 3:11

1 Tim. 2:5-6

"But again, in order to obtain forgiveness by deed, some price must be paid to God, and something must be provided as a covering for our sins. Sin has sentenced us to the just curse of a righteous law. The only deliverance from the curse that is upon us is that we be justified by way of a redemption; a price must be paid for the evils we have done. And this has been done by the blood of your Lord who willingly came and stood in your place, offering to die the death to which you had been sentenced because of your sins. He has, therefore, ransomed you from the penalty of your lawbreaking by shedding His blood. He has covered your warped, polluted souls with His righteousness, and because of this, God will pass by you and will not harm you when He comes to judge the world."

Gal. 3:10

Rom. 4:24;
Gal. 3:13

Matt. 20:28;
Mark 10:45;
1 Tim. 2:6;
Heb. 9:15

Christiana Now Understands

"This is wonderful!" exclaimed Christiana. "Now I am able to see that there was a lesson to be learned from our being pardoned by both word and deed." Then turning to Mercy and her sons, she said, "Let us endeavor never to forget this but to continually keep this in mind."

"But, sir," she asked, "is this not the truth that caused my husband Christian's Burden to be released from his shoulders and made him leap for joy?"

"Yes," Great-heart replied. "It was by his faith in what I have told you that those cords were cut, and in no other way could they have been severed. Because he was forced to carry his Burden all the way to the Cross, he was made certain of the Cross's true worth."

Eph. 2:8-9

"I thought that might be the case," said Christiana. "For though my heart has felt happy before, now it is ten times more joyful! I have to believe from my experience here, even though I have so little experience thus far, that even if the most burdened man in the world were here and were able to see and believe as I now do, his heart would rejoice with joy and freedom."

"Not only is there comfort and freedom from the burden we bear after seeing and considering these things," explained Great-heart, "but also an endearing affection grows within us because of it. For who cannot be deeply affected when he realizes that his redemption comes not only through a promise given to him but through a sacrifice made for him? So it is when one ponders the One who did this for us."

Her Heartfelt Response

"True," responded Christiana. "I think it makes my own heart bleed to think that He should bleed for me. Oh, Loving One! Oh, blessed One! You deserve to have me; You have bought me. You deserve to have all of me; You have paid for me ten thousand times what I am worth! It is no marvel that this moved my husband to tears and caused him to go onward so relentlessly. I believe he wanted me to be with him, but oh, vile wretch that I was! I let him go all alone. Oh, Mercy, if only your father and mother were here! Yes, and Mrs. Timorous also! And now I wish with all my heart that Madam Wanton was here too. Surely, oh, so surely, their hearts would be affected as well. Neither the fear of the one, nor the powerful lusts of the other, could prevail upon them to return home again; they would not be able to refuse becoming dedicated pilgrims."

1 Cor. 6:20; Rev. 5:9

There is cause for such admiration.

"You are speaking this way out of the height of your emotions," said Great-heart. "Do you think you will always feel this way? Besides, these truths are not communicated to everyone—not even to everyone who saw your Jesus bleed. There were those who stood by, watching the blood run from His heart down to the ground. Yet, they were so far from understanding that, instead of lamenting, they jeered at Him, and instead of becoming His disciples, they hardened their hearts against Him. Therefore, my daughter, all that you have received has been specially impressed upon your senses as you have been divinely moved to think on what I have spoken to you. Remember what was told you about the hen, that it is not her normal call that accompanies food for her chicks. You have, therefore, received this, not by normal means, but by special grace."

Matt. 27:34-44; Mark 15:25-32; Luke 23:34-37

Simple, Sloth, and Presumption

Now I saw further in my dream that they went on until they came to the place where Simple, Sloth, and Presumption lay sleeping when Christian went by on his pilgrimage. They were still there, a little ways off the other side of the road. Their hands and feet had been cuffed in chains, and they were hanging dead.

simple Sloth PRESUMPTION

Then Mercy asked their guide, "Who are these three men? Why are they left hanging there?"

"These three were men who had some very bad qualities," answered Great-heart. "Not only had they no intention of becoming pilgrims themselves, but they also hindered everyone else they could. They were slothful and foolish themselves, and they sought to persuade others to be like them, promising that in the end they would all do quite well. When Christian went by they were asleep, and now when you are going by they have been hanged."

Matt. 23:13

Look here how the slothful are a sure sign;
Strung up, 'cause holy ways they did decline.
A child would be a man and will so feign,
But weak grows strong when Great-heart sifts the grain.

"Were they actually able to persuade some to think like them?" asked Mercy.

"Yes," answered Great-heart. "They turned several out of the way. There was one, Slow-pace, who they were able to persuade. They also prevailed upon Short-wind, No-heart, Linger-after-lust, Sleepy-head, and a young woman named Dull. As if this were not bad enough, they also gave a bad report of your Lord, persuading others that He was a taskmaster. They also spread around an evil report of the Good Land, saying it was not half as good as some pretend it to be. They slandered His servants, saying the best of them were meddlesome and troublemaking busybodies. Further, they called the bread of God 'mere husks,' the comforts of His children 'mere imaginations,' and the travel and labor of pilgrims 'things of no purpose.'"

Matt. 25:24-25

Num. 13:27-33

"My," said Christiana. "If they were like this, I won't grieve for them. They have only gotten what they deserved. I think it is a good thing that they are hanging so close to the High-way so that others can see them and be warned. But wouldn't it have been better to erect a sign made of iron or steel and engraved with a description of their crimes so that others like them might be cautioned?"

"There is a sign," answered Great-heart. "You can see it if you walk over to the wall."

"I don't need to see any more," said Mercy. "Let them hang there; and let their names rot, and their crimes testify against them forever. I think it is a great favor to us that they were hanged before we got here. Who knows what else they might have done to trouble such vulnerable ones as we. Then she began to sing,

Prov. 10:7

"Now you three just hang there and be a sight
To all who against the truth shall unite;
And let those who come after, fear this end
If to the pilgrims they are not a friend.
And, oh, my soul, of all like these, beware,
Who, opposing the truth, do so declare."

CHAPTER 23

♦♦♦♦♦♦♦♦♦♦♦♦♦♦

The Dirty Spring

They went on until they came to the foot of the
Hill Difficulty, where, again, their friend Great-
heart took the opportunity to inform them what
had happened there to Christian when he
had traveled by. He took them first to the
Spring saying, "Look, this is the
Spring where Christian drank
before he began to go up this
Hill. It used to be clear and
good water, but, because
some did not want pilgrims
to quench their thirst here,
it is now dirty."

Ezek. 34:17-19

"I wonder why they would be so envi-
ous," asked Mercy.

"The water is drinkable if you use a good container to get it out," said Great-heart. "The dirt
will settle to the bottom, and then the water will
become more clear."

*It is difficult to
get sound
doctrine in
erroneous times.*

Christiana and her companions wanted to try
this, so using an earthen pot, they took some
water out and let it stand until the dirt had sunk
to the bottom. Then they drank it.

The Two False Ways

Next he showed them the two false ways at the
foot of the Hill where Formality and Hypocrisy
were lost. He explained, "These are two most dangerous paths. Two were cast away here when

By-paths though barred up will not keep all from entering them.

Christian came by. Even though, as you can see, these ways have been closed off by chains, barriers, and even a ditch, nevertheless, there are some who will choose to endanger themselves here rather than make the effort it takes to go up this Hill."

Prov. 13:15

"The way of the unfaithful is hard," said Christiana. "It is a wonder that they can get into those ways without breaking their necks."

"They will go ahead and take the chance. Yes, even if one of the King's servants happens to see them and warns them that they are going the wrong way and that they are in danger, they will answer insolently, 'We will not listen to the message you have spoken to us in the name of the Lord! We will certainly do everything we said we would.' No, if you look a little farther, you can see that enough warning signals have been placed in front of those ways. Not only are there chains, barriers, and a ditch, but there is even a hedge around them. Yet they will still choose to go there."

Jer. 44:16-17

"They are extremely lazy," said Christiana. "They don't want the trouble of the uphill way; it is just too unpleasant for them. Therefore they have fulfilled what is written, 'The way of a lazy man is like a hedge of thorns.' 'For he is cast into a net by his own feet, and he walks into a snare' rather than go up this Hill and the rest of the way to the City."

Prov. 15:19

Job 18:8

Climbing the Hill Difficulty

After this, they all set out to go up the Hill, but before they reached the top, Christiana began to pant and said, "It is difficult to breathe on this Hill. No wonder those who love to be comfortable choose an easier way!"

"I must sit down," said Mercy. At that time, also, the youngest boy began to grow faint.

"Come, come now," prodded Great-heart. "Don't sit down here; the Prince's Arbor is just a little farther up the Hill." Then he took Mercy and the boy by the hand and led them there.

When they had arrived at the Arbor, they were exhausted and **HILDIFHCULTY** very hot, so they were very happy to sit down and rest. Then Mercy said, "How sweet is rest to those who labor. And how good it is of the Prince to provide such resting places for pilgrims. Though I have never seen this Arbor, I have heard much about it. Only let us be very careful not to sleep, for I have heard it cost poor Christian dearly."

Matt. 11:28

Then Great-heart said to the boys, "Come, my fine young men, how are you doing? What do you think about going on this pilgrimage?"

"Sir," said the youngest boy, "I thought my heart would stop beating, but thank you for helping me. I now remember what my mother has told me—that the way to Heaven is like climbing a ladder, while the way to Hell is an easy slide downhill. I would rather climb the ladder to life than go easily down the Hill to death."

Prov. 16:25

"But going downhill is easy," said Mercy.

But the boy, whose name was James, replied, "I think that the day is coming when going downhill will be the hardest of all."

"You are a fine young man," said Great-heart. "You have given her the right answer." Mercy smiled, but the boy blushed.

"Come," said Christiana. "Here are some sweets for you to eat while you rest your legs.

Here is a Pomegranate that Mr. Interpreter gave me just as I was leaving his House. He also gave me some Honeycomb and a Bottle of Spirits."

"I thought he gave you something when he called you aside," said Mercy.

"Yes, he did," replied Christiana. "But, Mercy, it is just like I said. You also will share in all the good I receive because you so willingly became my companion." Then she gave them what she had, and they ate. And Christiana asked Great-heart, "Sir, won't you eat too?"

"No," he answered, "you are going on a pilgrimage, and I will soon return home. You will need what you have, but at home I eat the same food every day."

So after they had eaten, they chatted a while longer, and their guide said to them, "The day is wearing quickly away; if you are ready, let us prepare to be going." So they got up to go, and the boys went in front of them. They had gone only a short distance when Christiana remembered that she forgot her Bottle of Spirits, so she sent one of the boys back to get it.

Then Mercy said, "My, I think this is a place for losing things. Christian lost his scroll here, and now Christiana has left her bottle behind. Sir, what is the reason for this?"

"The cause is sleep, and, I might add, forgetfulness," answered Great-heart. "Some sleep when they should stay awake, and some forget when they should remember. This is the very reason why some pilgrims who stop at resting places sometimes end up the losers. Pilgrims should 1 Thess. 5:6 keep watch and be careful not to neglect what they have already received; for they are capable of forgetting even what has been their greatest source of joy. Often, because they have grown careless, their rejoicing ends in tears and their sunshine turns into dark clouds. Witness the story of Christian at this place."

A Stage for Warning

When they had come to the place where Mistrust and Timorous had met Christian and had tried to persuade him to go back with them out of fear of the Lions, they saw something that looked like a newly erected stage. Near the stage area and close to the road they could see a large floor engraved with verses telling why the stage had been placed there. It said,

Let him who sees this stage take heed,
Watching his heart and tongue;
Lest, if he won't, by here he'll speed,
As some before have done.

The following explanation was printed beneath the verses: "This stage was built as a place to punish those who through fear or mistrust will not go farther on their pilgrimage." On this stage the tongues of both Timorous and Mistrust had been burned with a hot iron for attempting to hinder Christian in his journey.

Then Mercy said, "This is very much like the saying, 'What will he do to you, and what more besides, O deceitful tongue? He will punish you with a warrior's sharp arrows, with burning coals of the broom tree.'" Ps. 120:3-4

The Lions and Giant Grim

So they went on until they came to within sight of the Lions. Great-heart was a strong man, so he was not afraid of the Lions. But when they had come up to the place where the Lions were, the boys, who earlier had run on ahead, now cringed behind him in fear. At this, their guide smiled and said, "How is it, my boys, that you love to go ahead when no danger is approaching, and love to go behind as soon as the Lions appear?"

1 Sam. 17:34-35

As they approached the Lions, Great-heart drew his Sword for the purpose of making a safe way for the pilgrims to pass. Suddenly, someone appeared who had seemingly taken it upon himself to jump to the aid of the Lions. "What is your reason for coming here?" he asked Great-heart. The name of the man was Grim, sometimes called Bloody-man, because he had killed pilgrims. He belonged to a race of Giants.

Then Great-heart answered, "These women and children are going on a pilgrimage, and this is the way they must go; and go they shall, in spite of you and these Lions."

"This is not their way," challenged Grim, "they shall not pass here. I have come out to withstand them and to prevent them from passing; to this end I will team up with the Lions."

Now, to tell the truth, because of the fierceness of the Lions and because of the harsh and threatening behavior of this one who backed them, this way had recently remained largely untraveled; in fact, it was almost completely covered over with weeds.

GIANT GRIM

Christiana reminded her companions that 'in
the days of Shamgar and of Jael, the main roads
were deserted. Travelers used the narrow, crooked
side paths . . . until Deborah became a mother to   Judg. 5:6-7
Israel.' Then Christiana spoke up, saying, "Even
though the High-ways may have remained
untraveled until now, and even though the travelers have in times past been forced to walk
through sideroads, this will no longer be the case
since I, too, am risen as a mother in Israel!" Then
Grim swore by the Lions that they would not
pass; he told them to turn aside since they would
not be allowed to get by.

But Great-heart made his first approach at
Grim and wielded his Sword at him so power-
fully that the Giant was forced to retreat.

"Will you slay me on my own ground?"
shouted Grim.

"This is the King's High-way that we are in,
and it is in His way that you have placed your
Lions. But these women and young pilgrims,
weak though they may be, will yet keep to their
way in spite of your Lions." And with that Great-
heart gave the Giant another powerful blow that
smashed the Giant to his knees. This blow also
broke his helmet and with the following one he
lost an arm. The Giant roared so hideously that
his voice frightened the women. Yet they were
glad to see him sprawling helplessly on the
ground. The Lions were chained, so could therefore do nothing themselves.

After Grim was dead, Mr. Great-heart said to
the pilgrims, "Come along now, and follow me;
the Lions will do you no harm." So they went
on, even though the women trembled as they
passed by them and the boys also looked as if
they might die. But they all got by without any
further incident.

CHAPTER 24

◆◆◆◆◆◆◆◆◆◆◆◆◆◆

The Gatekeeper's Lodge

By this time they were within sight of the gate-keeper's Lodge, and they hastily approached it because travel was dangerous in that area at night. When they had arrived at the gate, Great-heart knocked, and the gatekeeper answered, "Who is there?" As soon as Great-heart had said, "It is I," the gatekeeper came down to let them in.

GREAT HEART

He knew his voice because Great-heart had often come that way to conduct pilgrims on their journey. The gate was opened by the gatekeeper, and, seeing only Great-heart (for his charges were behind him), he said, "How are you doing, Mr. Great-heart? What brings you here so late tonight?"

"I have brought some pilgrims here to lodge as the Lord has commanded me. We would have arrived earlier had we not been opposed by the Giant who stood in support of the Lions. But after a difficult and tiring battle with him, I have killed him and have brought the pilgrims here in safety."

Great-heart Must Leave

"Won't you come in and stay until morning?" asked the gatekeeper.

"No, I will return to my Lord tonight."

"Oh, sir," said Christiana, "how can we say good-bye to you and allow you to leave us alone in our pilgrimage? You have been so faithful and loving, and have fought so resolutely and courageously for us, and have given us such unqualified support and such sincere and thorough counsel, that I will never forget what you have done for us."

"Oh, that we might have your company to our journey's end!" cried Mercy. "How can we who are so feeble hold out in a way that is so full of troubles without the help of a friend and defender?"

Then James, the youngest of the boys, said, "Please sir, decide to go with us and help us; we are so weak, and the way is so dangerous."

"I do as my Lord commands me," said Great-heart. "If He will appoint me to be your guide all the way through, I will willingly do so. But in this you failed at the beginning. When He told me to come this far with you, then you should have begged Him to allow me to go the rest of the way with you; He would have granted your request. However, for now I must withdraw. So, dear Christiana, Mercy, and my brave boys, good-bye."

Welcomed into the House

After Great-heart had departed, Mr. Watchful, the gatekeeper, asked Christiana about her Country and her people. She answered, "I came from the City of Destruction. I am a widow; my husband is dead. His name was Christian the pilgrim."

"Oh!" exclaimed the gatekeeper. "Was he your husband?"

"Yes, and these are my sons; and this is Mercy, one of my neighbors."

Then the gatekeeper rang his bell, as was his custom at such times, and a young woman came

humble MIND

whose name was Humble-mind. The gatekeeper said to her, "Go tell those within that Christiana, the wife of Christian, and her children and a friend are here on a pilgrimage." So she went in and told them, and oh what a sound of gladness there was within the House when Humble-mind announced the good news!

They all came running to the gatekeeper, for the little band was still standing at the door. Then some of the more serious-minded among them said, "Come in, blessed woman, come in, along with all who are with you." So they all went in and were shown to a very large room where they were asked to sit down. When they were seated, the members of the household were called to see and welcome the guests. When they came in and realized who their guests were, they greeted each one with kisses and said, "Welcome, 'objects of his mercy, whom he prepared in advance for glory.' We, your friends, welcome you."

Chrisians' love is kindled at the sight of one another.

Rom. 9:23

They Go to Bed

Because it was getting late, and the pilgrims were weary from their travels and faint from seeing the fight and the terrible Lions, they desired to go to bed as soon as possible. The family told them that they should first be revived by eating some meat; they had already prepared a lamb

Exod. 12:3, 8; with the customary fixings. After they had eaten
John 1:29 and had a time of prayer, they closed with the
Matt. 26:30 reading of a psalm.

"Please," said Christiana, "if we may be so
bold as to choose, let us stay in the same room
that my husband stayed in when he stopped
here." So they were taken to that room, and they
prepared for bed. Once they were in bed, Christiana and Mercy talked for a while.

"At one time," said Christiana, "I hardly gave a
thought to the possibility of my ever following
my husband on a pilgrimage."

"And," Mercy added, "you most likely never
thought you would be lying in the same bed
within the same room."

"Yes, and even less did I think that I might
ever have the hope of seeing his face again or of
worshiping his Lord the King together with
him—yet, I now believe I will."

"Listen!" said Mercy, "Can you hear sounds?"

"Yes, I believe it is the sound of joyful music
because we are here."

"Wonderful!" cried Mercy. "Music in the
House, music in the heart, and music in
Heaven—all for joy that we are here!"

Mercy's Dream

They talked a while longer and then went to
sleep. In the morning Christiana asked Mercy,
"Why were you laughing in your sleep last
night? I suppose you were dreaming."

"Yes, I was dreaming, and it was a sweet
dream. But are you sure I laughed?"

"Yes, you laughed heartily; but please tell me
about your dream," said Christiana.

"I dreamed that I was sitting all alone in a
lonely place, grieving over the hardness of my
heart. I had not been there for very long when I

saw many others gathered around me to see me
and to hear what I was saying. They were listening while I continued to bemoan the hardness
of my heart. Some of them began to laugh at me
while others called me a fool; and some began
pushing me around.

"Then I looked up and thought I could see
someone with wings coming toward me. He
came directly to me and said, "Mercy, what ails
you?" When he heard my complaint, he said,
"Peace to you." He then wiped my eyes with his
handkerchief and dressed me in silver and gold.
He put a chain around my neck, earrings in my
ears, and a beautiful crown upon my head.   Ezek. 16:9-13

"Then he took me by the hand and said,
'Mercy, come, follow me.' So he traveled upward,
and I followed until we came to a golden gate.
He knocked, and the gate was opened, and he
went in with me following behind. I followed
him up to a throne, upon which sat One who
said to me, 'Welcome, daughter.' The place had a
brilliant appearance, and it glistened like the sun.
I thought I saw your husband there. Then I
awoke from my dream. But did I really laugh?"

"Laugh?" said Christiana. "Indeed you did,
and well you might after seeing yourself in such
a setting. Allow me to say that I believe this was
a good dream. As you have already begun to find
the first part of it true, may you also surely find
the second part true at the end. 'For God does
speak—now one way, now another—though
man may not perceive it. In a dream, in a vision
of the night, when deep sleep falls on men as   Job 33:14-15
they slumber in their beds.' When we are in bed,
we don't need to lie awake to talk to God; He can
visit us while we sleep and cause us to hear His
voice. Our heart often awakens when we are
sleeping, and God can speak to us then, either by

words, by proverbs, by signs, or by allegories, just as well as if we were awake."

"Well," replied Mercy, "I am glad I had my dream; I hope that before long I will see it fulfilled—then I would laugh again!"

They Begin the New Day

"I think it is now time for us to rise and find out what we are supposed to do," said Christiana.

"If they invite us to stay awhile," said Mercy, "let's by all means accept the offer. I am very willing to stay here for awhile and get better acquainted with the women who are called Prudence, Piety, and Charity. I think they are very attractive and yet serious-minded."

"We will have to see what they will want to do," Christiana answered.

When they had gotten up and were ready, they came down to see their hosts. They were asked if they had been comfortable and if they had slept well. "I slept very well," said Mercy. "It was one of the best night's sleep that I have had in my life."

Then Prudence and Piety said, "We would like to persuade you to stay here for awhile; if you do, you will have whatever the House can afford."

"Yes," said Charity, "we are very willing to have you." So they consented and stayed there about a month or more and were of great encouragement to one another.

Prudence Quizzes Christiana's Sons

Because Prudence wanted to see how Christiana had taught her children, she asked for permission to question them. Christiana consented, and Prudence began with the youngest, the one named James.

"Come, James," she said, "can you tell me who made you?"

"God the Father, God the Son, and God the Holy Spirit," he replied.

Eph. 2:8-9

"Good boy. And can you tell who saves you?"

"God the Father, God the Son, and God the Holy Spirit."

Isa. 53:9;
2 Cor. 5:21;
Heb. 9:12;
10:11-14

"Good boy, again. But how does God the Father save you?"

"By His grace."

"How does God the Son save you?"

"By His righteousness, by His death and His blood, and by His life."

"And how does God the Holy Spirit save you?"

"By enlightening us, by reviving us with new life, and by keeping us."

Then Prudence said to Christiana, "You are to be commended for training your children like this. I suppose that I don't even need to ask questions of the rest, being that the youngest is able to answer so well. However, I will ask the next to the youngest a few questions."

Piety
PRUDENCE
AND
Charity

Then she said to the boy whose name was Joseph, "Come, Joseph; will you let me test you?"

John 14:16;
15:26; Acts 9:31;
Gal. 3:14; 1 Pet.
4:14

"Yes, with all of my heart," answered Joseph.

"What is man?" she asked.

"A creature that God has made with the ability to reason."

Gen. 1:26-27

"What does the word *saved* suggest?"

"That, because of sin, man has brought himself into a state of bondage and misery."

Gen. 3; Ps. 51:5;
Rom. 5:12, 18-19

"What do the words, *being saved by the Trinity,* suggest?"

"That sin is such a great and mighty tyrant that no one is able to pull us out of its clutches except God alone. Also, God is so good and loving to man that He will, indeed, pull him out of this desperate condition."

Ps. 49:7-9; 130:3

Exod. 34:6-7; Ps. 103:8-9

"What does God have in mind by saving such a poor creature as man?"

"The glorifying of His name, of His grace, and of His justice; and, also, the everlasting happiness of His creature."

Matt. 5:16; 1 Cor. 6:19-20; 10:31

"And who will be saved?"

"Those who accept His salvation."

Matt. 7:14; John 3:16, 18, 36; Rom. 11:16-21

After that, Prudence said, "Good boy, Joseph; your mother has taught you well, and you have been attentive to what she has said to you."

Next, she turned to Samuel, who was the next to the oldest, and said, "Samuel, will you also allow me to quiz you?"

"Yes, indeed, if you want to," he replied.

"What is Heaven?"

"A place and condition that is absolutely blessed because God dwells there."

Rev. 4

"What is Hell?"

"A place and condition that is absolutely woeful because it is the abode of sin, the Devil, and death."

Rev. 20:10, 14

"Why do you want to go to Heaven?"

"So that I may see God and be able to serve Him without weariness; that I may see Christ and love Him forever and ever; that I may have the fullness of the Holy Spirit living inside me, which I will never be able to fully enjoy here."

Rev. 21

At this she said, "You have done very well, also; you have learned well."

Then she looked at the oldest, whose name was Matthew, and said, "Matthew, may I ask you some questions also?"

"I am very willing," he answered.

"Then I will ask you if anything ever existed before God did?"

"No," he answered, "for God is eternal; nor is there anything that existed, besides Himself, before the beginning of the first day. 'For in six days the Lord made the heavens and the earth, the sea, and all that is in them.'"

Exod. 20:11

"What do you think of the Bible?"

"It is the holy Word of God."

2 Tim. 3:16;
Heb. 4:12

"Is there anything written in it that you cannot understand?"

"Yes, a great deal."

"What do you do when you come to the places that you don't understand?"

THE WORD OF GOD

"I remind myself that God is wiser than I am. I also pray and ask Him if He will please let me understand everything in His Word that He knows will be for my good."

"What do you believe about the resurrection of the dead?"

"I believe that they will rise the same as they were buried—that is, the same in nature but not in body. I believe this for two good reasons. First, I believe it because God has promised it, and second, I believe it because He is able to accomplish it."

1 Cor. 15:20,
42-46; Phil. 3:21;
1 John 3:2

Prudence Admonishes the Boys

Then Prudence said, "You have answered well." And looking at all of the boys, she said, "You must continue to be attentive to your mother;

she can still teach you more. It is also important that you listen attentively to whatever edifying conversation you might hear from others, because it is for your sakes that they talk about these good things. Be careful also to learn what you can from both the heavens and the earth. Most important, however, you must meditate frequently upon that Book that brought your father to his decision to become a pilgrim. As for me, my young men, I will teach you whatever I can while you are here, and I will be very happy to try to answer any questions you may have that serve the purpose of godly edification."

Josh. 1:8

CHAPTER 25

❖❖❖❖❖❖❖❖❖❖❖❖❖

Mercy and Mr. Brisk

After the pilgrims had been there for about a week, a young man whose name was Mr. Brisk came to visit Mercy. He was a culturally sophisticated man who professed the faith but who also stayed closely attached to the world. He came on several occasions to see Mercy, offering her his love and affection. Now Mercy had a very lovely countenance, and this made her all the more alluring to him.

Mercy had a way of continually keeping herself busy doing things. When she finished doing the necessary things for herself, she would find things to do for others, such as making socks and other items of clothing for those who had need. Mr. Brisk had no idea what she did with the things she made and seemed to be very impressed with the fact that he never saw her idle. He thought to himself, "I'll bet she would make a wonderful housewife."

In the meantime, Mercy told the women who lived in the House about Mr. Brisk. She asked them about him since they knew him better than she did. They told her that he was a very busy young man who professed to be religious, but that they feared that he was a stranger to the real power that comes from true faith in God. 2 Tim. 3:5

"If that is the case," said Mercy, "I will no

289

longer set my sights on him, for I never intend to have a weight tied to my soul."

Then Prudence told her that she would not need to do anything to discourage him; if she continued doing what she was already doing to help the poor, his interest would surely be cooled quickly enough.

So the next time he came and found Mercy working away, making things for the poor, he asked, "What? Are you always at it?"

"Yes," she replied, "either for myself or for others."

"And what can you earn in a day?" he asked.

"Oh, I do these things 'that I may be rich in good deeds.' For those who do these things 'will lay up treasure for themselves as a firm foundation for the coming age, so that they may take hold of the life that is truly life.'"

"Why? What do you do with them?" he asked.

"I clothe the naked," she replied.

At that, his countenance fell, and he never again visited her after that. When someone asked him why he had stopped visiting her, he answered that Mercy, while undeniably a pretty girl, was overly preoccupied with the problems of the poor.

After he had left Mercy, Prudence asked her, "Did I not tell you that Mr. Brisk would soon forsake you? He will probably even say negative things about you. For in spite of his apparent faith in God and his seeming love for you, there is such a difference between his disposition and yours that I doubt you will ever see him again."

"Though I have not spoken to anyone about this before, I have had more than one young man take an interest in me," said Mercy. "But even though none of them found fault with me personally, they have not appreciated my priorities. Therefore, we could never agree."

1 Tim. 6:18-19

Matt. 25:36

"In these days," responded Prudence, "people appreciate Mercy in name only. The practice, which is demonstrated by your priorities, finds few adherents."

"Well," said Mercy, "if no one will have me, I will die single, and my values will have to take the place of a husband. For I cannot change my nature, and to marry someone who is at cross-purposes with me in this matter is something I intend never to do as long as I live. I had a sister whose name was Bountiful. She married one of these base characters, and she and her husband never got along. My sister had resolved to continue showing kindness to the poor. Her husband deeply resented her resolve to follow Christ and the way of the Cross, and he eventually turned her out on the street."

1 Cor. 7:34

"And I suppose he was a believer too?" asked Prudence.

"Yes, such that he was. And today the world is full of his type—but I will have none of them!"

Matthew Gets Sick

Now Matthew, Christiana's oldest son, became sick, and his sickness became very serious. He was afflicted with terrible abdominal pains that sometimes were excruciating.

Not too far away there lived a man named Dr. Skill. He was a physician of longstanding prominence, so Christiana sent for him, and he came right away. When he entered the room and examined the boy, he concluded that he was suffering from

An illness of conscience Gripes. Dr. Skill asked Christiana, "What has Matthew eaten lately?"

"Eaten?" said Christiana. "Why, nothing but wholesome food."

Then the physician answered, "This boy has been tampering with something that is now lying undigested within him, and it will not go away by itself. He must be purged of it or else he will die."

"Mother," said Samuel, "what was it that Matthew gathered up and ate just as we were leaving the Gate at the beginning of the way? You know, there was an orchard to the left of the way, just over the wall. Some of the trees hung over the wall, and my brother picked them and ate the fruit."

"This is true, my child," said Christiana, "he did take some of that fruit and eat it. He was a naughty boy, and I scolded him for it, but he didn't listen to me."

"I knew he had eaten something that was not wholesome food," said Dr. Skill. "And to tell you the truth, that fruit is the most dangerous of all. It is the Fruit of Beelzebub's Orchard. I wonder why nobody warned you about it—many have died from it."

Then Christiana began to cry, and she said, "Oh, naughty boy! Oh, careless mother! What will I do for my son?"

"Come," said Dr. Skill, "don't give up hope; the boy may end up well again, but he must be cleansed and purified of the poison and vomit it up."

"Please, sir," pleaded Christiana, "do the best that you can with him, whatever it costs."

Dr. Skill's Medicine

"No," replied Dr. Skill, "my price will be reasonable." So he made a mixture that would cleanse Matthew's system and induce vomiting, but it was too weak. It was made from the blood of a goat, the ashes of a heifer, and some hyssop juice.

Heb. 10:1-3
Heb. 9:13, 19

When Dr. Skill saw that that remedy was too weak, he made another one better suited for his purpose. It was made *"ex carne et sanguine Christi"* (you know that physicians give strange Medicines to their patients!). It was made into Pills, along with a Promise or two and a proportional amount of Salt. He was to take them three at a time, fasting, in a cup of the tears of repentance.

Heb. 9:14
Latin for "from [the] body and blood of Christ."
John 6:54-57
Mark 9:49

When this remedy was prepared and brought to the boy, even though his cramps were severe, he was repulsed by it and didn't want to take it. "Come, come," said the physician, "you must take it."

"It turns my stomach," said the boy.

"I must have you take it," said his mother.

"I will vomit it up again," said the boy.

Turning to Dr. Skill, Christiana asked, "Sir, how does it taste?"

"It doesn't taste bad," he replied.

Then she touched one of the Pills with the tip of her tongue. "Oh, Matthew," she said, "this Medicine is sweeter than honey. If you love your mother, if you love your brothers, if you love Mercy, if you love your life, take it!"

Ps. 19:10;
119:103

So after a lot of fuss and a prayer for God's blessing upon it, Matthew took it. He responded favorably to it, and it purged out the poison and caused him to sleep peacefully. He was completely rid of the cramps, and in a short time, though still weak, he was able to walk with a cane. He went from room to room, talking with Prudence, Piety, and Charity about his sickness and how he was healed.

So after he was completely well, Christiana asked Dr. Skill, "Sir, what can I pay you for your efforts in caring for my child?"

He answered, "You must pay the Master of the College of Physicians, according to the rules made in that case and the services rendered."

Heb. 13:11-16

"But, sir," she asked, "what else is this Pill good for?"

"It is a universal Pill," he answered. "It is good for fighting all the diseases that pilgrims are susceptible to. When it is prepared well, it can keep you in good health at all times."

"Please, sir," said Christiana, "make me up twelve boxes of them. For, if I can take these, I will never look for another Medicine."

"These Pills are good to prevent diseases as well as to use as a cure once one is sick," said Dr. Skill. "Yes, I dare say, and will stand by my word, that if a person will use this Medicine as he should, it will make him live forever. But, Christiana, you must take these Pills only as I prescribe them. If you don't take them this way, they will do you no good at all." So he gave the Pills to Christiana for her own use as well as for her sons and for Mercy. He then warned Matthew to be careful not to eat any more green plums, and, after giving each of them a kiss, he went his way.

In a glass of the tears of repentance

Prudence Answers Matthew's Questions

As was told you before, Prudence had offered the boys the opportunity to come and ask her any questions they might have at any time, and she would try to answer them. Matthew, who had been sick, came and asked her why good Medicine usually tasted bad.

"To show how unwelcome the Word of God and its effects are to a carnal heart," she answered.

"Why does the Medicine, if it works well, have to purge us and cause us to vomit?"

"To show that the Word, when it is allowed to work effectively, cleanses the heart and the mind. Don't you see, what Medicine does to the body, the Word does to the soul." 2 Tim. 3:16

Looking at the fireplace, he next asked,

"What can we learn by seeing the flame of our fire lap upward while the sun's beams shoot downward?"

"By seeing the flames of fire go upward, we are taught to ascend to Heaven by fervent and hot desires. And by seeing the sun send down its heat and its beams of light and warmth downward, we are taught that the Savior of the world, though very high, reaches down with His grace and love to us below."

"Where do the clouds get their water?" asked Matthew.

"From the oceans," replied Prudence.

"What can we learn from this?"

"That ministers should get their doctrine from God."

"Why do the clouds empty themselves upon the earth?"

"To show that ministers should give out to the world the knowledge God has given them."

"Why is the rainbow caused by the sun?"

"To show that the covenant of God's grace has been been made effective for us by Christ."

"Why do springs come from the sea to us through the earth?" asked Matthew.

"To show that the Grace of God comes to us through the Body of Christ," answered Prudence.

"Why do some springs rise out of the tops of high hills?"

"To show that the Spirit of grace shall spring up in the lives of some who are great and mighty,

GREAT Grace

as well as in many who are poor and lowly."

"Why does fire attach itself to the wick of a candle?" asked Matthew.

"To show us that unless grace is kindled in the heart, there will be no true light of life in us."

"Why are the wick and the wax of the candle spent in keeping the candle lit?"

"To show that body and soul, and all we have, should be at the service of, and constantly spending themselves to keep the grace of God within us well maintained."

"Why does the pelican pierce her own breast with her bill?" asked Matthew.

"To nourish her young ones with her own blood," replied Prudence. "Likewise, Christ, the Blessed One, loved his young, his people, so much Rom. 5:8 that He saved them from death by His blood."

"What can we learn from hearing the cock crowing?"

"We can learn to remember Peter's sin and Luke 22:60-62 Peter's repentance. The cock's crowing tells us also that the day is dawning. Let it therefore remind you that the great and terrible day of God's judgment is before us."

They Prepare to Be on Their Way

It had now been a month since they had come to the Lodge, and they told those of the House that this would be a good time for them to journey on. Then Joseph said to his mother, "You should be sure to send a message to the House of Mr. Interpreter and ask him to allow Mr. Greatheart to be sent to us so that he may be our guide for the rest of our journey."

The weak may be used sometimes to call the strong to prayer.

"A good suggestion, son," she said; "I had almost forgotten." So she wrote a letter and asked Mr. Watchful, the gatekeeper, to find someone who would take it directly to her good friend, the Interpreter. When the Interpreter had received the message and had read the request, he said to the messenger, "Go, tell them that I will send him."

When the family members of the Lodge saw that the pilgrims had reason to go forward, they called the entire household together to give thanks to their King for sending such good guests to them. After doing this, they said to Christiana, "May we, as is our custom with pilgrims, show you something that you may meditate on when you are on your way?"

Eve's Apple

So they took Christiana, her children, and Mercy into the closet and showed them one of the Apples that Eve had eaten. She had also given it to her husband, thus causing them both to be cast out of Paradise. "What do you think this is?" asked Prudence.

Gen. 3:6

"It is either food or poison, I don't know which," answered Christiana. So they explained it to her, and she marveled.

Rom. 7:24

Jacob's Ladder

Next they took them to see Jacob's ladder, and right at that same time, there happened to be *Gen. 28:12* some angels climbing it. So they all watched with great interest. They were on their way to another place when James said to his mother, "Please ask them if we can stay here a little longer, for this is fascinating." So they turned back again and stood *John 1:51* gazing at this sight for awhile longer.

A Golden Anchor

After a while they were taken into a place where a golden Anchor was hanging. Christiana was instructed to take it down, and Prudence said, "Take it with you; it is absolutely necessary that you do so because you must lay hold of what you find inside the veil and be able to stand steadfast in the event *Heb. 6:19* of turbulent weather." So they gladly received it.

Abraham's Sacrifice

Next they took them to the mount upon which *Gen. 22* our father Abraham had offered up his son Isaac. They were shown the altar, the wood, the fire, and the knife, which have remained to be seen there to this day. When they saw this sight, they raised their hands in praise and exclaimed, "Oh! what a man was Abraham! He had such a great love for his Master; and he demonstrated such great self-denial."

In the Dining Room

After they had shown them all these things, Prudence took them into the dining room where there was a harpsichord. She picked it up and

began to play on it, turning what she had
shown them into this song,

"Eve's Apple we have shown you;
Of that keep quite aware.
You've seen Jacob's ladder too,
At angels you did stare.
An Anchor for you is meant;
But don't let these suffice
Until with Abra'm you present
Your highest sacrifice."

Great-heart Returns to Guide the Pilgrims

Now about this time someone knocked at the
door. The gatekeeper opened it, and there was
Great-heart. Those inside the House were filled
with joy when they saw him again, for his
appearance brought to their minds afresh his victory over Grim Bloody-man, the Giant, and also
their deliverance from the Lions.

Then Great-heart said to Christiana and Mercy,
"My Lord has sent provisions to refresh you on
your way—a Bottle of Wine, some parched Corn,
and several Pomegranates. He has also sent the
boys some Figs and Raisins."

When it was time for them to resume their
journey, Prudence and Piety walked with them
out to the Gate, and Christiana asked the gatekeeper if anyone had gone by that way lately. He
answered, "Only one who went by some time
ago and said that there had been a great robbery
committed on the King's High-way, on which
you are traveling. But the thieves have been
caught and will shortly stand trial."

When they heard this, Christiana and Mercy
became fearful, but Matthew said, "Mother, there
is nothing to fear as long as Mr. Great-heart is
our guide."

The Gatekeeper's Blessing

Then Christiana said to the gatekeeper, "Sir, I owe a debt of gratitude to you for all the kindness that you have shown me since I came here, and you have also been very loving to my sons. I don't know what I can do to repay your kindness, but please accept this small gift as a token of my appreciation. So she put a small gold coin in his hand.

And bowing to her, he said, "'Let your garments always be white, and let your head lack no oil.' Let Mercy live and not die, and don't let her works be few."

Then to the boys he said, "Flee the evil desires of youth, pursue godliness with those who are sober and wise; then you will make your mother's heart happy and receive praise from all of those who are serious-minded." So they thanked the gatekeeper and went on their way.

Eccles. 9:8

2 Tim. 2:22

1 Tim. 6:11

CHAPTER 26

◆◆◆◆◆◆◆◆◆◆◆◆◆◆

The Country Birds

Now I saw in my dream that they went forward until they had come to the brow of the Hill. Suddenly Piety cried out, "Oh! I forgot to give Christiana and her friends what I had intended to give them. I will run back and get it." While she was running back, Christiana could hear a most fascinating and melodious song. It was coming from a grove, off the right side of the way, not too far ahead. The words were much like these:

*"Through all my life is Your favor
So clearly shown to me,
That in Your house forevermore
My dwelling-place shall be."*

Ps. 23:6

And listening more, she thought she heard someone else answer, singing,

*"Why is the Lord our God so good?
His mercy is forever sure;
His truth has always firmly stood
And will from age to age endure."*

After hearing this, Christiana asked Prudence where the songs were coming from. "They are Birds that are native to our Country," explained

Song of Sol.
2:11-12

Prudence. "They rarely sing these songs, but in the springtime when the flowers appear and the sun shines warmly, you can hear them all day long. I often go out to listen to them and frequently keep tame ones in our House. They provide fine, uplifting companionship when we are feeling depressed. They also make the woods and the groves and the lonely places pleasant to be in."

Piety Gives a Gift
By this time Piety had returned. "Look," she said to Christiana, "I have brought you a record of all the things that you have seen at our House. When you start to forget them, for your edification and encouragement you can look at this and be refreshed in your memory once again."

Lessons in the Valley of Humiliation
After this they began to descend the Hill into the Valley of Humiliation. It was a steep Hill and the way was slippery, but, being very

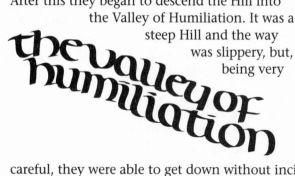

careful, they were able to get down without incident. Once they were down in the Valley, Piety said to Christiana, "This is the place where Christian, your husband, met with the foul Fiend, Apollyon. I know that you couldn't help but hear about the dreadful battle they had here. But you mustn't be afraid; you have Greatheart to conduct you and to be your guide, and we trust you will have an easier time than your husband did."

After Prudence and Piety had prayed for their trip and released them into the hands of Great-heart, their guide, he went ahead, and they followed close behind him. "We do not need to be afraid of this Valley," said Great-heart, "for there is nothing here that can hurt us, unless we invite it. It is true that Christian met Apollyon here and had a grievous battle, but that fight was the consequence of the slips he had made on his way down the Hill. Those who lose their footing there must expect battles here. This Valley has been given quite a bad name because of this fact. The average person, when he hears that some frightening thing has befallen a person in such a place as this, believes that the place is haunted with some foul Fiend or Evil Spirit. In truth, it is because of what they have done that such things befall them. This Valley of Humiliation is, in and of itself, as fruitful a place as any that the birds fly over. I am convinced, if we could somehow find it, there is something here that will confirm what I have said about why Christian was so severely afflicted in this place."

Then James said to his mother, "Look, there is a Monument standing over there, and it looks as if something is written on it. Let's go and see what it is."

So they went to the Monument and found this inscription on it: "Let Christian's loss of footing

on his way here, and the battles he fought in this place, be a warning to all who come after him."

"See there," said Great-heart, "didn't I tell you that there would be something in this vicinity that would indicate the reason why Christian was so hard-pressed in this place?" Then turning to Christiana, he said, "This is not a bad reflection on Christian any more than on many others who have likewise suffered. For it is easier going up this Hill than it is going down, and that can be said of very few hills in all these parts of the world. But we dare not accuse the good man; he is now at rest, and he did have a courageous victory over his enemy. Let Him who dwells on high grant that we fare no worse than he when we are tried.

"Now back again to this Valley of Humiliation: It is the best and most fruitful piece of ground in all these parts. It is fertile ground, and, as you can see, it is filled with Meadows. If one comes here in the summertime, as we do now, and doesn't know what lies ahead, but only knows what he can presently see, he will find it delightful. Look how green this Valley is and how lovely all the lilies are. Actually, I have known many from lowly occupations who have come out of this Valley in good condition. For 'God opposes the proud but gives grace to the humble.' It is a very fruitful soil, indeed, and produces fruit bountifully. Some have even wished that the remainder of the way to their Father's House were like this so that they might not be troubled any further with Hills or Mountains to climb up and down. But the way is the way, and it cannot be changed by our desires; eventually there will be an end."

Now as they continued to walk along and talk, they saw a Boy feeding his father's sheep. Although the Boy wore ragged clothing, he seemed full of life and happiness. He was sitting

Song of Sol. 2:1

Prov. 3:34;
James 4:6;
1 Pet. 5:5

Mark 4:1-9

by himself singing a song. "Listen to what the Shepherd Boy is singing," said Great-heart. They could hear him singing,

"He that is down needs fear no fall;
He that is low, no pride:
He that is humble ever shall
Have God to be his guide.

With what I have I am content
A little bit or much;
Contentment, Lord, is still my bent
Because You do save such.

Affluence to them a burden is
Who join the pilgrim's quest;
Here little, but hereafter bliss
From age to age is best."

Phil. 4:12-13
Matt. 19:24
Heb. 13:5

Then their guide said to them, "Do you hear what he has said? I will dare to say that this Boy lives a happier life and enjoys more of that Herb called Hearts-ease, than the one who is clad in silk and velvet. But let me continue with what I was telling you before.

"Our Lord once had a Country Cottage in this Valley and He very much loved to be here. He also loved to walk in these Meadows because the air is so pleasant, and the place is so free from the noise and hubbub of this life. All other places are full of noise and confusion, but in the Valley of Humiliation one can find freedom and solitude. Here also, he will not be so easily hindered in his times of meditation as in other places. This is a Valley that nobody but those who love a pilgrim's life will walk in. Although Christian had the misfortune of meeting Apollyon and fighting him for his life, in earlier times pilgrims have met angels here; they have also found pearls and have found words of life.

Hos. 12:4-5

"I mentioned that our Lord used to have a Country Cottage and that He loved to walk here. I will add that He has left a yearly revenue to the People who love these grounds and delight to walk in them. At certain times it is to be faithfully paid them for support; it serves to encour-

Matt. 11:28-30 age them on in their pilgrimage."

As they went on, Samuel said to Mr. Greatheart, "Sir, I can see that my father and Apollyon had their battle in this Valley, but where exactly did it take place since this Valley looks so large?"

"Your father had that battle with Apollyon at a place that still lies before us. It is in a narrow passage just beyond Forgetful Green. And, indeed, that place is the most dangerous place in all these parts. For if, at any time, the pilgrims meet with any violence, it is when they have forgotten the mercies they have received and how unworthy they are to have received them. This is the place where others have also been hard-pressed. But we can talk more about it when we come to it; for I am sure that there remains to this day some sign of the battle or some Monument that will testify that such a battle took place."

The Valley Suits Mercy Well

"I think I am as well in this Valley as I have been anywhere else in all our journey," said Mercy. "I

Humility is a think the place suits my spirit well. I love to be
sweet grace. in such places where there is no noisy rattling of coaches or the rumbling of wheels. I think it is possible here for one to think, without being disturbed about such things as who he is, where he has come from, what he has accomplished, and for what purpose the King has called him. Here one may his heart humbled and broken and his spirit melted until he has 'eyes like the

Song of Sol. 7:4 pools in Heshbon.' 'When they walk through the

Valley of Weeping it will become a place of
springs where pools of blessing and refreshment
collect after rains!' This is the Valley that the   Ps. 84:6
King will give to His own for vineyards. Follow-   Hos. 2:15
ing his encounter with Apollyon, Christian could
sing, and so it is with all His People who go
through this Valley."

"This is true," said Great-heart. "I have gone
through this Valley many times, and have never
been better off than when I was here. I have also
been a guide to many pilgrims, and they have
confessed the same experience. 'This is the one I
esteem: he who is humble and contrite in spirit,
and trembles at my word.'"   Isa. 66:2

A Memorial to Christian's Battle in the Valley

After a time, they came to the place where Christian's battle had been fought. Then Great-heart
said to the pilgrims, "This is the place; on this
ground Christian stood, and from up there Apollyon came against him. And, look—didn't I tell
you—here is some of your husband's blood lying
upon these stones to this very day. Also, notice,
the pieces of Apollyon's broken arrows. See how
the ground is still disturbed, and how even some
of the stones are split because of their blows.
Truly, Christian stood like a man and
was every bit as valiant

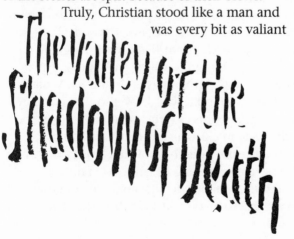

The Valley of the Shadow of Death

as Hercules himself would have been if he had been here. After Apollyon had been beaten, he retreated to the next Valley, the one that we will come to in a short time; it is called the Valley of the Shadow of Death."

"Look over there. Do you see the Monument?" Since it stood on the side of the way just a short distance ahead of them, they walked quickly over to it. They saw that it had some engraving on it which heralded Christian's battle and subsequent victory over his foe. It read:

Close to here was a battle fought,
So strange, and yet most true;
Christian and Apollyon sought
Each other to subdue.
The man so bravely took command,
He made the Fiend to fly;
Of which a Monument I stand,
The same to testify.

Into the Valley of the Shadow of Death
After they had passed by this place, they came to the border of the Valley of the Shadow of Death. This Valley was longer than the other, a place strangely haunted with evil things, just as many have testified. But these pilgrims went through it more easily, not only because it was daylight, but also because Mr. Great-heart was their guide.

Upon entering the Valley, they thought that they heard the groanings of dead men. What a very great sound it was! They also thought they could hear words of bitter lamentation by some who were in extreme torment. These things made the boys tremble in fear; Christiana and Mercy grew pale and began to feel faint.

But their guide encouraged them, and they were able to go on a little farther. They then

thought that they felt the ground begin to shake
under them, as if it might give way because of a
hollow place beneath. And although they could
see none, they thought they could hear the hiss-
ing of serpents nearby. One of the boys asked,
"Aren't we at the end of this miserable place
yet?" But their guide told them to take courage
and to look carefully where they walked lest they
might be taken by some snare.

Meeting the Dangers of this Valley

Now James began to feel sick, but I think the
cause was nothing more than fear. His mother
gave him three of the Pills that Dr. Skill had prepared and something to drink to wash them
down. After taking the Pills, he began to revive,
and so they continued on until they came
to the middle of the Valley. Christiana
said, "I think I see something ahead
on the road; it is of a shape that I
have not seen before."

"Mother, what is it?" asked Joseph.
"An ugly thing, son; an ugly thing."
"But, mother, what is it like?"
"I cannot tell yet, but it is getting closer."

James 4:7

"Well, well," said Mr. Great-Heart. "Let those
who are most afraid stay close to me." So the
Fiend came closer, and Great-heart met it. But as
soon as it came to him, it vanished from sight.
Then they remembered what they had heard
some time before, "Resist the Devil, and he will
flee from you."

So, being relieved, they went on. They had
not gone far, however, when Mercy looked
behind her and saw something that seemed to
her to most closely resemble a Lion. It was
approaching them quickly with ferocious roars—
with every roar that it gave, the entire Valley

echoed. All their hearts ached except the heart of their guide, Great-heart, who put himself between the pilgrims and the Lion. The Lion stalked ever closer, and Great-heart stood ready for battle. When the Lion saw that there would be a resistance made, however, he drew back and came no farther.

1 Pet. 5:8-9

They again went on, and their guide went before them. They soon came to a place where there was a huge pit, which they calculated ran the entire breadth of the way. Before they could prepare themselves to cross it, a thick mist came over them, and darkness fell upon them so that they were unable to see. "Oh! now what are we going to do?" cried the pilgrims.

Exod. 14:13

"Do not be afraid. Stand firm," answered Great-heart. "Wait and see how this will be put to an end also." So they stayed there because their path was marred. Then they thought they heard more clearly the noises and rushing sounds of their enemies, and the fire and the smoke from the pit were also much more easily discerned.

Then Christiana turned to Mercy, saying, "Now I see what my poor husband went through. I have heard a lot about this place, but I have never been here before now. Poor man! He traveled by himself almost all the way through here at night, and these Fiends were busy harassing him continually as if they would tear him to pieces. Many have talked about it, but no one can tell what the Valley of the Shadow of Death is like unless they have been in it themselves. 'Only the person involved can know his own bitterness or joy—no one else can really share it.' To be here is a frightening thing."

Prov. 14:10

Ps. 107:23

"We are like those 'who do business on great waters,'" said Great-heart. "On the waves of the sea 'they mount up to the heavens, they go

down again to the depths; their soul melts
because of trouble.' This is like being in the heart   Ps. 107:26
of the sea. We are like the one who said, 'to the
roots of the mountains I sank down; the earth
beneath barred me in forever.' But, 'let him who   Jon. 2:6
walks in the dark, who has no light, trust in the
name of the Lord and rely on his God.' As for   Isa. 50:10
me, as I have already told you, I have gone
through this Valley often and have been much
more hard-pressed than this. As you can see I am
still alive. I have nothing to boast in since I am
not my own savior, but I do trust that we will be
safely delivered. Come, let us pray for light to
Him who can lighten our darkness and who can
rebuke not only this, but all the Devils in Hell."

So they cried and prayed, and God sent light
and deliverance. There was no longer anything
substantial to impede them from going forward
on their way. They were able to cross the pit, but
they still had not gotten through the Valley.
They continued on and were annoyed by the
loathsome stench of the place; the stink was nau-
seating. Then Mercy said to Christiana, "It is not
nearly as pleasant here as it was at the Gate or at
the Interpreter's or at the House where we last
slept."

"Oh," said one of the boys, "it is not so bad to
have to go through here once. Think what it
would be to have to stay here always! And, for all
I know, one reason we must go this way to the
House prepared for us, is so that our home will
seem all the sweeter to us."

"Well said, Samuel," said Great-heart. "Now
you are talking like a man."

"Well," Samuel replied, "if I ever get out of
here again, I think I will more highly prize the
light and the good way than I have ever before
in my entire life."

"We will be out of here before long," Great-heart responded.

So they went on, and Joseph said, "Can't we see the end of this Valley yet?"

"Watch your feet," said Great-heart, "for you will soon be among the snares." So they watched their feet as they went on, and, sure enough, they were troubled by the snares. While they were among the snares, they saw a man cast into the ditch on the left side of the way; his body lay mangled and torn. Then Great-heart said, "That is one who was going this way; his name was Heedless. He has been lying there for a long time. There was another one with him when he was killed whose name was Takeheed, but he escaped. You cannot imagine how many are killed in this area, yet people are still foolishly venturing to set out carelessly on their pilgrimage without a guide. Poor Christian! It is a wonder that he escaped this place, but his God loved him. And besides this, he had a good heart; if he had not, he never would have made it."

The Battle with Giant Maul

They were now approaching the end of the Valley, and as they were passing the cave that Christian had seen when he went by, a Giant named

Maul came out. Maul had destroyed some young pilgrims with his deceptive arguments and reason. He now called Great-heart by name and said to him, "How many times, Great-heart, have I forbidden you to do these things?"

"What things?" asked Great-heart.

"What things!" shouted the Giant. "You know what things, but I will now put an end to your trade!"

"But before we engage ourselves, let us understand fully why we are fighting," said Great-heart.

Christiana, Mercy, and the boys stood trembling and did not know what to do. Then the Giant said, "You rob the Country and rob it by the worst of thefts."

"You are speaking in generalities," replied Great-heart. "Come to the specifics, man."

"You practice the craft of kidnapping," said the Giant. "You gather up women and children and carry them into a strange Country; this weakens my master's kingdom."

God's ministers are seen as kidnappers.

"But now," replied Great-heart, "I am a servant of the God of Heaven; my business is to persuade sinners to repent. I am commanded to make every endeavor to reach men, women, and children and 'to open their eyes and turn them from darkness to light, and from the power of Satan to God.' If this is the grounds for your quarrel, let us fight as soon as you are ready."

Col. 1:13
Acts 26:18

At this the Giant stepped forward, and Great-heart went to meet him. As he went, he drew his Sword; the Giant had a club. Without wasting any time they fell upon each other. At the first blow the Giant smashed Great-heart down on one knee. The badly shaken little band of pilgrims began to cry when they saw it. But Great-heart recovered and, with great determination, he wounded the Giant's arm. They fought like

Weak folks' prayers sometimes help strong folks' cries.

this for an hour, and at the height of the conflict, heat came out of the Giant's nostrils like steam coming out of a boiling cauldron.

In exhaustion, they both sat down to rest, and Great-heart used the time to pray. The pilgrims did nothing but sigh and cry during the entire time that the battle lasted. After they had caught their breath and rested awhile, they commenced fighting again. Great-heart, with a very powerful blow, sent the Giant reeling on the ground. "No, hold up, let me recover," Maul said. So Great-heart let him get up again, and they began their fight once more. At one point, when Great-heart realized that the Giant had just barely missed smashing his skull with his club, he ran toward the Giant with great fervency of spirit and pierced him under the fifth rib. The Giant began to faint so that he could no longer hold up his club. Then Great-heart gave a second blow that took the Giant's head off. The pilgrims rejoiced, and Great-heart also praised God for the deliverance that He had brought.

1 Sam. 17:50-51

After this, they erected a Monument and put the Giant's head on it. Beneath it they wrote for passersby these words:

He who wore this head was one
Who would pilgrims misuse;
He stopped their way, sparing none,
And did them all abuse.
Until I, Great-heart, arose,
The pilgrims' guide to be;
Until I did him oppose,
Who was their enemy.

CHAPTER 27
• • • • • • • • • • • • • •

They Reflect on Great-heart's Victory

Now I saw that they went on to the rise that had been formed to be a Lookout for pilgrims. From this same place Christian had first caught sight of his brother, Faithful. So they sat down here and rested. They also ate and drank and celebrated their deliverance from such a dangerous enemy. As they sat and ate, Christiana asked their guide if he had been hurt at all in the battle. "Only a few wounds," replied Great-heart, "and yet, rather than being a handicap, it is presently a proof of my love to my Master and to you. It will be a means, by God's grace, to increase my reward; so don't feel bad for me."   2 Cor. 4

"But weren't you afraid, Great-heart, when you saw him coming at you with his club?" asked Christiana.

"It is my duty to distrust my own ability," replied Great-heart, "so that I might have full reliance on Him who is stronger than all."

"But what did you think when he caught you with that first blow and sent you to the ground?" asked Christiana.

"Well, I remembered that my Master was treated thus, and yet it was He Who conquered in the end."

"You all think what you please," said Matthew, "but I will tell you what I think. I think God has been wonderfully good to us, both in bringing us out of this Valley and in delivering us out of the hand of this enemy. I see no reason why we   Ps. 18:17

should ever distrust our God again. In a place like this He has given us this incredible testimony of His love."

Rom. 8:31-39

Mr. Honest

After this they got up and proceeded on their way. Now, not far ahead of them stood an oak tree, and when they came up to it, they saw beneath it a pilgrim who was fast asleep. They could tell that he was a pilgrim by his clothing, his staff, and his belt. So Great-heart awakened him, and the old gentleman lifted up his eyes and cried out, "What's the matter?

One saint sometimes takes another for his enemy.

Who are you? What is your business here?"

"Come, sir, don't be so upset. There are none here but friends." But the old man got up, and, standing his ground, demanded what their business was.

"My name is Great-heart. I am the guide of these pilgrims who are going to the Celestial Country."

Then the man, whose name was Mr. Honest, said, "Have mercy on me. I feared that you were part of the band who some time ago robbed Little-faith of his money. But now that I have my bearings again, I can tell that you are more honest than they."

"Tell me," said Great-heart, "what would or could you have done to help yourself if, indeed, we were part of that group."

"Done?" said Mr. Honest. "Why, I would have fought for as long as I had breath left in me, and if I had done so, I am sure you could not have prevailed over me, because a Christian can never be overcome unless he yields himself to it."

2 Pet. 2:20; 1 John 4:4

"Well spoken, Mr. Honest," said Great-heart. "By this I know that you are right on the mark, for you have spoken the truth."

"And I can tell by your statement that you know what a true pilgrimage is," said Mr. Honest, "for all the others think that we will be the most quickly overcome of all."

"Well," said Great-heart, "since we have so happily met one another, I really want to know your name and where you have come from."

"I cannot tell you my name, but I came from the town of Stupidity. It is not too far from the City of Destruction."

"Oh!" exclaimed Great-heart, "are you then that countryman? I have half a guess who you are. Are you old Mr. Honesty?"

The old man blushed a little and replied, "Not Honesty in the abstract, but 'Honest' is my name. I can only wish that my nature will agree with what I am called. But sir, how could you guess that I am such a man, since I came from such a place?"

"I heard your name come before my Master," replied Great-heart. "For He knows all the things that are done on the earth. But I have often wondered how any should be able to find their way from your place since that town is even worse than the City of Destruction."

"Yes," said Mr. Honest, "since our town is shaded from the sun, we are more cold and senseless. But even if a man were in a mountain of ice, if the Sun of righteousness will rise upon him, his frozen heart will begin to thaw. And this is how it has been with me."

"I believe you, Mr. Honest," said Great-heart. "I believe you, and I know that what you say is true."

Then the old gentleman saluted all the pilgrims, and gave them a loving holy kiss. He asked all of them their names and how they had fared since they had first set out on their pilgrimage.

"You may have heard of me," said Christiana. "Good Christian was my husband, and these four were his children."

But you cannot imagine how excited the old gentleman was at hearing this. He skipped, laughed, and blessed them with a thousand good wishes, saying, "I have heard a great deal about your husband and his travels, and also the wars that he experienced on his pilgrimage. May it be a comfort to you to know that his name is revered and resounds all over these parts of the world. His faith, his courage, his patient endurance, and his sincerity in all that he undertook, have made his name famous."

Then he turned to Christiana's sons and asked them their names, and they told him. He said to them, "Matthew, be like Matthew the publican, not in vice, but in virtue. Samuel, be like Samuel the prophet, a man of faith and prayer. Joseph, be like Joseph in Potiphar's house, pure, and one who flees from temptation. And James, you be like James, the just, and like James, the brother of our Lord." Then they told him about Mercy, about how she had left her town and her family to come along with Christiana and her sons. Upon hearing this the old man said, "Mercy is your name, and by mercy you will be sustained and carried through all the difficulties that will assault you in your way until you come to see face to face the very Fountain of Mercy, in whom you will find consolation." All this time Great-heart was greatly pleased and was smiling upon his new companion.

Matt. 10:3
Ps. 99:6

Gen. 39

Acts 15:13;
Gal. 1:19

Poor Mr. Fearing

Now, as they began to walk along together, Great-heart asked the old gentleman if he knew someone called Mr. Fearing who had come out of his parts to go on a pilgrimage.

"Yes, very well," he replied. "He was a man who had a grasp of spiritual things within him, but he was one of the most troublesome pilgrims that I have ever met in all my days."

"Yes, I can see you knew him, for you have given an accurate portrayal of him."

"Indeed, I did know him!" said Mr. Honest. "I was a close companion of his. I was with him most of the time, and when he first began to think of what would come upon us hereafter, I was with him."

"I was his guide from my Master's House to the Gates of the Celestial City," said Great-heart.

"Then you knew him to be a troublesome one."

"Yes, I did; but I could bear it well, because men of my calling are often entrusted with conducting those of his sort."

"Well then, please let us hear a little about him and how he handled himself under your guidance."

"Why, he was always afraid that he would fall short of his desired destination," said Great-heart. "Anyone who spoke with the least bit of opposition in his voice frightened him greatly. I heard that he lay down and cried at the Slough of Despond for more than a month. He didn't dare venture forward, even though he saw several others go over before him. He wouldn't go even when they offered him a helping hand. But neither would he go back again. He said he would die if he didn't reach the Celestial City, and, yet, he was dejected at every difficulty. He stumbled at every straw that anyone cast his way.

Well, after he had lain there at the Slough of Despond for a great while, one bright, sunny morning—I don't know how—he finally ventured on and got over. Once over, however, he could scarcely believe it. I think he had a 'Slough of Despond' in his mind, a slough that he carried with him everywhere he went; how else could he have been the way he was?

"At any rate, he finally came up to the Gate that stands at the beginning of this way, and he stood there also for quite some time before he mustered the courage to knock. Whenever the Gate opened, he would draw back and let others go in, saying he was not worthy. He had arrived at the Gate before them, but they went in ahead of him. The poor man would stand there shaking and shrinking back. It was heartbreaking, no doubt, to see him there. And yet, he still would not go back.

"At long last, he took the hammer that hung on the Gate into his hand, and he gave a small rap or two. When someone opened to him, he shrunk back just as he had done before. So the one who opened the Gate stepped out after him, and said, 'You trembling one, what do you want?' With that he fell to the ground. The one who asked the question marveled to see him so faint and said, 'Be at peace, and get up, for I have opened the door to you. Come on in, for you are blessed.' He got up off the ground and went in, still trembling. Once inside, he was ashamed to show his face. After he had been entertained there for awhile, however, he was encouraged to go on his way, and they told him what direction he should take.

"So he went on until he came to our House, but when he arrived at the door of my Master, the Interpreter, he behaved just as he had done at the Gate. He lay there in the cold for a good while before he gathered enough courage to call on us. Yet, he still wouldn't go back, even though the nights at that time were long and cold. He had been given a note of introduction written to my Master telling him to receive him, to grant him the comfort of his House, and to provide him a strong and valiant guide because he himself was such a chicken-hearted man. Yet, in spite of all this, he was afraid to call at the door. So he slept outside in different spots until the poor man nearly starved! His depression was so great that, even after he saw several others get in by simply knocking, he was still afraid to venture the risk.

"At last, I happened to look out of the window and saw a man pacing in front of the door, so I went out to him and asked him what he was doing. But—the poor man—tears were running down his face, and I could tell what he wanted. So I went back inside and told those inside the House about him, and we took the matter to our Lord. He sent me back out to ask him to come in, so I did; but I must say that I had to work to get him inside. Finally, he came in, and my Lord was very gentle and loving with him. There was only a little food left on the table, but we put it on his platter to eat.

"When he presented his note, my Lord read it and then told him that his desire would be granted. So after he had been there for awhile, he began to feel encouraged and was able to relax and to be a little more comfortable. My Master, I am sure you know, has a very tender heart, especially toward those who are afraid. Therefore He dealt with him in the manner that would most encourage him.

"Well, after we showed him some sights around the place, he was ready to resume his journey toward the City once again. My Lord, just as He had done for Christian, gave him a Bottle of Spirits and some good food to eat. Then we set forth together, and I went ahead of him. He didn't have much to say; he just spent a lot of the time sighing.

"When we had come to the place where the three men had been hanged, he said that he feared that might be his end also. But he seemed happy when he saw the Cross and the tomb. He wanted to stay awhile and look, and after doing so, he was even somewhat cheerful for a time. When he came to the Hill Difficulty, it wasn't even an issue to him. He wasn't very afraid of the Lions either. You realize, of course, that his trouble was not with those types of obstacles; his fear had to do with whether or not he would find acceptance.

"I got him in at the House Beautiful, I think, before he was ready. Once he was inside, I introduced him to the women of the place, but he was ashamed to socialize with them. He wanted to be alone much of the time. Even so, he liked to hear good conversation and would often stand behind the door and listen. He also loved to look at items of historical interest. Once he saw them, he would ponder them in his mind for quite some time. He told me afterwards that even though he did not have the courage to ask to come in, he had loved being in the Houses that he had visited, both the one at the Gate and the Interpreter's House.

"When we left the House Beautiful and went

down the Hill into the Valley of Humiliation, he
handled it as well as I had ever seen any man in
my life. He didn't care how low he might have to
go, just so long as he would be happy in the end.
Yes, I even think there was some kind of empa-
thy between that Valley and him; for I never saw
him better in all his pilgrimage than when
he was in that Valley. He would lie down
there and hug the ground and kiss
the very flowers that grew there.
Suddenly he was getting up every
morning at the crack of
dawn, discovering what he
could as he walked back and
forth there.

Lam. 3:22-30

House Beautiful

"But when he came to the
entrance of the Valley of the Shadow of Death, I
thought that I might lose him, not because of any
inclination to go back—he abhorred the thought
of that—but because he was ready to die of fear.
'Oh, the demons will take me! The demons will
take me!' he cried. I couldn't convince him other-
wise. He made such a racket and carried on so
irrationally that if they had heard him, they
would have been immediately encouraged to come
and fall upon us.

"I became keenly aware of the fact, however,
that this Valley was more quiet when he went
through it than at any other time in my experience. I suppose that the enemies here had been
specially checked by our Lord and commanded
not to meddle until Mr. Fearing had passed
through it.

"It would be wearisome to tell you all that
happened, so I will just mention a few more
incidents. When he had come to Vanity Fair,
I thought that he was going to fight with all the
men in the fair. I feared that we would both be

knocked over the head there, he was so intensely angry at their foolishness.

"He stayed awake on the Enchanted Ground with no problem. But when he had come to the River where there is no bridge, he once again became distraught. He cried out, 'Right here and now I am going to be drowned forever and never enjoy the comfort of seeing that face that I have come so many miles to see.'

"Once again I noticed something unusual. The water level was lower at this time than I had ever seen it in all my life. So finally he went over with the water barely ankle deep. Once he was on his way to the Gate, I called out a good-bye to him and wished him a happy reception at the Gate. So he smiled and said, 'I will; I will.' Then I left, and I didn't see him again."

They Evaluate Mr. Fearing

"Then it seemed to you that he was safe at last?" asked Mr. Honest.

"Yes, yes, I never had a doubt about him. He was a man of choice spirit; he just always kept himself so low that his life was burdensome to himself and troublesome to others. He was more conscious of sin than most, and he was so afraid of doing injury to others that he would often deny himself those things that were lawful. He simply refused to cause an offense."

Ps. 88

Rom. 14:21;
1 Cor. 8:13

"But what can the reason be that such a good man lived his life so much of the time in the dark?" asked Mr. Honest.

"The primary reason," replied Great-heart, "is that the wise God wills it that way. Some must

whistle, and some must weep. In the book of Reve-   Matt. 11:16-19
lation the saved are compared to a company of
musicians that play on their trumpets and harps
and sing their songs before the throne. Mr. Fearing   Rev. 8:2; 14:2-3
was one who played a bass. He and his friends
make doleful sounds like a tuba. Their sounds are
more sorrowful than those of other instruments.
Even so, some will say that the bass is the ground
of music. And, for me personally, I don't care
much at all for a profession that doesn't begin
with a heavy heart. When the musician intends to
put all his instruments in tune, the first string that
he usually touches is the bass. God also plays
upon this string first when He is tuning the soul
to Himself. But Mr. Fearing's problem was this—
he was unable to play any other music except this
kind until he got to the last part of his trip."

"It is clear from your account of him that he
was a very zealous man," said Mr. Honest. "Difficulties, Lions, or Vanity Fair—he feared none of
them at all. It was only sin, death, and Hell that
were a terror to him because he had some doubt
about his own share in the Celestial Country."

"You are right; those are the things that were his
troublemakers. And, as you have observed, they
arose not from a weakness of spirit as to the practical living of a pilgrim's life, but rather from a weakness of mind. I can easily believe that, like the
proverb, he would have bit a burning ember if it
had stood in his way. But the things which
oppressed him, no one was ever able to help him
shake off easily."

"Hearing about this Mr. Fearing has done me
good," interjected Christiana. "I thought nobody
was like me. But I can see that there is some resem-
blance between Mr. Fearing and myself. We only
differ in two things. He was so severely distressed
that he couldn't contain it; I can keep it to myself.

Also his distress was so heavy upon him that he was unable to even knock at the Houses that were provided for his relief; but my fear made me knock even louder."

"If I might also express myself," said Mercy, "I wish to say that I see something of him also in me. For I am always more afraid of the lake of fire and the loss of a place in paradise than I am of losing other things. I thought to myself, 'If only I may have the joy of having a place there!' It is sufficient for me to lose all the world to win it."

Then Matthew said, "Fear is something that made me think that I was far away from having within me what it takes to obtain real salvation. But if it was like this for a good man like him, would it not also go well with me?"

"No fears, no grace," said James. "And even though there is not always grace where there is a fear of Hell, yet there is certainly no grace where there is no fear of God."

"A good statement, James," said Great-heart. "You have hit the mark. For 'the fear of the Lord is the beginning of wisdom.' And it is a certainty that those who lack the beginning have neither the middle nor the end. But let us conclude our discussion of Mr. Fearing after sending him this farewell:

"Well, Mr. Fearing, you did fear
Your God, and were afraid
Of doing anything while here
That would have you betrayed.
And did you fear the lake and pit?
Would that others do so, too!
And as for those who lack your wit,
They will themselves undo."

Rev. 20:11-15

Luke 9:23-25;
Phil. 3:7-11

Ps. 111:10

CHAPTER 28

◆◆◆◆◆◆◆◆◆◆◆◆◆◆◆

The Opinions of Mr. Self-will

Now I saw in my dream that they continued talking among themselves. After Great-heart had finished his discussion of Mr. Fearing, Mr. Honest began to tell them about

MR SELF WILL

another man whose name was Mr. Self-will. "He ventured to be a pilgrim, but I doubt that he ever came in at the Gate that stands at the head of the Way."

"Did you ever talk to him about it?" asked Great-heart.

"Yes, several times; but he always resorted to acting according to his true nature—self-willed. He didn't care in the slightest what a man, or reason, or example had to say. He did what his own mind prompted him to do, and nothing else could sway him."

"Please, tell me," said Mr. Great-heart, "what were his principles? For I imagine you could perceive them."

"He believed that he could follow the vices as well as the virtues of pilgrims and that, in so doing, he would not jeopardize his salvation."

"Hmmm," said Great-heart. "If he had said that it is possible for the best of us to be guilty of having vices while at the same time partaking of the virtues of pilgrims, I would not fault him. For, indeed, we are not absolutely exempt from the power of any vice except by one condition—that we watch and strive against it. But I perceive that is not the case with him. If I understand you correctly, you mean that he was of the opinion that he had permission to be like this."

Rom. 7:21-25; 8:12

Rom. 6:1-2

"Yes, that is what I mean," said Mr. Honest. "This is how he believed, and what he believed was reflected in what he practiced."

"But what were his grounds for believing this?" asked Great-heart.

"Why, he said his basis was the Scriptures."

"I would appreciate it, Mr. Honest, if you would tell us a few of his arguments."

"All right, I will. He said that because David, God's beloved, had taken another man's wife, that he could therefore do the same. He said that having more than one woman was practiced by Solomon, and so therefore he was justified in doing likewise. He pointed out that Sarah and the godly midwives of Egypt had lied, as did Rahab who was saved, and that he could therefore do the same. He also said that because the disciples went and took an owner's donkey at their Master's command, that he could do likewise. He said that Jacob got his father's inheritance by cunning and deceit, and that therefore he would be justified in doing the same."

2 Sam. 11

1 Kings 11
Gen. 12:13;
Exod. 1:19;
Josh. 2:4-7

Mark 11:1-3

Gen. 27

"Lofty arguments indeed! Are you sure he believed this?"

"I have heard him debate his point; he always uses Scripture in his arguments, too."

"This is an opinion that isn't fit to be allowed in the world!" exclaimed Mr. Great-heart.

"I want to make sure you fully understand me. He didn't say that just anyone could do these things. He believed that only those who had the same virtues as those mentioned in Scripture should be allowed to do the same."

"But what could be a more false conclusion?" asked Great-heart. "What he is saying is that, just because good men have sinned out of their own weakness, he can presumptuously justify doing it himself. It is like saying, if a child, because of a sudden blast of wind, stumbles over a stone and falls down and gets muddy, he might as well decide to lie down and wallow in it like a hog. Who would have thought that anyone could become so blinded by the power of lust? But what is written has to be true, 'They will stumble because they will not listen to God's Word, nor obey it, and so this punishment must follow— that they will fall.' His supposition that those who addict themselves to their vices may also have the godly person's same virtues, is a delusion as strong as the other. "It is just as if a dog should say, 'I either have or am able to have the qualities of a baby because I chew on his messy diaper.' To chew on the sin of God's People is no sign of one who possesses their virtues. It is difficult for me to believe that one who holds this type of opinion can truly have faith or sincere love for Him. I know you have made strong objections to his opinions, but what does he have to say for himself?"

"Well," replied Mr. Honest, "he says that to do these things in accordance with one's beliefs demonstrates a lot more integrity than to do them while holding a contrary opinion."

"A very subtle and wicked answer," said Great-heart. "For while letting loose of the bridle on our lusts is bad when our convictions are against doing so, how much worse it is to sin and to argue that it is fine to do so! The first has

1 Pet. 2:8

Hos. 4:8

momentarily stumbled, while the second justifies his sin and walks straight into a snare."

"There are many who share this man's opinions but who do not have his boldness to speak," said Mr. Honest. "Sadly, it's because of pilgrims like these that pilgrims in general have such little esteem."

"What you say is certainly true," replied Great-heart, "and it is lamentable, but, nevertheless, the one who fears the King of paradise will be victorious over them all."

Other Unsteady Walks of Life

"There are certainly strange opinions in this world," said Christiana. "I know someone who said that he was certain he would have enough time to repent when it was his time to die."

"Those who hold his view are deceiving them-

unsteady walks of life

selves," Great-heart responded. "If that same person were given a week to run twenty miles in order to save his life, he wouldn't wait until the last hour to do it."

"This is correct," said Mr. Honest, "and yet so many of those who consider themselves pilgrims do that very thing. As you can see, I am an old man. I have been a traveler on this road for quite some time, and I have observed many things. Why, I have seen some who have set out as if they would set the world on fire, and yet they have died in the wilderness within a few days. They weren't able to catch even a glimpse of the Promised Land.

"I have also seen some who have shown no promise at all when they first set out; one would have doubted that they could survive even for a day. Yet, they have proved to be very good pilgrims. I have seen some that have run forward hastily, who have, after a short time, run right back again just as quickly. I have seem some who have spoken very highly of a pilgrim's life at first, but then, in a short time, have spoken just as strongly against it. I have heard some who, when they first set out for paradise, have said that there is undoubtedly such a place; then, when they have almost gotten there, they have come back again saying that it doesn't exist. I have heard some brag about what they will do when they face opposition, but who have, in the face of even a false alarm, abandoned the faith and fled from the pilgrim's way."

Now as they were walking on their way and still talking, someone came running to meet them. He said, "If you love your lives, you had better change your course, for there are robbers up ahead."

Then Great-heart said, "Those would be the three who once plundered Little-Faith. Well, we are ready for them." So they kept to their way. They carefully looked around every bend in the road expecting to meet these villains at any time. But whether they had heard of Great-heart or whether they had found some other diversion, they never appeared.

They Come to Gaius's Inn

By this time Christiana longed for an inn for herself and the others; they were all quite weary. Then Mr. Honest said, "There is one just a little way ahead of us where a very honorable disciple named Gaius lives." The old gentleman's report sounded good to them all, so they decided to go there. When they arrived, they walked right in since it is not necessary to knock at the door of

Rom. 16:23

an inn. They called for the innkeeper and he came to meet them. Then they inquired as to whether or not they could stay the night there.

"Yes, you may, if you are true. For my House is available only to pilgrims." This made Christiana, Mercy, and the boys very glad, because the innkeeper was one who loved pilgrims. They asked for rooms, and he showed them one for Christiana and Mercy, one for her sons, and another for Great-heart and Mr. Honest.

Then Great-heart asked, "Brother Gaius, what do you have for dinner? For these pilgrims have come far today and are hungry."

"It is late," replied Gaius, "so it is not convenient to go out and look for food. But you are certainly welcome to whatever I have, if that is all right with you."

"Yes, we will be content with whatever you have in the House. I am sure that you never run out of what is beneficial."

Gaius then went down and spoke to the cook whose name was Taste-that-which-is-good. He instructed the cook to make a dinner for the pilgrims. After doing this, he returned to the pilgrims, saying, "Come, my good friends, I have welcomed you and am glad that I have a House to provide for you. While dinner is being prepared, why don't we enjoy one another's company by sharing in conversation."

They all were agreeable, so Gaius asked them who they were.

"The older woman is the wife of one called Christian, a pilgrim who went before us," said Great-heart. "And these are his four sons. The young lady is one of her friends who she persuaded to come with her on the pilgrimage. All of these young men take after their father and desire to walk in his footsteps. Yes, if they see any place where the old pilgrim has slept or if they see even so much as a footprint left by him, it brings joy to their hearts, and they desire to do those same things and in the same manner as their father."

What a Rich Heritage

Then Gaius, turning to Christiana and her sons, asked, "You are Christian's wife and children? I knew your husband's father and also his father's father. Many good people have come from this line. Their ancestors first lived at Antioch. Christian's forefathers were very worthy men; I suppose you have heard your husband speak of them. No pilgrims have done better in proving themselves to be men of great virtue and courage. They always sought to honor the Lord, to follow and point out His ways, and to support those who love Him. I have heard of many of your husband's relatives who have stood trial for the sake of the truth.

Acts 11:26
Acts 7:59-60
Acts 12:2;
Eusebius, *The History of the Church*, Book 2:9

Taste that which is good

"Stephen, who was one of the first members of the family from which your husband came, was stoned to death. James, another one of that generation, was killed by a sword. And I must not forget Paul and Peter, men of old from which your husband's family came. Then later there was Ignatius, who was thrown to the lions, and Romanus, who was cut to pieces; there was Polycarp, who stood tall as he burned at the stake. There were others, also: one who was hung up in a basket in the sun for the

See Ignatius's *Letter to the Romans* and Eusebius's *The History of the Church*, Book 3:36

See Eusebius,
*The Martyrs of
Palestine, 2.*

See *The
Martyrdom of
Polycarp.*

wasps to eat, and another who was put into a sack and cast into the sea to be drowned. It would be utterly impossible to count all the members of that family who have suffered injury and death for the love of a pilgrim's life. And it excites me greatly to see that your husband has left behind him four sons like these. I trust they will carry their father's name well and walk in his footsteps until they come to their father's end."

"Indeed, sir," said Great-heart, "these young men are likely to do just that; they seem to wholeheartedly embrace their father's ways."

The Family Line Must Be Extended

"Then it is as I said," replied Gaius. "Christian's family is likely to continue spreading all over the face of the earth. Christiana, therefore, should watch for some girls for her sons to marry so that the name of their father and the house of his ancestry may never be forgotten in the world."

"It would be a shame if this family should fall and become extinct," said Mr. Honest.

"It cannot fall," said Gaius; "however, it can be diminished. But if Christiana will take my advice, it will continue to prosper. And, Christiana, I am so glad to see you and your young friend Mercy here; you are both lovely! May I take the liberty of telling you that Matthew, your eldest, and Mercy would make a very fine couple. If I were you, I would want Mercy to be a closer relation."

Now, in this time and culture betrothals were arranged early, and the two became betrothed right then. Indeed, they were eventually married, but I will tell you more about that later.

A Discourse about Women

"I would like to speak now on behalf of women for the purpose of removing their shame," said Gaius. "For as death and the curse came into the world by a woman, so did life and well-being. 'God sent forth his Son, born of a woman.' And to show how much the women who came later abhorred the act of their mother, Eve, the Old Testament women earnestly desired to have children, with the hopes that they might possibly be chosen to become the mother of the Savior of the world. I will also say that, when the Savior did come, women rejoiced because of Him, before both men and angels. I never read about one man who gave any money to Christ, but the women who followed Him always ministered to Him out of their substance. It was a woman who washed His feet with tears, and a woman who anointed His body for His burial. Women wept as He was going to the Cross, women followed Him to the Cross, women followed Him away from the Cross, and women sat by His tomb when He was buried. Women were the first ones with Him on His resurrection morn, and it was they who first brought the news that He was risen from the dead to His disciples. So women are highly favored and show that they have their share in the grace of eternal life."

Gen. 3

Gal. 4:4

Luke 2

Luke 8:2-3

Luke 7:37-38;
John 11:2

John 12:3

Matt. 27:55-56,
61; Luke 23:27,
49, 55

Mark 16; Luke
24:22-23

CHAPTER 29

◆◆◆◆◆◆◆◆◆◆◆◆◆◆◆

Lessons from the Dinner Table

Now the cook sent a message to them that dinner was almost ready. As they came into the room, someone had spread a tablecloth, and he was now setting the table, putting the cups, plates, and silverware, the salt and pepper, and the bread and butter on the table. Then Matthew said, "The sight of this tablecloth and these preparations for dinner makes my mouth water and gives me a greater appetite than I had before."

"And, likewise," said Gaius, "let all of the teachings that edify you in this life give birth to a greater desire within you to sit at the dinner of the great King in His kingdom. For all of the preaching, the books, and the commandments that are given here are like the mere laying out of the table service and the setting of the salt on the table when compared with the wondrous feast that our Lord will prepare for us when we arrive at His House." Rev. 19:9

So it was time for dinner, and first the Offered-thigh and the Wave-breast were set on the table before them. This was to show that they must begin their meal with prayer and praise to God. David had stood lifting his heart up to God with the Offered-thigh; he had used the Wave-breast offering, where his heart lay, to lean upon his harp as he played. These two dishes were very fresh and tasty, and they all ate heartily of them. Num. 6:20; Lev. 10:15

Next they were brought a Bottle of Wine, as red as blood. Gaius said to them, "Drink freely, Ps. 25:1; Heb. 13:15

Deut. 32:14

Offered thigh &

Judg. 9:13;
John 15:1
for this is the juice of the true vine that gladdens the hearts of both God and man." So they gladly partook.

Next a Pitcher of Milk was brought out, and Gaius said, "Boys, you drink this pure Milk 'that 1 Pet. 2:2 you may grow thereby.'"

Following this, they brought out a Dish of Curds and Honey. "Eat freely of this," said Gaius, "for it will both cheer you and strengthen you with wisdom and discernment. This was our Lord's food when He was a child; 'He will eat Curds and Honey when he knows enough to Isa. 7:15 reject the wrong and choose the right.'"

After this a very delicious Bowl of Apples was brought to them, and Matthew asked, "Since it was fruit that the serpent used to entice our first mother, why is it alright for us to eat it?"

Then Gaius responded,

"Fruit it was by which we were beguiled;
Yet sin, not fruit, has our souls defiled.
Forbidden fruit eaten, corrupts the blood;
To partake when commanded, does us good:
Drink from His vessels, O church, His dove,
And eat the fruit of Him whom you love."

Then Matthew said, "I made an issue of this because I will never forget how sick I got from eating fruit."

"Forbidden fruit will make you sick," replied

the Wavebreast

Gaius, "but you need not fear that which our Lord has permitted."

While they were still talking, they were presented with yet another dish, a Bowl of Nuts. Someone at the table said, "Nuts can ruin tender teeth, especially the teeth of children." When Gaius heard this, he replied:

Song of Sol. 6:11

"Hard texts are nuts (I won't call them cheaters),
Whose shells keep their kernels from the eaters;
So open the shells, and you'll find the meat;
They're brought here for you to crack and then eat."

Relaxing with Some Riddles

After this they were all very happy, and they sat at the table for a long time, talking about many things. Then the old gentleman said, "My good landlord, while we are cracking these nuts, if you will, I would like you to solve this Riddle:

"There was a man, though some counted him mad,
The more he cast away, the more he had."

Everyone looked at Gaius, wondering what he might say. He sat still for awhile and then replied:

"He that bestows his goods upon the poor,
Shall have as much again, and ten times more."

Then Joseph said, "Really, sir, I didn't think you would be able to solve it."

"Oh!" replied Gaius, "I have been trained up in this way for a great while. Nothing can teach better than experience. I have learned from my Lord to be kind, and have found out by experience that I have gained by doing so. 'One man gives freely, yet gains even more; another withholds unduly, but comes to poverty.' 'There is one who makes himself rich, yet has nothing; and one who makes himself poor, yet has great riches.'"

Prov. 22:6
Prov. 11:24
Prov. 13:7

Then Samuel whispered to Christiana, "Mother, this is the House of a very good man; let's stay here for a long time, and let Matthew marry Mercy before we leave here."

Gaius, overhearing this, said, "I am certainly willing, young man." So they stayed there for quite some time, and Mercy was given to Matthew to be his wife. While they were staying here, Mercy, as she had always done, continued making coats and other garments for the poor. Because of this, she gained a good reputation among pilgrims.

But to return to our story, after dinner the younger boys wanted to go to bed since they were tired from traveling. So Gaius called for someone to show them to their rooms, but Mercy offered to take them instead.

They slept very well, but the rest of them stayed up all night—Gaius was such good company, they didn't want to part! After much talk about their Lord, about themselves, and about their journey, old Mr. Honest began to nod off. "What, sir? Are you beginning to get drowsy?" asked Great-heart. "Come, perk up; I have a Riddle for you."

"Let's hear it," said Mr. Honest.

So Great-heart said,

"He that will kill must first be overcome,
And he who would live abroad
must first die at home."

"Ha!" said Mr. Honest. "That is a hard one—hard to explain, and harder to live! But come, landlord, if you will, I will leave my part to you. Please explain it, and I will listen to what you say."

"No," said Gaius; "the Riddle was put to you, and it's only right that you should try to answer it. "

So the old gentleman replied:

"He first by grace must conquered be,
For his sin to be mortified.
And who, that lives, would convince me,
Unto himself must die."

1 Cor. 15:31;
Gal. 2:20

"That is right," replied Gaius. "Good doctrine and experience both teach this. For first, before grace discloses itself and overwhelms one's soul with its glory, that soul is altogether unable to oppose sin. If sin is Satan's cord that binds a person's soul, how can he resist strongly enough to break free from the bondage? And secondly, no one who acknowledges reason or grace believes that such a person can be a living testimony of grace while he is still a slave to his own sin."

Rom. 7:24

Old Men vs. Young Men

"That brings to my remembrance a story worth listening to. There were two men who left on pilgrimages; the one began when he was young, the other when he was old. The young man wrestled with powerful struggles with sin, while the old man's inclinations to sin had subsided because of the declining vitality that the course of nature brings. Yet the young man walked his steps as evenly and as easily as the old one did. Which one of them, would you say, walked more clearly

in the power of God's grace, since both seemed to be alike?"

"Doubtless, the young one," replied Mr. Honest. "For the one who goes against the greatest opposition demonstrates that he is the stronger one, especially, when he is able to keep pace with the one who does not meet with half as much opposition—and the older one certainly does not. Besides, I have observed that old men often pride themselves mistakenly, in that they tend to view their weakening inclinations to sin as some victorious conquest over sin in their lives. In this they deceive themselves. Indeed, old men who are full of grace are best able to give advice to those who are young because they have experienced firsthand the emptiness of most things. But, yet, for an old man and a young man to set out together, the young one is the most likely to have the advantage of discovering a wonderful work of grace in his life, because the old man's fleshly desires are naturally weaker."

Acts 20:7-12   So they went on talking like this until dawn.

Responses to Christ
When everyone was up, Christiana told her son James to read a chapter out loud to them all; so he read Isaiah 53. When he had finished, Mr. Honest asked why it said that the Savior would come "out of dry ground" and why "he had no

Isa. 53:2   beauty or majesty to attract us to him."

Great-heart responded, "In answer to the first question, I believe it's because the church of the Jews from which Christ came had lost nearly all the substance and spirit of its religion. To the second question, my answer is that the words are descriptive of how Christ looks through the eyes of unbelievers; because they lack the vision to see into our Prince's heart, they tend to judge Him solely by His outward appearance, which lacked any distinctive qualities. They are just like those who, being ignorant of the fact that precious gemstones are covered with a crust that looks quite common, will toss a precious gem away. Because they don't realize the worth of what they are looking at, they treat it just as they would an ordinary stone."

Hunting Down and Destroying Giant Slay-good

"Well," said Gaius, "now that you are here, and since, as I know, Great-heart is skillful with his weapons, why don't we go for a walk into the fields after breakfast to see if we can do some good. About a mile from here there is a Giant called Slay-good who, along with the band of thieves he leads, greatly disturbs travelers on the King's High-way in these parts. I know where his haunt is, and I think it would be very helpful if we could clear these parts of him." So they decided to go, Great-heart with his Sword, Helmet, and Shield, and the rest of them with spears and staffs.

When they came to the place where the Giant was, they found him clutching one whose name was Feeble-mind. He had grabbed the man from

the way and had taken him to his cave. Now the Giant was attacking the man and had every intention of picking his bones clean, since his nature was that of a cannibal.

As soon as he saw Great-heart and his friends with their weapons drawn at the mouth of his cave, he demanded to know what they wanted.

"We want you," replied Great-heart, "for we have come to avenge the lives of the many pilgrims you have killed when you dragged them out of the King's High-way. Therefore, come out of your cave."

So the Giant armed himself and came out, and they immediately began to fight. After battling for over an hour, they stood still a moment to catch their wind. Then the Giant asked, "Why are you here on my ground?"

"To avenge the blood of pilgrims," answered Great-heart, "as I told you before." So they commenced fighting once again, and the Giant forced Great-heart to lose ground. But soon he had gained it back, and in the strength of his will, he swung his weapon so forcefully at the Giant's head and sides that the Giant's weapon fell out of his hand. Then Great-heart struck him and killed him and cut off his head. They took the Giant's head, and also Feeble-mind, the pilgrim, and brought them back to the House. When they had come home, they showed the head to the family and set it up outside so that hereafter any others who might attempt to do as he had done would be afraid to try.

Feeble-mind's Story
Then they asked Feeble-mind how he had fallen into the Giant's hands. "As you can easily see, I

am a sickly man," the poor man replied.
"Because death had usually knocked at my door
once a day, I thought I would never be well at
home. So I decided to take on the pilgrim's life
and have traveled here from the town of Uncer-
tain where I and my father were born. I am a
man of no strength at all of body or mind. But
I still plan, if I can, to spend my life in the pilgrim's way, though I am barely able to crawl.

"When I arrived at the Gate at the beginning
of the Way, the Master of that place graciously
received me in and did not object to my weak
appearance or feeble mind. Instead, He gave me
some necessities for my journey and encouraged
me to persevere in hope until the end. When I
came to the House of the Interpreter, I was also
received there with much kindness. Because the
Hill Difficulty was judged to be too hard for me
to climb, one of His servants carried me on up.
I have received much encouragement from pilgrims even though none of them were willing
to tread as softly as I am forced to do. Even so,
when they came to me, they would tell me to
be of good cheer and that it was their Lord's will
that comfort be given to the fainthearted. Then
they would go on at their own pace.

"When I came to Assault Lane, there the Giant
met me and told me to prepare for a confrontation. But, alas! I didn't need a fight; I needed
something to raise my spirits and give me
renewed vitality! He came and took me away, but
I never thought that he could kill me. I hadn't
gone with him willingly, and so, therefore, when
we got to his den I believed that somehow I
would come back out alive. I had heard that in
virtue of the laws of God's providence, no pilgrim who has been taken captive by violent
hands, as long as he keeps his heart pure and

1 Thess. 5:14

345

wholly toward his Master, will die at the hands
of the enemy.

"I may look as though I have been robbed, and
so I have, but, as you can well see, I have,
indeed, escaped with my life, for which I thank
my King as the author, and you as the means.
I may well run into other violence ahead, but
I have resolved to go on. I will run when I can
run, walk when I cannot run, and crawl when I
cannot walk. As for me, I thank Him who loves
me, and I am fixed on my course. My way lies
before me, and my mind is beyond the River that
has no bridge, although, as you can see, I am
weak and feeble."

"Did you ever know a pilgrim some time ago
named Mr. Fearing?" asked Mr. Honest.

"Know him! Yes, indeed; he came from the
town of Stupidity, which is just north of the City
of Destruction, not far from where I was born.
We were well acquainted. As a matter of fact, he
was an uncle of mine, my father's brother. He
and I had similar dispositions. He was a little
shorter than I, but we were very much alike."

"I can tell you knew him," said Mr. Honest.
"I can also tell that you were related to each
other. You look like him and have a similar countenance. Your speech is even like his."

"Most people have agreed with you who have
known us both," said Feeble-mind. "Besides,
what I have seen in him, I have for the most part
found in myself."

"Come, sir," said Gaius, "enjoy yourself; you
are welcome in my House. And whatever you
desire, just ask for, and whatever you would have
my servants do for you, they will do it without
hesitation."

"This is an unexpected favor," replied Feeble-
mind. "It is like the sun that has come shining

out of a very dark cloud. Did Giant Slay-good intend for me to enjoy this favor when he stopped me and resolved to let me go no farther? Did he intend that after he had stripped my pockets clean that I should go to Gaius who is now my host? Yet it is so."

Now as Feeble-mind and Gaius were talking, someone came running to the door and cried out that, about a mile and a half from there, a pilgrim named Mr. Not-right had been struck dead where he stood by a thunderbolt.

"Oh no!" exclaimed Feeble-mind. "He reached me several days ago and wanted to be my companion. He was with me when Slay-good took me, but he was quick on his feet and escaped. But it seems he escaped to die, while I was taken to live."

The one you'd think to be killed outright,
Is often delivered from the saddest plight.
That very Providence whose face is death,
Often to the lowly gives life and breath.
I was taken, but he escaped to flee;
Hands crossed, gave death to him but life to me.   Gen. 48:8-22

CHAPTER 30

❖❖❖❖❖❖❖❖❖❖❖❖❖❖

Weddings before Leaving Gaius's House

Now about this time Matthew and Mercy were married. And Gaius gave his daughter Phoebe to James to be his wife. After the wedding, they all stayed for about two more weeks at Gaius's House spending their remaining time there as pilgrims do. When they were ready to leave, Gaius made a feast for them, and they ate and drank in joyous celebration. Now the time had come for them to leave, so Great-heart prepared to pay the bill for their stay. But Gaius told him that at his House it was not customary for pilgrims to pay for their stay. He took pilgrims in, but looked for his pay from the Good Samaritan who had made this promise to him: "'Look after him,' he said, 'and when I return, I will reimburse you for any extra expense you may have.'"

Luke 10:35

With that Great-heart replied, "Dear friend, you are faithful in what you are doing for the brothers, even though they are strangers to you. They have told the church about your love. You will do well to send them on their way in a manner worthy of God." Then Gaius said good-bye to all of them, including his daughter and Feeble-mind, to whom he gave something to drink as he went on his way.

3 John 5-6

Feeble-mind's Reluctance to Go with Them

As they were going out of the door, however, Feeble-mind acted as if he wanted to linger. When Great-heart noticed this, he said, "Come along with us,

Feeble-mind. I will conduct you on the way, and you will do as well as the rest of us."

"Alas!" cried Feeble-mind. "I want a suitable companion. You are all strong and vigorous, but I, as you can see, am weak; I choose therefore to come later instead, lest, because of my many illnesses, I would be a burden both to myself and to you. I am, as I said, a man of frail body and mind, and I often stumble and grow weak trying to cope with things that others are able to bear. I don't enjoy laughing and lightheartedness; I don't like bright, festive clothing; and dislike unprofitable conversations. No, I have such a tender conscience that the things that others have the freedom to enjoy cause me to stumble. I don't yet know all of the truth and am a very ignorant Christian man. Sometimes, if I hear someone rejoice in the Lord, it disturbs me because I am not able to do it, too. I am as a weak man among the strong, or as with a sick man among the healthy, or as a lamp that is despised. 'He that is ready to slip with his feet is as a lamp despised in the thought of him that is at ease.' So I don't know what to do."

Rom. 14; 1 Cor. 8:7-13

Job 12:5

"But, brother," said Great-heart, "I have been commissioned to 'comfort the fainthearted' and 'uphold the weak.' You must go along with us; we will wait for you and give you our help; we will deny ourselves of some things, both in opinion and in action, for your sake; we won't enter into doubtful disputes or controversies in front of you; we will be made all things to you, rather than have you be left behind."

1 Thess. 5:14

Rom. 14:13; 1 Cor. 8:9-13

1 Tim. 6:3-5

1 Cor. 9:22

Mr. Ready-to-halt Arrives Just in Time

Now all this time they had been standing at Gaius's door. Suddenly, while they were deep in their discussion, a man named Ready-to-halt

Ps. 38:17

350

came by with his crutches in his hand; he also was going on a pilgrimage.

When Feeble-mind saw him, he said to him, "Man, how did you get here? I was just complaining that I had no suitable companion, but you are just the one I would like. Welcome, welcome, Mr. Ready-to-halt; I hope you and I may be of some help to one another."

Ready-to-halt

"I would be very happy to have your company," he said. "And since we have been so blessed to meet each other, rather than part company, I will lend you one of my crutches."

"No," replied Feeble-mind, "although I am thankful for your generosity, I don't intend to be lame before I am lame. However, I think, if the occasion should arise, it would be useful in helping me fend off a dog."

"Well," answered Ready-to-halt, "if either I or my crutches can do you any good, we are both at your command."

So they all set forth. Great-heart and Mr. Honest went first, followed by Christiana and her sons with their spouses, and then Feeble-mind and Ready-to-halt with his crutches.

Recalling Christian and Faithful's Encounters

"Please, sir," said Mr. Honest to Great-heart, "now that we are on the road once again, tell us some helpful things about some of those who have gone on pilgrimage before us."

"Certainly," replied Great-heart. "I suppose that you have heard how Christian of old met with Apollyon in the Valley of Humiliation and also about his difficult time in getting through the Valley of the Shadow of Death. I think you probably have also heard about how Faithful was so hard-pressed by Madam Wanton, Adam the First, Discontent, and Shame—four of the most deceitful villains anyone could meet with on the road."

"Yes," answered Mr. Honest. "I have heard about all of this. But Faithful was assaulted most relentlessly by Shame, who never grew weary of his wicked aggression."

"Yes, for the pilgrim spoke the truth when he said that Shame, of all men, had the wrong name."

"But tell me, sir, where did Christian and Faithful meet Talkative?" asked Mr. Honest. "He was also a notable character."

"He was a confident fool; yet so many follow his same ways," replied Great-heart.

"He certainly desired to deceive Faithful," said Mr. Honest.

"Yes, and he certainly would have, but Christian showed him how to find out his true colors."

So they went on until they came to the place where Evangelist had met with Christian and Faithful, and Great-heart said, "Here is where Christian and Faithful met with Evangelist, who prophesied to them concerning all they would encounter at Vanity Fair."

"Is that right?" said Mr. Honest. "I'll bet that was a hard pill for them to swallow."

"Yes, it was," replied Great-heart, "but along with this he also gave them encouragement. They were a couple of lion-hearted men; they had set their faces like flints. Don't you remember how undaunted they were when they stood before the judge?"

Isa. 50:7

"Faithful suffered nobly," answered Mr. Honest.

"So he did, and noble things have come from it; for Hopeful and some others, as the story goes, were converted through his death."

"Well," said Mr. Honest, "please go on, as you are knowledgeable of many things."

"Of all those whom Christian met after passing through Vanity Fair, one called By-ends was by far the most troublesome."

"By-ends! What was he?"

"A very sly fellow, a downright hypocrite," replied Mr. Great-heart. "He was one who wanted to be religious in whichever way the world turned; yet, he was so cunning that he would certainly never give anything up or suffer for it. He conformed his religion to every fresh wind, and his wife was as good at it as he was. He kept changing from one opinion to another and, all the while, he kept defending himself in doing so. I have heard, however, that he came to an ill end with his by-ends; and not once have I ever heard that any of his children are esteemed by those who truly fear God."

Eph. 4:14

CHAPTER 31
◆◆◆◆◆◆◆◆◆◆◆◆◆◆◆

At Mnason's House in the Town of Vanity

By this time they had drawn to within sight of the
town of Vanity where the Vanity Fair is held.   Ps. 12:2
When they saw that they were so near the town,
they discussed with one another how they should
best pass through. Some said one thing, and some
said another. At last Great-heart said, "I am sure
you understand that I have often conducted pilgrims through this town. I have come to know a
man there; we can be 'guests at the home of Mna-
son, originally from Cyprus.' He is an old disciple,   Acts 21:16
and I am sure we can lodge there with him. If you
think this is a good idea, let's stop there."

"I agree," said Honest; "I agree," said Christiana; "I agree," said Feeble-mind; and so did the
rest of them. Now by the time
they had gotten to the town, it
was evening; however, since   (ƆNΛSON
Great-heart knew the way to
Mnason's House, they were
able to go straight to it. When they got to the
door, Great-heart knocked and called to Mnason
inside. Recognizing his voice, Mnason opened
the door immediately and invited them all to
come right in.

Then Mnason, their host, asked, "How far
have you come today?"

"From the House of Gaius, our friend," they
replied.

"I tell you, you have come a good distance. I'll

bet you are very tired; please, sit down." Turning to them, Great-heart said, "Yes, relax; my friend welcomes you." And so they all sat down.

"I do welcome you," said Mnason, "and whatever you want, please, just ask for it, and we will do what we can to get it for you."

"Our greatest need for awhile has been for lodging and for good fellowship," replied Mr. Honest, "and I hope we have found both."

"As for lodging, you can see what I have," responded Mnason, "but as for good fellowship, that will be known only after we spend some time together."

"Well," asked Great-heart, "would you please show the pilgrims to their rooms?"

"I certainly will," he answered. After he showed them to their rooms, Mnason brought them into his lovely dining room where they could fellowship and eat together until it was time to retire for the evening.

Mr. Mnason's Friends
After they had settled in and were feeling invigorated following their journey, Mr. Honest asked the landlord if there were any good people in the town."

"We have some," answered Mnason, "but there are only a few when compared with the number are only a few when compared with the number of those who are wicked."

Mr. Contrite

"But is there a possibility that we might see some of them?" asked Mr. Honest. "For the sight of good folk are to those going on pilgrimage, like the sight of the moon and stars to those sailing on the open seas."

Then Mnason stamped his foot on the floor, and his daughter Grace came in. He said to her, "Grace, my dear, please go tell Mr. Contrite, Mr.

Holy-man, Mr. Love-saint, Mr. Dare-not-lie, and
Mr. Penitent that I have some friends at my House
that would like to see them this evening." So
Grace went to invite them, and before long she
had returned with all of them. After greeting one
another, they all sat down together at the table.

"My neighbors," said Mr. Mnason, "as you can
see I have some guests in my House; they are pilgrims who have traveled quite a distance and
who are on their way to Mount Zion." Then he
pointed to Christiana and asked, "Gentlemen,
whom do you think she might be? This is Christiana, the wife of Christian, that well-known pilgrim who, along with his brother Faithful, was so
shamefully treated in our town."

They were amazed at this, and said, "We had
no idea that we would see Christiana when
Grace invited us to come; this is a wonderful surprise!" They proceeded to ask her how she was
doing, and if these young men were her husband's sons. When she told them that they were,
they said to them, "May the King whom you
love and serve make you as your father and bring
you where he now is in peace."

Then Mr. Honest asked Mr. Contrite what condition their town was presently in. "To be sure,"
answered Mr. Contrite, "our town is very busy during fair time. It is difficult to keep our hearts and
spirits in good health when we are surrounded by
so much distraction. Those who live in a place like
this, as we do, need to make sure they remain careful and alert every moment of the day."

"How are your neighbors?" asked Mr. Honest.
"Are they quiet and peaceful?"

"They are much more moderate now than
they used to be," answered Mr. Contrite. "You
know how Christian and Faithful were abused in
our town; but I would say that lately they are

more tolerant. I believe that the blood of Faithful has brought heavy conviction upon them, even up to this day. For after they burned him, they have been ashamed to burn any others. In those days we were afraid to walk the streets, but now we can show our faces. Previously those who professed the faith were despised, but now, especially in some parts of our town (for you know our town is large), those who hold to the faith are considered honorable."

The Pilgrims Recount Their Adventures

Mr. Contrite paused, and then asked, "Tell me, how has it fared with you in your pilgrimage? How has the Country treated you?"

"We have fared pretty much the same as most other travelers," replied Mr. Honest. "Sometimes our way is smooth, sometimes rough; sometimes it is uphill, and sometimes downhill. We are rarely certain of what is in store for us. The wind is not always on our backs, nor is every person a friend whom we have met in the way. We have already met with some obstacles worth remembering along the way, and we don't know if they are all behind us yet. But, for the most part, we have found the old saying to be true that says, 'We are hard-pressed on every side, but not crushed.'"

2 Cor. 4:8

"You spoke about obstacles; what obstacles have you met with?" asked Mr. Contrite.

"We have already been confronted three or four times," said Great-heart. "First, Christiana, her sons, and Mercy were attacked by two ruffians whom they feared would kill them. We have also had confrontations with Giant Grim, Giant Maul, and Giant Slay-good. Actually, we confronted the last Giant rather than be confronted by him. This is what happened: after we had spent a good while at the House of 'Gaius, my

host, and the host of the whole church,' we were
inclined to take our weapons with us and go see
if we could destroy any of the enemies of pilgrims.
We had heard that there was a notorious one in
the region, and since Gaius lived in the area, he
had a better idea of where the Giant's haunt was
than we did. So we looked and looked until at
last we found the mouth of his cave, a sight that
made us glad and caused our spirits to revive. We
approached his den, and lo and behold, he had
dragged this poor man, Feeble-mind, into his
den by brute force and was about to make an
end of him. But when he saw us, evidently thinking he might have some more victims, he left the
poor man in his hole and came out. We immediately began to fight him with all our strength,
and finally, he was brought down to the ground;
his head is now set up by the wayside to frighten
any others who might want to practice such
wickedness. As a proof of what I say, here is the
man himself who was like a lamb taken out of
the mouth of a lion; he will confirm my story."

"Yes, it's true; and the experience was costly as
well as comforting," said Feeble-mind. "It was
costly in that he came so close to ending my life,
and it was comforting when I saw Great-heart and
his friends with their weapons drawn to deliver me."

Mnason's Friends Speak Their Minds

Mr. Holy-man then spoke up, saying, "There are
two things that those who go on pilgrimage need
to have—the first is courage, and the second is a holy
life. If they do not have courage, they will never
hold fast to the way; and if their lives are lived
loosely, they will cause the name 'pilgrim' to stink."

Then Mr. Love-saint said, "I hope my admonition will not apply to you, but truly there are many
who travel on the road who show themselves to

Rom. 16:23

1 Cor. 16:13;
1 Thess. 3:7-8;
Heb. 10:23

Titus 2:6-8;
1 Pet. 2:12

be strangers to the pilgrimage rather than 'strangers and pilgrims on the earth.'"

Heb. 11:13

"This is true," added Mr. Dare-not-lie. "They neither dress like pilgrims nor have the courage of pilgrims. They don't walk uprightly, but their feet go all awry, making them walk off course. One foot goes inward while the other goes outward. Meanwhile, their pants are ripped and torn and dragging behind them, bringing disgrace and dishonor to their Lord."

"They should be very disturbed because of such things," said Mr. Penitent. "These pilgrims are not likely to receive the grace and the pilgrim's progress that they desire until such spots and blemishes as these are taken out of the way."

They continued to talk along these lines until dinner was ready. After dinner, they went right to bed because they were quite weary. They stayed a great while at the House of Mnason. In time, he gave his daughter Grace to Christiana's son Samuel to be his wife. He also gave his daughter Martha to Joseph.

The Pilgrims Stay Long in Vanity

As I said, they stayed here for quite sometime because the town was not as it had been in former times. The pilgrims came to know many of the good people of the town and served them in whatever way they could. Mercy, according to her nature, worked continuously to meet the needs of the poor. Both their full stomachs and their clothed backs caused her name to be honored and blessed, and in that place she was as a jewel in the crown of godly faith. To tell you the truth, Grace, Phoebe, and Martha were also very pleasant, and they, too, did a great deal of good. They were all very fruitful so that Christian's name, as was said before, would likely continue to live on, having great impact in the world.

The Great Monster

While they were staying there, a Monster had come out of the woods and had killed many of the people of the town. It had also carried off their children and had trained them to sidetrack other children, leading them into his clutches. No one in the town dared so much as to show his face to the Monster, and everyone fled when they heard the sound of him coming.

Matt. 18:6

The Monster was like no other beast on the face of the earth. Its body was like a dragon's, and it had seven heads and ten horns. It especially wreaked great havoc among the children, and yet it was governed by a woman. This Monster set certain conditions before men, and the men who loved their lives more than their souls accepted these conditions and came under the Monster's power.

Rev. 17:3

Mark 8:34-36

Now Great-heart and those who had come to visit at Mnason's House entered into a covenant with one another to go and engage this beast, so that, if possible, they might deliver the people of this town from the paws and mouth of this devouring serpent.

Great-heart, Mr. Contrite, Mr. Holy-man, Mr. Dare-not-lie, and Mr. Penitent picked up their weapons and went down to meet him.

The Monster at first was wild and unrestrained. He looked down upon these enemies with great disdain. But they so wearied him, being rugged fighting men, that they made him retreat, and they came home to Mnason's House once again.

I want you to know that the Monster came out and intensified his efforts to get the children of the town during certain seasons of the year. Consequently, during these seasons our courageous and worthy men would watch for him. Whenever he appeared, they would mount a continual assault, so that in time he was not only wounded, but was caused to be lame. He has not been able to wreak havoc on the townspeople's children as he had done formerly, and it is sincerely believed by some that this beast will die

Rev. 13:3   from his wounds.

Because of this, Great-heart and his friends were highly esteemed in the town, and, even among those still attached to the tastes and pleasures of the world, there were many who had great admiration and respect for them. Because of this, the pilgrims did not suffer much in the town. It is true that there were some of the baser sort who could see no farther than the end of their noses and who had no more understanding than dumb animals; these had no respect for them and took no notice of their courage and adventures.

CHAPTER 32
◆◆◆◆◆◆◆◆◆◆◆◆◆◆◆

Well, the time drew near for the pilgrims to continue on their way, and they began to prepare for
their journey. They sent for their friends and con-
ferred with them, and they spent some time committing one another to the protection of their
Prince. Their friends brought them some things
that they might need on their journey, things fit
for the weak as well as the strong, and things for
the women as well as the men. Then they set out
to resume their journey. Their friends accompanied them for a considerable distance, and,
before parting, they once again committed each
other to the protection of their King.

Acts 28:10

They Resume Their Journey
Those belonging to the pilgrims' company went
on with Great-heart leading the way. The women
and children, being weaker, were able to move
at only a moderate pace, and, because of this,
Ready-to-halt and Feeble-mind were encouraged
because they had others who could sympathize
with their condition.

Having left the townsfolk and having said farewell to their friends, they quickly came to the
place where Faithful had been put to death.
They stopped there and thanked Him who had
enabled Faithful to bear his cross so well. They
were thankful also that they had been so blessed
and strengthened by his outstanding example of
courage in the face of suffering. After this, they

went on a good deal farther, talking about Christian and Faithful and how Hopeful had joined Christian following the death of Faithful.

After awhile they came to the Hill Lucre where the Silver-mine was that had drawn Demas away from his pilgrimage, and into which By-ends was believed to have fallen and perished. So they stood and thought about it for awhile. Then they came to that old Monument, the Pillar of Salt, that stands over against the Hill Lucre, within view of Sodom and its smelly lake. They marvelled just as Christian had done before them, wondering why men of such learning and intelligence would become so blinded as to turn aside here. They took note that man's nature is not so much influenced by the misfortunes that others have suffered as it is by the allurements that act upon their foolish eyes.

Then I saw that they went on until they came to the River that was on the near side of the Delectable Mountains. This is the River where the beautiful trees grow on both sides of the way, the leaves of which, if taken inwardly, are good

Rev. 22:1-2 against digestive ailments. Here the Meadows are green all year long, and they provide a pleasant

Ps. 23 place where pilgrims may safely rest.

The Good Shepherd
Here in the Meadow by the River, there were pens and folds for Sheep, and a house built for the nourishing and raising of lambs, the babies of women who go on pilgrimage. There was someone here, entrusted with their care, who 'gathers the lambs in his arms and carries them close to his heart; he gently leads those that have

Isa. 40:11 young.' Christiana encouraged her four daughters-in-law to commit their little ones to the care of this Man, that alongside these waters they

THE GOOD Shepherd

might be sheltered, kept, loved, and nurtured, and that none of them might be lacking in the time to come.

Jer. 23:4

If any of the lambs go astray or get lost, this Man will bring them back again. He will also bind up that which is broken and will strengthen those who are sick. Here they will never lack food or drink or clothing, and they will be protected from thieves and robbers; for this Man would lay down his life before allowing one of these little ones committed to his trust to be lost. Here, too, the children will most assuredly receive good nurture and admonition and will be taught to walk in the paths of righteousness. And this, of course, is a blessing of tremendous worth. Also, here, as you see, are tranquil Waters, pleasant Meadows, delicate Flowers, and varieties of Trees that bear only wholesome Fruit—not Fruit like Matthew ate that reached over the wall from Beelzebub's Garden. The Fruit of these Trees produces health where there is none and sustains and increases health where it already exists. Understandably, then, the mothers were pleased to commit their little ones to his care. And knowing that their King was in charge of everything, including the hospital for young children and orphans, was a further encouragement in making this decision.

Ezek. 34:11-16

Matt. 6:19-21, 25-33

John 10:11

Their Decision to Go to Doubting Castle

As they continued on, they came to By-path Meadow and to the steps over which Christian had gone with his friend Hopeful, causing them to be taken by the Giant Despair and put into Doubting Castle. Here they decided to sit down and discuss what the best thing to do might be. Since they were strong and had such a mighty man as Great-heart for their guide, they wondered whether or not the best thing to do would be to make an assault on the Giant. Perhaps they could demolish his castle and set any pilgrims free who might be imprisoned in it. So they discussed the idea, but one said one thing and another said just the opposite. One questioned whether or not it was lawful to go on unholy ground. Another said it was alright if their purpose was good.

Then Great-heart said, "Although this last assertion cannot be universally true, still I have been given a command to resist sin, to overcome evil, and to 'fight the good fight of the faith.' And please tell me, with whom should I fight this good fight, if not with Giant Despair? I will therefore attempt to take his life and demolish Doubting Castle." Then he asked, "Who will go with me?"

1 Tim. 6:12

"I will," said old Mr. Honest.

"And so will we," chimed in Christiana's four sons, Matthew, Samuel, James, and Joseph. For they were strong young men. So they left the women on the road, and with them, Feeble-mind and Ready-to-halt along with his crutches to be guards until their return. For even though Giant Despair lived nearby, in that place, if pilgrims keep on the road, a little child might lead them.

1 John 2:13-14

Isa. 11:6

Confrontation with Giant Despair

So Great-heart, along with Mr. Honest and the four young men, went over the steps on their way to Doubting Castle to look for Giant Despair. When they came to the castle gate, they made an unusual clatter as they knocked at the gate. At that the old Giant came to the gate, and his wife, Distrust, followed him. Then he demanded, "Who is he and what does he want who is so hardy and presumptuous as to disturb the Giant Despair in this way?"

"It is I, Great-heart; I belong to the King of the Celestial Country, and I guide pilgrims to their place. I demand that you open your gates so that I may enter. Also, prepare to fight, for I have come to remove your head and to demolish Doubting Castle."

Now Giant Despair, because he was a Giant, thought no man could overpower him. He thought to himself, "Since I have conquered angels, shall I be afraid of Great-heart?" So he harnessed himself in all his gear and went out. He had a helmet of steel on his head, a breastplate of fire strapped to him, and iron shoes on his feet. He carried a huge club in his hand.

1 Sam. 17:4-7

The six men wasted no time, attacking him both from behind and in front. When Distrust, the Giantess, came to help him, old Mr. Honest struck her down with one blow. They fought for all they were worth, and Giant Despair was brought down to the ground, but didn't want to die. He struggled hard, and, as they say, had as many lives as a cat. But Great-heart pressed hard and overcame the Giant, refusing to let up until he had cut the Giant's head from his shoulders.

1 Sam. 17:50-51

Despondency and Much-afraid Are Delivered

Then they went about the business of demolishing Doubting Castle. This was not a difficult task now that Giant Despair was dead, but it still took them seven days to destroy it. Within the castle they found two prisoners, Mr. Despondency, who was nearly starved to death, and his daughter, Much-afraid. These two were brought out alive, but a huge number of dead bodies lay all over the castle yard, and the dungeon, also, was full of dead men's bones.

Josh. 6

Matt. 23:27

After Great-heart and his companions had completed this feat, they took Mr. Despondency and his daughter Much-afraid under their protection. They were honest people, in spite of the fact that they had been prisoners of that tyrant Giant Despair in the Doubting Castle. The men buried the bodies of the Giant and his wife under a heap of stones, but they took his head with them, and they brought it down to the road to show their companions what they had accomplished.

A Joyful Celebration

When Feeble-mind and Ready-to-halt saw that it was indeed the head of Giant Despair, they were filled with joy and merriment. It so happened that Christiana could play the violin, and her daughter-in-law Mercy could play the guitar. Since they were all so happy, the two began to play them a song. Ready-to-halt wanted to dance, so he took Despondency's daughter Much-afraid by the hand and began to dance right there in the road. True, he could dance only with the aid of a crutch in his hand, but you have my word, he did quite well. And the girl also was to be commended, for she danced to the music beautifully.

As for Mr. Despondency, the music wasn't of much interest to him; being that he was nearly starved, he was much more concerned about eating than he was dancing. So Christiana gave him something to drink and prepared a meal for him to eat, so that in a short time the old gentleman was feeling revived.

Now I saw in my dream, that, after all their festivities had ended, Great-heart took the head of Giant Despair and set it on a post by the side of the High-way, right next to the Monument that Christian had erected to caution pilgrims who were to come thereafter.* Then he placed a marble stone under it upon which he had written these words:

This is the head of him whose very name
In former times brought pilgrims to shame;
His castle's down, and Distrust, his wife,
Brave Great-heart has bereft of life.
Despondency, his daughter, Much-Afraid,
Great-heart for them also the man has played.
Whoe'er has doubts if he'll but turn his eye
Upon this post; may it his doubts satisfy.
This head, also, when doubting cripples dance,

Although the Doubting Castle is now destroyed,
And Giant Despair of his head is devoid,
Sin can rebuild the castle, make it remain
And bring Despair the Giant to life once again.

Shows that from fears they've found deliverance.

CHAPTER 33

••••••••••••••••

With the Shepherds on the Delectable Mountains

This done, they went forward until they came to the Delectable Mountains where Christian and Hopeful had been refreshed by the diversity of beauty to be enjoyed there. They also became acquainted with the Shepherds, who welcomed them to the Mountains just as they had welcomed Christian before them. When the Shepherds saw so many people following Great-heart (they were already well-acquainted with him), they said to him, "Great-heart, you have a large company with you; where did you find all of them?"

Then Great-heart replied:

"First, here's Christiana and her family,
Her sons and their wives, have moved steadily
As by a compass their lives did steer
From sin to grace, else they'd not be here.
Next here's old Honest who's on pilgrimage
And Ready-to-halt, too, with the advantage
Of a heart that's true, and so does Feeble-mind,
Who was not willing to be left behind.
Despondency's, a good man, now set free
And Much-afraid, his daughter, you can see.
May we now find provision here, or must
We go farther? Let us know on what we can trust."

The Shepherds replied, "This is a pleasant group. We welcome you here, for we have provisions for those who are feeble, as well as for those

who are strong. Our Prince is concerned about
Matt. 25:40   what is done for the least of these, so infirmities
can in no way limit or hinder our hospitality.

The Shepherds

So they took them to their palace
door and said to them, "Come in, Mr.
Feeble-mind; come
in, Mr. Ready-to-
halt; come in, Mr.
Despondency, and
Miss Much-afraid."

Then one of the Shepherds said to Great-heart,
"We call these by name since they are the ones
most prone to draw back; but as for you, and the
rest who are strong, we leave you to walk in the
freedom to which you are accustomed."

Then Great-heart, addressing the Shepherds,
said, "On this day I can see that the grace of God
shines in your faces. I can see that you are my
Lord's Shepherds, indeed, for you have not
Ezek. 34:21   poked and prodded these who have infirmities,
but rather, have strewn their way into your palace with flowers, just as you should."

So the weak and feeble went in first, followed
by Great-heart and the rest. When they had all
been seated, the Shepherds asked those who were
weaker, "What would you like to eat?" For it was
their habit to "warn those who are lazy; comfort
1 Thess. 5:14   those who are frightened; take tender care of
those who are weak." So they made them a feast
of easily-digested foods that were as nutritious
Rom. 14:1-4   and nourishing as they were delicious. After the
pilgrims had finished eating, they retired for the
evening, each to his respective room.

Sight-seeing on the Mountains
When morning had come, the Mountains were
lovely and the day was clear and bright. The
Shepherds were accustomed to showing some of

the special sights of the area to pilgrims, so, after the pilgrims had refreshed themselves and were ready, the Shepherds took them out into the fields and showed them the same sights that they had shown Christian.

The Man of Faith

Then they took them to see some new places. First they went to Mount Marvel, from which they could see a man in the distance who was tearing down hills by his words. They asked the Shepherds about him, and they answered that he was the son of the man named Great-grace (of whom you heard in the records of Christian's pilgrimage). They explained that his purpose in being there was to teach pilgrims that they can set their faith against whatever difficulties may confront them; they can topple them by faith. "I know him," said Great-heart; "he is a great man."

Matt. 17:20; 21:21; Mark 11:23

The Man in White

After this they took them to another place called Mount Innocent. They saw a man there who was completely clothed in shining white, and they saw two other men also, Prejudice and Ill-will, who were continually hurling dirt at him. But, interestingly, whatever dirt they threw at him would in a short time fall off again, and his garment

would look as clean as if no dirt had ever been on it. The pilgrims asked what this meant, and one of the Shepherds answered, "This man's name is Godly-man, and his garment shows the purity of his life. Now those who are throwing dirt at him are the kind that hate his good deeds. But, as you can see, the dirt will not stick to his clothes. So it will be with whoever lives a life of true purity and innocence in this world. Whoever would try to make such people dirty labors in vain. For God, after a little while, 'will make your righteousness shine like the dawn, the justice of your cause like the noonday sun.'"

1 Pet. 2:12

Ps. 37:6

THE GENEROUS MAN

The Generous Man

Next they took them to Mount Charity where they showed them a man who had, lying in front of him, a bundle of cloth. From this cloth he made coats and garments for the poor, who were standing around him. Yet his bundle of cloth never diminished in size. "What does this mean?" asked the pilgrims.

One of the Shepherds replied, "This is to show you that he who has a heart to help the poor will never run out of resources. For 'he who refreshes others will himself be refreshed.' And the flour that the widow used to make bread for the prophet did not cause her to have any less in her barrel."

Prov. 11:25

1 Kings 17:16

The Black Man and the Fools

After this, the Shepherds took them to a place where they saw two men, one named Fool and the other, Want-wit. The two were busily washing a man from Ethiopia with the intention of making him white. The more they washed him, however, the darker he appeared.

"What does this mean?" asked the pilgrims.

"A fool will attempt to change a person to make him like himself, not realizing that God is the originator of our differences. True righteousness has nothing to do with the outward appearance but is of the heart. Every effort to effect change in a person that disregards the need for change in the inner nature of the heart results in frustration and even greater unrighteousness. So it was with the Pharisees, and so it continues to be with all hypocrites.

1 Sam. 16:7

The Terrifying By-way to Hell

Then Mercy said to Christiana, "If it is possible, I would like to see the hole in the Hill that is commonly called the By-way to Hell."

Christiana revealed Mercy's desire to the Shepherds, and so the Shepherds took them to the door, which was in the side of a Hill. Upon opening it, they told Mercy to listen for awhile. So she listened and heard someone crying, "May my father be cursed for holding back my feet from the way of peace and life!"

Rom. 3:15-16

Another was crying, "Oh, that I had been torn to pieces before the time that my soul was lost!"

And yet another cried, "If I could only live again, I would surely deny myself rather than come to this place!"

Then it seemed as if the earth itself groaned

and quaked for fear under Mercy's feet. Her skin turned an ashen color and she came trembling away, saying, "Blessed are those who are delivered from this place!"

Mercy Receives the Unique Looking-glass

Now after the Shepherds had shown them all these things, they took them back to the palace and provided them with all they had in the House. Mercy longed for something that she saw in the House but was too ashamed to ask for it. Her mother-in-law, seeing that she did not look well, and concerned especially because Mercy was pregnant, asked her what the matter was. "There is a special Looking-glass hanging in the dining room," she replied, "and I cannot get it off my mind. I don't understand why, but I so earnestly desire to have it that I fear I may miscarry if I cannot obtain it."

"I will mention your desire to the Shepherds," said Christiana; "they won't deny your request."

"But I am ashamed of what these men will think if they know how I have longed for it," said Mercy.

"No, my daughter, it is no shame; rather, it is a virtue to long for such a thing as that."

The Word of God

"Then, Mother, if you will, please ask the Shepherds if they are willing to sell it."

James 1:23-25

1 Cor. 13:12;
2 Cor. 3:18

Now the Looking-glass was of great value, one in a thousand. If turned one way, it would show the exact image of the person holding it; if turned another way, however, it would show the very face and likeness of the Prince of pilgrims Himself.

John 19:1-4

I have talked with those who know, and they say that they have seen the very crown of thorns

John 19:16-34

upon His head by looking into that Looking-glass. They have also seen the holes in His hands, in His feet, and in His side. Yes, that Looking-glass has such excellence that it will show Him to those who earnestly desire to see Him. They will see Him whether He is living or dead, whether in earth or in Heaven, whether in a state

THE LOOKING-GLASS

of humiliation or in His exaltation; and whether He is coming to suffer or coming to reign.

So Christiana went to the Shepherds—Knowledge, Experience, Watchful, and Sincere—and said to them, "One of my daughters is longing for something that she has seen in this House. She is expecting a child, and she wants this thing so deeply that, if denied by you, she fears she will have a miscarriage."

"Call her, call her," said Experience. "She can help herself to whatever we have."

So they called her and asked, "Mercy, what is the thing that you would like to have?"

She was blushing as she replied, "The Looking-glass that hangs up in the dining room." So Sincere ran and got it and gave it to her. She gave them sincere thanks and said, "By this I know that I have obtained favor in your eyes."

They also gave the other young women whatever they desired. And they greatly commended their husbands because they had joined with Great-heart in slaying Giant Despair and demolishing Doubting Castle.

The Shepherds put a necklace around Christiana's neck, and they did the same for her four daughters-in-law. They also put earrings in their ears and jewels on their foreheads.

The Shepherds Send Them on Their Way
When it was time for the pilgrims to travel on, the Shepherds let them go in peace. They did not

give them the warnings and instructions that they had given Christian and Hopeful, however, because Great-heart was their guide. They knew that he was well-acquainted with the dangers on the way, and so could more appropriately warn them when danger was approaching. Also, by the time they needed to put them into practice, Christian and Hopeful had already lost the instructions and warnings that the Shepherds had given them. So this present group had an advantage over the others.

They went out from there singing this song:

"Oh, see what a fitting stage has been set
For relief of pilgrims who this world roam;
And how they've received us without regret,
Who make the other life our goal and home.
Whatever they have they're willing to give,
That we, though pilgrims, may joyfully live.
And upon us, too, such things they bestow,
That show we are pilgrims where'er we go."

CHAPTER 34

◆◆◆◆◆◆◆◆◆◆◆◆◆

Remembering Turn-away

After they had left the Shepherds, they soon came to the place where Christian had met a man named Turn-away who lived in the town of Apostasy. Great-heart said, "This is the place where Christian met one called Turn-away, whose turned back exposed the nature of his rebellion. Let me say concerning this man that he refused to listen to any counsel, and, once he was falling, no one could persuade him to stop. When he came to the place of the Cross and the Grave, he met someone who encouraged him to take a look. But he ground his teeth together and stamped his feet and said he had resolved to go back to his own town. Before he got to the gate, he ran into Evangelist who offered to lay hands on him that he might turn him back into the way. But Turn-away resisted him and showed great contempt for him. After that he escaped from Evangelist's hand and climbed over the wall."

Valiant-for-truth and His Conflict

Then they went on, and, just at the place where Little-faith had formerly been robbed, they met a man standing with his Sword drawn and his face all bloody. "Who are you?" asked Great-heart.

"My name is Valiant-for-truth," the man replied. "I am a pilgrim and am going to the

Celestial City. As I was on the way, suddenly three men came and surrounded me, and they gave me three alternatives. First, I could become one of them; second, I could go back where I came from; or third, I could die on the spot.

"In answer to the first, I told them that I had been a man of integrity for a long time, and so

they could not expect me to join the ranks of thieves.

Prov. 1:10-14

Then they demanded what I would say to the second alternative. So I told them that if the place I had come from had been advantageous to stay in, I would not have left it at all. But finding it altogether unsuitable, and very unprofitable for me as well, I abandoned it to come this way. Finally, they asked me for my response to the third alternative. I told them that my life had been payed for at great cost and that, therefore, it was of much too great a value to warrant lightly giving it away to them. Then I said that besides this, they had no right to set my choices and that they would imperil their lives if they chose to interfere further.

1 Pet. 1:18-19

"Then these three, namely Wild-head, Disregard, and Meddlesome, drew their swords, and I also drew mine. And we fought, one against three, for more than three hours. As you can see, they left me with some wounds, and they have taken away some of my belongings. They have just left; I suppose they heard you coming and decided to take off."

"Well, you were fighting against great odds, one against three!" said Great-heart.

"This is true," said Valiant-for-truth. "But it makes no difference; whether few or many means nothing to one who has the truth on his side. 'Though an army besiege me, my heart will not fear; though war break out against me, even then will I be confident.' Besides, I've read in some records how one man fought an army, and how many Samson killed with the jawbone of an ass!"

Ps. 27:3

Judg. 15:15

"Why didn't you cry out so that others might have come to your rescue?" asked Great-heart.

"I cried out to my King. I knew He would hear me and provide for me aid that eyes cannot see, and that was enough for me."

"You have behaved yourself in a most worthy manner," said Great-heart. "Let me see your Sword." So he showed it to him. When he had taken it in his hand and looked at it for awhile, he said, "Ha! this is a true Jerusalem blade."

"It is; let a man have one of these blades, and, with a strong hand to wield it and skill to use it, he can win a battle with an angel. He doesn't need to fear its power as long as he knows how to use it. It's edges will never grow blunt. 'It penetrates even to dividing soul and spirit, joints and marrow.'"

Eph. 6:17

Heb. 4:12

"But you fought a long time," said Great-heart. "It's a wonder you didn't grow weary."

"I fought until my Sword froze to my hand; it was then, when the Sword and my hand were joined together as if the Sword grew out of my arm, and when the blood coursed through my fingers, that I fought with the greatest courage."

2 Sam. 23:10

Faith

"You have done well," said Great-heart. "In your struggle against sin, you have resisted to the point of shedding your blood. Come, join us;

Heb. 12:4

come in and go out with us, for we are your companions." So they took him in and washed his wounds and offered him whatever they had. Then they went on together.

Luke 10:25-37

Valiant-for-truth Tells How He Became a Pilgrim

Great-heart was delighted to have Valiant-for-truth with them, both because he had a great love for those who knew how to fight, and also because there were many feeble and weak ones in their group. So he asked him about many things, first of which was where he had come from.

"I am from Dark-land," answered Valiant-for-truth; "I was born there, and my mother and father still live there."

"Dark-land," said Great-heart. "Doesn't that lie on the same coast as the City of Destruction?"

"Yes, it does. I'll tell you what caused me to become a pilgrim. A man named Mr. Tell-true came to our area, and he told us about the things that Christian, from the City of Destruction, had done. He told us how Christian had forsaken his wife and children and had taken upon himself the life of a pilgrim. He also reported how he had killed a serpent that had come out to resist him on his journey, and how he had finally reached his

destination. He described the welcome Christian had received at all of his Lord's lodgings, and especially when he came to the gates of the Celestial City. He said that Christian was received into the City with trumpet blasts by a band of Shining Ones, and that all the bells in the City rang for joy at his reception. He spoke of the golden garments that Christian wore and of many other things that I won't take the time to tell you

about now. In short,
that man told the story
of Christian and his
travels in such a way
that my heart burned
with intense yearning to
go after him as
soon as possi-
ble. My father
and mother
couldn't even hold me
back, and I left them and have
come this far on my way."

The Gates of the Celestial City

"You came in at the Gate, didn't you?" asked
Great-heart.

"Yes, yes; for the same man told us that all
would be for nothing if we didn't begin our journey from the Gate."

The Joy of Loved Ones Reunited in the City
Then Great-heart looked at Christiana and said
to her, "Christiana, see how the story of your husband's pilgrimage and what he has received as a
result of his quest has spread far and wide."

"Why, is this Christian's wife?" asked Valiant-
for-truth.

"Yes, she is. And these are her four sons."

"What, and they are going on pilgrimage, too?"

"Yes, they are truly following the same way."

"Well, it gladdens my heart," Valiant-for-truth
responded. "How joyful the good man Christian
will be when he sees these who had refused to go
with him, now coming after him to the Gates of
the Celestial City!"

"Without a doubt, it will be of great comfort to
him," said Great-heart. "For next to the joy of
being there himself will be the joy of being
reunited with his wife and his children."

"But," said Valiant-for-truth, "now that you have mentioned it, please tell me your opinion about something. Some question whether or not we will know one another when we get there."

"Well, do they think that they will know themselves when they get there?" responded Greatheart. "And if so, do they expect to rejoice upon seeing themselves in such bliss? If their answer to these questions is "yes," then why wouldn't they expect to know others and rejoice in their wellbeing also? Since our relatives are so near to us, like an extention of ourselves, even though that state will be dissolved when we get there, should we conclude that we will be more glad to see them there than to see them left out?"

Arguments Made against
Valiant-for-truth's Pilgrimage

"Well, I can understand your position with regard to this," said Valiant-for-truth. "Do you have any other questions you'd like to ask me about my decision to go on this pilgrimage?"

"Yes, I do; were your father and mother agreeable to your decision to become a pilgrim?"

"Oh no; they tried everything they could think of to persuade me to stay home."

"Why, what could they say against it?"

"They said it was an idle life, and that if I didn't have an inclination toward sloth and laziness, I would never be happy as a pilgrim."

"And what else did they say?"

"They told me that it was a dangerous way. Why, they even said that the way that pilgrims go is the most dangerous way in the world."

"Did they offer to tell you why they thought this way is so dangerous?"

"Yes, in great detail."

"Name some of them."

"Well," said Valiant-for-truth, "they began by telling me about the Slough of Despond where Christian nearly drowned. Then they told me that there were archers at Beelzebub Castle who were always standing ready to shoot those who might knock to gain entrance at the Wicket-gate. They also spoke of the woods and the dark Mountains, the Hill Difficulty, and the Lions. They told me about the three Giants named Grim, Maul, and Slay-good. They said there was a foul Fiend that haunted the Valley of Humiliation, and that he had nearly taken Christian's life. They also told me that I would have to go through the Valley of the Shadow of Death where demons prowl, where light is darkness, and where the way is full of snares, pits, and traps. Then they told me about Giant Despair and Doubting Castle and about the large number of pilgrims that had come to ruin there. Furthermore, they told me that I would have to travel through the dangerous Enchanted Ground. And, after all this, they said that I would come upon a River over which there was no bridge and that the River would run between me and the Celestial Country."

"And was that it?" asked Great-heart.

"Oh no. They told me also that this way was full of deceivers and other people who were just lying in wait to turn good pilgrims out of the path."

"Did they describe any of them?"

"Yes; they told me that Worldly-wiseman would be waiting there to deceive me. They also told me about Formality and Hypocrisy who are continually walking the road. They said that By-ends, Talkative, or Demas might draw near to snatch me away. They also assured me that the Flatterer would catch me in his net, or that, like empty-headed Ignorance, I might go to the gate and be sent back to the hole in the side of the

Hill and be made to go on the By-way to Hell."

"This certainly sounds like enough to cause dis-couragment," said Great-heart. "But did they end with this?"

"No, keep listening. They told me that many people of old had started on the way and had gone a great distance on it. These, they said, had wanted to see if they could find some of the glory there that, from time to time, so many had so enthusiastically talked about. They said, how-ever, that large numbers of them had come back again, feeling very foolish for ever having set foot outside their door toward that path. They said that the whole Country was relieved at their turning back. Then they named several who had done just that—Obstinate and Pliable, Mistrust and Timorous, Turn-away and old Atheist, among others. They said that some of them had traveled far to see what they could find, but that not one of them had found so much as a feath-er's weight of benefit from their efforts."

"Did they try to discourage you with anything else?"

"They weren't finished yet. They told me about someone named Mr. Fearing who had been a pilgrim. He was so gloomy that he never experienced a happy hour. They also said that Mr. Despondency had almost starved as a pil-grim. Oh yes, I almost forgot about Christian, who has been so talked about. They said that after all of his undertakings for a celestial crown, he had most certainly drowned in the black River and had never taken another step farther, sug-gesting that stories to the contrary were a cover-up of the real truth."

He Remains Undaunted

"And none of these things discouraged you?" asked Great-heart.

"No; they didn't seem to me to be worthy of consideration."

"How did you come to that conviction?"

"Why, I still believed what Mr. Tell-true had said, and that belief carried me through all the questions and doubts thrown at me by others."

"Then this was your victory, even your faith!"   1 John 5:4

"This is true," replied Valiant-for-truth. "I believed, and therefore I stepped out and started on the way, fighting all who would set themselves against me, and, by believing, I have now come to this place."

Who would true valor see?
Let him now come here;
He will always steadfast be,
Whether stormy clouds or clear;
is no discouragement
To make him even once relent
From his avowed intent
To be a pilgrim.
Those who will him surround
With their dismal story
Do but themselves confound;
More is his strength and glory.
No Lion can cause him fright,
He with a Giant will fight,
And he will have the right
To be a pilgrim.

No Devil nor foul Fiend
Can ever daunt his spirit;
He knows he at the end
Will life inherit.
Then whims will fly away,
He'll fear not what men say;
He'll labor night and day
To be a pilgrim.

CHAPTER 35
◆◆◆◆◆◆◆◆◆◆◆◆◆◆◆◆

On the Enchanted Ground

By this time they had come to the Enchanted Ground where the air naturally caused one to become drowsy. It was all overgrown with briers and thorns, except for where there were Enchanted Arbors scattered here and there. Some say that if anybody sits down or stretches out to get some sleep in one, there is a strong chance that he will never get up or awaken in this world again. For this reason, they went across this ground staying very near to one another. Great-heart went first because he was the guide, and Valiant-for-truth pulled up the rear, fearing that some fiend, dragon, giant, or thief might possibly come and attack them from behind. So they went on, each with his Sword drawn and ready in his hands; for they knew that this was a dangerous place. They tried to be as encouraging as they could. Great-heart told Feeble-mind to follow right behind him, and Despondency was kept close to Valiant-for-truth.

Isa. 5:5-6

Now they had not gone far when a very heavy mist, along with thick darkness fell upon them. For awhile, each could barely see the person standing right next to them. Because of this, they were forced for some time to feel for one

2 Cor. 5:7 another by listening to each other speak; for they walked 'not by sight.' It would be obvious to anyone that this was tough going even for the best of them; how much worse, however, for the women and children who had tender feet and hearts. Nevertheless, moved along by the encouraging words of the one who was in the lead and the one who guarded the rear, they managed to move on at a reasonable pace.

The way was muddy in this place, and traveling through the mud was very tiring. And in all this area there was not so much as one inn or place to buy food whereby the weaker ones could be refreshed. So along they went, grunting and puffing and sighing, and as one would trip over a bush, another would get stuck in the mud. Some of the children even lost their shoes in the mud. One would cry out, "I have fallen down," another, "Hey, where are you?" and a third, "The bushes have caught hold of me, and I don't think I can get away from them."

Finally they were able to come to a warm Arbor that offered rest and refreshment to the pilgrims. It was finely fashioned above them, and was beautified with greenery and furnished with benches and armchairs. There was also a soft couch upon which the weary could sit and rest. I am sure you know, all things considered, that this was quite tempting. For the pilgrims were already beginning to feel frustrated and defeated by the terrible condition of the way.

In spite of this, not one of them expressed so much as a gesture or word to stop there. Indeed, as far as I could tell, they carefully gave heed to all of their guide's advice. He had so faithfully warned them about all the hazards and of the dangers associated with each of the hazards they reached, that usually when they were approaching them, they roused their spirits and encouraged one another to deny the flesh. This Arbor was called The Slothful's Friend, and its purpose was to allure, if possible, some of the pilgrims into resting when they became weary.

Great-heart's Map

Then I saw in my dream that they went on in this solitary place until they came to a spot where one can easily lose his way. Now, when it was light, their guide could readily tell them how to avoid the routes that would send them the wrong way, but in this darkness, he was forced to come to a standstill.

He had a map in his pocket, however, that showed all the ways that lead to or from the Celestial City. So he struck a match (for he never went without them) and began to study his map. It instructed him to be careful to keep to the right side of the way in that area. If he had not taken the time to look in his map, in all probability, they would have drowned in mud. For just in front of them, and, ironically, right where the way looked cleanest, there was a pit filled with mud. The pit was so deep that no one knew its depth, and it was put there for the purpose of swallowing pilgrims and destroying them.

Then I thought to myself, "Whoever goes on pilgrimage must have one of these maps with him so that he may look at it when he doesn't know which way to take."

God's Word

The Two Sleepers

So they went on in this Enchanted Ground until they came to another Arbor which was built by the side of the High-way. There in the Arbor were two men who were fast asleep. Their names were Heedless and Too-bold. They had come a long way on their pilgrimage, but, being weary from their journey, they had sat down to rest here and had fallen fast asleep.

When the pilgrims saw them, they stood still, shaking their heads, for it was obvious to them that the sleepers were in a desperate plight. They discussed with one another what they should do, whether to go on and leave them in their sleep, or to step over to them and try to wake them up.

HEEDLESS and TOOBOLD

They decided to try and wake them, if possible, but with the understanding that they would be very careful themselves not to sit down or in any way seek to enjoy the benefits offered by the Arbor.

So they went in and spoke to the men, calling them by their names, for Great-heart seemed to know them; but they made no answer. Then Great-heart shook them and did whatever he could to disturb their sleep. Finally, one of them said, "I will pay you when I get my money." When Great-heart heard this, he shook his head. Then the other one said, "I will fight as long as I can hold my sword in my hand." At that, one of the children laughed.

"What does this mean?" asked Christiana.

"They are talking in their sleep," Great-heart replied. "No matter what you do to them—whether you strike them or beat them, they will answer you in this fashion. A long time ago someone said to a drunkard, 'You will be like one sleeping on the high seas, lying on top of the rigging. "They hit me" you will say, "but I'm not hurt! They beat me, but I don't feel it! When will I wake up so I can find another drink?"' This is what they are like. You know that when people

Prov. 23:34-35

talk in their sleep, they will say anything. These men speak incoherently now; their words aren't directed by any faith or power to reason. But this only reflects the condition they were in between the time they began their pilgrimage and when they sat down here.

"Here, then, is the trouble: When heedless ones go on pilgrimage, the odds are better than twenty to one that this will be what happens to them. For this Enchanted Ground is one of the last refuges that the enemy to pilgrims has placed; you can see that it is almost at the end of the way. For this reason, it gives the enemy a greater advantage. He thinks, 'When will these fools have a stronger desire to sit down than when they are so very weary? And when will they be more likely to be weary than when they have almost reached their journey's end?' So I say that this is the reason why the Enchanted Ground is placed so close to the Land of Beulah and so near to the end of their race. May pilgrims always watch themselves carefully so that what has happened to these men will never happen to them, for as you can see, no one can awaken these two."

They Are Helped

Then the pilgrims, trembling with fear, desired to go on. They asked their guide to light a lantern so that they would have light on the rest of their way. So he lit the lantern, and they went on by its light, even though the darkness was still very great.

2 Pet. 1:19
The light of the Word

The children, by this time, were miserably tired, and they cried out to Him who loves pilgrims, asking Him to make their way more comfortable. Shortly thereafter, when they had gone a little way farther, a wind arose that drove the fog away so that the air became more clear. They were not yet off of the Enchanted Ground, but, at any rate, they could see one another better, and it was also easier to see the way that they should walk.

They Meet Stand-fast

Now when they had almost reached the end of this ground, they could hear just a little ahead of them the voice of someone who sounded deeply concerned. So they went on, trying to look ahead. Suddenly they saw a man on his knees, with his hands and his eyes lifted toward Heaven. It appeared that he was speaking earnestly to the One who was above, but they were unable to hear what he was saying. They approached him very quietly since they did not want to disturb him. When he had finished talking, he got up and began to run toward the Celestial City.

Then Great-heart called after him, saying, "Hello, friend! If you are on your way to the Celestial City, as I think you are, let us enjoy your companionship."

So the man stopped, and they approached him. As soon as Mr. Honest saw him, he said, "I know this man."

"Who is he?" asked Valiant-for-truth.

"He comes from the area where I used to live. His name is Stand-fast; he is certainly a very fine pilgrim."

So they came together, and Stand-fast said to old Honest, "Hello, Mr. Honest; is that really you?"

"Yes, just as sure as you are standing here, it is I."

"I am so glad that I have found you on this road," said Stand-fast.

"And I was so glad to see you, too, and on your knees," replied Mr. Honest.

Stand-fast blushed a little and asked, "You saw me?"

"Yes, I did; and the sight caused my heart to rejoice."

"Why, what did you think?" asked Stand-fast.

"Well, what else could I think but that we had come upon an honest man on the road, and that, therefore, we would soon be able to enjoy his company."

"Well, if you thought correctly, how happy I am! But if I am not as I should be, I alone must bear responsibility for it."

"That is true," replied Mr. Honest, "but your concern for yourself only confirms to me more than ever that things are right between the Prince of pilgrims and your soul. For He says, 'Blessed is the man who always fears.'" Prov. 28:14

The Danger of the Enchanted Ground

"But brother, please tell us why you were on your knees," said Valiant-for-truth. "Did you need mercy to help you with a struggle, or what?"

"Well, as you know, we are on the Enchanted Ground. And as I was journeying along, I was thinking about what a dangerous road this is and about how so many who have come all this way on the pilgrimage have been stopped and destroyed when they got to this place. I was also thinking about the manner of death in which people are destroyed here. Those who die here do not die from any kind of violence; their death is not grievous to them. For the one who falls away by going to sleep, begins that journey with comfort and pleasure. Yes, they rest satisfied in obedience to the will of that disease."

"Did you see the two men asleep in the Arbor?" Mr. Honest interrupted.

Prov. 10:7

"Yes, yes, I saw Heedless and Too-bold there; and for all I know, they will lie there until they rot."

Stand-fast's Struggle with Madame Deception

"But allow me to go on with my story," said Stand-fast. "As I was thinking, someone approached me who was dressed in very pleasing attire, though she was a little old. She presented herself to me and offered me three things—her body, her purse, and her bed.

Prov. 7

"Now, to tell you the truth, I was quite weary and very sleepy, not to mention the fact that I am as poor as a church mouse; she may have known that fact. Anyway, I resisted her over and over, but she just smiled and let my rebuffs pass right by her. Then I started getting angry, but that didn't matter to her at all. She just continued to proposition me. She told me that, if I would submit to her, she would make me great and happy, for she said, 'I am the mistress of the world, and men are made happy by me.'

This vain world

"Then I asked her her name, and she told me it was Madame Deception. This made me want to distance myself from her all the more, but she kept following me with her enticements. Finally, I fell on my knees, and with hands lifted up, I cried to Him who had said He would help me. Evidently, just as you were approaching, she went on her way. When I saw her leave, I continued to give thanks for this great deliverance. I know she didn't intend any good for me, but, rather, she wanted to stop me from going any farther on my journey."

"Without a doubt her intentions were bad," said Mr. Honest. "But, wait a minute; as you have talked about her, it occurs to me that I have either seen her or read some story about her."

"Perhaps you have done both," said Mr. Stand-fast.

"Madame Deception!" exclaimed Mr. Honest. "Is she a tall, attractive woman with somewhat of a swarthy complexion?"

"Right, you are; she is one that matches that description."

"Does she speak very smoothly and give you a smile at the end of every sentence?"

"You got it again; this is exactly what she does."

"Does she not keep a large purse at her side, with her hand in it, eagerly fingering her money like it is her heart's delight?"

"Yes, that is so. You couldn't have described her better if she had been standing here all this time."

"Then," said Mr. Honest, "the one who drew a picture of her was a good artist, and the one who wrote about her said the truth."

The Truth about This Woman

"This woman is a witch," said Great-heart, "and it is because of her sorceries that this ground is enchanted. Whoever lays his head down in her lap might as well lay his head on the chopping block, and whoever gazes upon her beauty is counted as the enemy of God. She is the one who maintains those who are the enemies of pilgrims in their wealth and splendor.

James 4:4;
1 John 2:15

And she has bought many men off so that they turned from the pilgrim's life. She is quite a talker, and she and her daughters are always yapping at the heels of one pilgrim or another, constantly promoting and praising the virtues of this present life. She is bold and impudent, always ready to talk with any man she can find. She laughs poor pilgrims to shame, but highly commends the rich. If there is someone shrewd enough to gain wealth, she will brag about him from house to house. She loves parties and feasting, and is always at one banquet or another.

1 Tim. 6:10

"She has passed it around in some places that she is a goddess, so there are some who worship her. She likes to entertain, and she has opened houses of gambling and corruption. She boasts that no one can throw a party like she can. She promises to use her powers to bless all those, and their children, who pledge to her their reverent love and loyalty. On a whim, she will toss gold out of her purse in some places and to some people as if it were mere sand. She loves to be sought after, spoken well of, and held close to the hearts of mankind. She never grows weary of showing her powers and merchandise, and she loves them most who think the most highly of her. She will promise crowns and kingdoms to those who will take her advice; yet she has put many on a leash of bondage and has brought ten thousand times more into Hell."

"Oh!" cried Stand-fast. "What mercy I received when I was able to resist her; for where might she have drawn me?"

"Where?" asked Great-heart. "Only God knows; but one thing is certain, she would have drawn you 'into temptation and a trap and into many foolish and harmful desires that plunge men into ruin and destruction.'"

1 Tim. 6:9

"She is the one who turned Absalom against his father and Jeroboam against his master. She also persuaded Judas to sell his own Lord, and she prevailed with Demas to forsake the godly pilgrim's life. No one knows all of the mischief she works. She causes dissensions between leaders and those they govern, between parents and children, between neighbor and neighbor, between a man and his wife, between a man and himself, and between the flesh and the spirit.

2 Sam. 2:15;
1 Kings 12
Luke 22:5
2 Tim. 4:10

"Therefore, Mr. Stand-fast, do like your name commands, so that 'you may be able to stand your ground, and after you have done everything, to stand.'"

Eph. 6:13

This discussion brought about a mixture of joy and fear among the pilgrims, but, eventually they burst into song, singing:

"What danger is the pilgrim in!
So many are his foes!
How many ways there are to sin
No living mortal knows.

Some shy away from the ditch, yet can
Lie wallowing in the mire;
Some, though they shun the frying pan,
Go leaping into the fire."

CHAPTER 36

◆ ◆ ◆ ◆ ◆ ◆ ◆ ◆ ◆ ◆ ◆ ◆ ◆ ◆ ◆

Arrival in the Land of Beulah

After this, I watched until they had come into the Land of Beulah, where the sun shines night and day. Once they arrrived, being quite weary, they decided to rest for awhile.

Rev. 21:22-25; 22:5

This Country was commonly traveled by pilgrims, and, because all of the orchards and vineyards here belonged to the King of the Celestial Country, His pilgrims were allowed to freely partake of anything of His that their hearts desired. It took only a short time for them to feel rested and refreshed. Even though there were bells ringing and trumpets playing melodiously, making it impossible for them to sleep, they still felt tremendously renewed, as if they had never before slept so soundly.

The continual talk of those who walked the streets here sounded like this: "More pilgrims have come to town! Many passed through the water and were let in at the golden gates today!" Then someone would exclaim, "Here comes a legion of Shining Ones into town; that tells us that there are more pilgrims on the road, for the Shining Ones have come here to wait for them and to comfort them after all the sorrow they have experienced on the way."

Then the pilgrims got up and walked back and forth enjoying everything. Their ears were filled with heavenly music, and their eyes were delighted with celestial visions! There was absolutely nothing here in this Land that was offensive to their ears, their eyes, or their sense of touch, of smell, or of taste; nothing that was at all offensive to body, mind, or spirit. It was only when they tasted water from the River through which they were to pass, that they thought it tasted somewhat bitter; but even that proved sweeter once it was down.

Death is bitter to the flesh but sweet to the soul.

There was a record kept here of all the pilgrims of old, and it included all the famous acts that they had done. The ebb and flow of the River was much talked about here, too. It seemed that some had been able to cross it when it was nearly dry, while others were forced to cross it when it had overflowed its banks.

The children of the town would go into the King's Gardens and gather bouquets for the pilgrims and bring them to them with sincere affection. Henna, spikenard, saffron, calamus, and cinnamon grew here, and there were also trees of frankincense, myrrh, and aloes, and all the best spices. These wonderful fragrances and spices were used to perfume the bedrooms during their stay here; and with them, also, their bodies were anointed in preparation for their crossing the River when the appointed time had come.

Heb. 9:27

A Messenger Visits Christiana

Now as they rested here, waiting for their hour to come, a Messenger from the Celestial City came into town creating a great deal of excitement. He carried something of great importance for one called Christiana, the wife of Christian, the pilgrim. After inquiring about her, he found the

house where she was staying, and he presented
her with a letter, the contents of which said: 1 Cor. 15:54
"Greetings, good woman! I bring you news that
the Master is calling for
you and expects you
to stand in His
presence,
clothed in immor-
tality, within the
next ten days."

The Messenger

After the Messen-
ger had read the let-
ter to her, he gave
her a token to assure her
that he was a true Messenger and that he
had come to instruct her to make
preparations to leave. The token
was an arrow with a point sharpened with love
that easily found its way into her heart. It so
worked in her that by the appointed time, nothing could restrain her from going.

When Christiana saw that her time had come,
and that she would be the first of her companions to cross over the River, she called for Great-
heart, her guide, and told him what was
happening. He told her that he was genuinely
happy to hear the news and that he would have
rejoiced, also, had the Messenger come for him.
Then she asked him to advise her on all the preparations she should make for her journey. So he
told her what to do and what to expect on her
journey, and then he assured her that the rest of
them would accompany her to the riverside.

After this she called for her children and gave
them her blessing. She told them that it was a
comfort to her that she could still read the mark
that was set in each of their foreheads. She said
that she was so glad to see them with her there

and, also, so happy that they had kept their garments so white. Last of all, she bequeathed to the poor what little she had and admonished her sons and her daughters to be ready for the Messenger when he came for them.

Rev. 3:4-5

After she had finished talking to her guide and her children, she called for Valiant-for-truth and said to him, "Sir, you have shown yourself in every place we have been to have a true heart. My King says, 'Be faithful, even to the point of death, and I will give you the crown of life.' I would also request that you keep an eye on my children, and, if at any time, you see any of them weaken, please speak encouragingly to them. For they have been faithful, and the promise will be fulfilled for them when they reach their end."

Rev. 2:10

She gave Stand-fast a ring and then called for old Mr. Honest. She said to him, "Here is a true Israelite, in whom there is nothing false." Then he said, "I wish you a pleasant day when you set out for Mount Zion, and I will rejoice if I see that you are able to cross the River with dry shoes on your feet."

John 1:47

"Whether wet or dry, I long to be gone," she replied. "For no matter how the weather is in my journey, once I reach my destination I will have enough time to sit down and rest and dry myself off."

Then that good man, Ready-to-halt, came in to see her. "Your journey here has been difficult," she said, "but that will only serve to make your rest even sweeter. Therefore watch and be ready; for the Messenger may come at an hour you don't expect."

Matt. 24:44

After him, Despondency and his daughter, Much-afraid, came in to see her. Christiana said to them, "You should always remember to be thankful for the deliverance that you received

from Doubting Castle and the hands of Giant
Despair. The result of that mercy is that you have
been brought here safely. Be watchful, and cast
off all fear; be sober, and keep your hope until
the end."

1 Thess. 5:6-8
Heb. 3:6

Then she said to Feeble-mind, "You were delivered from the mouth of Giant Slay-good so that
you might live in the Light of the Living forever
and see your King in everlasting peace and consolation. Before He sends for you, however, I would
advise you to repent of your tendency to be
afraid and to doubt His goodness. If not, this
fault could cause you embarrassment when you
stand before Him."

Christiana's Departure

Now the day of her departure had finally arrived.
The road was full of people who wanted to see her
off on her final journey. But what a surprise to see
all the banks beyond the River full of horses and
chariots—they had come down from above to
accompany her to the City Gate. So she went
ahead and entered the River, and, with a wave
good-bye to those who had followed her to the riverside, she was gone. The
last word that anyone
heard her say was, "Lord, I
am coming to be with You and to bless You!"

So her children and friends returned to their
places, for those who had waited for Christiana on
the other side had carried her out of their sight.
When she called at the Gate and it was opened to
her, she entered with all the joyful celebrations
that her husband, Christian, had experienced
before her. Her children wept at her departure, but
Great-heart and Valiant-for-truth played joyfully
on the harp and cymbal. So all departed to go to
their respective places.

Ready-to-halt's Departure

In time, a Messenger came to the town again, and this time his business was with Ready-to-halt. He found him and said, "I have come to you in the name of Him whom you have loved and followed, even though on crutches. My message is to tell you that He expects you at His table to dine with Him in His Kingdom on the day after Easter. Therefore, prepare yourself for this journey."

Then he gave him a token to guarantee that his message was true, and he said, "I have severed your silver cord and broken your golden bowl."

Eccles. 12:6

After this, Ready-to-halt sent for his fellow pilgrims and said, "I have been sent for, and God will surely visit you also." He wanted Valiant-for-truth to make out his will. Having nothing to bequeath to those who would survive him except for his Crutches and his best wishes, he said, "I bequeath these crutches to my son with a hundred warm wishes that he will walk in my footsteps better than I have done."

Promises

Then, after thanking Great-heart for all of his guidance and kindness, he left for his journey. When he came to the edge of the River he said, "Now I will no longer need these crutches, since there are chariots and horses waiting across the River for me to ride on."

The last words he was heard to say were, "Welcome life!" So he went his way.

Feeble-mind's Departure

After this, Feeble-mind heard the sound of the Messenger's trumpet at his bedroom door. The Messenger came in and said, "I have come to tell you that the Master needs you, and that in a very short time you will see His face in splendor. Take this token of the truth of my message: 'Those looking through the windows grow dim.'"

Eccles. 12:3

Then Feeble-mind called for his friends and told them the message he had received. He said, "Since I have nothing to bequeath to any, what reason would there be in my leaving a will? As for my faint heart, I will leave that behind me; I will have no need of it in the place where I am going, nor is it worth bestowing on the poorest of pilgrims. Therefore, when I am gone, I desire that you, Valiant-for-truth, would bury it in a garbage dump."

This having been done, the day came in which he was to depart. He entered the River as had the others. His last words were, "Hold out, faith and patience!" So he went over to the other side.

After many days, a Messenger came for Despondency, bringing this word to him: "Trembling man! You are summoned to be ready to see your King by the next Lord's day, to shout for joy for the deliverance you have received from all your doubts."

Then the Messenger said, "To prove my message is true, take this for a proof: 'The grasshopper drags himself along.'"

Eccles. 12:5

Despondency and Much-afraid's Departure

When Despondency's daughter, Much-afraid, heard what had been done, she knew it was her time to go also.

Then Despondency said to his friends, "You know in what condition my daughter and I have been, and in what a troublesome manner we have behaved ourselves all along the way. Our will is that our depressions and slavish fears will never be received by anyone, from the day of our departure and forever. For I very well know that after our death they will offer themselves to others. To be frank with you, they are spirits which we entertained when we first began to be pilgrims and could never shake them thereafter.

They will walk about and seek to find other pilgrims who will receive them, but for our sakes, keep the doors shut to them."

When the time had come for them to depart, they went to the riverbank. The last words of Despondency were, "Farewell, night! Welcome, day!" His daughter went through the River singing, but no one could understand the words of her song.

Mr. Honest's Departure

Then, after awhile, it came to pass that a Messenger was in town inquiring for Mr. Honest. So he came to the house where Mr. Honest was staying, and he delivered these lines into his hands: "You are commanded to be ready within one week to present yourself before your Lord at His Father's house. And here is the token that my message is true: 'And all the daughters of music are brought low.'"

Eccles. 12:4

So Mr. Honest sent for his friends and said to them, "I will die, but will not make a will. As for my honesty, it will go with me. Let those who come after be told of this." When the day that he was to depart had come, he set out to go across the River. At that time the River was overflowing its banks in some places, but Mr. Honest in his life-time had asked a man named Good-conscience to come and meet him there. Good-conscience was there and lent him a hand, helping him over. The last words of Mr. Honest were, "Grace reigns!" And so he left this world.

Valiant-for-truth's Departure

After this, there was much talk in town that Valiant-for-truth had been given a summons by the same Messenger who had come to the others. He had been given this token that the summons was true: "Your pitcher is shattered at the spring."

Eccles. 12:6

When he understood it, he called for his friends and told them about it. Then he said, "I am going to my Father's, and though I have come this far with great difficulty, I do not regret any of it. I give my Sword to the one who will succeed me in my pilgrimage; I give my courage and skill to the one who can take it. My marks and scars I will carry with me to be a witness for me that I have fought the battles of the One who will now be my rewarder."

Gal. 6:17

When the day had come that he must go on, many accompanied him to the riverside. As he went in, he said, "Where, O death, is your victory?" And as he went down deeper, he said, "Where, O death, is your sting?" So he went on over, and all the trumpets sounded for him on the other side.

1 Cor. 15:55

Stand-fast's Departure

Then there came a summons for Stand-fast. He is the one that the rest of the pilgrims had found upon his knees in the Enchanted Ground. The Messenger brought it to him open in his hands. The content of the message was that he must prepare for a change of life, for his Master was not willing that he should be so far from Him any longer.

Stand-fast wondered deeply at this, and the Messenger said, "No, you don't need to doubt the truth of my message, for here is a token of the truth of it: 'The wheel is broken at the well.'"

Eccles. 12:6

Stand-fast called for Great-heart, who had been their guide, and said to him, "Sir, although it was not my good fortune to have been in your company for long during the time of my pilgrimage, yet, since the time I met you, you have been helpful to me. When I came from home, I left behind me a wife and five small children. I know

that you will go and return to your Master's
house in hopes that you may yet be a guide to
more of the holy pilgrims. So please, I beg you,
when you return, please send for my family and
tell them all that has happened to me. In addition, tell them about my happy arrival at this
place and of the blessed state that I have more
recently come to. Tell them also about Christian
and Christiana, his wife, how she and her children came after he did. Tell them of the happy
ending she came to and where she has gone. I
have little or nothing to send to my family,
unless it is my prayers and tears for them. And
that will be enough if you are able to share these
things with them and get them started on the
way."

Stand-fast's Final Words

When Stand-fast had finished putting his things
in order, his time of departure came. A great
calm had come over the River at the time that he
came to it, and when he was about halfway in,
he stood for awhile and talked to his companions that were still on the bank.

He said, "This River has been a terror to many;
yes, the thought of it has often frightened me,
too. But now I see that I am standing easily; I am
standing on the same thing that priests who bore
the ark of the covenant stood on while Israel
Josh. 3:17   went over this Jordan. The waters are indeed bitter to the palate and cold to the stomach. Yet,
the thought of what I am doing, and the glorious
escort that awaits me on the other side, warms
my heart like a glowing coal. I now see myself at
my journey's end; my days of toil are over. I am
going now to see that Head that was crowned
with thorns and that Face that was spit upon for
me. I have formerly lived by hearing and by

faith,
but now
I am going to
where I will live
by sight and will
be with Him in
whose company I delight. I have always loved to
hear my Lord spoken of, and wherever I have
seen the print of His shoe on the earth, I have
desired to set my foot, too. His Name has been to
me as a priceless treasure—sweeter than all perfumes. His voice has been music to my ears, and
I have more earnestly desired to see His face than
those who would most desire to see the light of
the sun. I have gathered His Word which became
my food, and used it as a remedy against fainting
along the way. He has held my course steady,
and I have forsaken all my sins. Yes, He has
strengthened my steps in His way."

Now while he was talking to them, his countenance changed, and after saying, "Take me, for I
come to You!" he was gone, and he ceased to be
seen by them.

Matt. 27:29
Matt. 27:30
Rom. 10:17
1 Cor. 13:12;
2 Cor. 5:7

Rev. 22:4

Ezek. 3:1-3;
Rev. 10:8-10

Isa. 40:29-31

The Joy That Awaits Us

Oh, how glorious it was to be able to see there beyond the River and in the upper regions the vast numbers of horses and chariots, with trumpeters and flutists, with singers and musicians playing stringed instruments—all present to welcome the pilgrims as they crossed the River, following one another to enter at the beautiful Gate of the City.

As for Christiana's four sons and their wives and children, I did not stay long enough to see them go over. I did, however, hear after I left that they were still alive, building up the church in the place where they were left for a time.

Should I have cause to go that way again, I may give to those who desire it an account of what I have left out in this story. In the meantime, to my reader I say, "Farewell."

T   H   E   E   N   D

GENERAL INDEX

◆◆◆◆◆◆◆◆◆◆◆◆◆◆◆◆◆◆◆◆◆◆

SCRIPTURE INDEX
◆◆◆◆◆◆◆◆◆◆◆◆◆◆◆◆◆◆◆◆◆◆◆◆

OLD TESTAMENT

DISCUSSION QUESTIONS
◆◆◆◆◆◆◆◆◆◆◆◆◆◆◆◆◆◆◆◆◆◆◆◆◆◆◆◆◆◆◆◆

The following questions are suitable for use in a small group or classroom setting. Some of the chapters may be discussed together to fit the time available.

6 weeks: 1-2, 3-5, 6-8, 9-11, 12-14, 15-17.
9 weeks: 1, 2-3, 4-5, 6-7, 8-9, 10-11, 12-13, 14-15, 16-17.
14 weeks: 1, 2, 3, 4, 5, 6, 7, 8, 9, 10, 11, 12-13, 14-15, 16-17.

CHAPTER 1
1. Why did Christian leave his home and family? What was Christian's Burden? What role did the Book play? How did the Evangelist help him?
2. What hindrances did Christian encounter as he journeyed to the narrow Gate? What arguments were made to try to convince him to go back? What made the Slough of Despond so difficult?
3. Why did Christian keep going despite all the obstacles? According to Christian, what are the benefits of the eternal Kingdom?
4. What kind of arguments might Obstinate use today?
5. What could you say or do to answer those arguments?

CHAPTER 2
1. Why did Worldly-wiseman's advice sound so appealing to Christian?
2. What three things did Evangelist say that Christian should abhor in Worldly-wiseman's counsel?
3. What does Galatians 3:10-11 say that refutes Worldly-wiseman's advice?

4. In what ways can morality be a poor substitute for faith?
5. When has the desire for relief from guilt tempted you to take shortcuts? In those situations, what would have been a faith response?

CHAPTER 3
1. In what ways does Good-will symbolize God's love?
2. What in Interpreter's visions made Christian fearful? What gave him hope?
3. What do Passion and Patience represent? Why is Passion such a strong influence in our lives?
4. In what situations does Passion distract you from doing God's will?
5. What can you do to develop Patience for the good things that God provides?

CHAPTER 4
1. How did Christian lose his Burden?
2. What was Christian given by the Shining Ones in place of his Burden? What does each gift represent?
3. What "false Christians" did Christian meet? How did they justify their actions?
4. What "false Christians" are prevalent today? How do difficult experiences distinguish false Christians from true ones?
5. How can the Scroll (God's Word) help us reject false Christians, overcome fears, and stay on the right path?

CHAPTER 5
1. How were Discretion, Prudence, Piety, and Charity helpful to Christian?
2. Where might you find people like this?
3. How does sharing your Christian journey with other believers help strengthen your faith?
4. At one point Christian says, "When I want to do what is

best, that is when I struggle the most." When has that been true for you?

5. Where is your Palace Beautiful where you can find supportive people, rest, help, instruction, and hope?

CHAPTER 6

1. Who is Apollyon? What arguments does he use to try to convince Christian to turn back?
2. According to Christian, why are some Christians not delivered from fear, danger, difficulty, or death?
3. What did Christian use to defeat Apollyon?
4. What did Christian use to make it through the Valley of the Shadow of Death? According to Ephesians 6:18, how is prayer a part of a Christian's armor?
5. At what times are you most aware of Satan's attacks? How can you utilize the armor of faith?

CHAPTER 7

1. What temptations had Faithful encountered on his pilgrimage? How was Moses a temptation? What was the temptation of Shame?
2. How was Faithful able to resist each temptation?
3. What temptations are prevalent in our world?
4. Which of these temptations is the most difficult for you to resist?
5. What steps can you take to resist that temptation?

CHAPTER 8

1. What kind of a person was Talkative?
2. Why did Faithful want to talk with Talkative at first? What changed Faithful's attitude toward Talkative?
3. What was Talkative's error?
4. What should be the relationship between what a person professes and how he or she acts? (See James 2:17, 26.)
5. What can you do to make your faith more than empty talk?

CHAPTER 9

1. What enticements did Vanity Fair offer Christian and Faithful? According to Matthew 4:1-11 and Luke 4:1-13, where and when did Jesus encounter these enticements?
2. How did Christian and Faithful respond to the merchants? What caused the commotion at the Fair?
3. Why did everyone turn against the pilgrims? What kinds of opposition do Christians face today?
4. What worldly enticements do you face? What opposition have you encountered because of your stand for Christ?
5. Evangelist told Christian and Faithful that their "sufferings were not mistakes." How can this truth help you resist temptation and live for Christ?

CHAPTER 10

1. Describe Mr. By-ends's religion. Why did he reject Christian's beliefs?
2. What rationalizations did By-ends and his friends give for their life-style? What makes their reasoning so appealing?
3. How did By-ends and friends react to Christian's arguments?
4. These men tried to embrace both the world's values and God's. Why is that impossible? (See Luke 16:13.)
5. When are you tempted to think like Mr. By-ends or one of his friends? What can you do to avoid their way of thinking and life-style?

CHAPTER 11

1. What did Demas try to get Hopeful and Christian to do? Of what truth did Lot's wife remind them?
2. What finally caused Hopeful and Christian to leave the path?
3. What did Hopeful and Christian do to Despair? How did they resist giving in to this Giant and then finally escape? How did remembering help?

4. When has your path become rough? What causes you to become discouraged?
5. What can you do to escape despair?

CHAPTER 12

1. How did the Shepherds help Christian and Hopeful?
2. What warnings did the Shepherds give? What did they do to encourage the pilgrims and give them hope?
3. Who are the "Shepherds" today? In what ways could a "Shepherd" help you in your Christian walk?

CHAPTER 13

1. What was Ignorance depending on to enter the Gate at the Celestial City?
2. Why is this man called "Ignorance"?
3. Why would Little-faith be admitted to the Celestial City? What could Little-faith have done to become a victor?
4. At what times do you have "little faith"?
5. What can you do to increase your courage?

CHAPTER 14

1. How did Hopeful and Christian get tangled in the net?
2. How could they have avoided their predicament?
3. List some of the false teachers in our world.
4. How can we discern truth from error?
5. What can fellow believers do to keep each other alert and on the right path?

CHAPTER 15

1. What was Hopeful like before he began his pilgrimage? What made him decide to begin?
2. What holds people back from following Christ?
3. When Hopeful gave his testimony, the story of how he came to Christ, what were his main points (outline)?

4. Following Hopeful's outline, describe your journey of faith.
5. With whom should you share your testimony?

CHAPTER 16
1. What did Ignorance believe about God? Why wasn't that enough to get him into Heaven?
2. What did Christian say in response to Ignorance's confession of faith? What is true faith?
3. What causes people to "backslide"?
4. What can you do to avoid backsliding?

CHAPTER 17
1. What final barrier did Hopeful and Christian have to cross before entering the Gate to the Celestial City? What happened in the process?
2. What were the pilgrims told they could expect in Heaven?
3. How did Heaven make all the problems of the journey worthwhile?
4. Why were Hopeful and Christian welcomed at the Gate? What happened to Ignorance?
5. How can the reality of Heaven help you in your present path?